T0128953

SCENES
from the
CATASTROPHE

MICHAEL WASHBURN

SCENES FROM THE CATASTROPHE

iUniverse books may be ordered through booksellers or by contacting:

iUniverse
1663 Liberty Drive
Bloomington, IN 47403
www.iuniverse.com
1-800-Authors (1-800-288-4677)

ISBN: 978-1-4917-9670-2 (sc)
ISBN: 978-1-4917-9671-9 (e)

Library of Congress Control Number: 2016907847

Print information available on the last page.

iUniverse rev. date: 06/05/2020

Table of Contents

Preface

About ten years ago, I began writing fiction intensively. It was an exhilarating move after many years in publishing jobs that required little initiative or imagination. I recently made the decision to round up some of my short stories and publish them together as a book.

This book consists of stories, not equations or position papers. Character, plot, and description have taken precedence over any social or political message or subtext. But a number of the tales do share general subject matter with others, and this made it easier to give them an order within the manuscript. The early part of the book contains stories depicting relations within and among social classes. The middle part features tales about the state of cultural institutions such as the Fourth Estate, the book publishing industry, and academia. In the last part, the reader will find stories depicting total societal breakdown, the end result of myriad processes of decay.

While I do not presume to have invented a "fictional world," a few characters do appear in more than one story. One character, Al Duchamp, a sensitive film director with a touch of Artaud's anguish about him, has served varied purposes. I have given him a role in "The Diversion," a tale with a more or less omniscient narrator, and have made Al the narrator of "The Ordeal" and the collection's titular story, "Scenes from the Catastrophe."

Michael Washburn
April 2016

Acknowledgements

A number of the stories in this collection previously appeared in literary journals. "The Reckoning" first appeared in *The Long Story*, "In the Flyover State" in the *New Orphic Review*, "Foxley's Progress" in the *Bryant Literary Review*, "Break-in on Woodward" in *Still Point Arts Quarterly*, "The Prank" in *Meat for Tea*, "In the Proudest Country" in *34th Parallel Magazine*, and "The Envy of Nations" in the *Brooklyn Rail*. The author thanks the editors of these publications for permission to reprint the stories.

Break-in on Woodward

At the end of a dim hallway on a lower floor of the museum, a doorknob turned, the door it was attached to swished outward, and four young men in leather jackets warily moved inside. Malik, Gus, R.E., and Twan looked around in the dimness for a couple of minutes, allowing their eyes to adjust, before setting off furtively across the polished marble floor of the long hallway toward the front of the building. Every so often, they paused to listen, but save for their own motion, the paintings and statues appeared to exist in a state of perfect stillness and quiet. When they had advanced to the hallway running along the front of the building, they probed the depths of the two intersecting corridors, not afraid, but intensely alert.

"Haywood could get in a whole lot of trouble for this," said Twan, referring to the guard who, on his last day on the job, had discreetly unlocked the door through which they'd come and had disabled the motion sensors. Twan was carrying an empty green gym bag whose twin handles had a Velcro clasp.

"Well, what the hell are they gonna do, fire him?" Malik retorted.

"No, I'm sure he'll go to jail," Twan rejoined.

"Probably a step up for him."

They were all aware of the dangers of being here. But of the four young men, only Gus really had reservations about this adventure. For the others, it was a welcome diversion, preferable by far to playing pool, watching football, or getting high in the basement of someone's parents' house or in an abandoned building in a part of the Detroit ghetto that looked bombed out. Gus had a little sister and brother to feed and he didn't care to think of what would happen to them if he went to jail. Nonetheless, what Gus felt now had little to do with his family's or his own welfare and everything to do with the fact that Malik was on parole and could be incredibly brutal

1

to others. In Gus's mind, Malik was a guy who, if he were in a lifeboat with room for one more and there were two guys floundering in the water, would let them both drown to assure himself lots of leg room. But Malik was crafty about money, and money was why they were here tonight. Money was the thing that nobody else in their world, besides Malik, could make or manage with any acumen or foresight. Hence Gus had banished his reservations and agreed to come along. But as he looked back down the dim corridor along which they'd crept, part of him wanted to bolt. Dash back out there into the November air and hug his black leather jacket while sprinting all the way back to the drab room where his brother and sister shared a mattress or crashed out in the dingy, grimy, chipping bathtub on nights when bullets came through the walls.

After an exchange of whispers, the party agreed on the need to go up at least one level to find what they were after. They moved up a flight of stairs and emerged from the stairwell at another intersection of dimly lit halls. On this level, there were paintings hanging from the walls, not the kind you can cart around on foot, but big framed rectangular scenes of white people in leafy, rural places that looked kind of like parts of America that Gus had seen, on TV mostly, yet looked different, alien. He was unsure how the people in these paintings would sound if you talked to them. But he imagined their talk would be kind of formal, like characters on the PBS station he'd occasionally flipped past, and they wouldn't ever curse.

Now Malik led the way into a wide room with the most florid paintings facing each other across spotless wooden panels on which the impact of feet, however tentative, produced sharp echoes in the dim spaces all around. When Gus and R.E. tried to tiptoe, to walk as they would in a hangar full of slumbering Marines, Malik laughed. Nobody was around and the motion detectors were disabled. The party moved through this room and into another impressive chamber, similarly adorned, before making a right into yet another big room and toward the center of the museum. They paused inside this room, taking in the treasures mounted on the walls. Then Twan handed the bag to R.E., moved off in search of a men's room, and ended up ascending another level.

Gus marveled at the figures in a few of the paintings here. A number of the women in these pictures were nude, yet these women's appearance did not appear overtly erotic. They had big bodies and looked entirely unselfconscious about aspects of their figures that would deny them a spot in today's skin mags. They had just settled right into figures that were natural for them, and if they cared a whit how others might interpret their looks, you couldn't tell from their faces. On the other hand, Gus had to admit, a number of these white people were svelte. The women were in ponds or lakes, or in a few cases you couldn't see any background at all, just a lady pulling on or off a slip or a dress. People lounged on elegant terraces or walked to and fro on the banks of a river. In other paintings, people stood in lush gardens, appreciative of but not overwhelmed by the curving and leaning masses of green around them, or walked down paths in settings far removed from any city. They chatted with a gardener, or milled around on a pier against a background so lush you might think any talk or action by people was quite beside the point. The point was to stand there and exist. *Renoir* was the name Gus read in the captions for a few of the paintings. In the other rooms, he'd spied the name *Rembrandt*.

On the floor above, Twan ambled down a hall, turned, started down another hall, realized there was no restroom down this way, whirled, and walked back the way he'd come. Then he made out another hall perpendicular to this one, on the far side of the hall he'd entered from. He navigated a course through the dimness, wishing his footfalls were quieter though he told himself it didn't matter.

Now Gus gazed at one of the paintings, a rendering of a pair of women in a garden of some kind, clean, lush, and sprawling. He turned his gaze to another, showing a few women's progress through a country footpath in summer. Malik and R.E. were smirking behind his back, but he didn't care. Another painting captured a woman standing nude in brilliant light, or perhaps she was ambling through a patch of grass that just reached her privates, it was impossible to tell for the bottom left of the canvas was a frenetic blur. The young woman's look was sweetly innocent and Gus could not help gaping at the fullness of her breasts, almost perfect in their roundness. Gus was thinking maybe Renoir had a gift.

"You'd sho love to get your lips 'round those titties and suck, wouldn't you?" Malik said.

"Fuck you," Gus answered.

Slowly but certainly, Gus was beginning to make associations. He did not know what country was the setting of the scenes he was witnessing.

But he could not help thinking that the painters of some of the works he'd viewed here spoke to a way that people everywhere were sometimes, people of all races and classes and religions. There was a quality about these paintings that hit you hard, something that was just so, what was the word, come on, he knew the word . . . something so *domestic*. Yes, that was it. These scenes were from a time before modern problems, crime, riots, insolvencies. Before the infrastructure we know today. And before squad cars or fire trucks or sanitation crews riding in trucks. Still, Gus felt he knew scenes kind of like these, didn't he, in their general sense if not in their particulars.

As Malik and R.E. smirked, Gus recalled a place where he'd liked to pass his afternoons. It was not a nice place. By some accounts Gus had read, the city's obligations to its pensioners had made it divert money that otherwise would have gone toward everyday services, like fighting fires or collecting trash. But people did not know just how bad things were. Gus thought of a yard behind a decrepit structure of bricks with a rusting sheet of corrugated tin at the top. The structure of the house had lost its integrity years ago. It was rapidly crumbling and collapsing. Bricks littered the rancid dirt and grass behind the building, amid bottles and cans and wrappers, in a space where anyone who walked without shoes would end up with cuts and shards of grass lodged in the channels and grooves of feet's tender undersides. Roughly thirty yards behind the crumbling rear of the house was where the bush began in earnest. Vines had overwhelmed stumps of concrete and the beginnings of a brick edifice where there had been a patio of sorts years ago, and vines crept outward from the looming branches and stalks, the organic structures that rose, converged into a mass of gnarled green and brown that denied passage to the sun's rays. A sighing came through the trees. In the yard, it was neither light nor dark, but shadows were present and they advanced toward the remains of the house in the waning day. In those hours when Gus sat there, on the skeleton of a grimy rusting deck chair, clutching a bottle of beer, hardly anything disturbed him except for a gust, a mangy cat limping while holding aloft a paw in which the nails had grown into the pads, or, on one occasion, a girl with matted hair who strode barefoot over the grounds in defiance of the shards and rocks, and addressed him as Angus when making her offer.

Upstairs, Twan had begun to grow quite frustrated until at last in the dimness he spied signs with universal male and female images and he knew which way to turn. He'd lost his trepidation in his growing feeling that aside from his three friends, these halls and rooms were as abandoned, starkly vacant, as anyplace in the universe.

Suddenly, Gus had a total change of mind. He thought, *No, no, ain't no way where I live is anything like these paintings. Ain't no way!*

Twan imagined the rooms all around him to be vacant, but he was wrong. In an office down the hall, a fifty-one-year-old guard named Harry Budzynski sat at a desk staring at characters on the screen of a Dell computer. Harry was a member of a poor Hamtramck family pummeled by the city's financial woes and in particular by the problems when it came to paying retirees' benefits. The city had managed to meet this obligation, more or less, by diverting some of the funds set aside for basic things like police departments, firehouses, garbage crews, and even water or electricity in certain of the most barren, neglected areas. So many people in the city now didn't even bother to call the police even when something horrible happened, for they would merely be stringing themselves along, adding to the trauma, if they waited up to an hour just for cops to arrive, write stuff down in a notebook, then leave.

As for Harry, he had a father with Parkinson's who needed 24/7 care, and the makeshift arrangement at home wasn't working. The private aide Harry's family had hired was irresponsible and unreliable and wasn't available for the old man more than fifty or so hours a week. Harry was in the midst of desperate online research into how he could go about setting up a Medicare trust for his father, with a couple of Medicaid-appointed helpers minding the old man. Harry thought it was impossible to make another arrangement, particularly now that Detroit's pensioners, by some estimates he'd read, were going to have to eat about ninety percent of the city's losses. But Harry loved his dad and he had to *try*. For the past couple of nights, he had sat hunched forward over the computer in the office set aside for the guards' use. Though Harry had passed most of his time in the museum standing at the entrances to rooms or instructing visitors to use pencils rather than pens when they wrote or attempted likenesses of the paintings, he had spent enough time in the office to become familiar with a few of the other guards, such as Walt, Rick, Danny, and Haywood, who had finished his last shift at the museum a few hours ago. Even if Harry hadn't been so busy with his research, he wouldn't have cared enough to find out why they let Haywood go. It was probably repeated lateness or something. Well, at least Haywood had shown Harry how to turn off motion sensors.

Now, as Harry did his research with quiet intensity, he heard an odd noise. The office was not far from one of the broad, curving stone stairways and the noise came to him almost like a stirring in the upper reaches of a silo. Harry reached into a drawer of the desk at which he sat, withdrew the Glock 32 pistol he'd carried on his person since a mugging two years before, and got up, straining his ears. The heights and depths of the vast place beckoned to him. The silence felt really weird. He was getting old and he couldn't tackle a four-year-old. But investigate he must.

Gus whirled around the room below looking at the paintings, ignoring the snickers of his pals, thinking that something made the places he knew, the trash-strewn yards and the barren lots, different from the scenes depicted here, and it wasn't just the bottles and wrappers and butts. A quality of these scenes disturbed him.

Upstairs, Twan was glad the others hadn't seen him get so anxious, like a little kid, when he'd had trouble finding the men's room. He started toward the door in the dimness.

Downstairs, Malik and R.E. were almost rolling on the floor at the sight of Gus turning around, gaping, at the paintings that dumb crackers who'd been dead for centuries had made.

"Just you hold on for a second there, fella," said a voice behind Twan's back. At that moment, one of the overhead lights in the hallway flickered on. Twan rotated his body, slowly, so as not to excite anyone, until he was gazing at a plump middle-aged white man in the type of uniform he'd seen Haywood wear on occasion. The man appeared to be breathing with difficulty, but was pointing a Glock 32 at Twan's chest. When the man gave a series of orders to the intruder, his voice rose as if he were fighting to assert his authority and barely edging out the terror in his own head. Twan nodded earnestly.

Because Malik and R.E. had managed to contain their laughter, they were just able to catch faint noises from upstairs, the sounds of a white man giving orders if they weren't mistaken. They looked at each other. They looked at Gus, now frozen with a deadly serious look, his contemplation arrested like a jerk-off session in a foxhole when a whistle announces the commencement of an assault. At a signal from Malik, they moved into formation behind him and the three began to creep noiselessly across the wood floor, out of the room, right toward the short stairwell. Malik moved so lithely and quietly that each part of his physique seemed autonomous, able to act and pause, act and pause. As they neared the top of the stairwell, Malik's left hand lifted his black leather jacket up toward his shoulders and his right hand fluttered onto the handle of a .357 Smith & Wesson Magnum with duct tape holding together the checkered, honey-hued grip. Moments later, they emerged from the stairwell into a scene that evoked, for them, the Rodney King beating and the Trayvon Martin killing all at once. The white guard was standing over their prone friend and pressing a heel on Twan's shoulder while demanding information. You could see from Twan's look that he was terrified and the heel was pressing, digging.

"Drop it, mothafucker!" Malik thundered as he swept fearlessly across the floor toward the two.

Harry, who'd felt himself on the verge of a heart attack for the past two minutes, was so startled he dropped the Glock. Emboldened, Twan pushed himself up, socked Harry in the gut with a right hook, then pushed the middle-aged man toward the wall so hard that Harry's head slammed into the stone. Harry keeled forward, moaning, just barely able to prop himself off the ground with hands that were already numb, unresponsive, like rubber appendages. He wheezed and tried to draw breath. Malik kicked him hard in the face and he flopped onto his back and looked up at the bright light in the ceiling.

Malik stood above the guard, pointing the Magnum at his face. Harry thought Malik was going to kick him again.

"Is there any other guards in this place, mothafucker?" Malik demanded.

Nobody else saw the point of a question to which the answer would be the same no matter what. It was like asking "Are you a cop?" But Malik wanted an answer and the barrel of the Magnum was long and wide. Gasping, wheezing, straining his eyes, Harry managed to rotate his head. Again he expected a kick, but Malik's demeanor appeared to ease ever so faintly. He picked up Harry's gun, handed it to Gus, and instructed him to watch the guard. Then Malik, Twan, and R.E. set off in search of a statue or painting that might be worth a few million but would not require a crane or a truck to take out of here. The three of them entered the stairwell and disappeared.

Gus thought, *This is such fucking bullshit.* It would be corny if he tried to get in touch with the feelings of the captive or vice versa. But Gus didn't have to worry, because Harry was quite unable to talk at this point. He just lay there, sputtering, coughing up blood and phlegm, his sad desperate eyes pleading with his captor not to shoot him. For the half hour that Gus was alone with Harry Budzynski, they did not exchange more than a couple of sentences, once when Harry asked Gus not to point the gun at his face, and once when he begged Gus to pull him to the wall opposite the one he had gotten slammed into, to prop him into a sitting position. Pitying the crumpled heap of a once proud, working-class American male, Gus put the Glock aside and granted both requests. Then he picked up the Glock and rubbed the barrel with his left hand, studying the reflection from the overhead light with interest. When Harry began to murmur, Gus pointed the gun at his face and got the overweight white man to shut up. As he watched the immobilized guard recoil, Gus felt a twinge of pleasure.

But during a part of tonight's adventure that the others had already forgotten about, something had begun to clamor for Gus's attention. They had talked briefly of Haywood. This did not prompt Gus to recall Haywood, whom he'd met only once, but rather to recall a scene that he didn't think Twan and R.E. had any inkling of, as of yet. In this memory, Gus was lying on a mattress in someone's basement, it might have been Twan's, taking drags from a Pall Mall. A few feet to his right there was another mattress. Who was on it? He thought it was a girl named Jasmine and a young man whose name he'd forgotten. A far more important fact: Tonight was Halloween and the city was on fire. Sirens screamed and the police moved to and fro, but there was a half-hearted feel to it all. You heard but the faintest echoes of all that down here in this basement, where logs snapped and dissolved in a fireplace ten feet down and to the right of Gus's feet. The flames jumped and danced and briefly illuminated a boot, a belt, a torso, a lock of hair, the skin of a penis, the glistening barrel of a Colt or Magnum. Gus wanted to rotate his head to the right until he had a full view of what was happening on the other mattress, but he didn't want to alienate anyone. He wrestled with his options until someone decided the issue for him. The boot that collided with the head of the man going at it with Jasmine was attached to Malik. The bastard had strode right in here and now he towered over the tangled lovers with hands protruding from the sleeves of that hard black jacket of his clenched tightly. With alacrity, the man on the mattress shifted and folded his body into a kneel and all but begged Malik not to blast him. There came a pause while the standing man considered this entreaty. Malik's grin practically reached opposite ends of the room in the seconds before another kick shattered the kneeling fellow's jaw and sent him scurrying, in something between a hop and a crawl, through the passage at the end of the room opposite Gus.

The scene had lain there, one of the jagged shards of memory on the dusty floor of Gus's mind, until tonight. At last he was beginning to make connections. With a bit of effort, he recalled the name of the man whom Malik had driven from the basement, it was Bobby, and now he recalled another night, perhaps four months after the incident, when he'd spied Haywood sitting in the dimly lit bar in Corktown, talking with a man who looked kind of like Bobby. With further effort, Gus recalled Haywood on a couple of occasions venting about a fat white sonofabitch he had to deal with at work and realized that in all likelihood, the quivering, bleeding mass Gus now stood over was the object of Haywood's loathing. Which meant—

"Man, ain't you finished that mothafucker?" came a voice from the top of the stairwell. Malik, Twan, and R.E. emerged into the hallway. Twan and R.E. each held a handle of the gym bag which had the tops of a few canvases and the upper reaches of a bust poking out of it.

"Malik, I think somebody *wanted* us to run into this—"

"Shut your mouth, chump," said Malik as he swept past the others toward the prone body of the guard.

At last Harry's breathing had evened a bit and his body had begun to straighten out. But now, in terror, Harry's eyes rotated up and to the right, toward the tall form of the gangster who leered and seethed at him. Malik did not waste a second. He kicked Harry in the face and then, in that moment when screaming signals overrode the guard's nervous system and particles of water joined at the base of each eye, followed up with blows to the temple and gut. R.E. and Twan laughed, gently set the gym bag on the spotless floor, and moved over to positions on either side of Harry. Spit began to fly as blows rained down from three directions, tearing Harry's clothes and flesh and drawing cries akin to those Gus had heard once from a pusher whom Malik had enlisted to help move crack on the street and whom Malik had then caught skimming from the proceeds. But to Gus these cries sounded infinitely more desperate, more hopeless than when Malik had beaten that poor bastard in a trash-filled lot behind a house.

Yes, Gus thought as he recalled the earlier beating, that lot was a scene all right, a filthy, garbage-filled, run-down, messed-up domestic scene. Not unlike certain others.

"Pleeaasse stop! Uuuuggghhhhh!!!" Harry moaned.

Malik laughed and delivered a kick that knocked out a couple of the guard's front teeth. R.E. kicked the guard's left shins to bloody mulch. Now Twan unzipped his pants, whipped it out, and began pissing on the guard.

Gus shut out Harry's wails as his thoughts reverted, abruptly, uncontrollably, to the scenes of white people in lush verdant settings, white people chatting or stolling or bathing in the subtlest light which made their pale hues glow, and he couldn't piece things together and figure out why he experienced a stab of anger and felt so upset. Was it because those people were so much richer than he'd ever be?

"Pleeaasse! Please stop it. Pl—"

The guard spat red pulp while groping for something with his right hand. Malik stomped on the hand, again and again and again, as if it were a tiny rat that wouldn't die.

"Pleeaasse..."

Now the guard's voice became feebler and trailed off.

"Please, please, please. Ain't he polite?" Malik said.

The three obligingly ramped up their beating. Harry tried to talk, spat blood, rolled his eyes toward the ceiling.

No. Oh, no. Gus decided that, in fact, the people in the paintings were like people here in this city, with the critical difference that the painters' subjects did not depend on government services to make things a certain way. The settings way out in the country, many miles from anywhere, were clean and agreeable because the people who lived there kept them that way, out of pride, just perhaps, out of a conscious or unconscious idea of duty that did not depend on having crews, or "vital services," making rounds. Yes, that was it. And some people today had dared to think the memory, the images of such times and places worth preserving. With a bit of effort, Gus could imagine himself standing in clean air, breathing deeply, exulting, basking in soft light.

Now Gus called to Malik, who spun around. Without warning, Gus raised the Glock and fired. The gun practically bolted out of his hand as the roar reverberated through the polished halls all around. R.E. and Twan froze, gaping. He thought they would try to recover the Glock but neither of them moved toward where it lay on the floor. R.E. and Twan bolted for the stairwell. Gus retrieved the Glock and tried to shoot Twan in the ass but missed. Within seconds they were gone, the bag full of looted art already forgotten. Gus turned back to where Malik stood with a hand at his neck to stop the blood from spurting. At the last split-second, Malik had turned so that the bullet had shaved off a big chunk of tissue on the left side of his esophagus and passed down to the nether reaches of the hall. Now Malik stared at Gus, with hate in his eyes, for a few seconds before his knees began to buckle.

Harry Budzynski was alive. He moaned, spat blood. When the paramedics came, they had a temporary dilemma about whether he was worth trying to save, but they acted professionally and spirited him off to Detroit Medical Center where, contrary to expectations, he proved his toughness and resilience and eventually made a partial recovery. He would never quite walk straight again and would require injections of Ketorolac daily for years to come. It is hard to say whether he came out of it better than Gus who, though able to cut a deal with prosecutors who wanted him to testify against Twan and R.E., would be in trouble with associates of the gangsters he'd once considered his friends.

Harry and Gus both enjoyed a spell of local and national fame as the duo who had thwarted the theft of their city's artistic treasure. There were talk show and radio appearances, carefully planned tours and occasional spontaneous encounters around the city with crowds in awe of Harry and his savior. But their heroism, and the promotion of it, became a bit of an awkward topic in the face of the decision taken by the city's financial planners seven weeks after the break-in. To fend off the creditors of the bankrupt city and begin to get it out of its fiscal hole, they decided to auction off a large number of the works in the museum's roughly $2 billion collection. Attention spans waned, and the organizers of the events showcasing Harry and Gus felt firmly that if they couldn't sell more than fifty seats per appearance, then the tours were a losing proposition.

Those People

Bob Hughes was having lunch with two fellow police officers in a college town in Ohio on a Friday morning in May. The café where they ate was a quiet place where a few kids from the college sat at the opposite wall, engaged in some kind of conspiratorial talk. When the waitress came to their table, she flashed a grin so enticing that Bob had a flashback to his wife, Anne, on their honeymoon in Orlando half a decade before. This was a girl from the town, Bob guessed, not one of those young people from the college with all their highfalutin' ideas about race and gender, money and the social hierarchy.

Carl Schmidt, one of the other officers, leaned toward Bob and lowered his voice, saying:

"You hear them? I'm damn sure one of them kids is dealin' dope. I can't believe they'd talk about it right here, fifteen feet away from us."

Bob smiled indulgently.

"Kids'll be kids, Carl. Think about your son Paul. I don't think he's always your idea of virtue."

"Maybe not. I still think you're too lazy-fair toward them kids."

"You mean *laissez-faire*, Carl. How's your sandwich?"

"I expect a little more if I'm gonna pay eight seventy-five for a BLT, to be honest with you."

"You're always honest, Carl. It's one of your endearing traits."

"My what?"

"Miss? Some more coffee, please?" called Mike Dobbs, the third cop at Bob's table. The girl strode over again, flashing that look that would stir a thousand associations if Bob let himself slip into a dreamy state, casting aside all his responsibilities. She refilled Mike's cup before ambling back to the counter where a handmade sign reminded patrons that tipping was not a city in China.

"I don't know why they passed me over for promotion again, what with me and Linda needin' a playpen for our second and not goin' to Disneyworld since '99."

"Well, let me and Anne take a look in our cellar. I don't know about a playpen, but we might be able to help out with a basket for the first few months," Bob offered. He wanted to add, *Jesus Carl, they can't give you a promotion based on where you're at in your life.*

"That might help."

Mike, thirty-eight and a bachelor, tried to hide his self-consciousness during discussions of this nature. He scarfed down his sandwich, gazing through the window to where a woman pushed a stroller past the awning of a thrift shop beneath a sky of cobalt blue. He appreciated the quiet around the campus over the past week or so, as people hunkered down over their books in preparation for finals, and the only arrest he'd made was of a bum who fell asleep at the library downtown and grew menacing when asked to leave. It was a relief. Mike felt such anger at the college kids, at times, that he got a little afraid of what he might do. Lately the emotion had been getting worse.

Carl droned on about how tough things were now with only one income for his family, prompting Bob to think again how undisciplined such talk was, to wish Carl would have a little more sense about these things.

A call came over the walkie-talkies:

"Possible 2-11 in progress at First National Bank, Broad and Second Streets."

That was two blocks away! Bob was the first one out of the café, the kids in the corner watching with unfathomable expressions as the cops scurried. He raced down Broad Street, thinking back to reports of robberies at the same bank in March and April, wondering whether this was the same robber, knowing that if there was one thing he'd learned as a cop, it was never to underestimate how dumb a criminal might be—very possibly, the employees had recognized the guy the moment he'd walked in, and had raised the alarm. Now Bob was nearing the intersection of Broad and Third as he felt sweat dampen the back of his shirt, passing the veterinarian and thinking that Anne had mentioned that the dog was long overdue for an appointment there, and all around him the air was so clear and calm, kids walked alongside their mothers in the street with looks suggesting that order prevailed in their universe. He charged down the block where the bank stood, trying to assume a calm demeanor before coming into view of those beyond the huge windows of the façade. Carl took up a position outside the bank while Mike urgently shooed pedestrians and cars away. Nothing seemed out of order as Bob strolled into the bank, where a dozen people were in line before a counter with two tellers on the job. Surreptitiously, Bob scanned the faces of the customers, a middle-aged woman with dyed copper hair, a young guy whom Bob recognized as a mechanic at the body shop three blocks from here, a businessman, two more middle-aged ladies, and behind them the man in the dark green jacket, sporting an afro, whom the two tellers must have recognized from the hits on the bank earlier in the year.

At this point, Bob would have had his sidearm drawn, but his department had come in for scathing criticism, not to mention the threat of lawsuits, after its officers failed to follow the rules of engagement deemed proper by the minority activists and coalitions that recruited heavily at the college. If anything went down after Bob took the initiative to draw his gun, then whatever the outcome—dead suspect or dead cop—guess whose fault it would be. Resting his palm on the grip of his gun, Bob advanced toward the man in the green jacket who grinned queerly, gazing straight ahead. But no one was surprised. The man wheeled and reached into his jacket, but before he could steady his weapon, he and Bob were dancing, dancing, spinning in an assertion and resistance of force, a call and response, the gun firing at the ceiling, spinning toward the lobby as screams and gasps rose. Bob lay on the ground with the perp's left hand clawing at his throat. Then the man rose, like a partner in sex getting up to go urinate, stood calmly, and with great poise fired a round into Bob's chest.

Once again, Carl Schmidt was in trouble. It was time to report to Captain Davis, with or without a PBA rep at his side. He strolled through the corridors with a sense of resignation, trying not to think about Carl Jr. clinging to the edge of his basket, howling in need of a fresh diaper when

Carl was out of diaper money for the week. At least Anne Hughes, Bob's widow, was too distracted to think of asking for the basket back. His weary resignation grew as he sat across from Captain Davis and the man began berating him for his conduct toward the demonstrators who had swarmed into the streets on the day of the governor's visit weeks before. The politician had just given a talk at the college, a widely booed and jeered talk, and nearly all the protestors were kids from the college pursuing the man for his stances on abortion and gay marriage.

At the end of this harangue, Carl Schmidt handed over his gun and badge, strode out of the dingy precinct, and sat at the wheel of his '85 Chevy, his face in his hands, shame and rage welling within him, in the grip of a force he had barely the vocabulary to convey. He sat there muttering until the lot was empty save for the old Chevy, then he slowly turned the key and started driving in the direction of a small white clapboard house beside a vacant lot on the corner of Arch and South Streets.

James Hughes, the child of Bob and Anne Hughes, imagined things were different at his friends' houses. He stood in the middle of the living room with the Christmas tree adorned with so many plastic sleighs, ribbons, bells, and tiny stuffed animals, and he thought *I can't believe this happened to our family,* and he wasn't sure how to process the loss, he just knew things weren't supposed to be this way, there was supposed to be a dad here, how could there not be. He gazed out the window at the twilight of 4:30 p.m., where two of the neighbors were carrying a pair of sleds up the steps of their house and stomping their boots with each footfall. All the boy knew was that Christmas was meant to be a certain way under the immutable laws of the cosmos and his house was practically alone in not being right. His schoolmates had not relented a bit in their abuse, not even a bit, after Bob's death, but rather than engage with them, James had grown introverted and sullen.

He studied one of the ornaments, a replica of Santa Claus in a sleigh pulled by four reindeer, he meditated on the details of this ornament that seemed meant to convey the joy and intimacy of this holiday in its every nuance, its every angle, Santa's grin and the cute beady eyes of the four animals that took pride and pleasure in their commission, the sixteen feet galloping in unison. The ornament seemed assured of its place in the world that had made it, but James was not right, this was what his classmates kept repeating, they taunted him ceaselessly, they told him he was like a boy with a vagina or a talking skeleton, he was not right, he was so sullen because if he opened up, he'd wail and cry, and so he had turned into this mannequin that they could scorn and kick and spit on without ever provoking a response. *How can this be real? How, how can this be real?*

The years went by. The mocking never ended.

When James was a bit older but no less distraught, he and Anne sat in the same living room where the current year's Christmas tree, a far cry from former ones, tended to underwhelm all their visitors. It was short and pathetic in terms of ornaments this year, the nicer ornaments having been pawned. Soon Ray and Linda Guthrie would be coming over. They'd all heard about Carl, that poor failed cop, about the course of all his struggles, but maybe Ray and Linda's visit could rekindle some of what Anne knew ages ago, when she did not feel so sad and middle-aged all the time, when James was a blip on a sonogram and she dreamed of the vacations the family would take, the times they'd share in the sweet hereafter, to quote the title of a movie Anne had seen, a sad and bleak movie, yet the title had a resonance to it.

"Are we going to see Carl, mom?" asked James.

"No . . . no. Carl decided to go away, James."

"We're never going to see Carl again, then."

"No."

Ray and Linda made their appearance in the squat ugly house, sitting across from the widow and the boy with the unprepossessing tree in between. Ray looked dead tired. At this time, he was working double shifts in an effort to forestall threatening letters from the bank concerning the home where once they had organized an event or two for working families in the valley, but whose condition now made Linda jealous as she sat in this living room, spartan though it was, across from Anne and her boy who always said *please* and *thank you*. Ray had a perspective on the life of the miners. He had funerals on his schedule. Just the week before, one of them died while attempting to clear drainage pipes in the depths of a mine, when the roof collapsed, only days after the Mine Safety and Health Administration's inspectors had declared the mine to be safe.

Ray had black lung disease, as did John Reynolds and an untold number of their fellows. Old John was not expected to live long, a pity, since the illness was detectable years earlier when the mobile health inspection teams made their rounds, administering blood tests. Unfortunately, you had to be an active miner to undergo a test, so John's semiretirement made him ineligible. Whom are we kidding here, Ray wanted to know. He described conditions in the depths of the mines.

"It's like the bottom of the ocean, down so deep that all is blackness around you, and you wouldn't see a predator until it swam up and bit you in the nose. You eat and breathe coal dust."

But it was a job, and Anne had made a promise to someone. She asked Ray about the life of the mine, the hours men worked, and whether there might be an opening for a boy she knew who had his sights set on an IT training course at the community college next fall, but desperately needed income now.

"I can sure ask around, Anne, but don't go promisin' nothing yet," Ray answered.

Anne spoke highly of the youngster who had babysat James when she went out on dates a few years before, and who now was trying to support his own family. He hid the truth beneath a veneer of nonchalance such as Bob used to display in his belief that a lack of confidence was unmanly.

"I said I'd inquire, now don't lean on me no more."

Linda's expression to her husband said *cool off.* James had little to contribute here. He would have liked to ask about the young man who'd babysat for him and to whom he looked up like a little brother, full of awe. To James the world was like the vast unapproachable merchandiser that published catalogs advertising one or another way of life: Here is the garb of an outdoorsman—a logger, a fisherman, a construction worker, and here are the habiliments of a golfer, an investment banker, all of them compelling in a way he couldn't articulate, and beyond a price range he could consider.

"Y'all heard about Carl Schmidt," Ray said.

"Yes, we heard about Carl. I guess he cared more about who he was professionally than any other part of himself," Anne replied.

"He brought down that offender who preyed on the college co-eds—three assaults and two rapes in the month before Carl laid the cuffs on him."

That evening, quite by chance, a few students were talking in the lounge on the campus in that Ohio college town, a lounge where you were no longer allowed to smoke. Just an hour before, they'd been working in one of the computer rooms by the south dining hall, along with a dozen others, until one of the college employees, a big man with fat ruddy cheeks who lived in the town, poked his head in to announce that he had to close the room for the night. But the kids kept typing away, working on papers or surfing the web, acting as if he wasn't there, until he grew incredulous and bellowed:

"Did you *hear* me? I *have* to shut down for the night!" *What is it with these kids?* he thought. *It's like I don't exist.*

At length, they'd grudgingly begun to shut down their computers and pack up, barely acknowledging the clown of a man in his dark blue windbreaker and flannel shirt and fouled blue jeans, wondering whether they really had to obey him at all. To them, he was a lot like Shelly Knowles, the fifty-something woman who swiped the kids' cards at the entrance to the dining hall, making a point of trying to greet every kid by name without looking at the card. Sometimes her memory worked, sometimes not. Once when Lacey Worth's boyfriend, Paul Fisher, had just gotten back an advanced calculus exam with a bright red "F" on it and Shelly addressed him as Steve, he'd come back with "It's *Paul*, you dumb cow!" He pressed ahead in the line as Shelly held her head in embarrassment, saying, "Oh, I've got to get all these names straight!"

No longer able to surf the web and chat with their friends by e-mail, Lacey Worth and Michelle Danby sat in the lounge with their sociology, or as they termed it, "soche," textbooks propped before them, sipping mocha lattes. Lacey asked Michelle how many shirts she'd bought at the department store in Columbus over the weekend. Lacey herself had gotten five.

"I got three shirts and a scarf," Michelle replied.

They weren't too fixated on the texts assigned for their soche class, which required them mainly to talk about their changing emotions, their attitudes toward men, sex, and society, and to devise experiments to test one or another theory. On one occasion, the professor told the class to act like social deviants, to see what it felt like to be a deviant, so Lacey and Michelle and a few of their friends decided to dump garbage in the campus library. They emptied several big bags onto the floor, then raced out of the library, the alarm going off and the clerks behind the desk, middle-aged women from the town, gaping in bewilderment. Lacey and Michelle thought it was the most fun they'd had since the anti-Bush protests a number of months before, when they and a dozen others used chalk to cover the walls and pavement with oodles of multi-colored graffiti, creating hours of work for the minimum-wage grounds crew. That was nearly on par with the time when about twenty women protested misogyny by lounging topless on the steps of the library, greeting the pair of cops who showed up gawking at them and their signs with, "What's the matter, piggy?" "Hey piggy, you didn't know women could spell?"

Lacey and Michelle were not going to take guff from anyone, not from overbearing boyfriends, prying parents, or the conservative blowhards who dared set foot on this campus on occasion. Not from anyone who didn't know what it is to be oppressed.

Lacey and Michelle were oppressed.

Their soche professor spelled it all out for them, with the help of *Race and Gender*, Third Edition, with its pithy proclamations about the structures preserving outdated privilege, society's mechanisms of subordination and control. One smug boyfriend had quipped that Lacey was going to graduate with a "degree in victimhood," and he was her boyfriend no longer. She needed a man who evinced the proper respect, sensitivity, and empathy for Lacey's status as an oppressed woman.

The two friends were pretty psyched about the coming rally down in the podunk town where the state's death chamber was, the death chamber whose next guest—if all went as planned by prosecutors and the governor—was one Cecil Jones, who had gunned down a cop named Bob Hughes. Geez, didn't all those cops have dumb names. It was important to save the latest victim of the system while relaying a message to the pigs in power. Lacey and Michelle were going to get a ride from one of their wealthy friends, but in the meantime there was the matter of making signs, · and perhaps fliers to distribute, with figures about capital punishment, and the perfect sound-byte had to be crafted in the event that the cameras might alight on Lacey or Michelle. To be honest, they didn't really feel like going back to the supermarket in town anytime soon. Folks there were so slow and out of it! The last time they went there, they'd stood sweltering on line for upward of twenty minutes while the lone checkout girl worked herself into a frenzy ringing up bunches of kids with kegs for an off-campus party. Meanwhile, one of the employees, a fat guy with a beard in a black t-shirt, seemed totally worn out by the humidity, and he'd slumped over by a heap of boxes in the corner, panting and heaving while trying to steady himself, and one of the kids on line said, "When I start a business, I want an employee JUST LIKE THAT!", causing an uproar among the kids. They could find cardboard for their placards somewhere else, Lacey decided. How she disliked coming to these odd corners of the town where blue-collar folk turned up unexpectedly, like the fiftyish man in a gray parka who happened upon Michelle and her musician boyfriend when they were standing on a corner freezing, waiting for the bus, an hour late, that would take them to Columbus. "You waitin' on the bus? You look like your ears are red." They ignored him, but he noticed the boyfriend's guitar case. "I'm just tryin' to help," he said. A pause. "Are you in a band?" he asked the boyfriend. "What the fuck do you care if we're in a band?" was the reply. "Whatever," the odd man said before taking off.

Just two months later, on the day of the rally, throngs of kids climbed into the cars idling on a patch of turf by the campus, to begin the trip toward the death house in that redneck part of the state they loathed. Later in the day, they gathered outside the death house on the outskirts of Lucasville, wondering what sort of opposition they'd face in this land of cow towns and reactionary politics. Under Lacey's arm was a copy of the *Times Literary Supplement* with an article by Margaret Drabble in which the author voiced her loathing for America, berating those insular and unenlightened people with their judicial system that still meted out the death penalty, in contrast to all the other industrialized nations. All around, kids were handing out flyers, while signs made from cardboard kited from the back of the supermarket reminded onlookers that death is irreversible. As with other causes, this was about more than one man's guilt or innocence, about more than the justness of execution in this case. The matter had snowballed into a referendum on any number of topics ranging from policy in the Middle East to programs for the homeless. The signs were rhetorically quite diverse.

On the far side of the police mounted on horses in the street was a little counter-demonstration, consisting of family and friends of a widely forgotten cop. Anne Hughes stood quietly with no idea how to address the death penalty's opponents. Beside her were Mike Dobbs, who had gotten fired from the police force in the town where most of these kids attended college. Anne's son was required to be at work. Ray and Linda Guthrie would have been here, but the black lung illness had encroached so far that Ray could not talk without his respirator or move without his mechanized wheelchair, and he needed Linda around all the time.

At this point, the protestors began to direct their attention to the counter-demonstration, such as it was, a few of them slipping past the cops stretched a bit too thin down the street. One of the kids from the college, a long-haired dreadlocked white guy in Birkenstock shoes, approached the barrier on the far side of the street and began yelling and gesticulating at the counter-rally.

Mike Dobbs glared at the protestors, and though no one would ever accuse him of excessive emotional sensitivity, he felt the anguish of the widow beside him as if he were a puppet of skin looking at the body it had been pulled off. The kids were determined to exacerbate the wounds. A few feet away, the guy with dreadlocks stood there, not exactly engaging with any member of the counter-rally but hurling abuse like a water-cannon. Anne's face was in her hands, she was beginning to cry, Mike doubted she had ever really been ready emotionally for anything since Bob's death, but had just sort of coasted along in the hope that she'd somehow adjust, silently and organically, to the new reality. When she saw this. . . . Now the cops had pushed the guy with dreadlocks back to the throng outside the death house. And it suddenly came, whistling, with such an innocuous sound that it took a moment to process. A barrage of eggs flew across the barrier, hitting Mike's arm, splattering on the cardboard signs, landing on Anne's khaki trousers as she wept. Mike studied the kids with their signs and their flyers, as all the memories came racing back, all of what he had seen and heard from friends, and friends of friends, up at the college town.

When I start a business, I want an employee just like that!
It's Paul, you dumb cow!

What the fuck do you care if we're in a band?
Hey piggy, you didn't know someone with breasts could spell?

He slipped under the barrier and walked toward the part of the rally that seemed most aggressive, where Lacey, Michelle, and Paul were waving signs and hooting and cheering on the egg throwers who did not stand their ground, but flung their charges before melting into the anonymity of the crowd, where they received plaudits and hugs from their comrades. That wasn't how Mike's father had brought him up. You have something to say to someone, you say it and you stand your ground, boy. *Don't be a coward.* Mike decided he was going to avenge his fallen comrade, Bob Hughes, by killing some of these kids right here, right now.

Yes, he decided, vengeance would be his. He advanced toward the kids.

Then a hand fell on Mike's shoulder. When he spun around, he was looking at James Hughes, whom he'd thought could not tear himself away from his shift. But here he was. Maybe James would help him kill the kids. But James said, "*No, Mike.* I know how I used to be, and I know where I'd be now without a mentor. Kids are kids, Mike. This isn't the way."

"Let go of me," Mike said. He recognized the part of Bob Hughes that looked out at him now, the calm reasonable part.

"Really. Fuck off," Mike added.

He continued toward the crowd before the death house, hesitated, started, and paused again.

Hey piggy . . .
You cow . . .
I want an employee just like that . . .
Hey piggy . . .
Piggy piggy piggy piggy pigg-yyyy!

James, who seemed to shut out the furor around him, tightened his grip on Mike, continuing: "It's easy to screw up when you're that age. Let's show them we're not what they think we are. Come on now."

"No! *No!*" Mike was thinking about what he could do when he got the dreadlocked guy's head in a vise, or one of those egg chuckers, those goddamn chickenshit bastards . . . Mike Dobbs had the strength of three of those creme puffs put together, and he aimed to show it.

"Mike. You're only going to provoke them further. This isn't what my dad would have wanted, and it's not what I want. Follow me now."

And Mike felt a twinge of uncertainty, in the face of this calm youngster in whose features he saw his dead friend looking out at him, imploring, in the friendly but resolute way Bob always had.

Hey piggy . . .

You dumb cow . . .

Piggy . . . piggy . . . piggy . . .

Now the voices in his head joined with the sensory impression of signs in the crowd: "Bigots Fuck Off!" "Racists Go Home!" and an image of a certain cartoon character in a policeman's garb with a look of distress contorting his snout, the air of a doomed villain, and the words: "How's your pork?"

He paused a final time, then the matter was decided. Mike pushed past James Hughes, walking in the direction of Paul Fisher, Lacey's boyfriend, ready to help Paul understand a few things, and soon he was inches away. But then he felt the strong arms of three state troopers forcing him to the ground as a fresh salvo of eggs went sailing over the barriers.

In the Flyover State

The small Cessna jet began its descent above a gently sloping field in a vast canyon. Mountains loomed to the north and east. To the south were tributaries of a powerful river, and to the west lay the distant forms of trailers on the perimeters of coal mines. At this hour, the trailers were empty. The workers had gone home to enjoy cooked meals and episodes of their favorite melodramas. But for the plane, it was deathly still in the canyon. The plane banked, swerved, evened its course gracefully as the pilot mentally charted a route across the field.

Besides the pilot, forty-four-year-old Harry Van Zant, the plane contained two young executives of a tech company on their way home to San Luis Obispo from a meeting in Denver. Natasha Pruitt and James Fletcher were both in their early thirties, and were both rising quickly within their firm. Natasha wore her blonde hair short and had a cutting, at times shrill, voice. James was tall but gangly and meek, with a pair of rectangle-rimmed glasses and Clark Kent cheekbones. Friends and co-workers occasionally noted the irony of this resemblance, because they knew James was never going to morph into Superman, no matter what test might come before him. He was a talker and a thinker. Colleagues who had worked with James throughout his four years with the firm could not recall him cursing, raising his voice, or speaking ill of anybody.

They were quite lucky that there was still a bit of light left. Harry skillfully guided the plane to a course roughly through the middle of the field as he deployed the landing gear, grateful that there were hardly any rocks out here. Neither of his passengers voiced alarm as the plane touched down, roared onward for a couple of hundred feet, and came to rest. Harry leaned back in his seat, sighed with relief. When he turned his head around, they were sitting calmly, on either side of the aisle, looking at him.

"It's the left turbofan. Might just be a bird but it's totally jammed. We didn't have a choice here," Harry told the pair of executives.

All three climbed out of the plane. The canyon appeared almost as barren as the moon. From here, the trailers way off in the distance looked like Legos. A winking light atop one of them did not reassure anybody. The barrenness had a forbidding quality and enhanced the feeling that precious time was ebbing away and they were completely stuck. As a cool breeze swept over the field and caressed their hair, James began fishing in his pockets for his cell phone. Before he could begin to use it, Natasha pushed her hair back, away from her cheeks, and turned to confront the pilot.

"Harry! Are you aware of how this affects anyone? I have to be at a meeting with the CCO at exactly nine-thirty tomorrow—"

Harry took a step back, putting the flats of his palms forward.

"Ms. Pruitt, I'm very sorry, but like I said—"

"How could a bird have caused this? You're a fucking incompetent pilot!"

"Ms. Pruitt, please understand—"

James turned toward them, started to say something, but thought better of it. Before Harry could finish, Natasha turned, walked over, and stood by James ten yards from the plane, reaching for her own cell phone inside a front pocket of her black slacks.

"Oh hell, I left it in my briefcase," she said and started back toward the plane.

"Wait, never mind, I've gotten through," said James.

Now James was talking to a local dispatcher.

"No, no, it's not really an emergency, but we had to land and we're stuck out here. In a canyon somewhere. I don't know—I think I see some trailers about a mile west of us."

At the other end someone was recording, processing all of this. Natasha was fuming but James didn't find the situation so dreadful, all things considered. Who knew what might have happened with a less experienced pilot.

"Three of us," James said, and then, because Natasha was nudging him, added, "and we *really* need to get back to California."

Again James paused, listening, then he said: "What do we tell them about the engine, Harry?"

"It's not the engine, Mr. Fletcher, it's one of the turbofans. I'm not sure what the problem is and it's going to take hours to do a proper inspection," he began.

"—which obviously you can't do in the dark," Natasha finished for him.

Harry nodded.

"So, we shouldn't even think about departing until some time tomorrow at the very soonest."

"Once again, Ms. Pruitt, I'm very sorry—"

"Oh, shut the hell up!"

Easing the cell phone into a pocket, James moved ever so slightly closer to her and talked in a low voice, trying to soothe and conciliate. For the next half hour, the three stood shivering in the breeze caressing the grass across the floor of the canyon. Finally, with the light almost totally gone, they were just barely able to make out a plume of exhaust rising behind a battered station wagon. When it pulled up in front of them, they saw that the driver was not a cop but a woman in her late forties or early fifties in jeans and a brown flannel shirt. She had ruddy, weathered flesh and an ingenuous grin.

"Bob's over on the other side of town, and his deputy's not on duty, so they sent me," said this lady, who went on to introduce herself as Linda.

The two young executives looked at each other. It was just their luck to get stranded in Pin Point, Nevada, with exactly one sheriff and one deputy, plus Linda, at its disposal.

"Thanks for coming to the rescue, Linda. We don't know exactly how long we're going to be here. Is there, uh, like, a motel somewhere?" James said.

"Well aren't you in luck, honey. There's a place about thirty minutes from here, and it's the sweetest little hotel you ever saw. Why don't y'all hop right in?" Linda beamed.

Natasha went back to the plane to collect her briefcase, which had her laptop and cell phone in it, and then she and James climbed into the station wagon.

"Coming, Harry?" James asked through a window.

"If it's all the same to you, I think I'd like to stay here with the plane," Harry said.

"All right. We can reach you on your cell, correct?"

"Of course you can, Mr. Fletcher."

James spoke in a comradely tone to Harry, but Natasha gazed stolidly ahead from her position on the rear seat. Harry must be wondering about what would happen when they made it home, and no man would want to be him right now, James thought. Seconds later, the station wagon was plowing ahead through the quiet field, dodging the mountains as it veered off to the northwest. James could tell that this whole experience was an unthinkable imposition for Natasha. They were many miles from any train route or, he could hardly bear to think of it, Greyhound bus route, but she'd been slow to accept the inevitability of passing the night here. In the current age, when forming or dissolving corporate empires was a matter of seconds, the thought of having trouble getting oneself to an office park in time for a meeting dared hardly rear its head.

They rode on in the gathering dark. At length, ramshackle structures began to flit past the station wagon on either side, momentary apparitions amid the vast loneliness of fields. The car made a turn onto the main street of what passed for a town. In reality, James saw now, the town was two rows of buildings mostly fashioned from weathered boards with crude thatch roofs. It wasn't a town to speak of, but it would do for one night. It had to. He wanted to try to assuage Natasha a bit, to tell her that they could very well have landed in the midst of jagged mountains with nothing and nobody around for miles, and perhaps Harry did deserve just a bit of credit here, but James saw this wasn't the time to try to persuade Natasha of anything. Just let her annoyance run its course, as it must eventually. That approach had worked well enough when she'd yelled at an intern not long ago. Then again that was an episode James would really rather not recall. *You really mustn't take it personally. She's like that with the interns,* he'd told the quivering twenty-one-year-old, who somehow didn't seem to find that reassuring.

They had barely pulled onto the main street when Linda brought the station wagon to a halt. They were parked before the hotel, one of the few buildings here with more than one floor. At the sight of this building, its porch and plain wooden banisters and plaque between two upper-floor windows bearing the numerals **1875**, a barely perceptible relaxing of Natasha's tension and anger registered on James. Here was, at the very least, the thrill of something she didn't encounter every day. Here was an Old West hotel at the mouth of a dusty, neglected street. Linda turned her head back toward the executives. She was smiling ingenuously. If driving all the way out there to pick them up and bring them here had messed up Linda's evening, you wouldn't know from her face.

"So I'll leave you folks here, and hope you've got things sorted out by mornin'. If you need me, just holler," she said, pressing a card into James's hand. The card had information for an amateur florist business on it, along with her cell number.

"Thanks, Linda," James said in his nice Clark Kent voice.

"If you get bored up at the hotel, you might saunter on over to Zeke's place," Linda said.

"Where's that?"

"Four clicks up the street here on your left. You can see it from here," Linda replied.

Natasha titled her head toward James, nodded slightly.

"Thanks again," he said to Linda.

The two executives climbed out of the battered vehicle and proceeded up the steps and into the lobby of the dingy hotel. At the desk they found an elderly couple. Natasha pulled out the corporate card and got them two rooms on the upper floor. When they climbed the stairs and broke apart into the two rooms at the front of the hotel, James found to his dismay that the dingy walls, which had a blue background imprinted with images of daisies, were as thin as props hastily hammered together for a high school play. He found it more than a bit unseemly that he and Natasha would be lying down just inches from each other, even if a wall divided them. Well, they didn't have to think about that now. Before going out, he really must freshen up a bit. He moved in front of the sink and the mirror surmounted with a decal of a cowboy on a horse. The horse was rearing back on its hind legs at about a 45-degree angle as the cowboy swung a lasso with his right arm. James took off his glasses, rinsed his face, stood studying his dripping visage as feelings of awkwardness surged. *I'm going out on the town with Natasha Pruitt. Doing something, you know, social with her.* In the past, he'd had his share of drinks and laughs in Natasha's presence, but in the company of many other employees, at an official event marking a colleague's promotion or moving on from the firm. This was different and he wasn't sure how to feel about it. But the alternative was languishing in this dingy room with the thin walls and the peeling decal of a cowboy in action. Besides, in a vague way, James felt protective of Natasha, though she might vocally object if he said so.

But something complicated that protective impulse, oh yes. At times James couldn't help thinking about Vince, the guy James had had to fire. Vince was a young guy the firm had hired to write and edit copy for brochures and press releases. Technically he was to report to both James and Natasha, but Vince's cubicle adjoined Natasha's, so it was Natasha who managed Vince from day to day. And she did more than that, far more. Natasha was in close contact with her boyfriend throughout much of the day, some would say too close, for it was fairly common for workers passing by her cubicle to hear her exclaim "I love you!" with the phone pressed tightly to her ear. She also dashed off e-mail to the boyfriend regularly, and here is where the trouble developed. It seemed Vince could not refrain from peering over her torso at times and looking at what she was writing, and the content of some of the e-mail explicitly mocked Vince and his work. Vince clearly did not understand all the intricacies of the C-130 and C-140 software systems, as evidenced by the errors that kept turning up in his copy. Nevertheless, the notion of an employer or supervisor who made fun of her subordinates during business hours was a new one on Vince. After five weeks of abuse, to his face and through the electronic method, Vince burst out, "Natasha, if you do not speak to me more professionally, I am going to get up and walk out of this building and you won't see me again!"

Poor Vince. But Vince was wrong about Natasha, James figured. She was as flamboyant about her likes and dislikes as about her professional goals. Power to her. In any event, the phone sex with her boyfriend had ceased lately and there were whispers that Natasha had gone through a breakup.

Minutes later, they set out up the road in the dark, still in their work clothes except that they had shed their sports jackets and James had taken off his tie. It was chilly out but the walk was ninety seconds door to door. Soon they were standing before Zeke's, a saloon in a rectangular brick and cement building with a Budweiser sign in one window and a pair of swing doors, just like in those old Westerns, James thought. Contrary to one of Natasha's remarks on the way over here, they had built some things in this town since the 1800s. Natasha's look said, *I don't know about this.* They walked into a smoky space where the first thing you saw was a jukebox, followed by a bar running the length of the west wall. A dozen tables with three or four chairs apiece divided the bar from a raised platform with a microphone on a pole. About twenty people were at the tables, miners, ranchers, and other blue-collar folk unwinding after work, and a handful of cowboys sat at the bar. Behind the bar, a forty-five-year-old lady with stringy brownish hair that might have been ravishing before the gray set in was serving draft beers and whiskies. James and Natasha made their way to a table equidistant from the bar and the stage. James was a bit worried but he saw now that Natasha's look had mellowed just a bit, as if part of her might be willing to give this place a chance.

Though James had no idea what they served here, he asked Natasha what she wanted to drink. In her cutting manner, she said that to save them both some time, she'd better accompany him to the bar. When they got there, they quickly drew the attention of one of the fellows on a stool, a man in his early forties with black hair and a physique that was full without quite being fat. He wore dungarees and a white long-sleeved shirt made of coarse fibers.

"Well what're you two Fortune 500 folks doin' in these parts?" the man inquired.

James grinned.

"We had a bit of a transport malfunction, sir. Our plane had to land unexpectedly."

The man laughed.

"Oh, you don't have to call me sir. You can call me Merle, or good 'ol boy, or hayseed, or redneck, or you can call me asshole if you like!"

James laughed. To his surprise, Natasha joined in the laughter.

"Hey Sally," Merle called to the bartender, who looked over from the other end of the bar.

"This MBA type here just called me 'sir'!"

Now it was Sally's turn to chuckle.

"Get these two here a round on my tab, would you?" Merle called to Sally.

"Oh, you don't have to—" James began.

"No. No, I insist. One for you and one for the missus—excuse me, for the young lady here," Merle said.

James thought Natasha might erupt, but she laughed again. When Sally slid down the bar in their direction, James ordered a Woodpecker for Natasha and a Bud draft for himself. When they had their drinks in hand, Merle raised his glass of beer in a toast.

"Welcome!"

Now to the guests' amazement, Sally reached under the bar and produced a big hat, a Stetson, James thought that was what they called it. She held it out to Natasha.

"Come on, hon, I know this'll just look swell on you," Sally urged.

With another laugh, Natasha put on the big hat.

"When in Rome," she said.

James and Natasha made their way back to their table. But they weren't about to settle down with their drinks just yet, because Natasha had discovered the jukebox. Leaving James to guard her drink, she walked over to the area near the entrance while fishing dollar bills out of her wallet. When she reached that side of the room, James saw her engage in conversation and even flirt a bit with a burly man, about thirty-five, in overalls and boots, and a younger guy in jeans and a red and black checkered flannel shirt. Natasha found four dollars bills in her wallet. Soon she had programmed the juke to play "Born on a Bayou," "Rolling on a River," "Bad Moon Rising," and "Fortunate Son." Then she retreated to the table where James sat grinning and sipping his beer. By the time John Fogarty's voice came from the speakers, wishing he were back on the bayou, rolling with some Cajun queen, Natasha had drained her Woodpecker and was ready for another. More patrons were arriving so it made sense to get over to the bar now. Natasha nodded at Merle as she stood waiting for Sally's attentions. She did not want to use the company card for this purpose, so she opened a tab on her personal credit card, which she handed over to Sally, not without reluctance. How Natasha loved that credit card. As a platinum member, she enjoyed all kinds of perks and privileges.

·It didn't take long for the saloon to fill up. People noticed the white-collar interlopers but generally refrained from staring. James and Natasha talked about work for a bit, then they talked about Harry Van Zant, and their exquisite misfortune in ending up here, James taking the position that it wasn't Harry's fault at all, Natasha insisting it was. There were questions James really wanted to ask. He had a pesky curiosity about her. Was Natasha single? If so, did she want to stay that way? But he had lived in the corporate world too long to commit elementary mistakes of the kind that had proved fatal to others. He enjoyed himself without reservation until she said, quite abruptly, "Why don't you go get me another." Even in his mildly altered state, James was taken aback that she'd spoken to her colleague as if he were a waiter. But he picked himself up and ambled over to the bar.

They had a couple more rounds before someone turned off the juke. Having heard all of her requests, Natasha didn't mind. But both of the executives were surprised at the appearance of a woman, on the cusp of thirty, with luscious dark hair that Cezanne might have painted and flesh so supple and luminescent that it looked eager to nurture life and produce new life. She wore a purple shirt with sleeves down to her elbows, and, like most people in here, a pair of jeans. Most eyes in the place were on her as she passed amid respectful quiet from the entrance to the platform with the mike on it. A bass guitar player and a drummer followed her onto the platform and took a few minutes preparing. Then the young woman's lovely voice filled the smoky space. It was a voice that married clarity, perfect enunciation, with a caressing softness and effulgence that could transport the listener back to the womb. James and Natasha sat in something close to a trance as the singer outdid the Cowboy Junkies in her covers of "Blue Moon," "To Love Is To Bury," "200 More Miles," "Dreaming My Dreams With You," and "I'm So Lonesome I Could Cry." During the last number, in particular, the singer emulated and surpassed the languid cadences of the vocals of that band's lead vocalist, Margo Timmins. The singer in this remote smoky place allowed the instrumental rhythms to lull the listeners for so long that when her voice resumed, it was like the return of the caressing hand of a lover who knows exactly what her partner longs for. "Have you ever seen a robin weep . . ."

"Beautiful," Natasha murmured. The Stetson had slid a bit toward her right ear, so that the humor of her wearing it was even more pronounced. But she was oblivious to this. Here, James thought, was a side of Natasha, open, ingenuous, admiring, that he could never have suspected. Though she had often declared her love for her boyfriend over the phone, you had to be on the receiving end of that love to have any appreciation for it. Otherwise it was a distant, flimsy bridge over torrents of nastiness. James and Natasha would gladly have paid to extend this experience throughout the evening, but the woman on the stage went through a few more numbers before thanking the audience and the tavern's owners and making her way down and around the audience toward the bar. Patrons began to leave.

Minutes later, the woman who had filled the space with her lovely voice was seated over a drink at one of the tables closest to the juke. James thought he recognized the two men at her table as the fellows he'd spotted Natasha flirting with earlier. Now Natasha's look seemed to ask, *What do you think? Feeling brave?* A voice in James's head pleaded vainly that it was unseemly for Natasha or himself to drink any more. From a certain point of view, they were even now on a corporate outing together. But it was clear that Natasha wanted to invite the singer over to their table for a drink. Well, why not, he figured. He had a bit of a buzz at this point, but it wasn't like he was plastered. James picked himself up, ambled over to the other table, and broke into the conversation with all the politeness he could muster. He felt pleasant surprise when the vocalist agreed to join him and Natasha. The two fellows seemed mildly resentful but they didn't challenge James or follow him and the singer. At the executives' table, the woman introduced herself as Bethany.

Natasha sent James back to the bar where he got a Woodpecker for her, another draft beer for himself, and a Jack-and-diet for the singer. As he returned to the table, James saw that the crowd had really thinned out. There were maybe fifteen people in the place, the bartender included. As James sat down, he found Natasha in animated discussion with Bethany. He soon perceived envy on Natasha's part, mingled with another element.

"That was, bar none, the best cover of 'Blue Moon' I've heard. Believe me when I say it leaves others in the dust."

"Why thank you."

"You have a lovely voice. I wish I could sing like that."

"Have you ever taken any lessons?" Bethany asked.

"Oh, no. But I just might. You've shown me what a voice can do."

"Again, thank you, Natasha."

"You're quite welcome."

"You and James here seem like real nice folk."

"You will stay here and enjoy this one on us," Natasha said, pushing the Jack-and-diet across the table. It wasn't really a question.

James noticed that the two men from Bethany's former table, the thirty-five-year-old fellow in overalls and the kid in a flannel shirt, had maneuvered themselves over to one of the immediately adjoining tables. They were not participating in the conversation at the executives' table, but they were not exactly absent from it either. He heard the younger of them address the older as Gary. For her part, Bethany seemed mildly astonished at the generosity of the white-collar strangers. Who were they, and why were they so taken with her? Natasha, who appeared obsessed with Bethany, wanted to keep drinking. By this point, Natasha must have lost count of the number of Woodpeckers she'd put away. They'd been here for hours now. She'd flirted with the man in overalls and his young pal, she'd mingled on the way to and from the restroom, she'd sat there in rapt attention during the performance, slamming her glass down at the end of a number. Modesty was never a hallmark of hers in the first place.

"So tell me, Bethany."

"Yes ma'am," said Bethany, a faint, shy glimmer in her easy blue eyes.

"Tell me what it is you do when you're not singing."

Bethany chuckled.

"Oh, well, that's most of the time. I'm here once a week at the most, you know."

"Right, so tell me how you fill up the rest of your life, Ms. Laura Ingalls Wilder," Natasha pressed.

"Ms. who? What? I don't get it," Bethany said.

"I asked you a simple question. What do you do when you're not here?"

"Well what do you imagine, now?"

"I asked you a simple question."

"I said I don't get it."

Natasha stared. This was not how one spoke to Ms. Natasha Pruitt.

"I said I don't get it, miss," Bethany added.

"I asked you a very simple question. Why the hell don't you give me a straight answer?"

"I take care of my six- and four-year old boys."

Natasha titled her head back and laughed a raw, rasping laugh.

"Oh, now that figures, right? While professional women go to work, Miss Bethany here yanks up her shirt and offers her naked titties for the brood to come and suck on!"

"Natasha," James murmured.

"You dumb fucking country cunt. You don't have any function except to please the men in your life, do you, you stupid cow," Natasha exclaimed, and tossed the remainder of her drink in Bethany's face.

"Natasha!" James shouted, leaping to his feet, attempting to wipe the stunned singer's face with his bare hands, apologizing profusely. Gary and the young guy were on their feet and everyone was looking toward the executives' table in astonishment.

"Guys, guys, please, I'm so sorry, she's been under tremendous stress lately. You know what, she's in shock from the emergency landing," James blurted, forgetting that two lies are less convincing than one.

Gary and his sidekick were briefly too incredulous to move. If James had done this thing, they'd know exactly how to react, but this was a lady here.

"Guys, I'm so deeply sorry. Here, the next round's on us," James put in, thrusting a heap of bills into Bethany's left hand. Bethany herself was the calmest person in the place.

"Come *on!*" James hissed in Natasha's ear, pulling her to her feet. He began half-coaxing, half-shoving her in the direction of the exit. But before he could get them both to the exit, she whispered that she felt sick and couldn't leave now. Everyone was staring and the scene could erupt into violence at any moment. But James led Natasha to the restroom, between the end of the bar and the wall supporting the juke, and he stood guard at the door while she was inside, presumably vomiting. Gary and the younger guy, whom somebody had addressed as Chris, looked coldly at James. In a quick movement, James drew up to the bar and asked Sally as politely as he could for the credit card she'd been holding. Though naturally Sally showed none of her former warmth, she handed it across the counter. Sally had a big heart and she both liked and pitied James. But when he moved back in front of the restroom, Gary and Chris looked ready to jump him. To his surprise, he heard faint noises suggesting that Natasha was doing something with her iPhone. When she emerged he led her swiftly out into the cool air.

"What on earth were you thinking? I know you're drunk, but—" he began.

"Just shut up. Those hayseeds were feeling me up with their eyes all night."

"No they weren't."

"Yes, they were, James. And I refuse to pay them."

"You already have."

"No, I just took care of that."

So Natasha had cancelled the payment. James guessed this made them thieves. But James had long ago lapsed into a mode of thought where he did not consider himself to have done right or wrong. There were things he did right and things he would right later, in the pleasant environs of a well-run modern office. But the reality of the offense hit home and for the briefest of moments, as he considered what a shitty thing they'd done and other aspects of their experience that night, James's mind lingered in a flyover state, a rarely glimpsed and long neglected place between the assumptions that guided his interactions with men and women, with colleagues, superiors, and diversity trainers, from day to day.

Though he had his right arm slung around Natasha, it was only to keep her upright, there was no romance in it. Just another minute and they'd be back in the hotel. Soon enough, they climbed the rickety wooden steps and passed into the lobby, where only the grandfatherly member of the couple they'd met before was on duty. James asked the elderly gentleman how far away the police station was. He asked whether the old man knew anyone who could provide a ride in the morning down to the field in the canyon where the jet was. No sooner had James begun to shepherd Natasha up the dusty stairs when noises outside distracted him. He turned to peer through the tall rectangular windows in the double doors. A little crowd had followed the executives here from the tavern. He saw Gary, Chris, Merle, six or seven others.

James turned back to the stairs. Natasha had retreated up to her room. He whipped out his cell phone and tried the dispatcher he'd talked to a matter of hours ago. The ringing and ringing seemed to mock him. For all he knew, the dispatcher might have been in the tavern during that whole scene. Yes, that was probably the case. He thought of asking the old man for help but this was just too ludicrous. James decided to bite the bullet. He walked out onto the porch.

"Thief!" "Cheat!" "Scumbag!" called some of the people in the crowd.

James looked Merle in the eye.

"What do you good fellows want?"

"I think Gary here would like a word with you, sir," said Merle.

Gary got to the point.

"You brought the situation about and you have to face up," the man said.

"Sir, I am very deeply sorry for how my colleague behaved. As I said before, we have both been under extreme stress—"

"Excuses!" Chris broke in.

"You brought the situation about and you have to face up to it like a man now. Whyn't you stand up and be a man? We ain't goin' home and you'll never sleep a wink with the ten of us under your window," Gary pressed.

Face up to it like a man. When had anyone ever spoken to James Fletcher this way?

He thought about the distance between his room and the street, about Natasha hiding away in a room with flimsy walls, about the theft they'd committed that night. He studied the faces on the street before him.

"You know it's her we're mad at," Gary said.

"You'll have to go through me," James answered.

They gazed in fury at the prim executive on the porch.

"All right, then."

James removed his glasses, then stepped down from the porch. He'd heard about fights where the opponents circled each other endlessly, but Gary was too enraged to let that happen. Gary moved in fast. James swung wildly, and his fist grazed Gary's chin before the man in overalls slammed James in the gut so hard that James made only a quick hoarse noise like a reaction to an onscreen event in a hushed theater. When James swung his right arm with all his force, he actually got the satisfaction of hearing something crack, of a faint acknowledgment of the blow at a point within Gary's jaw. Gary kneed James in the groin and followed up with a punch so hard James thought his head would snap right off. Instead he staggered back a few paces, teetered in desperate fear, then dropped to his knees. Gary moved up and kicked his opponent so hard in the face that he split James's left cheek. As James lay on the ground, Gary gave him three hard kicks to the rib cage.

While Gary and the others wandered back toward the tavern, Merle approached the executive lying on his back in the dust. He helped James into a sitting position on the steps of the hotel's porch, disappeared into the hotel for a minute, returned with some napkins and ice, and spoke gently to James about the way things were, here in the flyover state. Merle could not go very far toward easing the pain, but at the very least, James felt he himself had not totally failed tonight.

A little more than two months later, the offices in San Luis Obispo had undergone nothing less than a reconfiguration. The higher-ups in the company had seen fit to open a new annex at the far end of the vast parking lot abutting the complex containing James Fletcher's office, and they had also handed out a few promotions. So James had a bit of a walk in store for him when he received a call one bright afternoon summoning him to the new annex, which he had barely glimpsed. When he had finally traversed the parking lot, he saw that they'd really spared no expense. The annex was something, all right. Here was a gleaming, ultramodern complex of vast black and silver cubes and cylinders. Light glinted off the pristine ultrasmooth rectangles and curves at innumerable points. You entered the annex through a lobby flanked by two stern-faced guards hired from an elite security company. Marveling at the ambition that had inspired this place, James strolled through the lobby and into an elevator that took him to the third floor. James walked down a corridor, made a left, and pursued another corridor to a corner office. He went inside.

"Hello, Natasha."

"Hi James, how are you?"

"Not bad at all, thank you."

"James, you have been a highly dedicated employee for more than four years. A number of glowing comments have turned up in your evaluations. But as you know quite well, we're in a highly competitive industry, and sometimes we have to make tough decisions," Natasha began.

Ten minutes later, James walked back out into the parking lot, fuming. He spun around a couple of times, nearly falling, his face buried in his hands. He couldn't begin to accept the decision. It was incredible that he had barely gotten a chance to talk on his behalf. There were points he badly wanted to make, objections he urgently needed to raise. But accept the decision he must. The looks of the men guarding the entrance were hard, intimidating.

Comfort Zones

For Marci Rupp, the town in Iowa to which she had moved after accepting an associate professorship at a prestigious liberal arts college was not at all a hardship post. Yes, it was a provincial backwater burg where people said "sir" and "ma'am," soda was "pop," and a bag was a "sack," but the town was so picturesque in the fall, postcard-worthy, so gorgeous that if she lived just half a mile closer to the campus, she would stroll to work through the streets lined with red and orange foliage rather than drive. People complained about town-gown relations, but that was easy to forget amid the colors of a fall in Central Iowa. Above all, Marci appreciated the quiet of her house on the fringes of town, where it was easy to lose herself amid her piles of books and papers dealing with aspects of medieval life, a subject she taught to freshmen and sophomores, or as she invariably called them, first- and second-year students. The students, admittedly, were mixed. Some were history majors in need of credits, some were mildly curious about the subject, and some were fanatics belonging to an underground society on campus that staged reenactments of jousts and battles, complete with lovingly crafted swords, pikes, axes, and halberds.

Naturally, Professor Rupp had an area of specialization within this field, and it was class and gender. Her doctoral thesis had drawn heavily on the work of medieval historian Eileen Power, and she was the author of widely cited papers explicating the development and enforcement of class divisions and gender roles in the English and French towns of the 13th and 14th centuries. Back at Reed College, Marci's former employer, one of Marci's colleagues had sneered at the idea of working in this "hick town," which must have pretty unprogressive attitudes about gender or any other topic you could name. But the college itself was as progressive as any in the country, and offered a supportive environment for someone who dreamed of influencing the direction of a field and was bright and driven enough to pull it off. One of her new colleagues had accused her, half-seriously, of political correctness, but she dismissed the charge and quickly forgot it. Things had been going rather well for this rising star one evening in October when Marci heard pounding on her front door.

Even in a place as relatively peaceful as Portland, Oregon, Marci's city instincts would have kicked in immediately, and she would have called 911. But this was a cow town in the middle of Iowa. The very worst thing to happen here in living memory was when a college kid got plastered and mouthed off in a bar, and one of the locals introduced the kid's ass to his foot.

Hesitantly, but not fearfully, Marci opened the door to reveal a guy in his mid-twenties, with jet black hair combed straight back and a pale intense face, obviously a blue-collar guy from town, not a student. In fact, she had seen him on the street just the other week, outside the movie theater, not far from where Patricia Knowles, a professor of African American Studies, had had an encounter with a local in a rusty red pickup who'd called her a racial epithet before driving off. Marci had no idea of this fellow's name or occupation. He looked a bit scared, but even more embarrassed. Marci was not afraid of him.

"Oh ma'am, I'm really sorry to bother you," he began.

"What is it, sir?"

He spoke in a technical language she could barely follow—something about axles and CV boots—but she understood that he'd cut his left hand badly while fixing his car. (Never having owned a car before moving here Marci did not know what CV boots were.) She looked over his shoulder out into the driveway, and there indeed was a brown Chevy, hidden behind the neighbors' broad white house from the view of anyone on the street.

"Could I please use your bathroom for a minute?" he asked.

She glanced at his left hand, which was indeed bleeding profusely.

"Yes, yes, of course."

She pointed it out to him. He breathed thanks to her and hurried past through the living room, turned at the tall oak bookcase, and made a left into the pristine bathroom with a lavender rug and a shower curtain with prancing unicorns on it. The door closed, she heard water running, and the man grunting and emitting oaths as he tended to his hand. Suddenly she wondered if that was a siren she'd heard in the distance a minute ago—yes, it must have been—and thought maybe she should call the police. Who knew what had really happened to this guy's hand and why he'd stopped here? But no, this was not some drifter, it was someone from town, someone everybody knew, a kid with a house and a job and a family. Surely Marci's city instincts (she was originally from Boston) were driving her beyond rationality.

Now the guy came back into the living room, calmer, but still pale and nervous. Before she could make a gracious gesture ushering him to the door, he asked, "Could I sit down for just a minute?" in so polite and humble a tone that her wariness receded still further, and she felt almost solicitous toward the stranger.

"Oh, of course," said Professor Rupp with a gesture at the cozy couch where she stretched out in the evenings with stacks of papers and blue examination booklets. He eased onto the couch, extending the hand that wasn't bandaged.

"I'm Drew, by the way."

"Marci."

"Thanks for helping me, Marci."

"Not at all."

His breathing eased as he lay back in the couch and studied the bandage for a moment.

"I've seen you in town, Drew. What do you do?"

She could not have imagined the effect this question had on Drew. He gazed at her.

"It's not a trick question, Drew," she said with what she hoped sounded like levity.

He raised his head, eyes wide, stammering:

"I, uh, I work at Jake's Tavern and I do construction work a few days a month. They're both new jobs. I worked at the garment factory until they laid me off."

"Are you married?"

"Ah, well . . . I was. I'm separated."

She nodded. Drew had such an air of wounded innocence about him. He gazed ahead, taking in the four bookshelves and the heaps of papers on the desk and the table between the windows at the east wall, to his right.

"I've never seen this many books in one place before."

There was a childlike awe in his voice that she found endearing.

"You must have been to some libraries and bookstores in your life."

"Oh, well . . . when I was in elementary school, sure. How long does it take you to read a book like that?" he asked with a gesture at *Race, Gender, and Class*, Fifth edition.

She could not help smiling at his innocence of all things scholarly.

"A few hours, maybe."

"Gosh."

"Well, I grew up reading."

"I sure wish I had time to read."

In spite of herself, Marci felt proud of how much her vocation and her house impressed Drew. Marci so rarely had any company here at all. As awkward as the situation was, Marci felt an impulse to impress the young man even more, to make him see the magnanimity of the white-collar class Drew might have disdained. Marci offered him a glass of wine. He gratefully nodded. She rose and moved into the kitchen, thinking of the bottles of merlot she'd bought from the one store on Main Street that sold wines worthy of the name. How often did this kid ever get a taste of anything like that? She figured he probably had developed no appreciation of wine at all. His voice followed her as she reached for the wine and a corkscrew.

"If my friends saw me reading, they wouldn't get it. They'd ask me if I was bored, or just broke."

"Really? Your friends don't ever read?"

"Nah, every Friday and Saturday they're out lookin' for some hole."

Some *hole?*

"Excuse me?" Marci said, nearly dropping the bottle on the gleaming tiles of her kitchen.

"Oh, ma'am, I'm sorry, I meant, like a date, you know?"

Marci breathed deeply, steadying her grip on the bottle.

"It's okay, Drew, just could you please not use abusive or derogatory language about women in this house? Or anywhere for that matter?"

"I'm really sorry, ma'am."

"All right."

"So I was sayin', I don't really read much. But I do know parts of the Bible pretty well."

Surprise, surprise, thought Marci.

"What about your ex, what does she do?" the professor asked, handing him a glass of wine and sitting down in the oak chair across from him.

He shifted slightly, as if at an inappropriate question.

"She tends bar on occasion . . . 'till recently, she mostly cooked and cleaned for me. Why do you ask?"

"I'm interested in social roles, that's all."

"Angie was a good lady," Drew said with sadness in his voice.

"Was?"

"Yes, she took real good care of me and our boy Zack."

Marci doubted that Angela had had much choice in the matter. Her role had been handed to her. At this point, Professor Rupp recalled a line from a medieval manual addressed to women, written by the Ménagier of Paris and quoted in Eileen Power's book, *Medieval People*:

"Cherish the person of your husband carefully . . . for 'tis your business."

"Yeah, I actually wanted to go home after a shift instead of going drinking with my buddies, 'cause she sure knew how to look after me."

"I'm sure she sensed that she was expected to, Drew."

"And thus you shall persevere and guard him from all discomforts and give him all the ease that you can, and serve him and cause him to be well served in your house."

"It was like that for a couple of years, I came home dead tired and she had dinner ready for me and Zack, and she brought me beers while I watched *Friends* and *Cheers* reruns and ball games, and she liked taking care of us. I felt like it made sense, like there was—what's the word?—there was, like, a good match between her needs and mine."

"Symmetry?" the professor offered.

"Yeah, that's it. Symmetry. We loved each other and we loved Zack and each of us had something to offer the other two."

"May I ask why you're not still together, then?" the professor ventured, a bit moved by the simplicity of this crude man's sentiments, even as she recoiled from his primitive attitudes.

"Oh, well . . . Things got really nasty all of a sudden. I started coming home and she began acting angry and resentful, like she didn't want to do this duty no more."

This duty? *This duty?*

In a carefully controlled voice, the professor said, "You know, it wasn't up to you to dictate her duty. There may have been other things in her life that she needed to devote her time to . . . she may have started feeling a strain, Drew. You really may have not been thinking about her needs enough."

"I don't know. I guess so. But whatever was going on, life wasn't what I was used to anymore."

The Ménagier of Paris had written, "*I counsel you to make such cheer to your husband at his comings and goings and to persevere therein.*" That was six centuries ago, and such attitudes were as antiquated as the lances and halberds of medieval reenactors. Yet Drew had enforced a code not unlike the Ménagier's. Clearly, Angela had followed no such counsel when she realized what her own life was becoming. *Bravo for her*, thought Marci.

Something was very wrong with Drew. It struck her that Drew's face was as pale and unsettled as when he'd first entered. He carried right on.

"We argued, and it got so bad a couple of times that our neighbor told me the next morning he'd been an ass hair away from calling the police. Excuse my French."

At this, Marci nearly chortled—your *French*, Drew?

For a moment, he looked lost in his recollections, not seeming to care who Marci was or how she might react to the ignorant opinions he spewed, not even knowing why he was sitting in her living room on this crisp night in October. It had all seemed to fall away. Though he was exceedingly odd, the chummy good nature of the young man had muffled the voice telling Marci something was horribly wrong. But something was—and Drew was no good, he was a social Neanderthal not deserving of any empathy at all.

"Did it occur to you that maybe your wife—Angela—wasn't satisfied with domestic chores? That she felt a need to do things that were interesting and challenging, and your expectations made that practically impossible?"

Drew had lived for twenty-five years without thoughts of this nature occurring to him, and all other things being equal, he would have gone another quarter of a century the same way. Now, Drew had no defense.

He probably could not spell *patriarchy*, let alone justify the concept. She thought of ordering him to leave. Then, as his dark eyes roamed over the room, something deeply unpleasant occurred to Marci: She'd tolerated, even encouraged, Drew's presence here because she had not had company, of any kind, since moving in three months before. He drank his wine and shifted nervously, again seeming mentally disorganized to an extent well beyond what a minor hand injury would have caused.

"Well, I don't know if Angie would have taken the kind of opportunities you're talking about, even if they had been available. I just know I was working 'till I could hardly stand up to put food on the table for my wife and boy and pay the rent, and I was dog tired when I came through the door. Dog tired."

His conversation was all about himself; he was the center of his own universe, she thought.

"And then Angie started going out on the town with this skanky lady named Marsha Hoyt," he added.

Marci wondered if she'd ever spotted Marsha Hoyt, in the window of a bar, on the street clinging to some man's arm, standing at a pool table laughing hoarsely.

"I heard a lot of talk about it, oh yeah, there was wild talk, and it always found its way to me."

"Have a care that you be honestly clad, without new devices and without too much or too little frippery," the Ménagier had warned.

As she recalled those lines from Eileen Power's book, she thought Drew seemed driven by similar attitudes.

"Things got to the point where I had to tell Angie, look, Marsha is bad news, everyone's talking a lot of shit, you've got to cut this out for both our sakes."

As the Ménagier had written: *"When you go to town or church go suitably accompanied by honourable women according to your estate, and flee suspicious company, never allowing any ill-famed woman to be in your presence."*

Drew explained, in unnecessary detail, the demands of taking care of Zack, demands that grew after he got laid off at the garment factory, and he began working extra shifts at the bar, seven days a week, desperate for all the tips he could swing. To this day, he cared about Angie and did not want others to have a poor image of her, though he'd been upset by the growing frequency of her foul moods when he came home and there was no supper ready and he collapsed on the couch because she didn't want him in bed. Zack was experiencing ostracism more and more at school, and when he went to a birthday party, kids mocked him for the cheapshit present he brought, a little Harry Potter action figure, not even properly wrapped, but thrust into a brown paper bag. Marci wanted to roll her eyes. Without doubt, it would require more patience than Marci could summon to make Drew see how he'd laid down a restrictive code owing much to that which oppressed women in the Old World thanks to the Ménagier of Paris. If this rube weren't still taking up time here, Marci could be having all the wine to herself, meditating on her next research project.

He continued:

"A few months after we separated, I saw Angie going around with Bob Pointer, and the rumors started to fly—I heard all about Bob taking her out on the town, treating her like a queen. Bob's divorced, with a boy and a girl, Jared and Sarah, but he's done all right for himself. He owns the other construction firm in this county, the one that won't hire me. I knew she was digging for his gold, but I had to keep paying child support way beyond my means, hundreds upon hundreds and thousands upon thousands—and I have no idea how much of it, or whether any of it, was ever spent on my son, but the law is the law."

Marci Rupp studied the depths of those dark eyes, where his desperation was still visible but had segued partly into a bitterness that must have characterized all disciples of the Ménagier of Paris in such circumstances, all the petty male tyrants who had held sway in the Old World as in this one. Drew seemed to shift anxiously at a sound far off in the night—*was it a siren?* This jolted Marci in a way she hoped he didn't notice. Now it occurred to her that he'd been sitting an awfully long time in this space to which she had not invited him, and never would have, for certain. He was so mentally disorganized. What had really happened to his hand?

"Drew, I—I don't want to sound disrespectful—but a lot of your attitudes about Angela, about your marriage and your responsibilities to Zack, strike me as entirely out of date."

He sat there letting her probe the depths of his dark eyes. Then she thought *He doesn't want to move. I could insult him to his face and he'd nod and say, Yes, ma'am.*

"Will you excuse me for a moment?" she asked, in a tone she might have used with a student taking up time in her office in the Humanities Building two and a half miles from here. Then she disappeared, not into the bathroom, but into her bedroom, where she stealthily lifted her phone's receiver and dialed 911, then lay the receiver on the bed. Even without her saying anything, they'd trace the call and send the police here immediately.

She emerged into an empty room. The front door was ajar, she saw, reaching it just in time to glimpse Drew as he accelerated down the driveway and into the street and turned right onto a road that would lead eventually to a network of streets leading to the expressway. That expressway was several miles away. Within seconds, she heard the sirens again. For a mile, they followed Drew as he desperately weaved past slower cars. Finally his car reached a roadblock and officers, lacking patience for his refusal to give up, ended his life with a furious fusillade. The money in the car eventually made its way back to the payroll office he'd robbed.

As for Marci Rupp, aspects of their strange encounter and their conversation soon faded from her mind, leaving her with the satisfying sense that Drew had gotten pretty much what he deserved, that here was one oppressor who would not be oppressing anyone ever again.

The Forgotten Case

Dan Bede was determined to talk to the young woman sitting near him in the campus lounge. But he felt the old fear that had kept him from making more than a handful of acquaintances at this liberal arts college amid the cornfields, where students lived in such proximity that it practically took an effort *not* to get to know people. There's nothing worse than a moral coward, Dan thought. Moral cowardice is so much lower than the physical kind because it means you're not brave enough to take an action when the possible consequences are relatively limited, when there's no physical danger.

The girl had a compact body and arching brows conveying seriousness and intelligence. Her straight yellow hair fell to the upper edges of her thick white sweater. She was sitting cross-legged on a bench in her booth, one of two booths near the lounge's façade, reading a sociology textbook. The light coming through the big glass façade threw all her features into relief. Dan had seen her in here a couple of times, either in that booth or the adjoining one in which he now sat. She always had that keen, alert look. He guessed that if you were lucky enough to be in a relationship with her, you'd never get suspicious about jokes your friends might be making about her IQ. Not that Dan had any friends. Enough dithering, he decided.

"Hey. You know, uh, it seems like every time you're here, I'm here," Dan said, leaning a few inches toward her booth with a grin he hoped didn't look nervous.

She lifted her eyes from the textbook and rotated her face toward him. There was such disdain in her look, you might have thought Dan was a stripper trying to impress people with a tiny appendage.

"If you're trying to pick me up, I'm a lesbian."

"Oh, I, uh— No! I wasn't trying to pick you up or anything. I was just, like—"

"Tell me: Why are all men on this campus such pricks?"

"I—I'm *not a prick*! I'll let you get back to soche."

He hoped she might at least appreciate his use of the local vernacular for "sociology," but she turned indifferently back to the textbook.

Dan hurried out of the lounge and into the cool sunlight of a fall afternoon in the upper Midwest. The weather was changing markedly, in this first week of October 1992, but it was still warm enough for guys to toss Frisbees around on the grass in shorts and t-shirts. On the far side of the field, kids sat on benches facing the edge of campus, the road, and the town where nearly everybody disliked the college students. Dan was sure the Frisbee throwers saw the humiliation in his face as he hurried up the path leading to the library. He was practically running by the time he made it up the long ramp to the library's front door. Dan moved inside, past the checkout desk and the rows of periodicals where he'd discovered poems by a man named Bukowski in obscure little journals, past stacks filled with books on various periods of European and American history, and reached the quiet area at the back of the building. One of the comfy chairs was empty. Dan collapsed into it, closing his fingers around his face.

As he listened to cars and pickups rumble by on the road twenty yards from the library's glass rear wall, Dan reminded himself of what he'd overheard a psych major say one afternoon in the dining hall. A *catastrophe event* is a trivial occurrence that gets magnified, often to ludicrous proportions, within the mind of someone in a particular kind of state. People overlook or underestimate the role of catastrophe events in driving behavior, and the extremes to which they push some of us. It was up to Dan now to parse recent events in his life and figure out why he might be so vulnerable to such an occurrence. He realized he didn't have to go back far. All kinds of events that had been unimaginable to a teenager growing up in West Virginia had crowded the past week. There was the evening when a few of the politically active feminists blew loud whistles in the dining hall every twelve seconds to call attention to the frequency of rape in America. Dan hadn't been sure why it was necessary to blow whistles the whole evening after they'd made their point, or what people here on this campus in the cornfields were supposed to do about rape, but he hadn't dared voice his dissent. They ruined his meal, all right. There hadn't been such disruption in the dining hall since the L.A. riots were going on, six month earlier, and radical students had stood on tables giving speeches or harangues. People said race was the real issue on this campus, but Dan didn't believe it.

Then was the incident just three days ago where he'd been sitting up at the front of the library with one of his British history textbooks open before him, and a girl had walked right up, grabbed the book, and run out of the library without a word. He'd chased her out of the building and down the ramp, lost sight of her, and then found his $40 textbook face down in the mud near the ramp's entrance. Then he'd spotted the girl, in a cluster of students by the lounge, talking nonchalantly. When he approached her, she walked away. One of the other students, noticing Dan's bewilderment, told him that an assignment for a sociology class had required the girl to act like a social deviant, however she might interpret that phrase, and to record what the experience felt like. Just two days before that incident, the rarest of events happened. The few Republicans on the campus managed to bring a renowned conservative intellectual to the campus to give a talk. So rare were visits by conservatives that Dan couldn't even recall the previous one. In a reception at the lounge following the talk, a few of the feminists had removed their clothes and walked around with pink triangles taped to their privates.

But none of these events had unsettled Dan quite as much as an incident in his Intro to Social Theory class the other day. The professor, a dreadlocked lady known to all her students by her first name, had ordered the class of sixteen women and five men to conduct an experiment. She told the men to get up and leave the room. They were to wait a couple of minutes and come back in, and when they returned, they had to pretend they were women. Dan and the four other guys dutifully got up and left. When they came back into the room, their exaggerated prissy movements, which they thought were the natural consequence of the professor having ordered them to *act*, made the five guys the target of such psychological violence that Dan had wanted to cry. *Misogynist! Pig! Gynophobe! Cock-centered insecure male oppressor! SCUM!*

Now that he had placed the catastrophe event in context, had recognized it as part of a pattern of things that you just had to try to get used to here, Dan was able to study peacefully for a while. The library was a clean place with big cushions. He passed a lonely hour in the dining hall, eating his dinner alone as other kids talked happily. Then he returned to the library, went downstairs to the computer room, found a station, and took out his notebooks. Dan always tried to get here pretty early because the four computer rooms on campus filled up fast every evening. If you had a paper due and you couldn't find a station, you'd better have a portable typewriter. Nobody envisioned a time in the near future when most young people would have laptops. At this juncture, Dan had an assignment due for Classical History I and another for British History II. For the former, he had to draw up a list of questions he'd distribute to the other students on the morning they had him scheduled to lead the class discussion. For the latter, he had a twenty-page paper to turn out, on British perceptions of Russia at the time of the Crimean War.

He got to work on the questions for the discussion. Dan's reading of certain passages of Herodotus left no doubt in his mind that what purported to be acts of faith, like the offering up of cattle, had a highly commercial aspect to them. In style and in content, they were prototypical business deals, however Herodotus or his characters might refer to them. Dan wondered what the others in his class might think of this reading. As he was pondering how to phrase the question, an instant message flashed on the screen before him: "Greetings from afar!"

At first, Dan did not recognize the sender. The name was styled JFields. Did Dan know anyone with that initial and surname? Then he thought, *Of course, of course!* It was Jeff Fields, a popular kid who was active in the Black Students Association, the Multiethnic Coalition, and the Progressive Alliance. Dan had never been in a class with Jeff, but had met him quite briefly at a party. He knew Jeff had a large circle of friends and was big in the party and drinking scenes.

Dan didn't really have time to chat, but he couldn't help thinking of his failure to make friends on this campus and the reasons for that failure. He wondered how he could contemplate snubbing a well-meaning person yet again. His fingers hit the keyboard.

DBede: Hey what's up?
JFields: Wassup Dan. Where are you?

DBede: Dawson Library. Got a lot to do.

JFields: Studying all night. You work too hard, man.

DBede: Yeah, I know. I've got a big British history paper due. What're you up to?

JFields: Not a whole lot. I'm hangin here with Laura Timmerman.

So Jeff was in one of the other computer rooms, with another student Dan didn't know but thought he might like to know. A second-year student from Chicago, a little weird, about midway up the popularity scale. Dan saw a cursor blinking before "LTimmer" inside the chat box.

Dan engaged in a bit of banter with Jeff, establishing nothing except that he was glad to have gotten a station in here, he was under a fair amount of pressure, and he was looking forward to the weekend. Implicit in that last bit of information, Dan hoped, was his readiness and availability to hang out with people as soon as Friday afternoon came. Dan imagined a scene. He envisioned Jeff, Laura, and himself in a dorm room, on a floor Dan had thought he'd go through his life without ever exploring, Jeff in a chair and Dan on the bed with Laura, raising Coronas in a toast, laughing, getting up to dance to the tune "Love Shack" from the radio by the bed. Then he chided himself for getting so excited so quickly.

JFields: How come you eat alone in Gaines Hall every night?

Dan paused. Gaines was the dining hall where, indeed, he sat most nights shoveling the bland undercooked fare into his mouth. Dan thought for a moment, trying hard to recall seeing Jeff there. No memories came. Did everyone on campus know of Dan's loneliness, his alienation? Then he thought, no, Laura probably eats there. She said something to Jeff. He tried to remember where he'd ever seen Laura there, but now new messages were filling the space before his eyes.

JFields: Did your friends all leave and go to a different school? Why don't I see you more often at Howard parties? In truth I don't think I've ever seen you there.

Dan exhaled in relief. Jeff wasn't making any nasty insinuations about him, the popular kid just wanted to know why Dan had hardly made any effort to take advantage of the opportunities all around him on this cozy campus. Parties at the Howard Center were one way to meet people, even if some students panned the new building for reeking of suburban malls. Dan rebuked himself for making it necessary for Jeff to pose this question.

> DBede: I want to get out there, I really do, I know there are lots of amazing people there. I'm just on kind of a funny schedule sometimes, you know, with all these papers and exams and such. Sometimes I sleep when I should be getting out. Plus, honestly, I'm not always sure what to wear.
>
> JFields: You're self-conscious about what to wear?
>
> DBede: Yeah, I admit it.
>
> JFields: Well, I assumed as much.
>
> DBede: Huh?
>
> JFields: I said that's what I thought, bro.
>
> LTimmer: I hear that's not the only thing you're self-conscious about.
>
> DBede: I don't understand.
>
> LTimmer: No, I don't think you have much of a clue about anything, boychick.
>
> DBede: Huh?
>
> JFields: Do you eat alone in Gaines Hall every single night?
>
> DBede: No, Jeff, of course I don't.
>
> LTimmer: Really?
>
> DBede: I don't want to sound dense or anything but I'm lost here.
>
> JFields: So tell us, Dan, what do you do on the nights you don't eat in Gaines?
>
> DBede: I usually order Mexican from Jimbo's in town. Or I order pizza from one of a couple places.
>
> JFields: Really? Are you a big pizza eater, Dan?
>
> DBede: Yeah.
>
> JFields: I mean, do you really devour that stuff?
>
> DBede: I can't spend too much money, but I do like pizza whenever I can get it. People can come to my room and share it if they like.
>
> JFields: Do you like your pizza hot and wet?

DBede: Huh?

LTimmer: Is that all you can say? Huh?

DBede: I don't get it.

JFields: We were just talking about pizza.

DBede: What do the two of you want? I'm not trying to be short with you.

JFields: We want to know about your taste in pizza. Although you're obviously not Italian. You're about as far from black as a guy can be.

DBede: Huh?

LTimmer: Do you want to see me naked?

DBede:

DBede: Sorry I hit return before I was done.

LTimmer: That's okay.

DBede: What were you saying?

LTimmer: Do you want to see me naked.

DBede: Sure.

LTimmer: What's stopping you?

DBede: I don't understand.

LTimmer: You don't know about all the naked dinners and parties on and around this campus.

JFields: Never been to a naked party, man?

DBede: No. Is there one coming up?

LTimmer: I'm surprised you haven't been to one, because rumor has it you are really a bold and uninhibited person in certain situations.

DBede: Huh?

JFields: Going to fuckin slap you if you say that again.

DBede: Sorry. Really sorry. I just would like some clarification of what Laura said.

LTimmer: We just want to know why you'd ever be reluctant to show off. It's totally out of character, Dan.

Dan had no idea what to say. Didn't they know how shy he was? He badly wanted to know what Jeff and Laura were after and why Laura was flirting with him. At the same time, he had an anxious queasy feeling as he thought of how little time remained to compose his questions for the upcoming class and write his history paper. He withdrew his eyes from the screen and breathed deeply, deliberately, for a few moments before looking around the room. Dan had been unaware of his setting for a while now. Most of the young people in here were hard at work on papers, their eyes never leaving the flickering, flashing characters before them. At one of the stations, behind and to the left of Dan, somebody was watching him pretty intently. Yes, Dan realized, Matt Gardner was regarding him with interest.

Dan guessed Matt wasn't thinking about his lovely girlfriend from Kansas at the moment, or the paper on Brecht he'd come here to write. Matt was studying the changing expressions of the young man across the room with unease. Perhaps he could tell something was happening to Dan Bede, the timid guy hardly anybody knew. Maybe it was obvious to Matt that somebody was harassing Dan. Maybe Matt was weighing getting up and going over to Dan's station, but doubted that Dan would recognize him or get the purpose of his intervention. Dan returned his gaze to the screen and resumed typing.

> DBede: Laura, I'm just not sure that I get your point. I am shy a lot of the time. But I've never shown any inhibitions. Please understand, both of you, it's not like some Puritan ethos keeps me from doing things. It's really not like that at all.
>
> JFields: You're not repressed?
>
> DBede: No!
>
> JFields: So if we dared you to do something, right now, you'd do it?
>
> DBede: Yes.
>
> LTimmer: You didn't get my point at all. You're a really shy person, inhibited in some ways, but not at all in others. In fact people say you're really argumentative in class. Your answers to the prof go way beyond what's required and you like to contradict people when they've expressed an idea.
>
> DBede: I do not enjoy contradicting others. I do have disagreements sometimes but I always cite a source and show them why I don't agree.
>
> LTimmer: Really?
>
> DBede: I swear.

JFields: Obviously you haven't taken any psych classes. If you had, you'd know that your outspokenness is a repressed form of sexual longing and aggression.

LTimmer: You're a lonely person.

DBede: Okay. I really have to get back to the paper now.

JFields: You're lonely, and 1,300 people are looking at you in this lonely dejected state and laughing.

LTimmer: Pathetic loser.

DBede: Please let me go!

JFields: No, chump.

LTimmer: Come on. Tell us the truth about your social life.

JFields: Be brave, Dan.

DBede: If I tell you, will you let me get back to what I need to be doing?

JFields: Sure.

DBede: All right. You probably know anyway that I've never gotten a date for one of the formals. So what do I do? I stand by the wall kind of half-furtively looking at women I'm interested in, hoping they'll notice me. Then if they do see me standing there, I feel like my dick is this rubber appendage I have no control over and piss just slides right out.

JFields: You're joking.

DBede: I'm not joking. Why do you think I skipped the last formal? I just sat in my room clawing my face, wishing I had a gun to put in my mouth.

JFields: Harsh, man.

LTimmer: That would give you a break from pizza.

DBede: I'm so lonely all the time I don't know who'd go to the formal with me or what I was thinking when I did attend. You can't just show up and expect to get a dance.

LTimmer: That's exactly what I do.

DBede: Is it?

LTimmer: Every time. I show up and within minutes I've got several guys approaching me. I just take my pick.

DBede: Well it's different for

DBede: Never mind.

JFields: What?

DBede: Never mind. I almost said something sexist. I didn't mean it.

LTimmer: Oooohhh.

DBede: Really I didn't. I apologize. I'm so very sorry.

JFields: You were telling us about your social life.

DBede: What else can I tell you?

JFields: How often do you jerk off?

DBede: Twice a day, usually.

LTimmer: That's it?

DBede: That's it. What more can I tell you?

Matt Gardner noticed that Dan was crying as his fingers assailed the keys.

JFields: Poor chump. Poor privileged white turd.

DBede: You said if I confessed about my social life, you'd let me get back to my paper.

Now there came a series of words, from both of Dan's interlocutors but mostly from Jeff, words that Dan wanted to dissolve as soon as the characters fell into sequence on the screen before him. He did not wish to recognize the hurtful words, syllables, letters, he wished he could make them disappear before he began to process their meaning, before they could resonate in his psyche. The words kept coming. Dan turned to the clock above the door. He could barely believe how much time had passed. Even though he'd partially avoided the barrage of words, he was so upset he knew he could hardly think about Herodotus or British history again tonight. But that paper was due! Dan resolved he'd flee to his dorm room, pass an hour breathing deeply on his bed, then try to write the paper out longhand, or at least cobble notes together. In the morning, he'd have half an hour between the opening of the computer room and the start of his classes. Enough time, maybe, to type the paper and the questions about Herodotus.

Dan threw his belongings into his backpack and fled the room without a word. He spent the rest of the night sitting on his bed, his fingers clawing his cheeks, or sitting at his desk, trying ineffectually to marshal barely coherent thoughts into order on the pages of a spiral notebook.

Late in the afternoon on the following day, Dan sat in the booth in the student lounge, hoping the girl who'd spurned him wouldn't walk in. He could not begin to process or describe what he was feeling. Dan had no idea how he might react to rudeness, even if there was a basis for the rudeness. The girl did not appear, but this left Dan vulnerable to memories of the classical history class that morning. Memories of his fumbling, stammering attempts to form questions. "So, uh, do you think some of what Herodotus is depicting is, like, reminiscent—I mean not reminiscent, I mean, like, what's the word, adumbr—a dumb—" Memories of the professor, who had praised Dan's work in the past, looking silently on. Of one of the young women, Jessica, speaking in a tentative voice, trying to help Dan clarify what she thought he meant. Of getting really annoyed at Jessica, wanting to scream at her for acting like he needed help when it was his discussion to lead, his turn to set the agenda for once. A memory came from later on that same morning, when he'd turned in that misbegotten mess of a paper to his British history prof, who wore a gentlemanly smile.

The memories stopped when Matt Gardner entered the lounge and walked up to the booth.

"Dan. Everything okay?"

Dan looked at the near-stranger.

"Dan, man, you've got to file harassment charges."

"Why would I do that."

"Because you're a victim of harassment."

"Am I?"

"Obviously!"

"I couldn't prove it."

"I watched you walk out of there. Then I went over to your station and I printed out the entire thread!"

Matt held up a pile of white pages filled with crisp, laser-printed text. Dan immediately tried to snatch it, but Matt jerked the pile away.

"Give me that!"

"No, Dan."

"Tear it up!"

"This is evidence."

"Did you read it?"

"Enough of it."

"It's none of your fucking business, Matt."

"You're right. It's the administration's business. You are going to file charges and there will be disciplinary proceedings."

"No!"

"Dan, listen. I don't know how many ethics classes you've taken, but you've got to understand that if people don't act on things like this, the standards of interpersonal relations degenerate and the whole community suffers. I'm telling you this for your sake and because I don't want this to be a school where this kind of crap goes on."

"I'll think about it."

"No, Dan. If you wait they'll want to know why you didn't act immediately."

In the evening, the school's diversity officer, Sonia Drake, overheard a couple of the assistant deans talking about a complaint filed against a student who was prominent in a few vocal organizations on the campus. This was potentially explosive. The administrators Sonia heard talking were pair of middle-aged white women from the town. Sonia looked down on them, to say the least, and she felt totally unabashed about pressing them for more information. Madge and Nancy told her everything.

Just twenty minutes later, Sonia was on the phone with Jeff Fields, telling him what was afoot and some of the possible consequences if people decided the charges had merit.

"Well, what can I do?"

"There are really only so many things a black man charged with a crime on a white campus can do."

On the following day, Stan Harding, the Dean of Students, received a file from Madge containing formal harassment charges filed by Dan Bede. Included was the printout of Dan's exchange with Jeff and Laura. There also came, in the same pile of interoffice mail, something that took priority over Dan's complaint. It was a report of racial harassment, filed by a student then vetted and taken to the next level with a countersignature by the school's diversity officer, Sonia Drake. Scanning this document,

Dean Harding understood that an African-American student, Jeff Fields, had reported an incident in which a white student, Daniel Bede, had tried to block Jeff as the latter attempted to enter the lounge, had claimed the facility was for whites only, and had pummeled Jeff with racial epithets and obscenities. Dean Harding recoiled in his oak swivel chair. Just when the school was trying to get grants and the annual national rankings were under preparation, look what had to happen. With growing impatience, the dean read the charges filed by Dan Bede, put the case file down, and sent a message to Sonia asking to schedule a meeting ASAP.

"Parts of this thread are upsetting," Dean Harding said to the intense professional woman on the other side of his desk.

"Nothing in there could be remotely as upsetting as receiving racial abuse from a bigoted, privileged young man," said Sonia.

"The investigation is ongoing. You're talking like it's a fait accompli."

"Are you questioning my honesty, Stan?"

"Oh no, of course not. I just mean, due process requires—"

"Let me amend my earlier statement. Nothing could be as upsetting to you, and to the campus community, as a takedown in the national rankings. As I believe I've made you aware before, they've introduced a diversity metric, and God help a school that makes national headlines for failing to take appropriate steps in the face of a complaint."

"That's precisely why I said Dan Bede's complaint is upsetting."

"No, Stan. I'm talking about Jeff's complaint. Dan obviously concocted his in order to obscure the real issue. Dan knew he was in deep shit and he better do something. It's smoke."

Dean Harding listened to his diversity officer with growing dismay.

"Well. At least give me a little more time to go over all this."

"Sure, sweetie."

Sonia left.

While Dean Harding appreciated all of the concerns Sonia had raised, he had enough vestigial pride to object to her presumed superior knowledge of the two cases and her dictating what he must do. He picked up Dan's complaint again. Some of the exchange he found lighthearted in spirit, even amusing. Then he read further.

JFields: I mean, there's guys that have been with you in the showers at the rec center, and believe me, to a man, they're pretty fucking horrified. And they've captured some truly horrific things.

DBede: Jeff, I totally don't understand. Why are you being so nasty to me?

JFields: Listen, chump. Let me fill you in on what people here on this campus have gathered about you. You're a scrawny little runt and you try to hide your insecurities by embarrassing others in class.

DBede: I've been totally honest and told people exactly why I don't agree with them. I've always got evidence to back up a point.

JFields: Well, you may think so.

LTimmer: He's joking by the way. No one ever took a picture of you in the shower.

DBede: Okay.

JFields: Even so, it's in your interest to listen.

DBede: I'm listening.

JFields: Good. You little white turds have been ruling this campus and this society forever. Well, not you, of course, but you're still a turd. Anyway, you should disregard what Laura said because they did get a picture in the shower. A number of them, in fact. And I know this guy who went with his girlfriend to an adult bookstore, I mean the most X-rated bookstore in Chicago, and the owner says can I help you? And he says, I'm looking for something a little different. Not just the usual cock and cunt. Can you help me? And the owner says, you mean it? My friend says, I'm totally serious. Do you have what I want? The owner says, yes, but I have to go to the back to get it. So the owner goes all the way to this little room in the back, and when he returns he's got this magazine. I'm not even going to tell you the title. And he opens it and there's a section called "College Meat" and there's a picture of this little scrawny white guy in the shower, he's got this tiny, tiny thing, like the knot at the bottom of a balloon. And he's standing in the shower, naked, looking at his dick with this sad face!

LTimmer: Ha!
DBede: Jeff
DBede: Jeff I don't understa
JFields: Yes?
LTimmer: What are you going to do, Dan, cry harassment?
JFields: Don't do that, chump. We know where your room is. You go crying to the administration, you'll never get another night's sleep.

Dean Harding put down the printout. He picked up Jeff's complaint and read through all the things Dan had allegedly said to Jeff. Then he turned to his computer and opened his inbox. He sent a brief note to Sonia, turned back to his desk, and picked up the New York Times. A few minutes later, he noticed a new message in his inbox, from Sonia. She'd pasted into the body of it two queries she'd gotten from wealthy alumni, asking whether she knew when the new college rankings were coming out, and whether she was privy to any embargoed news. There was also a message from a researcher at the magazine that compiled and published the rankings. Dean Harding inferred that Sonia knew the researcher personally. The subject line of Sonia's message read, "Make a New Plan, Stan." Because she hadn't sent this message by clicking "Reply" on Stan's note of a few minutes before, only two people in the world could know the meaning of that line.

Dan received written notice via campus mail that Dean Harding wanted to meet with him following a complaint of racial harassment. The notice added, almost as an afterthought, that any investigation of charges Dan himself had recently filed was on hold pending an inquiry into the alleged racial incident. It referred Dan to a document he'd had to read and sign way back during orientation, outlining exactly what constitutes racial harassment, and the college's policies toward such an offense. Accompanying the notice was Dan's British history paper with a bright red "F" on it.

Dan walked into town, bought a container of rat poison at the hardware store, and made his way back to his room. Complaints of an odor from the room led the resident advisor and two members of the grounds crew to dig out a key and enter the room. Dan went in an ambulance to the hospital in town where they declared him comatose.

Dean Harding sat in his office with a grim look on his face. The sad middle-aged couple across from him didn't seem to follow anything he was saying. To Dean Harding, the man had a gnomelike appearance, with a stumpy body inside a beige trenchcoat, and untrusting eyes peering out from a coarse face partly concealed by a thick, uncouth black beard. The woman might have been pretty once, in a past buried under days spent ruining her complexion with donuts and Oreos. Now she had sagging red cheeks and stringy hair of a vulgar yellow he would never have dignified as blonde. Studying them with distaste as he talked in a near monotone, Dean Harding wondered whether Dan Bede was the first person in his family ever to attend college.

"It's inconceivable to me that a couple, in 1992, would not discuss the evils of racism with their son," he said.

While the official met the parents, Matt Gardner walked into a room in the hospital and tried hard not to avert his eyes from what was in the bed. He wondered whether Dan would ever stand and speak again, indeed whether there was any point in trying to communicate with Dan. But he tried.

"Hey, Dan. I just want you to know your parents are here, they came by to see you this morning, and now they're talking with the dean in his office. They're going to come back in an hour or so and I think your mom's going to bring you some cookies."

His mother knew the kind of chocolate chip cookies Dan liked. She'd sent a box of them during his first week at the college so many months ago. They were a little stale by the time they arrived, but the thought was nice. The idea was that Dan would offer them to the new acquaintances on his floor at the dorm, and they'd enjoy the cookies together, and the other kids would say, That guy down the hall, Dan Bede, he's a really nice guy.

After the Bedes left his office, Dean Harding reclined in his swivel chair and stared at the ceiling, thinking they reeked of Middle American boorishness, they were a pretty loathsome couple. The dean pulled the two complaints, Dan's and Jeff's, out of his desk again. He compared the dates on them. October 7 and October 8. This wasn't going to work, the dean decided. He tore up the covering sheet for the earlier complaint, the one Dan had filed, picked up his phone, called Madge into his office, and greeted the assistant dean with the sternest of looks.

"We've had this conversation before, Madge. You know you can't submit a complaint to me without the relevant statutes from the student handbook attached."

"So sorry, sir."

Madge looked pitifully contrite as he handed the complaint to her, sans covering sheet, and she went to get it ready for resubmission. Dean Harding thought Madge was a townie and a moron, if those things were not one and the same. Now Dan's complaint would have a later date than Jeff's, and with fall break coming up, there was all the more reason Dan's couldn't receive priority. The dean thought himself clever, and lucky. He thought, *God, imagine a world where people do virtually all their correspondence by e-mail.*

On the following day, the hospital staff called the mortician's office, asking them to send the van.

Matt Gardner sat in the booth in the lounge that Dan had once occupied, drumming his fingers on the table, looking around with a growing feeling he couldn't name.

Jeff Fields spent the night partying with Laura Timmerman and Sonia Drake, drinking beer from plastic cups, laughing, dancing to the song by the German band Snap! with the refrain, "I've got the power!" Jeff whooped when Laura told him that some health-conscious students were trying to raise awareness about binge drinking.

"There's some weird shit happening on this campus," Jeff said.

The Prank

Jason had a devious look. He was ready to do it again.

The stranger sitting at the bar about fifteen feet from Jason and myself seemed so insufferably prim. Oh, yes, he had the air of the stockbrokers who move into our town and think they're entitled to tell the people of northern New Hampshire what to do. The bartender, Dale, was busy serving the two young couples down at the end of the bar where the juke sits. Honestly, I doubt that Dale would have made any effort to stop Jason even had he been aware. If Dale never saw the prissy stockbroker in the $800 suit again, fine with him.

Jason and I were sitting at a table with a little round gray top with scars where bored kids had dragged their pocket knives this way and that. The two young couples were talking happily among themselves and not bothering with anyone else. When Dale got done attending to them, he served a mixed drink to a young lady with clipped rust-colored hair, wearing faded jeans and a blue and purple pullover, a cute girl who got noticed much more in these parts than she ever would in New York, where I've never been, but where I hear the clubs have lines running down the street and around the corner. This girl had chatted briefly with the stockbroker in the fancy suit, who was watching her though she'd probably forgotten him already. After she got her drink, that cute girl was going to turn around and saunter back over to her cluster of friends at the back, where the board games lie piled on a chipped wooden shelf.

The man in the fancy suit looked down the bar in the hope that the young lady would notice him again, decided it wasn't happening, and gazed around kind of aimlessly while taking sips of his draft beer. At length he got up and walked to the end of the bar, past the juke, and into the restroom, giving Jason his chance. My buddy stole down to the bar, whipped out the flask he kept in his jacket, screwed off the little black top, and poured horse urine into the draft beer on the counter. The beer quickly settled, its complexion just a tad darker. As Jason returned the flask to his jacket, he looked around hurriedly.

The stockbroker came out of the bathroom, sat down, seized his glass, and took a long swill. Then he had this look, as if a model he'd been admiring had just shat right in front of him. Though we sat behind him, we were just far enough to his left to relish that look, and the sight of him pitching forward, half-spitting and half-puking his beer out on the counter, whirling on his stool until he faced the back of the bar, collapsing forward with his hands on his belly. One of the young women at the end of the bar cried out. Her partner, a handsome guy in a black and red flannel shirt, got up and approached the stockbroker as the latter rose to his feet. Soon the prim man was shoving and cursing at the young man who'd come to help him, as if suspecting *him* of tampering with the beer. The man in the flannel shirt veered confusedly between trying to help the stockbroker and deflecting his flailing limbs. The stockbroker bellowed, "You fucking bumpkin! Goddamn rube! Got nothing better to do, huh?" I couldn't quite see Dale, back there behind the bar, but I'm pretty sure the bartender was trying hard to avoid laughing.

The next time Jason and I hung out, we got to talking about this middle-aged lady named Sarah Prentice who kept urging Jason to join a Bible discussion group. Obviously Jason would rather not have dealt with Mrs. Prentice at all, but he depended on mowing her lawn for income. He had to stand there in the kitchen of her little house as she dug into her purse, a process that took long enough for her to remind him that her son had gone through a phase like where Jason was right now in his life, lacking direction and purpose, but had come to appreciate how much God loves us, to crave forgiveness. Jason must understand that if he failed to straighten out, he'd end up sweeping floors for a living or reporting to his parole officer, she warned. There's Mrs. Prentice in her kitchen, digging in her purse for money, talking sanctimoniously to my best friend, and there's Jason thinking, *Please don't bore me with this bullshit anymore, you old bitch!*

"Can you cut her out of your route?" I asked Jason.

"No, man. Out of the question. It's thirty-five a week we're talking here."

"Well that's about your monthly Netflix fee, plus three Stellas."

"Like I said—it's out of the question, Zach. Until I get a few more customers."

We were sitting in a tavern three miles from the outskirts of town, an establishment whose origins as a barn were pretty evident. It was a long rectangular building with twelve thick rafters propping up a sloping shingled roof. There was hay amid the dirt and dust on the ground, as if they'd never had time to sweep the place out properly. About half of the stools at the tables lining the middle of the tavern had occupants. At the bar, about twenty feet in front of us, truckers and farmers were unwinding, some no doubt enjoying the absence of a nagging spouse. At a table under the next rafter to our right, a pair of cute college girls were drinking and giggling.

Now Jason spotted Martin Riggs. Here was a man who really wasn't so bad if you could look at him, you know, objectively. Martin didn't buy up all the plots of fertile land, or get a corner on the export markets and drive prices down so far nobody else made enough to eat. His manner was reserved and polite. Yet he made people feel small by tithing so much more in church than anyone else in his row, and by being pretty selective about who could date his eighteen-year-old daughter. Even so, Martin wasn't someone you could imagine anyone wanting to hurt. Well, it wasn't pain, exactly, that Jason planned to cause here. Not for the first or the last time, I was feeling kind of ambivalent about Jason's antics.

I drank my Corona, considered the situation, then addressed my friend.

"Why not skip it tonight, Jason? People are just chillin' out. Let's just talk about movies or the NHL or whatever. Let's act mature."

"Sanctimonious prick," Jason retorted.

"No, man. I'm watchin' out for you."

He looked at me curiously.

"You chickenshit, Zach?"

"I'm not chickenshit, Jason. I'll walk right up to any many in this tavern and speak boldly to his face."

"I just may call you out."

"Do it."

"But you won't let me do this."

"No. Not tonight."

"Chickenshit!"

"I guess we define courage differently."

He sneered. Sometimes I hated Jason. I drank some more of my Corona anxiously as my friend cast looks around the tavern. As if on cue, Martin Riggs got up and ambled across the dusty floor toward the men's room.

"Come on, let's just chill out, and the next round will be on me," I urged.

Jason fixed me with his unsettling look, the skin on his face clenched.

"I've got sixty hours of mowing lawns to look forward to, and I don't fucking well appreciate your telling me I can't have a little fun."

I stared at my friend, knowing how little effect anything I said could have, resenting him even as I wanted to see him go ahead. Now his face grew just a tiny bit less tense.

"Hey, Zach. You know what Mrs. Prentice told me last time?"

"What'd she tell you, Jason?"

"She said, 'If you go on as you are, you'll know a despair you never thought existed in this universe. If you live with maturity and purpose, you'll come to see that God's design is not a big prank.'"

I had to chuckle at that one. It was pretty good. Mrs. Prentice wasn't keeping science and theology separate in her wizened head. Emboldened, perhaps, by my chuckling, Jason cast final furtive looks around the tavern before sliding off his stool and over to the bar. Within seconds, the flask was out. But Jason didn't want a scene this time. He added just a tad. It was just enough to cause Martin to make a face once he took his seat again and resumed drinking. Martin seemed as happy as before, but I, and the two co-eds a few feet away who'd watched, could barely keep the hilarity from our faces.

I knew I could turn away from Jason forever, of course. I could hang around with friends enrolled in IT courses at the community college, or clerking at one of the two law firms in the county. But then my Fridays and Saturdays, irreplaceable evenings of my vanishing youth, would be so staid there'd be no memories to cling to, no emotions to mourn.

Jason was wild, and funny in his way. Plus, I'd struck out with a girl I'd met by chance on one of the nights I wasn't with Jason. This is primarily a story about Jason, but I will say a word about Rachel. She was a slender lass with long dark hair and the most artless, open look you'd ever see on a person's face. She needed makeup like a Hemingway story needs revision by the members of a Sarah Lawrence creative writing seminar. I felt the stirrings of something pretty profound when I was with Rachel, so you can imagine how I felt when she broke off our relationship before it really began. I couldn't stand being lonely. Here, in the form of Jason, was a salve, a drug, available to me for nothing at all. Only later did it occur to me that Jason might have been why Rachel rejected me.

The next time we cruised in Jason's Mercury, my friend wanted to know more about Rachel, how I'd met her, and why I'd ever consider her a competitor for my time. I told Jason about how I'd gone to see a movie the old-fashioned way, and I mean the really old-fashioned way, not in a theater owned by a big chain, but in a shack outside town. You walk in and find yourself a seat among five rows of folding chairs facing a screen. They don't collect money at the door. They place a jar on a little table beside the screen, putting their faith in this quaint honor system. If people put money in the jar, great, but there's no enforcement. Of course Jason wanted to know what movie all the God-fearing folk had gathered to watch. Was it a XXX porno, he asked with a grin.

"For your information, it was *Oklahoma!*" I told my friend.

"Oh, yeah, *Oklahoma!*" Jason exclaimed.

This led to the two of us belting out, in unison, *"Oh what a beautiful morning, oh what a beautiful day! / I've got a beautiful feeling, everything's going my way!"*

Jason drove on through the night until we finally reached our surprise destination. The roadhouse was squat and ugly. Its planners did not have aesthetic criteria in mind, but the fulfillment of base needs. Such needs the blonde girls in denim or leather jackets provided to truckers who raced from point to point in the night with dangerous levels of speed in their veins. Here were fellows you wouldn't dare look at funny if they sprouted wings. I could hardly imagine why my friend felt the need to take me here on this occasion. Maybe he really resented my spending time with Rachel and he needed a way to say, *You think I'm déclassé, Zach? Well, have a look in here.*

We took a seat a few yards from the bar, but in the end our distance to the bar didn't matter. For the bar was quite busy, and on those occasions where people got up to go to the john, they tended to have a drinking companion seated inches away, noticing all occurrences within a discrete shell of space and time. I hoped that Jason had at least begun to heed the counsel put forth by Mrs. Prentice and other of his elders. I liked to think there was hope for him after all. I found his behavior kind of cowardly and contemptible even as it amused me.

As soon as I spotted the target, I knew he was just that. The poor sap who was about to undergo humiliation to ease the sadness and boredom of this kid I hung out with. This victim had an unshaven face, heaps of stringy black hair, and a paunch. I couldn't see his eyes for he wore shades even indoors. He also wore a black leather jacket, and to be fair, it looked natural on him, not like a costume.

I wanted to banish Jason's impulses, to swat them like gnats. Everything that was decent and grown-up in me yearned to call others' attention to his plan, to force Jason to stop. But I didn't say a word. I lay back in my seat and watched that man in the black leather jacket, fighting to keep a smirk out of my face. The moment was horrible and hilarious.

The biker got up and walked down toward the restroom. Jason rose, glided across the barren unwashed boards to the counter, whipped it out, and poured. Then he was back at my side, the best friend I could hope to have in this life, the flask a barely detectable bulge in a breast pocket of his army green jacket. The scruffy man in the black leather jacket came back, sat down, and took a long quaff from his glass. A couple of the bikers on nearby stools watched with looks we couldn't make out. Had they seen Jason?

The biker, the socially unmentionable man in the dark jacket, set down his glass, grinned, recoiled, paused, reeled further at what had invaded him, then paused again. I looked at Jason. The stranger leaned forward, spat about a gallon of liquid out onto the floor in front of him, and pointed a finger at the youngster sitting beside me.

"*Ha ha ha ha ha ha ha ha ha ha ha!!!*" he burst out.

The others joined in. They whooped, bellowed, guffawed, pointed, slapped their thighs. I wondered how much Jason would hate me in coming days, if he had any, for failing to take note of how many people had been watching. I'd been so oblivious to almost everything as I'd silently cheered on my friend.

"Do you see that genius sitting over there?" the biker exclaimed.

Dozens, no, scores of eyes rotated in our direction. I feared I'd piss myself.

"This kid wanted to make me feel small in front of everyone, people! I wonder how many people he's done this to!" he exclaimed, with a gesture toward Jason, who might very well have been shitting himself.

"Yes, that guy singled me out as a biker loser and he put something in my beer! I stood right there at a crack in the door and watched him do it. I thought it was whiskey, and I should just go along, but now I know he put piss in my beer! You know what, people? It's the most fucking hilarious thing I've ever seen!"

All around us was such thunder, such hilarity, that I almost hated myself for not joining it. At the same time, I wondered how much time I had before they set on us. I stammered. I looked at my toes.

"Jason—"

He didn't say anything, but the look he gave me admitted something we both knew. Ignoring all the fervid eyes around us, Jason picked himself up and with his customary fast motions removed himself from the situation, leaving one subject for all the eyes in this place.

I tried to smile, gave it up, mumbled, stuttered, studied my feet some more, picked myself up, moved across the floor to the restroom. I was in there for a really long time trying to get things going. At last I got it done and reemerged into the scene my friend had bravely vacated. I was thinking maybe I'd been so stiff, so wrong about the patrons of this place.

A face appeared before me. Now the biker in the dark leather jacket wore a totally different look. His smile had flattened out. The hairs on his face and neck, which had held such scruffy charm, looked so unruly you might have thought he'd been living in the woods for months. Though his eyes were still hard to see, I could tell they were peering out fiercely from behind their dark shields as if they were the repository of all this stranger's intelligence, and his anger.

"Going somewhere?"

My heart made itself heard as I gazed at the rectangles of his shades and picked up a few of his pals in my peripheral vision, sitting on their stools, appraising me.

"I'm just rejoining my friend," I said in a tone that strained to sound innocent.

"The guy who put piss in my beer."

"I tried to stop him, I begged him not to."

Louder, louder came the thudding inside me as unsmiling faces all around continued to measure me.

"I doubt it but I'll tell you one thing. You're begging now, boy."

He grinned.

I slid around him, not expecting to get far before something stopped me. To my astonishment neither he nor anyone else made an attempt.

Outside, in the Mercury, Jason wanted to know whether I was o.k.

"Ah, nothing. Let's blow," I said, trying to sound casual as ever.

"You sure it's nothing."

"Nothing. Nothing at all. I worship you, man. Seriously."

Jason went right on working for Mrs. Prentice when he wasn't out with me. I couldn't imagine why she kept on this cocky prankster, let alone why she bothered trying to get him to follow other young men who'd become Christians and begun living in radically new ways. Whenever I met Jason there was the same flippant attitude, the same disdain that was quick and sharp but never quite witty. My friend could not hide his contempt for the people who paid his wages, who made his life here in this town possible. But Jason relied on me, and I on him. I was still lonely and sore. We hardly needed to make plans in advance of an outing, we just met up like migrating finches.

We found ourselves, once again, at Dale's bar, where we'd humiliated the prissy stockbroker. Now, I just said how much I relied on Jason. Tonight the truth was that I'd been thinking about how much I valued Jason's company, even as other thoughts were arising quietly. I enjoyed his antics but I knew he really should have matured a bit more by now, and if he didn't there was something pretty fucked about him. I sometimes thought I didn't want Jason to do the prank again. Right now I couldn't fathom my friend's thoughts. He'd taken out his cell phone and was examining a text from some girl.

I was on my fourth beer when I saw him set down his cell phone on our table and begin staring at a stranger at the counter. The man was in his mid-forties, neither tall nor short, in jeans and a dull green-gray flannel shirt. His hair was light brown, serrated into ridges. He had a brash manner and laughed often at the jokes of another stranger, a balding man in a raincoat who looked almost like a schoolteacher. I glanced at Jason and saw the devious look, the probing of possibilities in his alert brown eyes. Carefully, furtively, he moved his head from left to right, right to left. The forty-something got up from his stool. I knew my only chance of stopping Jason was before me now.

"Jason, I don't really know how to say this, man."

"What, Zach?"

"I don't know, I just feel like we can't, you know, be on the same road forever, or something."

My friend gave a devious grin.

"Fuck off, prude."

"I mean it."

"*I meeeaaannn it,*" Jason mimicked.

"Jason, you've been the most loyal friend to me, man. It's hard to say this. I'm just so terrified something's going to get in the way—"

Jason got up, walked casually over to the bar, produced the flask, and gave the middle-aged stranger something extra to whoop about when he got back.

"Can we go now?" I pleaded as soon as Jason was at my side again.

He grinned again, with a real hint of malice. I imagined my friend saying, "Look down, chump," imagined seeing that he'd tried my shoelaces to a leg of the table while I'd been checking out the babes in here. But I must have misread my friend, for he indulged me. We left without settling our tab at the bar. We'd done this a couple of times before and it was cool, we'd apologized and settled later, but this time it felt really awkward, for Dale had been nice to us lately. A minute later we were in Jason's Mercury once again, gliding up the drive out in front of the bar. The drive straightened out and merged with the road leading out of town, to the north, skirting hills it was way too dark to see.

"Can we speed up, please, buddy?" I asked as I watched the lights of Dale's bar recede, not quickly enough, in the passenger's side mirror.

My window was down and it was cool. The weather wasn't unpleasant, but the road was so barren and endless. Now Jason looked smug again, as smug as I'd ever seen him. Maybe he hadn't heard me, or maybe he'd grown resigned to my windy talk. I didn't know how to speak to my friend anymore.

"So why are you in such a hurry?" Jason inquired.

I thought of lying to him, telling him I'd reconnected with Rachel, the girl who dumped me, but I knew how easily Jason could verify such information. It turned out not to matter. Jason pressed down on the gas just enough for the whirring in the dark spaces around us to advance to a groan. Still the road seemed so intimidating in its vastness and still I yearned for the car to gain speed.

"Zach, man. It's like some fucker's flipping a switch inside you back and forth and you can only speak when it's on. You've been my buddy all these years and now it's like you're not sure of anything. Not ever our friendship."

"Jason, I'm sorry, it's not our friendship I've been concerned about. It's something a lot more specific."

"What?"

"Well for one thing, you damn near fucking got me killed that night at the roadhouse. Did you ever think about that for one second, shithead? That it wasn't so classy to do what you did and cut out of there while I was in the men's room? Huh, Jason? DID YOU *EVER* THINK ABOUT THAT?"

"Oh, fuck off."

Before I could respond, I noticed something back there on the road, coming up unmistakably behind us. A pair of headlights.

"Speed up."

"Why?"

"See those lights?"

"Oh, wow, never seen that before."

"Come on, Jason, it might be cops."

"So?"

"So we had six beers and didn't pay for them! We could go to jail!"

"You want me to drive over the limit so the cops'll leave us alone?"

"It might be—I don't fucking know! Let's just pull off somewhere!"

Jason thought I was being silly in the extreme. I wanted to plead some more. Within seconds, the driver behind us made the argument moot. The car surged up behind us, segued with grace into the left lane, surged further, like Phar Lap overtaking a lesser steed, and, before Jason could react, moved back into the right lane not six inches from the Mercury's bumper.

"Fuck!" Jason said.

The Mercury slowed down rapidly but the car ahead was in sync from moment to moment. The driver ahead of us knew exactly what he was doing. His moves were so fluid, so assured, you might have thought he'd visited five establishments before tonight where someone had put piss in his beer, and had prepared for this. Still cutting speed, Jason eased the Mercury onto the right shoulder. The vehicle slowed until it rested on the mix of dirt and pebbles lining the road. Jason depressed the brake all the way, but did not put the car in park. The other car was just inches in front. In the spaces between actions I heard my heart, as insistent in its protests as ever. I wanted to urge Jason to swing the car right back into the right lane and floor it. If Jason did it right, we just might escape.

But Jason sat there, breathing hard, his eyes fixed on the silver-blue Ford and the figure emerging now from the driver's side door. He rolled down his window. Perhaps it was a reflex that made him act as he would when pulled over by a cop.

The stranger's feet crunched on the pebbles. Jason stared straight ahead. A face appeared in the rectangle of space by my friend's head. We'd both seem this face before, oh yes. The man in his mid-forties with the dorsal-fin hair and the bluff manner regarded us with a curious, oddly indulgent look. In his blue eyes I detected a tender and patient quality, putting me in mind of a certain substitute teacher I'd had for just three days, way back in third grade.

"Why, evenin' fellows. I don't know what gives. You cut right outta there without payin'. You guys late for a double date?"

Still Jason looked ahead, his hands clutching the wheel.

"You fellows cut out of Dale's so fast, I guess we all thought you were tryin' to get down to Massachusetts before the last liquor store closed. But you're not headed south," he added.

Even now Jason looked straight ahead.

"So maybe you are chasin' girls? the stranger persisted.

At last Jason spoke.

"Mister, I know this isn't going to convince you for a second. But I just want to say, I never meant—"

"Oh, I know, a girl texted you and you wanted to get to her before she changed or mind or another fella won her attention. I get it, young man. Maybe you think I was born the age I am now," the stranger said.

Jason wanted to speak, to clarify, to try to preempt inevitable words.

"If you remember how people at this age—" Jason began.

"Forget it! I mean it, son, put it out of your mind. I don't fault you for getting horny. But I do fault you for being in such a hurry you left this on the table for any fella to help himself to!"

The man help up Jason's cell phone.

"Oh dear God—"

"Dear God is right! Don't you ever forget how much God cares for you and looks after you," the stranger said, understanding tinged with gravity in his voice.

"Thank you, mister."

"My name's Chuck."

"Why, thank you, Chuck. I'm Jason."

Jason was panting as the stranger turned, walked back to his car, got in, and moved back onto the road. His breathing did not even out until the taillights of the Ford were almost too tiny to spot, the silver-blue chassis indistinguishable against the plains and sky. I gave my friend a calm, consoling look to let him know he must feel no pressure to talk. We drove on up the wide empty road until we reached the ramp leading to the parking lot of our favorite tavern.

Inside the tavern, we found a pretty low-key scene. The first person we noticed was Melissa Hoyt, in her customary jeans and tank top. She had a reputation for not being safe to insert any part of your anatomy into. That hadn't kept Jason from having flings with Melissa lasting two, three, four months, or a night or two. When Melissa saw us come in, her look as she pushed back her long dark locks reminded me that in her mind, she was always available for Jason or vice versa. I thought she gave me a quick appraising look. A few feet from Melissa, Martin Riggs, the man Jason had recently played his prank on, sat at the bar with a dreamy look. Two seats to Martin's left, Tara Jones, a woman Jason had hurt and humiliated a couple of years before, sat sipping a mixed drink, probably a Jack-and-diet, and exchanging pleasantries with Andy Fowler, the bartender. I don't know what Tara told people about Jason, but I doubt Jason cared. To his mind, she was a pretentious girl who preferred foreign films to real movies. During their brief relationship, Tara had roped Jason into wasting irreplaceable hours of his life on Bergman and Antonioni, and she'd bawled when he told her he liked torture porn and didn't want to date her anymore. A month after the breakup, a big guy named Steve Fuchs had kicked Jason's ass in a lot behind a bar, and Jason wasn't the only one who found the timing suspicious.

As for Andy, he was one of three bartenders who had shifts here in the evenings. I was glad when we got to enjoy this place without Andy present, because Jason had insulted Andy for what seemed, to Jason, like deliberately slow service. Jason had left a tip of one penny on the counter. I could never tell whether Jason's slights rankled or not. There were rumors that Andy had paid someone to slash the tires of Jason's Mercury one night last year. Usually we had the schedule down, but I guessed Andy was filling in for someone tonight.

Jason and I took seats allowing us a perspective on the bar and the patrons that was quite familiar. Here was where we'd sat on the night Jason had humiliated Martin.

I got up to go to the bar. I spoke to Andy in a way that I thought communicated some of what I felt, and some of what I hoped he could feel tonight, an easy familiarity, a lack of interest in what may or may not have happened on past nights. Andy gave me an odd distant look. I wondered what he had going on later. Maybe he was going to go home with Tara tonight, and his dalliance with her made it more than a bit awkward to talk to anyone who knew the lout I'd accompanied here. It hardly seemed worth pursuing.

I returned to our table with a couple draft beers. Jason was struggling to process everything.

"I, uh, I don't know, Zach. Maybe it's just that God really wants to forgive us but we have these childish expectations about what he will or won't reveal. Maybe he really wants to extend the chance for us to admit our mistakes and see his decency. I know you've never heard me talk like this. I know. I'm sorry. I—I—"

His voice was really cracking now, drawing looks from people at the bar.

"I wish I'd been mature enough, not even necessarily to get these things, but just to think about them a little more, you know? I've been ignoring what all the older, sensible people around me have been telling me. I'm so sorry, Zach. I am so deeply sorry for being such a little punk. I—"

"Jason! Hey. It's o.k., man. I went through the same kind of phase. You know you don't have to explain yourself to me."

Tara and Andy were both looking at us, and I thought it was kind of rude, but I kept my gaze on my friend's wondrous eyes. There was a lot more he wanted to get out, but now Melissa, uninhibited Melissa, took the choice from his hands.

"Hey honey, you don't have a date tonight?" she asked while striking a pose at the fringes of our space.

"Get lost, you fucking skank," Jason said.

"I don't get it, honey."

"Melissa, you belong to a part of my life that doesn't matter anymore. I've come round to a new understanding of God's role. I really don't appreciate you coming over here to violate this sacred moment!"

"But Jason, the last time we were together, you said—"

"I was drunk!"

I could see that Melissa wanted to argue, but she read a certainty in Jason's eyes she hadn't thought possible. So she turned and treated us to a view of her swishing buttocks as she moved toward the exit.

"Zach, I'm sorry you had to see me do that, but it's impossible to express what I'm feeling now. Please understand. I'm not the most articulate guy, so please just believe me."

I could filled it all in for him. *I'm just a poor guy with a high school degree who has suddenly come to realize just what a horrible immature little bastard I've been to everybody. I'm speechless in the face of understanding and kindness.*

Sometimes I really, really hated Jason.

I drank my beer, then went to get us a new round. Our drinking had an intensity, a determination that Jason found kind of reassuring. Even as I did my best to respond articulately to my friend at this unique juncture, I could not help wondering whether others in the tavern might have been able to talk more encouragingly. But Tara and Martin were drinking in a resolute way, as if they themselves had plenty to take in tonight. We had three more rounds before Jason got the idea it was time to snap a few selfies, to preserve these moments. He'd left his cell phone in the car. He got up and went outside, leaving me once again among people who weren't thrilled with him. I felt so vulnerable, for I had no idea how convincing the others found Jason's revelatory mood. Maybe Martin would seize this opportunity to tell me what he thought of both of us.

Martin called to me from the bar.

"Hey Zach, haven't seen you in a while, buddy. Your next one's on me, o.k.?"

Martin liked me. A better educated man than myself could not have found the right words, so I just nodded. Tara took a draft beer from Andy and brought it over. I thanked her in a tone I wanted to sound coolly blasé.

The scream outside was so loud, so desperate, I thought a child had gotten run over. But the voice had the unmistakable taint of a normally brash young man whose demeanor had gotten a most unexpected shove in the other direction.

Jason burst through the door looking as if all his skin had blistered and run madly. Blood and garb covered him. But Jason's flesh had no cuts at all. No, someone had stood above him and emptied a bucket onto him. In the garb coating my friend, I could see what looked like clumps of hair, long dark hair that might just have belonged to Melissa Hoyt.

"*Iiiiieeee—yaaahhh! HELP ME!*" my friend screamed.

Chuck, the stranger who had reunited Jason with his cell phone earlier tonight, followed him through the door. The man had the same mirthful, indulgent look as before, but he clutched a silver Glock pistol in his right hand.

Tara screamed. Martin dropped his beer and the glass shattered on the floor.

"You! Get out from behind there!" the man bellowed, pointing the Glock at Andy's face.

The bartender obeyed. Tara began weeping. Andy and Martin looked terrified. My friend gibbered, cried, and pissed himself.

"So, Jason, you thought you were going to have a bit of fun at a stranger's expense once again."

Jason looked at Chuck through gaps in the garb. To my surprise, Jason was able to form words, to marshal them into a sequence.

"You killed Melissa Hoyt! You sick fuck! You do that and come down on me for a fucking *prank*!"

The man snickered.

"You're not the prankster here tonight, got it?"

Jason gibbered and wept, entering an excruciating call and response with Tara. Her crying was louder but Jason's shock was more pitiable, more abject.

"Now, Jason, notwithstanding what I just said, I believe you have been guilty of some pretty malicious behavior. I'm afraid I can't let you walk away from this, boy."

Jason gibbered, the surprising facility for words quite gone.

"Now, I do think I'm entitled to a bit of fun and sport. So, pick one."

Chuck raised the Glock until it was level with Jason's streaming face. He was blocking the door, and was not near enough for us to rush him without some or all of us getting killed.

"No matter how much of a punk and a lout you've been, I bet you do have a bit of moral sense, Jason. You are capable of some moral calculation, if you try. Tonight's the night you prove your ability to recognize hypocrisy, to single it out for punishment. This town's full of folks who think they're superior, and we've got four of them right here. So take a look around. Pick one. Who's it gonna be?"

The stranger kept the Glock exactly level with Jason's face.

Warily, my friend looked around at me, at Martin, at Andy, and at Tara. I couldn't believe he considered any of us really rotten, but we'd all been snobbish and condescending to Jason at one time or another. We all breathed laboriously as some kind of thought process went on behind his sullied features.

"No," Jason muttered.

"Choose one now, or those cow chips in your blond head will be all over this tavern. Don't deny me my fun. Do it now."

"No."

"Pick one now, Jason, or I'll shoot everyone in this place, starting with you."

Panting, wheezing, Jason looked around again. Sweat mingled with the blood and garb. When he stopped looking around, he was gazing right down the Glock's cool cylinder.

"All right. Tara!" he said.

Chuck pointed the Glock at Tara. The heaving inside her orange blouse betrayed such terror that I felt an urge to dart in front of her, if only for a moment.

Then the stranger laughed and pointed the gun at the ceiling.

"He just tried to sacrifice Tara. Maybe you're all getting a sense of this youngster's nature."

There came a silence in which everyone knew quite well what we were all thinking. Then Chuck held out the Glock toward Tara. He couldn't have shot her, for the weapon hung from the curve of Chuck's index finger. We all believed his offer was sincere, and it was astounding. Tara could have seized the weapon and blown Chuck's head off. We gaped at Tara, unable to draw breath.

She stared at the weapon, sobbed, wiped her eyes, cried some more, finally shook her head.

I could tell how badly Chuck wanted Tara to act, but he could see there were just too many conflicts going on beneath her pretty brunette scalp. He extended the gun toward Andy, whose conflicts played out subtly yet unmistakably. The bartender looked at the weapon with terror and awe, dropped his gaze to his feet, looked up again with a hopeless dullness in his eyes, then shook his head.

Next, Chuck made the offer to Martin. The prosperous but obtuse New England citizen whom Jason had humiliated in front of so many people grinned in embarrassment, fidgeted, shuffled his feet, and finally said, "Nah, I can't."

Chuck offered me the weapon.

I seized it and pumped four rounds into my best friend's skull.

Then and Now

Everyone in the family wants to know why the university fired me. The question is particularly urgent now that my father has died and preparations for the funeral are underway. No one can agree on who should speak at the funeral or for how long. My cousins, aunts, and uncles are trying to fit my firing the other day into a narrative about my life in general, and my relationship with my father in particular. They see it as yet more evidence that I'm a member of that loathsome species, the intellectual ne'er-do-well. How do I make them see this event differently? I can hardly tell them that its roots lie in my earliest interactions with authority. It wouldn't make any sense to them. It barely makes sense to me.

I'm not even sure how to broach the topic with most of the relatives. Take my uncle, for example. I tried to write a draft of a letter in which I addressed him as "Brad," but it felt exceedingly awkward, even though we are both old enough that I should be able to drop the word "uncle" from my salutations. Of course I am not really old, just forty-three. There are so many uncrossable lines in this family that I just never know how to proceed. I haven't even addressed the issue here, which is that Brad had expectations when I finally got a teaching position at a university here in Boston. He and my father both thought, *At last Mike's got a job he couldn't mess up if he tried.* And look at me, not sixth months later. I'm trying to scrounge beer money by advising kids on their resumes, and through a bit of freelance proofreading. I was pretty dependent on my father for many years, and I knew how much he disliked other people's constant questions. *Why doesn't Mike have a job? Why is he still unmarried?* All of this grew more noxious as the Mike in question aged, as his eyes grew bleary and his paunch swelled. My father was so deeply conscious of our status as members of an old and venerable New England family.

Brad, and others in the clan's Midwest and West Coast branches, heard much griping from the old man in the aftermath of my firing. They tried to fit the event into a narrative they could understand. I'd been through trauma when I was young, I'd gotten DWIs and gotten fired from jobs all over the city, and I'd never straightened out. I'm a loser. There are truths here, I'll grant.

Look, I don't blame my father for how I've turned out. Oh, no. I'm grateful to him for many things and particularly his early encouragement of my interest in journalism. Maybe he even pushed a little too hard. You can't really expect a sixth grader to write articles about the curriculum, and about what they call the "culture wars," from an informed perspective. But my father had opinions on the subject, and he urged me to meditate on it and produce articles for the student paper at my private school in Cambridge. I guess my father's intentions were good enough. But there were topics that interested me far more. Law enforcement, for one.

In the fifth grade, they took us on a day trip to a police station in downtown Boston. We met a number of the officers, including some muscular young men with a cool reserved manner. One of them was a stocky blond guy with gigantic biceps. I talked with him briefly about where we were from and the purpose of our visit. I kept thinking that the gun and billy club hanging from his belt were so big, they appealed for an attention our eyes didn't want to grant. His manner and that of his fellows suggested, to my mind, the sober anticipation of scenes I'd never see, in rooms or on streets I'd never visit. A big middle-aged officer gave us a tour of the place. He even took us into the cell area. One of the kids was curious.

"Do you have anyone locked up now?"

"Yeah, we got a guy in one of the cells," the smiling officer answered.

It's amusing to think some of us actually expected him to take us to the cell in question. I remember it was really cold that day, even by Boston standards, and the precinct had such a drab, lonely air that visitors might wonder about the interior lives of the people who worked there, never mind the prisoners. But I felt pure awe.

I thought about the experience every day. My assumption was that all cops had the same guarded professionalism as the officer who took us around the precinct and let us enter the cell area. I came to see cops not merely as people who had entered law enforcement, but as a race with attributes of courage, seriousness, and professionalism denied to most of us. Cop shows played their inevitable role, as did an incident a few months after that visit. Officers responded quickly when a young perp pushed a stick through a window of our house on Garfield Street, got it under the strap of my mom's purse, and moved the purse out of the window and down to the sidewalk. The teen was walking a few blocks away, almost nonchalantly, purse in hand, when the patrol car caught up. I know, there's nothing unusual about any of these experiences. There was something banal and boring about my respect for and fascination with cops.

But then I became interested in law enforcement on a global level, and conflicts at various hotspots around the world. One such place was South Africa, which was in the midst of one of its bloody border wars with communist-backed insurgents. Mind you, I have never been an apologist for apartheid. I could go on for thousands of words about the evils of racist social policy and abusive policing. At the time, I just knew that events in South Africa were really big and important.

My social studies teacher, Mr. Duncan, encouraged me to be adventurous. My father pushed me. I wrote to the South African embassy in Washington. Two weeks later, I got a package in the mail with newspapers from Johannesburg and Cape Town and some official literature about the country. This was long before the information age. There I was, a boy in a classroom in Cambridge, Massachusetts, listening to rain fall on the mud outside the window, staring at pictures of tanks and armored personnel carriers, of people in a geopolitical situation of unfathomable complexity for someone my age. The faces of the men in the pictures conveyed the cool professionalism of the cops I'd met.

"You really ought to pursue the subject, Mike," Mr. Duncan said.

"Okay. What else I can do?"

"I'll tell exactly what you can do."

My teacher encouraged me to write to my contact at the embassy, one Donald Barclay, and ask whether he could help coordinate an interview with someone who had a perspective on the dramatic events over there. This would make for a pretty impressive paper. I wrote a letter, with the input of my father and teacher. To my further amazement, Barclay wrote back, making an offer. He was liaising with a TV news crew that planned to interview members of a security force about to deploy to a town on the

Angolan border. I could send Barclay a question, and a member of the news crew could put it to one of the interviewees. I realize now how much sense this made from a PR standpoint. "Mike, a sixth grader in Cambridge, Massachusetts, would like to know…" But imagine my wonder at the time.

I remember when the segment aired. There we were in the living room of the house on Garfield Street. We stared at the TV in awe as the camera alighted on a column of young men standing by a wall in a concrete square, preparing to move into armored personnel carriers. I thought they were somewhere between commandos and police officers. They were members of a security force whose task was to keep order in a contested town on the border. Their outfits, deep blue with all manner of black straps and holsters, looked both alien and familiar. And their weapons! Those Israeli-made semiautomatic rifles would have made *Robocop* look dated, and it was still years before that film's release. After a few dozen words from the reporter about the border war and the mission of these young men, the reporter approached one of them. A thin fellow with a blond crew cut, chewing on something. The reporter asked about what lay ahead and about the preparedness of the force. The young man said there was danger from insurgents as well as upstarts who didn't like the government in Pretoria. But he wanted everyone to know most of the locals would welcome the security they brought. He said they'd been training for months for this eventuality. The interviewer moved down the line a few places, to another young man, with thick black hair, stockier than the first. He looked at the reporter earnestly enough. If he was feeling any fear, I sure couldn't see it. She asked him his name. He said, Marcus Smits. Where was he from? Johannesburg. Marcus Smits wore a look conveying both earthiness and intelligence. There was a faint bleariness in his round face, a mild imprecision to his speech, that I could imagine growing in different scenes as he drank. Here was not a celebrity or a comic book hero. Marcus Smits was a real person. I was aware of the horrors of apartheid, but at the moment this young man didn't strike me as an agent of apartheid. Marcus Smits was someone I could relate to.

"We have a question maybe you can answer. It's from a sixth-grade boy in America, in Boston. He wants to know, to your mind, what's the single most important thing you and your force can accomplish?" the reporter asked.

Marcus considered this for a moment.

"This boy, what is his name?"

"Michael."

After another momentary pause, Marcus looked at the camera.

"Michael. Listen, my friend. You're really far away, but this planet is very much the same in its general qualities if not in its particulars. Your city needs protection from the forces of disorder and the same is true over here. My mates and I have undergone many months of training in order to protect people from bad guys. If I do my job, there won't be a single civilian casualty at the border."

My family gave me the most abominable kind of attention. They were looking at me, trying to construe my reaction at an emotional moment, a time of direct personal rapport with a stranger who was at risk. I ignored them. I studied the features of the stranger who had addressed me earnestly, respectfully, almost as a fellow adult.

I haven't witnessed many acts of heroism in my life. My imagination has had to extrapolate from what seemed like solid information. Having pictured the young Cambridge cop getting out of his car, running, and tackling the purse thief, it wasn't hard to imagine another scene. I saw Marcus Smits dashing across open space between buildings, his semiautomatic raised, gesturing and yelling to his comrades. Crouching at the side of a building. Returning fire. Helping another officer drag one of their wounded to safety.

I followed the border war for a few weeks, but my attention faltered as my paper's due date neared. I got busy trying to fix spelling errors and awkward sentence structures.

After turning in the paper to Mr. Duncan, I couldn't help wondering. The BBC and the New York Times could report on the course of the war, but what was the fate of Marcus Smits? I wrote to Donald Barclay again. He gave me the address of the municipal authority in the area the force had gone to defend. Barclay didn't have the name of anyone in particular, but he was sure somebody could answer inquiries.

My father congratulated me. He coached me on how to frame my inquiry.

"You're not writing as a student, Mike, but as a journalist. This is an official inquiry about a source of yours!"

On my father's insistence, I included a reference in my letter to the Freedom of Information Act, which was then relatively new. At that age, I couldn't have explained to my father that FOIA requests were meaningless in a foreign jurisdiction. I did what my father told me to do.

Once again, I achieved a surprising result. The 9" x 12" manila envelope that came through the mail four weeks later had a return address with words I didn't yet know. I tore it open and pulled its contents into the light coming through the windows on Garfield Street. Here was a photograph and a pile of papers. The face in the photo wasn't a face as you and I understand the term. The temples, chin, and upper reaches of the forehead were there. At the top of the photo I made out a fringe of wispy black hair. Otherwise, a mess of scarlet tissue, twisted and ripped by high-velocity rounds, filled out the space where those earnest features had been.

My father didn't know how to react. I was the victim of my own curiosity, of course, but he'd so actively encouraged me. Maybe it wouldn't have happened if he'd spotted the words "Department of Forensics" on the envelope. Of course, none of this would have occurred if my father hadn't gotten such withering criticism from my mom. Yes, here's a whole other problematic part of my life I haven't mentioned before. She never forgave my father for being morally weak. When they were in their twenties and recently married, they lived in New York. My mom pursued her Ph.D. in Classics at Columbia while my father taught mathematics at City University. This was during all the tumult over open enrollment. Protestors used to burst into my father's classroom and demand to address the class about their cause.

> Protestor: "We demand to speak to the class now about the enrollment issue."
> My father: "I do sympathize with you, but I'm teaching a class here."
> Protestor: "I said, we demand to address the class, right now."
> My father: "Well, ah, we'll put it to a vote, okay?"

Always implicit in the protestors' conduct was a threat of physical violence, and some of them even carried bats. My father never ordered them to get out. I don't think a class of his ever voted against giving the floor to the protestors.

In the years following my early efforts at journalism, my relationship with my father declined to the point where we barely spoke anymore. But I don't resent the man now. I haven't been able to commit myself to many things for long, but I've pursued the craft of writing doggedly enough to have published work in glossies that pay upwards of $1,000 per article. And I landed a job as a writing instructor at one of the more reputable universities in our city.

But the world today is a little different from when I was in the sixth grade. Identity politics are too much with us. Look at the eruptions on my campus this month when one of the student groups invited a noted scholar and cultural critic, Walter Henderson, to come and give a talk on campus. Henderson's work is cited pretty often, but he has drawn ire for his unapologetic defense of the traditional curriculum against multiculturalists' demands for the expunging of Dead White European Males. When the announcement came that Henderson was going to give a talk, the reaction was immediate. The Black Students Association, the Multiethnic Coalition, and the Progressive Alliance all called for the invite's revocation. Implicit in their demands was a threat of mob violence, the disruption of lectures around campus, and calls for the ouster of the university's president such as happened recently at the University of Missouri. The furor had been going on for over a week when my letter appeared in the campus newspaper.

The content of my letter wasn't provocative. I didn't even really address the speaker's views on the traditional curriculum. I quoted Voltaire's famous utterance about defending to the death a person's right to speak.

Not inflammatory, right? Or so I thought until the afternoon when something pretty astonishing happened during one of my classes in Boalt Hall. I was in the middle of an excursus on D.H. Lawrence's short story "The Rocking-Horse Winner." Where might a boy's emotional intelligence turn when the adults around him have cut him off? Suddenly a twenty-year-old student, Jerome Price, rose from his seat in the middle row.

"How dare you invite that racist motherfucker to speak here?"

Startled, I made eye contact with the impudent youngster.

"Get your facts straight before you speak so boldly. I did not invite Walter Henderson to speak here."

"You defended his right to speak on this campus."

"That is entirely correct, Jerome. I defended his right to exercise his constitutionally protected right to free speech, at an institution theoretically devoted to the exchange of ideas."

"No racist has a right to speak at a school we're paying for."

The *we* in Jerome's statement referred to the students collectively, very much including himself. This was a little too much for me.

"Walter Henderson is not a racist. He has already explained why he places one set of cultural priorities above another, as you'd know if you could be bothered to read any of his publications on the subject. I might add that you, sir, are not in any way paying for the visit. You are the beneficiary of a generous athletic scholarship. If it depended on your academic abilities, Jerome, you'd never have set foot on this campus. Sports is the only thing keeping illiterates like yourself enrolled!"

Yes, those were the words heard by sixty-seven pairs of eager young ears.

If the situation happened again, I would not change a word. Does that sound like bravado? It is.

Or, to use another term, courage.

It's fine for others to speak before me at the funeral. Maybe the family will deny me a chance to talk at all. Well, that's okay. I'd rather be dead than be a coward. It's fine for the family to hate me, as long as they do it for the right reason.

Lotus Eaters

From where the boy sat on the dune, it was easy to take in the middle third of the beach, where all the nude sunbathers were. He watched them move up from the waves crashing on the shore to the space near the foot of the dune, just beyond the depression where thorny bushes obscured the approach to the beach. If he looked to the right, he saw the far more crowded public section where nobody was naked, and if he turned his gaze the other way, to the north, he could just make out colored specs near the foot of Corn Hill, the shapes of his parents and the German family with whom they spent most of their waking hours here on Cape Cod.

But he seldom shifted his gaze from the women below, one of whom had a clipped punk haircut, or so he classified it. The others were brunettes whose locks cascaded to the tops of their bare shoulders. They were sitting on blankets in the sun save for one of them who was trying, not very competently, to steer a narrow one-person sailboat twenty yards out at high tide, and another woman at the edge of the water yelling suggestions to the one on the boat. The boy, Matt Mills, had tried to spy on the sunbathers from a position not far from his parents and their friends, but whenever he walked close enough to get a good look, one of the women would grow suspicious and stare at him, and he had to pretend to be retrieving a shell or a piece of driftwood before retreating north up the beach. Now he had an ideal position, with a comprehensive view, a place no one could reproach him for occupying—a wooden platform halfway up the dune with a bench on it.

Suddenly one of the sunbathers got up and repositioned herself so that Matt could see most of the front of her body as she covered herself with suntan lotion. Though it was hard to tell at this distance, she appeared to be making eye contact with him. Now the sun caught Matt so directly, the force of the hot carnal moment was so strong, that these things obliterated all his sense of himself and he felt he was not *from* anywhere.

Twenty minutes later, the middle third of the beach was empty. Reluctantly, Matt picked himself up and studied the northern third long enough to determine that his family and most of the Germans had retreated to the houses atop Corn Hill. After a final survey of the beach, he ascended the black wooden steps encrusted with sand and bits of seashells until he stood atop the dune where he seemed to command the highest position on the planet, feeling like a Greek god from one of his coloring books as he overlooked all the dunes and seas of the earth. He ambled up the sandy path between the thin green stalks until the row of cabins came into view, cabins where affluent doctors from Boston sat drinking Chilean and South African wines, and lawyers who barely dressed down even on vacation sat emotionally exhausted after hours of quarreling with a spouse, and people like Matt's parents were grateful for a chance to assert their middle-class status by renting space for a week.

Nobody was visible on the row of porches as Matt sauntered to number 7, and walked into a modest living room where his mom sat talking to a woman he'd never seen before. They were discussing books. Immediately Matt noticed that they were both smoking and thought the visitor must have encouraged his mom to resume a habit she'd claimed to have kicked the year before. With an inward sigh, he climbed the bare wooden stairs to the second floor, and entered his room with a window facing the dunes and approaches to the beach, where he lay down on his bed and thought of the women he'd spied on and felt the inexorable reactions within his young body begin.

The next day, his mom asked Matt to run an errand for her. She'd lent Nicole, the woman who was here yesterday, a copy of *Orion*, the literary journal Karen Mills wrote for, and today she needed it back. She wanted Matt to run down to Nicole's cabin on the other side of Corn Hill. So out the boy headed into the perfect day where all was silent and the fronts of cabins were like faces staring in the knowledge of his prurience, making the boy hot and nervous in every pore as he proceeded down the hill, barely registering the architectural splendor of some of the rich people's houses grafted onto the imperfect circle of a hill or the jagged crest between the road and a cluster of trees. Reaching her building, Matt reflected that Nicole was at least his mom's age, maybe a year or two older, yet she didn't have a husband and kids.

When Matt entered, he reeled from a sweet aroma in the air that he would have instantly recognized had he been older. Directly across from the front door, Nicole sat on a couch, barefoot, in a black shirt and dark trousers, her blonde hair not tied back as when he'd seen her yesterday, but falling past her shoulders, not rich like his mom's, but kind of wispy. A television stood on a table beside the door, but she hadn't been watching it. On the coffee table before her were an overflowing ashtray, some issues of *Cosmopolitan*, and a couple of paperbacks. She gestured at the latter with the expression of an embarrassed pupil explaining why she hasn't done her homework.

"I promised myself I'd read *Moby-Dick* in its entirety once I got here," she told the boy, "but I've put it aside after a few pages."

Matt glanced at the fat novel lying face-down on the glass beside the overflowing ashtray.

"That's a few pages more than I've read," he replied.

She was making eye contact with the boy now.

"What sort of stuff do you read?" Nicole asked.

"Oh, Greek myths. *Mad* magazine. Comic books."

"You're into the good stuff," she said, the smile evolving into a grin. "What can I do for you, Matt?"

"I, uh . . . My mom asked me to pick up the magazine she lent you yesterday. She needs her editor's address."

"She needs her editor's address? My God. And I thought she was here at the Cape to *relax*," Nicole replied.

"Well . . . she does. But she also sits up typing stuff and sending it out to editors. So she needs the magazine."

"Yes I know, she's quite a literary sensation," Nicole muttered with what sounded to the boy like jealousy in her voice.

He found his gaze wandering over the ashtray and the three others in different corners of the room that Nicole had equally neglected to empty, the dog-eared paperbacks, the heaps of notebooks filled with a crabbed handwriting, and the bottles in a cardboard box by the foot of the kitchen counter.

"Are you a writer?" he heard himself ask.

"Heh. Is someone who casts bait all day and never catches anything a fisherman?" she asked.

"Huh?"

"Nothing. Yes, I'm a writer, but not quite in Karen's league. I'm an aspiring writer, if you know what I mean," she added as Matt noticed, in the light coming through the east window, that Nicole had reached an age when he thought people had long become whatever they were destined to be.

"Here's the *Orion* issue—and tell your mom thanks, and I thought her piece about Paul Celan was wonderful," Nicole put in.

Matt accepted the magazine and turned to go when he heard Nicole say, "One more thing, Matt."

He turned around and faced the woman who sat all by herself in this house by the sea, smoking and thinking about things.

"Do me a favor."

She turned and reached for something behind the couch, then turned back to the boy and extended a stack of typed pages bound with a paperclip. When he approached her to accept it, that cloying smell assailed him once more.

"Could you give that to your mom and tell her I'd be grateful—if she can find just a moment—for her opinion on it."

The boy nodded and left the house, quickly mounting the slope of Corn Hill toward the row of neat cabins in the setting sun.

The following evening, Matt's parents had decided to entertain the German family. Gerhard Ahl was here with his wife, Ulrike, and their three daughters. As so many times before, Matt had hoped to avoid the embarrassment of people seeing Allan, his brain-damaged older brother, prance about and twitch his fingers maniacally as others nervously carried on their conversations. At the moment, things were not quite so bad. Allan lolled against a wall, the one with the "First I lived here" inscription, staring ahead without seeming to register any of the buzz of conversation or the shuffle and pouring of drinks all around him in the comfortable if spartan cabin. But one of the German girls gazed at Allan and whispered into her sister's ear. Matt loathed whisperers. He'd crush their skulls if he could get away with it. Besides the German family, the Girards were here, a mathematician friend of Matt's father who taught at MIT, his wife, and their son and daughter. Matt overheard snatches of the banalities thrown about:

"—have an essay coming out on the early Sontag—"

"—that's my father's *Festschrift*, everything he published at Harvard and Chicago—"

"The couple in the cabin next door are an active couple, if you know what I mean—"

"It gets so damn crowded in July, you'd think you were on the Côte d'Azur!"

"Why don't we get away, go to Provincetown on Friday?"

Yet like a gull circling back to a shape that had piqued its interest on the rocks below, Matt returned his gaze to the younger two of the three German daughters, Anya and Katie, standing on the fringe of the crowd of guests, with looks suggestive of a shared knowledge denied the adults. He wandered over and confronted Anya, the middle daughter.

"Don't you think that if you have something to say, you should say it out loud, to everyone?" he demanded.

"Why?" she asked with a look of affronted innocence.

"Because you're doing something sneaky," he retorted.

"Weren't you doing something sneaky when you spied on those naked ladies on the beach?" she asked.

"How do you know what I was doing?" Matt demanded, feeling an invisible hand begin to close around his esophagus.

"We could see you, both of us. And I think your parents noticed you too, before they went back up. Your dad was really embarrassed."

"I was minding my business. I wasn't watching anyone," he stammered.

For the first time, Katie spoke.

"Don't you think if you're going to do something, you should be brave enough to be open about it?" she asked in that precise, elegantly modulated English the three girls shared.

"If you think it's funny that Allan's brain-damaged, it might have something to do with your own insecurities," he proclaimed, repeating a phrase he'd held in reserve after years of teasing in parks and playgrounds.

"How do you know we were talking about Allan?" Anya broke in.

"Never mind," Matt answered. "Is there something funny about him?"

"There's nothing funny about him at all, Matt. It's just something our father said the day we got here—"

Now for the first time, something tentative crept into Anya's voice—what exactly?

Matt glanced over at the jovial, middle-aged computer scientist standing between Mary and Vincent Girard and Matt's parents, holding aloft a glass of Chardonnay and pontificating about something President Carter had just done.

"What did he say?" Matt demanded.

The girls looked at each other, then thirteen-year-old Marc Girard came over and asked whether he could interest anyone in a game at the ping-pong table on the back porch.

Matt sauntered over to the punch bowl across from where Allan lolled against the wall, noticing with distaste that his brother was drooling again.

Matt sat in the hot crowded car wishing to hell that his father had not made the decision to visit Provincetown today. On his left, Marc Girard sat staring out the window at the scenery, while on his right, Allan sat and gibbered and repeated bits of phrases he'd heard from the other three in the car. Not wanting to tell him to shut up in so many words, everyone ignored Allan or gently reached out to push his spasming fingers to his lap.

On the exit leading to Provincetown, Matt realized that his mom had planned to have the Ahls over again while he, his father, Allan, and Marc were in the coastal town, and that he'd left not only his *Mad* issues but other of his cherished possessions—his baseball cards, WWII comics, and the radio with which he stood in the corner of the spare wooden room trying to follow Red Sox games through the static—strewn on the chair and dresser and floor where those horrible girls might walk in and find them, and God knew what they'd do before his return. Now the riders were approaching the teeming downtown, where investment bankers in white designer shirts and tan shorts strolled with their arms around the waists of woman ten or twelve years their junior, kids munched on pink and white and chocolate ice cream, and guys in their early twenties gathered at counters buying draft beers before sauntering over to the boardwalk to take in some skin.

After they'd parked, Marc said that he wanted to linger at the nautical museum, so Mr. Mills said fine, and he and his sons set off in the direction of the boardwalk. At intervals, some of the attractive young couples turned and stared at Allan, who hopped like a kangaroo, clapped for durations too brief to have meaning, and gibbered and drooled in the clear crisp air. They proceeded amidst the happy talk and for just a moment, Matt found himself able to quit thinking about the party and the girls who were like the talking idols of one of the more caustic deities in his coloring book. It was a good thing. Ever did those girls drive home the awareness that he wasn't—what was the term?—that he wasn't terribly *bright*. When the three got to the promenade, Matt gazed out into the infinity of blue with a sail just visible here and there, and they sauntered to the end of the pier jutting perpendicularly from the promenade and stood in awe of the majesty of the ocean.

"Matt, why were you so rude to the Ahls last night?" asked Mr. Mills, in the sententious academic tone his son loathed.

Matt protested that he wasn't aware of having been rude, or at least of having initiated any rudeness, which in his mind was by far the more important consideration.

"Yes, Matt, but when we have guests over, you need to act with forbearance. Their interests are more important than yours."

"Forbearance?"

"With patience. You have to go out of your way to be a good guest. Do you get what I'm saying?"

"Sure I do. You're saying people can be as nasty as they like to me, and I can't say anything back to them."

"Something like that," said Mr. Mills, gazing at the boy through those glasses that to Matt made him more distant than those sails way out there in the blue.

"Well, that's easy for you to say," the boy replied.

"Come on, Matt. I'll buy you and Allan some ice cream in a minute. I'll be your Ahab if you be my loyal Starbuck," Mr. Mills put in.

"Meaning what?"

"Meaning you have to repress whatever rebellious impulses you may feel. Not necessarily succeed all the time, but try."

Matt decided to let this go. He wished he were back at the nautical museum with Marc.

They started back toward the promenade. Suddenly the sky was not in the right place, Matt felt his whole body keeling violently to the right, farther, closer to the edge of the pier.

"Allan! ALLAN! NO! *STOP!!!*"

His grinning brother was pushing him hard toward the twenty-foot drop to the water, green with scum at the fringe of the rocky shore.

"*NO!!!*" he screamed.

In a split second, he jolted the right half of his trembling body forward fast enough to grasp the chain linking the stone pillars lining the pier before his body could go spilling off into the clear air. He swung his left half and then his ankles around the chain as Allan leaned over him murmuring nonsensically, still with that grin spread across his face.

"Hey!" the father said upon finally realizing that his sons were not anywhere near him and turning around to see Matt hanging onto the chain below the gibbering assailant.

Now that Matt knew Allan's design, there was no way it could succeed—everything had depended on that second, that moment of utter surprise in the crisp air under the perfect cobalt sky. Cursing and crying hoarsely, Matt disentangled himself and got up and faced his brother and negligent father.

Minutes later, they stood on the sidewalk holding ice cream cones, Allan letting the ice cream fall and dribble across his chest, not really enjoying it at all, and Matt not inclined to help him. When they had finished the joyless ritual, their father rounded them up along with Marc Girard and then they were in a car winding through the hills away from the perfect town in the undiminished light of 3:30, Allan snorting and muttering his mush of gibberish and names of relatives and of pets the family had had over the years, Matt staring ahead in rage, Marc silently embarrassed to be thrust between them on the back seat. Matt could only sit there glowering at the brain-damaged boy as they turned into Corn Hill, parked, and emerged from the driveway toward the row of nearly identical cabins.

Within minutes Matt was sitting on the edge of his bed wishing he could hit that gibbering retard who did such enraging things and then sat there with his doltish look, rocking back and forth, letting out the name of a cousin or a cat that had died five years before. Matt sat there on the edge of his bed, his hands like those of a man desperate not to be tossed from atop a bull, ignoring his father when the latter called him to come down to dinner, and there was a tacit understanding between them, that Matt was in one of the moods he'd come to know so well in later years filled with depression and ineffectual therapy. No one seemed to appreciate how close he had come to plummeting off that pier and dashing his head on a rock or getting impaled on a sunken anchor's hook. At length, the boy grew tired of sitting there, picked himself up, and sauntered down the stairs and out onto the wooden porch. He descended onto the sand and looked around. As it sank, the sun appeared like the tent of a circus whose final act was to set everything ablaze. The shadows of the row of cabins seemed enormous, he thought as he wandered southward gazing at the bland spartan façades masking the debauchery of the middle-class folk from Cambridge or Lawrence or Brookline or Watertown, until he came to a porch where one of the neighbors, a man Matt didn't know by name, languished on two front steps with a glass of something potent just beside him, wearing a straw hat. He was the type who might have had a copy of the *Wall Street Journal* in hand if seated on his couch back home, but he'd come here to disregard everything and partake of the sky and the view like that from Mount Olympus, and Matt hardly knew how to construe his odd expression. The boy tried to imagine the scene behind the façade of this cabin, a woman and maybe a guest or two seated at the table in the rear sipping Chardonnay and chatting about what they'd purchased in Truro or Provincetown, or maybe the wife was out with friends and a kid sat scratching away at the wooden walls, something brief and caustic that rhymed. Or maybe not. Matt wandered off away from the row of cabins, toward the bush where the buzzing rose and fell like the heave of a startled man's chest, the only manic sound in the dunes glowing in the orange light, the dunes where no one walked, the last nude sunbathers having retreated into their cabins in the last hour or so. As the boy listened to the sound of the waves rising and smashing against the shore strewn with random footprints hundreds of feet below, he inhaled the crisp air and felt his rage dimming ever so slightly. He could not maintain his wish to kill his brother, he felt those moments on the pier blur and distort into the present moment of clarity in which he sensed that the sun fell on a body that had not been designed to suffer, and how much more acute was the awareness of all the adults around him, how much more precious the aesthetic, evanescent perfection of each moment, each gesture and word in this place, as the memory of the pier fell and smashed into millions of fragments and he knew he could no longer hate Allan, could no longer harness the old revulsion. It was just like that moment on the hot wooden platform halfway up the dune. The sensations that came now obliterated motive, memory, identity. This place was for pleasure, little else had meaning or purpose.

Matt walked back into his family's cabin and climbed the bare wooden stairs and marched into his room, lying down and allowing thoughts of the women on the beach to flood his mind once more, the individual bathers segueing into a carousel of sensual delight as a breeze found its way through the window and the mellow rustling of the curtains lulled him.

On the following evening, with two more days to go at the Cape, Matt's parents, having exacted an apology for his sullenness toward his brother, organized a final party at the cabin. His father poured drinks and let out a classical allusion, a Homeric reference Matt would not grasp until years later. Besides the usual crowd, Matt soon noticed another guest wandering among the Ahls and Girards, recognizing this new arrival as Nicole, the woman with the dog-eared books and overflowing ashtrays, who had asked his mom to comment on her piece of fiction. Clad in black from head to foot, her slender aging figure maneuvered among the guests, dipping and turning in lithe movements, keeping her drink aloft, slipping in and out of the boy's vision like a frog in the reaches of the buzzing green stalks south of here. Nicole always knew exactly what to say, whether her interlocutor was a twelve-year-old girl or a middle-aged mathematician. For a while the boy stood around restlessly, then he spotted Marc with a grown-up drink in his hand, and slid over to his quasi-friend. Marc's mind flitted among levels of intelligence that seemed permanently off-limits to Matt, who was alternately eager to ingratiate himself and put off by the bespectacled boy's superiority. Matt made some remarks about the Ahl girls—he could hardly decide which of them was the worst—to which Marc countered that Matt was not mature enough to know and understand them. He could hardly have said something more calculated to piss off his friend.

"It's not them I'm really interested in," Marc added.

"Huh?"

"How old would you say Gebhard is?" Marc asked.

"Oh, I dunno, fifty-four maybe."

"You may be right for once."

"So?"

"Heh. Typical Matt response. 'So.'"

"What's your point?"

"There's no point really, I'm just a little curious about Gebhard, the Gebhard we don't see in front of us here."

Marc was making no sense, so Matt gave up hope of intelligent conversation and walked about until he found his mom tending to Allan, who seemed as remote as ever, lolling against the wall and making a mess with his fruit punch. Brushing up against his mother, whispering and receiving her whispers, Matt finally learned of the subject matter of what he'd brought over and thrust into his mother's hands. It was an account of a woman who had to take Seroquel and Depakote daily to stave off attacks of debilitating depression, the revulsion at finding herself trapped with an aging and deteriorating body while her friends fell in love and got married and brought children into the world, the horror at her position in time and the impossibility of grasping anything in her wasting and weakening hands, the humiliation of dates with men who dismissed her even as she gazed into imaginary vistas in which she bore their names, futures that could never begin to materialize. Nicole had written an account of one day when this character failed to take her meds because of the toll they exacted on her creative self, on her ability to drag a pen across a page. She'd wandered into one of the most risqué cafes in Brooklyn Heights, where the sights of closed windows had led her to the conclusion that all the diners here, the wealthy men and women of the Heights, were going to give their money to a fascist candidate, and it was up to her to dissuade them immediately. After the waiters told her she was making a scene and tossed her out, she got a ride from her brother, her responsible and successful brother, up to her mother's house in one of the toniest parts of Stony Brook, New York. Things went fine until she wandered the streets of the suburb, got into an argument with a preppy-looking girl out walking her dog, and broke the girl's jaw.

Now about $30,000 in debt, thanks to legal fees, the protagonist of Nicole's story hoped to find peace and tranquility and serenity conducive to good writing in seclusion in a quaint cabin near the beach.

His parents were sophisticated readers, but even without the story, they'd known exactly who Nicole was.

"Have another glass of Chardonnay," Matt's father said, extending a glass to the aging but still shapely woman in black.

"Thank you," came the raspy voice.

Foxley's Progress

August 20, 2014

Dear Lance,

This letter has come with no return address. As you realize who the author is, you may have an impulse to tear it up. I want to start off by asking you to hold off on assigning any blame for what has happened. I beg you to pause, reflect, and try to develop just a bit of perspective. Even at this distance, I feel the force of the tragedy and I'm achingly aware of what it has done to your life. Please, please don't blame me. I don't even know for certain whether this letter will ever come before your eyes, but my nights in these shitty little motels will be easier to get through if I can just try to help you reach some kind of understanding. I have to try.

When I first met your mother, Mrs. Vivian Foxley, I already had an idea of the world in which she was raising you. Competitive is a fair enough word. At the age of eighteen, you were showing promise academically, and particularly as a writer. You loved to read. But you lacked focus and needed a strong person to guide you and bring what was nascent into full bloom. In other words: You were eighteen. People believed in your promise but many complex and competing influences were at work and not all of them were healthy.

When I first set foot in your ornately furnished house in Brooklyn Heights, your mother was just getting done entertaining another guest, a neighbor some ten years her junior named Emily Mitchell. Emily was telling your mom about what happened when she and her husband brought their three-year-old boy, Jimmy, to see your prep school's psychiatrist and childhood development specialist, Kate Walsh. A few people had noticed that something wasn't right with Kate's mood that day. Still, it was a bit of a jolt when Kate spent a few minutes trying to administer some cognitive tests to uncooperative, irritated Jimmy, tests where you have to make simple deductions and recognize and identify things, and then brusquely turned around to the parents and proclaimed: "You'll never get him into any private academy in New York. You'll have to start thinking about special schools for retarded children."

Vivian of course was shocked to hear this story.

Well—it was bad enough news for Jimmy, and I'm sure that Emily Mitchell took an extra mouthful of Prozac as soon as she got home that afternoon. Emily was still in a tizzy. When she and her husband made the rounds of cocktail parties in Brooklyn Heights, I'm sure that psychologically she had something akin to a scarlet "A" emblazoned on her forehead.

I didn't mean to get derailed here, Lance. But it's worth noting that these parties are the domain of parents who groom their kids for prep schools, Princeton, the big investment banks, and the partnerships of white-shoe corporate law firms. At these functions, it simply does not do to go around looking like you're marketing damaged goods. You have had to attend your share of these parties, and you know how parents stand behind and to one side of a son or daughter, place a hand on the child's shoulder, and tell the other parents that so-and-so has a summer job on Wall Street or is interning at a publishing house. There have been times when Mrs. Vivian Foxley stood alone in the lobby or on the back porch of her brownstone, thinking herself unobserved, the fingers of her moist hands trembling as she unscrewed the cap of a tube of tablets and thought about an exam you had to take or a paper you had to write.

Particularly the latter. Though Vivian was not the first to take note of the increasingly feeble grasp of English usage and grammar among so many young people nowadays, she was prone to thinking about it more and more, perhaps partly because on some level she knew that she'd fallen short of her own family's expectations. At a remote point in her past, Vivian fancied herself a modern-day Virginia Woolf or Edith Wharton, but then she found that martinis and daytime soap operas have their allure. One thing she did become quite serious, deadly serious, about was making sure that you, her only child, her dearest Lance, learned to write well. There was still plenty of time for you to figure out what to do with your life, but one thing this lady understood was what E.O. Wilson calls the unity of knowledge and the universal value of language as a conveyor of it. So she invited me into the tea room of your impressive brownstone and served me a cup of Gevalia coffee and we talked for a bit. She said she'd heard that Bryce Allen was a wonderful writer and that I was also a patient, involved tutor. It did not take long for me to agree to become your tutor, not at the fees Vivian was offering. But don't think that was the only consideration. I made her show me a few of the papers you'd written for Mr. Irving's English class. A trained eye can quickly assess usage and style, and above all a writer's connection with what he or she is writing. If you'd been a hopeless case, as I think you know some of your classmates are, I would have handed the papers back to Vivian and walked out of there and never given her or you another thought.

But I saw promise in your writing, and I was pretty confident about taking you on and guiding you, Lance. God knows I liked you well enough. You weren't one of these excessively privileged kids one meets at an academy such as yours. I'm thinking of your classmate, Chase Sutter, and encounters I had with his overbearing mother, Mrs. Beverly Sutter. The Sutters were the first people your family became acquainted with following your move down from Boston when you were just eight. Although I have always thought Beverly is a lovely name, in this case it belonged to a woman whose cawing, raspy voice worked back and forth over you as if you were a protrusion that needed to be sandpapered away. Moreover, there was something oddly ambivalent about her at times, as I'm sure you found, Lance. She wanted her son Chase to succeed, in a conventional sense at least, just as much as any mother in this milieu, yet she chafed at other parents' restrictions on how much TV their kids could watch, and disparaged parents for allowing their son or daughter to turn into a "bookworm." (Don't you adore that phrase?) She was, I think, quietly resentful that Vivian, though never really serious about having a literary career, managed to work her way up to a senior editorial position at one of the more prominent book clubs, while Beverly worked as a human resources parasite somewhere. As for Chase, he was cocky and rude in the way that only the most insecure young men can be. He was also a vicious bully, from what I have heard. He mocked your bookishness. More on the Sutters later.

Yes, there were many odd and disharmonious influences at work on you in your younger days, Lance. I said the Sutters were the first people your family really befriended upon moving to New York, but that may not be strictly accurate. For you and your investment banker dad and your doting mom had barely planted your feet on the grimy pavements of Brooklyn Heights when a business acquaintance of your father's, the vice president of a publishing house, introduced your parents at a cocktail party to one Peter Osterman. Ah, yes. Imagine your mother's delight at getting an introduction to a writer with a growing reputation both here and in Europe, an author who'd already won lavish praise for his slender novels combining elements of hard-boiled detective fiction with a modern French style and sensibility. His four novels to date were a farrago of introspection, *roman à clef,* and metaphysical inquiry in which Osterman's many antecedents, from E.A. Poe to Raymond Chandler to Henry Miller to Georges Simenon, reared their figurative heads with varying degrees of subtlety. What a coup, your mom thought, just to be able to say to people that she knew Peter Osterman socially. That she knew a literary family.

A friendship blossomed with this literary family, which consisted of the writer, his Norwegian second wife, also a writer, and their son Noah. You became such good friends with Noah, I recall, that the Ostermans began taking you along on trips to their summer house, on the shore of an exquisite lake in Michigan. Noah got a lot of encouragement from his dad to become a writer, but Peter Osterman wasn't always kind about the few samples of your writing that he saw. For her part, Vivian never gave up on the idea of having a son who was better read and more intellectual than those of the women she hung out with down at the squash club. Your mother was also bringing home books for you, from best-sellers to avant-garde curiosities. Sometimes they were books published in the last few years, sometimes they were what unlettered people, like Beverly Sutter, refer to as "the classics." You took a necessary step in your artistic orientation when you began to develop an acquaintance with Dostoyevsky. You loved to read. I bolstered Vivian's efforts by giving you lots more to read, works by Salinger, Capote, Dubus, Carver, Wolff, John Fante, John Hawkes, John Cheever, and John Sayles, and then I got you on a Bukowski kick. And I relentlessly criticized your writing, where it was windy and where it was gauche, hammering you just as relentlessly when you used too few words as when you used too many.

Meanwhile, your mom and Beverly Sutter hung out a fair amount at the squash club and the more modish restaurants on Montague Street. Beverly made no secret of the fact that she wasn't thrilled with you. It's a little hard, trying to fathom the attitudes of a woman so committed to conventional success for her own son, Chase, and alternately distrustful and jealous of literary pursuits, which have such an ambiguous status for practical people like Beverly. On the one hand, she wanted Chase to be able to speak and write well, but on the other, she thought reading would ultimately distract her boy from what mattered. Chase was a popular kid, but also a limited guy who thought of reading as a punishment. When your mom tried to reason with Beverly, the latter invariably began saying, in an extremely shrill voice, that Kate Walsh had assured her that Chase showed promise in his early evaluations and the last thing she must do was allow her boy to become a bookish nerd, as, by implication, Vivian had done with you. Beverly had values and she stood by them. Hail to the post-literate age.

During your mid-teens, I was tutoring you, you were fighting to get your grades up at the prep school, and Vivian kept ending up in awkward positions at her job. I don't think she's ever told you this one anecdote, Lance. But she told me. Oh yes, she told me in detail about the time that she went into an editorial meeting in the Midtown offices of the most prominent book club on the planet, carrying portions of a translated manuscript of an author she and I both revere. The other editors at the meeting took turns plugging one or another diet book, smut novel, or ghostwritten celebrity biography. Then when the time came for Vivian's presentation, she said the name Dostoyevsky, and the eyebrows of the executive director, seated at the end of the table, immediately went up.

"Is that one of these new Eastern European writers?" he asked.

It's true, Lance—that's what he asked your mom.

All eyes were on Vivian. She could not tell her boss what she was thinking, right to his face, in front of twenty other editors. No, she sure couldn't.

Vivian thought for a moment.

"Ah, no, he's actually 19th century, but this is a new translation," Vivian said, laying stress on the last few words.

The editorial director of the world's most prestigious book club nodded, processing this information, as the subordinate editors seated around the table quietly exhaled.

Hail to the post-literate age.

Amid all the hostile forces at work, your mom's hope and faith in you never wavered for an instant, Lance. Never, not once. I want you to know that. It's critical that you regard everything that's happened in this light. And, it goes without saying, I never gave up on you. I continued to coach you as a writer, giving you as much tough love as I thought an eighteen-year-old could take. Meanwhile, Beverly Sutter insisted to your mom that Bryce Allen was a criminal whom her son should have nothing to do with, any more than top-flight restaurants in the Heights should allow homeless people to walk in off the street and take up tables. But at her urging, I continued to tutor you and to tell you exactly what I thought of your writing, whether you wanted to hear it or not. You forged ahead, your work improved, and I could hear the resentment in Beverly's voice when she sat in your mother's tea room and described the crabbed, awkward, misspelled disasters that ensued whenever Chase Sutter put pen to paper.

During your junior year of high school, your family kept up a precarious, complicated relationship with the Ostermans. It wasn't the highest point of Peter Osterman's career, what with his sales in a slump and an appraisal of his *oeuvre* coming out in one of the glossy weeklies. You might say that sounds like exactly what his career needed at that point, an essay drawing national attention, but then you've never brought yourself to read the magazine in question, Lance. Here was an acid rebuke not just to Osterman's serial use of clichés, but to the limpness, the laziness that characterized so much of his prose, which often read more like a Cliffs Notes summary of someone else's plot than like narrative. A measure of the accuracy of this appraisal was that everyone carefully avoided mentioning it at dinners and parties. But I suspect Vivian was thinking, "My son can't write, Peter? No—*you* can't write."

Having said all of this, Peter was a better friend than Beverly in some respects. He was outwardly warm toward Vivian, and he kindly, perhaps condescendingly, agreed to put in a word for you that helped you land an internship one summer at New Era Press, which billed itself as a progressive publisher and a home for authors not deemed commercially viable by the conglomerates. I guess in Peter's thinking you may not have been a writer but there were still ways for you to be involved with books.

So you got the internship at this place, but it wasn't quite what you hoped or expected. The founder and editorial director was an aging fellow whose family had fled the war in Europe when he was a little boy. No one questions his social conscience or his aptitude for publishing works that otherwise might never make it into print, but you quickly came to learn about his judgment in other areas. He hired an office manager named Martine who dealt brusquely with the interns and whom you sometimes overheard making off-color jokes or talking about killing white people. When you went to the editorial director to complain, he gazed at you across his desk with a distant look as if he couldn't fathom what you were upset about. Then he informed you that Martine was "signifying," expressing a certain attitude without actually meaning it. You told him you took offense and had a circular conversation with him, yielding nothing. But this wasn't what got you fired. All of the interns were powerless in the scheme of things but there was a so-called "head intern," a young woman from Seattle, a living embodiment of what they call youth culture. I would have said that putting a twenty-two-year-old in a position of authority is always a questionable proposition, but this young woman brooked no defiance as to how the other interns would do things. She made them say "No problem" rather than "You're welcome" when talking to outside callers, and, weirder yet, she required them to make all the personal pronouns in their readers' reports gender-neutral. She talked as if those were obvious things to do. So, when you wrote, in your report on a manuscript, "A character in such a situation may find his options painfully limited," she made you change it to "their options," even though you were referring to a fictional situation in a manuscript where the protagonist was in fact male. When you protested, she went right to Martine, and you walked between them as they faced each other in the hall outside the intern area, talking with smirks on their faces. So much for your internship.

But your writing continued to improve. You wrote with economy, yet avoided the workmanlike, dot-connecting banalities found in Peter Osterman's prose. I don't think I have ever seen jealousy so peculiarly manifest as it was on Beverly Sutter's face when she stood in the tea room of your brownstone and Vivian showed her a copy of the new edition of the prep school's literary magazine, which had published a story of yours. "The Gift," a tale set in the Australian outback, made the reader feel the presence of bloodied forms writhing and crawling through dry heat. In your early *oeuvre*, I believe that only your Vietnam War story "To Return to the Fields" surpasses it. I'll bet that the tales compare favorably to anything Peter Osterman produced at the same age or even years later. Let alone Chase Sutter. Your work was brilliant and it came as no surprise when, during your final year at the prep school, you won a partial scholarship to Princeton based largely on your creative writing. Your mother was not the only one who began to imagine how a literary aptitude might dovetail with professional success rather than just acting as a distraction.

That fact brings us to the next chapter in this sordid history. I recall Vivian telling me of the spontaneous decision Beverly made, one afternoon, to have Chase "do literature." Beverly abruptly got up off her bloated behind, went out from the Sutter residence to the nearest Barnes & Noble, and returned with a big pile of "the classics." Here were *Pride and Prejudice*, *A Tale of Two Cities*, *Wuthering Heights*, *Crime and Punishment*, *The Brothers Karamazov*, *The Great Gatsby*, *The Scarlet Letter*, *1984*, *Animal Farm*, *Brave New World*, *To Kill a Mockingbird*, *Ethan Frome*, *The Sun Also Rises*, and *In Cold Blood*. She dropped them on the desk in Chase's room and said, Get going, Chase darling. I want you to read these over the next few weeks and then you should be able to write stories that will make Lance Foxley want to crawl under a desk and stay there. And your publication history will quickly overtake his.

The books on the pile on Chase's desk looked so new and fresh, with their spines uncracked, their pages not yet smudged or creased. To Beverly and perhaps also to Chase, they said: *Possibility*. Chase began making his way through the books and obeying at least the letter of Beverly's second commandment, to write. But when Beverly read the stories and essays her son produced, even she knew right away there could be no question of submitting them to the prep academy's literary journal, let alone to the prestigious national ones where you, Lance, now sought entry. Still, I don't think Chase quite anticipated her reaction. Nor did she expect his reaction to her reaction. If it is a gross mistake to underestimate an upper-class mother's vanity, it is a fatal error to fail to gauge what a teen lacking experience in life, in its vagaries and vacillations, may do in response to the kinds of words Beverly uttered to her boy.

In Chase Sutter's mind, the newness and freshness of that stack of books on his desk were sort of akin to the sleekness and coolness of a revolver's barrel, on those occasions when he'd held one. It's hard to get your hands on a gun legally in New York City, as everyone knows, but there are subways that thunder past narrow platforms at all hours of the day and night. Chase had Beverly's feedback in mind when he made his way down to the station at two in the morning. They said later that the train practically cut Chase in half.

Here's the kicker, Lance. The first of two. Here's what no one has told you. After a couple of your stories came out, Beverly approached me with the same request your mother had made before. I asked to see a bit of Chase's writing, received it electronically as attachments, mulled it over, and wrote back saying that Chase's mom had forced on him pursuits that were not antithetical to developing gifts as a writer, but were not conducive to such gifts either. I fail to see how this is any different from what Beverly had been telling her boy all along, but I can't know what went through Chase's mind when he logged onto Beverly's account and read the message. But don't believe anyone who suggests that I may have sent really malicious, hurtful messages. In any event, I'm in trouble again.

Ah, Lance. Please refer to my earlier comment about vanity. I think you can understand it well enough now. You, or perhaps it was Vivian, should never, ever have granted Beverly's request to let her see early drafts of a few of your tales. You missed so many hints about Beverly and you never suspected that she might keep versions of the stories and might claim later that her son was the author and you, the plagiarist. Some people just might believe her. But guess what, Lance? Kicker number two is that I still have the earliest drafts, the ones you e-mailed over to me when the tales were just hot pulpy matter that had trickled out of your fecund imagination onto your screen. I also have our exchanges of e-mail in which I gave you ideas for revisions. Anyone will agree, upon reading these exchanges, that it is extremely unlikely that Chase and not you wrote the stories. You thought I deleted all of these things, but I kept them, and the e-mail account I'm using now isn't under my name, so they're going to stay my property for the time being, at least until you need to present them in court. (I am not privy to your current e-mail address, hence this letter.)

I'm going to have to stop writing now because I'm exhausted and it's only two more hours before the trucker in the next room brings home a drunken lady and the heavy breathing and banging resume. If I'm going to sleep at all, it has to be now.

In closing, please don't blame me or your mom for what has happened, and please, please, whatever you do, don't blame yourself. And don't trouble yourself about the lies Beverly tells.

It will probably take quite a while for all of this to go away and for you to find some time to isolate yourself and write. It may take years.

But some things won't change a bit, Lance. I'll still be a proud anachronism in a post-literate age, I'll be grateful for having been your tutor, and I'll always, always be proud of your progress.

Best wishes,

Bryce

P.S. I hate to bring this up, Lance, but I never got a check from Vivian for our last session. Crashing in these motels and eating at Hardee's is tough enough as it is. So I really need you put some cash in the mail. Send it to my brother in Maryland. There's only one Felix Allen living in Salisbury. Maybe you can add a little advance on the next two lessons. Will you do it now, Lance buddy?

Another Manhattan

"Let's sue the bastards!" Robert Schor, the editor of a popular Greenwich Village-based weekly, the *Village Oracle*, yelled into the phone in his office.

It was a bald statement from a man who was proud of having a master's degree in journalism and who embraced progressive principles both in politics, and in the daily management of his office. Schor believed passionately in what goes by the phrase "brand integrity," even when the quest for it eclipsed other areas of his work life. As he sat in his office yelling into the phone, he rued how much of his time he spent dealing with corporate lawyers. It was one call after another, and the journalists, stringers, and deputy editors he managed were lucky to sneak past his receptionist, Marlene, once a week to grovel for his time. The amount of time he spent editing copy, living up to his job description, dwindled daily. Yet Schor felt driven by an urge to enforce brand integrity by driving into bankruptcy any newspaper that dared to ape elements of the *Village Oracle*'s name, logo, layout, or content. The lawyers he put to work were up to the job, they'd better be giving what Schor was paying, and their skill in suing infringers gave Schor a *frisson* he could compare only to the thrill of sex.

On this dreary Wednesday afternoon in March, Schor was sitting at his desk holding the phone to his ear and sliding the cap of a pen off and back on endlessly. The woman at the other end of the line was a young partner at one of the global law firms. The firm wasn't Paul Weiss, but it was a respected and feared litigation shop. Schor's discussion with the junior partner turned from a pending lawsuit against a community newspaper on Long Island to plans to meet for lunch at the Bryant Park Grill one of these coming weekdays. The woman said Monday would work. Schor consulted his mental calendar for a moment and said sure.

He had, in fact, been planning to have lunch that day with an old friend, David Tanenbaum, who edited a small literary journal, but he could push that appointment to the evening. If Dave refused to speak to him again, so be it. The woman was delighted. As he listened to this lawyer, he thought she must have only just made partner. She must be barely out of her twenties. Well, Robert Schor, a modern, enlightened man, would never entertain any of the thoughts some clients might have if they imagined the firm had passed their file to a partner who had yet to prove herself.

Schor hung up the phone and gazed at his hands for a minute. The next matter wasn't going to be easy. Tanenbaum was such a Luddite, the man didn't even have e-mail. If you wanted to communicate with him, you had to call him on a land line of the ancient building on West 4th Street in whose basement Tanenbaum folded and stapled the pages of his little quarterly journal. Well, best to get it over with. He called up Tanenbaum. Schor's apology made reference to the death of an uncle and the changes this event necessitated in Schor's father's will. Grudgingly, Tanenbaum said he'd meet his friend on Monday evening, when Schor would have legal gibberish coming out his ears. Schor chuckled at how unwittingly right this prediction was.

Just as Schor was settling down to edit a film review, the peeling green rectangle covered with yellowed clippings across the room swished toward the wall as a young assistant editor named Will Herrick ambled into the office. Herrick was a thin, sickly-looking kid with small dark eyes. He dressed like a hipster, with battered jeans and old t-shirts inside a mud-colored flannel shirt. Upon moving to New York from Ohio, Herrick had been desperate to join an alternative weekly, rather in the way that a man in solitary confinement thinks about sex or filet mignon. Out of dozens of promising candidates for the job, Schor had hired this youngster because of his earnestness and the strength of a few clips from Herrick's college newspaper—impassioned editorials about the need to double the budget for visiting speakers or the need to recruit firebrand professors willing to sacrifice personal popularity for the truth. But he'd had kind of an odd relationship with Herrick in the few weeks the kid had been on the job. Herrick felt entitled to waltz into Schor's office and trumpet his opinions about literally any topic, as if Herrick were the publisher, rather than a beardless assistant editor.

"Did you read the piece on stop-and-frisk?" Herrick demanded.

"Ah, the what?"

"The piece I got this freelance guy Ben Sanders to write, comparing stop-and-frisk to apartheid policies," Herrick pressed.

"Oh . . . no, man. Haven't looked at it yet. I've got a lot going on."

"Well the city council vote is in two days, and if you don't sign off in, like, 10 minutes, the piece won't come out tomorrow."

"Ah, well now . . . is it a good piece, in your opinion, Will?" Schor asked.

"As good as anything you've run in the last three years."

"Then run it. I don't need to read it."

"Rob—"

"It may just be my personal vanity but could you not address me as Rob? Robert if you must, or even, dare I say it, Mr. Schor."

Herrick nodded gravely.

"Run the piece. I trust your editorial instincts."

"Well thank you, Robert."

"Anything else, kid?"

"Yes, I was going to ask you about the piece on the new developments in Times Square. It's already a rich man's playground, and now they want to build another goddamn office park where a famous strip joint used to be," Herrick said almost breathlessly.

"That I *do* need to read. Leave it on my desk."

He didn't want to say this to Herrick in as many words, but the weekly's corporate owners would be aghast if the paper embarrassed or criticized the developers, who, in point of fact, were not the enemy. They were big donors to progressive political candidates. If they transformed Times Square, making it into a haven for the wealthy, they deserved gratitude.

"Okay."

"On another subject, there's a protocol for coming into my office."

"Noted, Robert."

"And Will?"

"Yes, Robert."

"You know you can get a can of Axe deodorant for about five bucks."

Herrick's look of plain dumb shock said he had no idea how to react and it was the sort of comment you expect people to know not to make.

When it came time to meet the young lawyer at the Bryant Park Grill, Schor revved himself up by thinking of the fruitful actions he'd pursued against infringers of the *Village Oracle*'s intellectual property. Little community newspapers on the Jersey Shore and Martha's Vineyard would never dare use either word from this paper's name again, or feature anything even remotely resembling the *Oracle*'s corporate logo on their front page. The newest lawsuit was the continuation of a glorious venture. As his feet tapped on the marble of the floor inside the Bryant Park Grill, Schor looked, not without envy, at tables crowded with exquisitely dressed men and women, bent in hushed but intense discussion. He looked beyond three tables running down the middle of the place and spotted his lunch date, Emily Lofton, by herself at a table on the far side, abutting the window that afforded a view of benches and steps and a wide green field that in better weather would have been decked out with nearly naked youngsters. She had shoulder-length brown hair and wore a gray dress and sports jacket. On her face was a polite reserved expression. Here, Schor thought, was someone who had never bounced a check or bellowed abuse at a driver in her life.

After shaking hands and ordering wine and entrées, the conversation quickly moved to recent developments on the legal front. Emily described a situation where the other side couldn't figure out what it wanted to do.

"I'll bet those conniving little fiends will make their move soon enough," Schor muttered between bites of chicken Florentine.

"I actually don't think they have a strategy at this point, Robert. They're a little, sixty-five-hundred-circulation paper on Long Island, and I think quite obviously, for them, there's still something of a mental block to get past here."

"I don't get it," said Schor.

"They're really struggling with the legal aspects of this at all, Robert. There's a lot they don't get. They can't assimilate the concept that it's legally actionable for them to call themselves the *Port Washington Oracle*. They don't understand how any part of that could be someone else's property, let alone that they could be facing a ruinous lawsuit."

"Is that all?"

The young lawyer chewed her food for a moment with a somber look before replying.

"I don't think they can afford to retain counsel for the time it's going to take them to fight this," she said.

"So that's their reaction, then. That's all."

"Not quite all. They keep going on about the decline of print journalism and about how they're the only voice in the county for hard-hitting investigative—well, now, Robert, it's possible you may have heard arguments of this nature before. I do have to say, I imagined that you of all people might sympathize with an underdog independent paper that speaks truth to power."

Robert nearly spat his Merlot all over his pristine white and gray-striped Brooks Brothers shirt.

"Indeed I do, Emily!"

"That's what the *Village Oracle* is all about, isn't it?" she asked in a gentle voice.

"Of course. Who's ever said otherwise?"

He leered at her.

Emily Lofton gave him a bewildered look as he chewed his chicken. She crossed her legs.

"Is there something you want to ask me, Robert? Something a little outside the scope of our discussion so far?"

He locked eyes with her, his mind reeling as it stumbled back over his words and body language in the moments leading up to this one. There had been things on his mind but he'd semi-consciously considered it quite a breach of etiquette to mention them.

"I'm wondering, Emily—is it hard to make partner at your firm?" he asked in a cautious voice.

Her pretty brown eyes narrowed ever so slightly.

"What makes you ask?"

"I'm trusting the firm with a rather important responsibility and I have a right to do a bit of my own due diligence here," he said, feeling quite clever.

"Well, I would say that we have an excellent record of promoting people—and we rank higher on the diversity index that most firms in the AmLaw 500," the young lawyer replied.

The pause before Schor spoke again added to her perplexity.

"You may have misunderstood where I'm coming from here. I'm all in favor of diversity—but I don't think it's necessarily a good thing for promotions to be easy," he said.

"You don't?" she replied with almost a cross look.

"Excuse me," Robert said and got up to scurry to the men's room, leaving the bewildered young lady to guard his briefcase.

When he came back, he slid into his chair, sipped the exquisite Merlot, and locked eyes with her again.

"I want to have the most aggressive, most ruthless law firm in the world on board for this lawsuit. This is *brand integrity* we're talking about here. I don't *ever* want people to confuse my paper with some dipshit fly-by-night in East Bumblefuck. I want you to *épater* the fucking cocksuckers who are ripping off our logo and our style. Have I made myself clear now?" he said as a bit of spittle shot from his mouth.

The lawyer recoiled and clutched the edges of her chair as if it were all she could do not to pitch backward and fall over. Then she seemed to check herself, as if embarrassed by her overreaction. Schor noted all of this with interest.

"Emily, are you a little terrified of me?" he asked.

Equanimity returned to her face, a smooth professional manner reasserted itself.

"I'm not the slightest bit afraid of what you are right now, Robert," she said.

He did not ask her to expand on this cryptic answer, but it rankled just a bit. For the remainder of the lunch, they talked about the mechanics of the lawsuit. When he reflected on it later, Schor took her remark to mean that she didn't find his posture as an aggressive corporate go-getter entirely convincing, that he just wasn't quite there yet. Surely that was all she meant. He had no doubt at all.

Schor met up with Tanenbaum that evening in a darkened tavern off Seventh Avenue. Tanenbaum was a tall, bearded, often unpleasant man who talked of little besides literature and philosophy. To be fair, Tanenbaum had talent, however slight. One of Tanenbaum's stories was about a meeting of two businessmen in a room whose location the author never discloses. It might be another planet, or it might be Switzerland, or it might be hell. Schor had liked that aspect of the tale, though he didn't get much else about it.

Tonight, Schor would have preferred an elegant wine bar to this dive, but Tanenbaum was of modest means and could never hide his distaste for the city's more yuppified corners.

"So, David, how's the writing going?" Schor asked as they sat there in the dimness with Bud drafts before them.

Schor already knew the answer to this question. Tanenbaum's work was too outré for most editors. Unfortunately for Schor, Tanenbaum quickly guessed an ulterior motive.

"My stuff isn't moving at all, Robert. How's *your* writing going?

Schor took in a draught of beer as his eyes darted left and right, as if for a means of escape.

"Ah, well, upon reflection, David, that piece you were going run in *Intuitions*"—here Schor referred to the quarterly his friend produced, on the puniest of budgets—"isn't really right for your publication. I've been thinking there's another market that makes more sense."

Tanenbaum stared at Schor. It was a particularly cold, hard, unforgiving look.

"You want me to go home and slit my wrists over the kitchen sink?" Tanenbaum asked.

"Oh for God's sake, what kind of fucking *non sequitur* is that?"

"You think *Intuitions* is worthless, a steaming pile of pseudo-literary crap, and by extension you think I'm worthless."

"Are you so fucking hypersensitive that a decision to pull a story is a verdict on whether you should live or die?" Schor demanded, as a few heads around them in the dimness rotated their way.

"Yes."

"God. I'm kind of sorry I came out tonight."

"Tell me, Robert."

"Excuse me?"

"Tell me."

"Tell you *WHAT?*"

"I want to know who picked up the story while you fostered the illusion you'd written it for me."

"Oh, for Christ's sake."

"Tell me."

"Fuck you."

"Was it *The New Yorker*?" Tanenbaum asked.

Schor looked around again, mumbled, spluttered, finally nodded.

"And what are they laying out for it, five grand?" the bearded writer pressed.

"Yeah, that's about right."

Tanenbaum nodded.

"Well I'll just try to be philosophical about this," he said.

"I have no doubt that *Intuitions* is going to flourish. Your circulation's going to go way up," Schor offered.

"Maybe in another Manhattan," Tanenbaum said with a somber expression.

"Huh?"

"You should know that sentiments are beginning to turn, Robert."

Schor knew that when Tanenbaum began speaking cryptically like this, it was best to wrap up the evening as smoothly and diplomatically as possible. But he could not resist digging under the surface of this last remark just a bit.

"Really? I suppose this is a Time/CNN poll you're referring to?"

"Please, Robert. I know whereof I speak."

"Do you, now? Well, I suppose you encounter more real New Yorkers than most people. What is out there?" Schor asked with a look toward the lengthy window framed by the façade of the seedy tavern, beyond which bundled forms in coats and winter hats moved busily down the street toward Seventh Avenue, or the other way, toward the Hudson River.

"I just love the way you say 'real New Yorkers.' Thanks, pal. Maybe I will go home and cut my wrists," Tanenbaum replied.

"Fine. Let's drink to that," Schor said, raising his glass.

Three nights later, Schor was rather ecstatic over having told Herrick to kill the piece on the Times Square property. Schor delighted in what this decision did to Herrick. It was about time that little punk who'd barely stopped getting acne understood the chain of command in this office, Schor thought.

After work, he'd made his way to a wine bar over on Eighth Avenue, a few blocks from the wildly popular Standard Hotel, where Schor had spent many an evening getting tipsy. Right now he wanted something a little more subdued than the Boom Boom Room at the Standard, he needed a venue for reflection. This place was dark, with lithe forms in black clothing moving all around and jazz coming from the speakers. There was the comfort of knowing Tanenbaum, that surly bastard, wasn't going to walk in.

Schor had a few glasses of a crisp Belgian beer, enjoying the melodies of Duke Ellington and Charlie Parker, before he noticed the nubile young woman seated a few feet away, at the longest strip of the counter, running perpendicular to the part where he sat. Her dark hair stretched across the sides of her head and flowed down into a bun at the base of her pale neck. Her eyebrows were high and thin and her cheekbones, too, were a bit higher than on other faces, giving a faint impression of haughtiness. But her expression was blasé. For her, going out in the evening had lost its novelty quite a few years ago, but she presumably knew the bartender and a few of the other patrons. Her attire, at least what Schor could see from where he sat, was casual: a beige tank top with thin straps and a drooping neckline exposing a good part of her thin white brassiere. Nothing adorned her ears or fingers.

So pale, so ghostly was this lass, you might think she'd lost half the blood in her body, yet Schor found her exquisitely lovely. Schor did something staggering in its originality. He offered to buy the young woman a drink. She made eye contact with him, but did not smile.

"Hmm. I've never heard *that* before," she said.

"I'm a writer and invention is what I do," he said with a grin.

"Are you, now? What sort of writer?"

"The best kind, a journalist."

"Really? Would I have seen your byline anywhere?"

"Possibly. Ah, one more for the lady here," Schor said as the bartender moved down to his end.

The bartender replaced her empty glass with another one full of a gleaming amber liquid. The young woman's eyes said, *I don't remember telling you I wanted another.*

"I'm the editor-in-chief of the *Village Oracle*," Schor boasted.

"Ah, yes, that weekly. I can't say I like what it's become," she replied.

"Well, you know, we cover the bar and club scene in every issue. If you're bored with this place, you'll find plenty of suggestions."

"Did I say I'd grown bored of this place?" she asked, in her even voice.

"No, I mean, like, if you ever get bored," Schor fumbled.

"Ahh."

The delightful music had stopped. Schor excused himself, walked over to the juke at the back of the place, slid in a few dollars, and made selections. Soon Duke Ellington's voice filled the place again, urging "Do nothing till you hear from me . . ."

"Can I make a suggestion?" the young lady asked when Schor had reclaimed his seat.

"Of course."

"Quite a few years ago, the *Oracle* ran some pieces about the occupation of Tompkins Square Park. I thought those were good stories. You might catch up with some of the people who were in those protests, let readers know what they're up to now."

Schor laughed softly.

"Why, if we're thinking of the same protests, those were decades ago! You're telling me you read the paper then?"

"No, of course not. I've done some research on modern protest movements, as part of my graduate studies," she informed him.

"Really? Where? Columbia?" he gushed.

"Ah, no, not Columbia. City College."

"Oh well, close enough, eh?"

"I guess."

Schor couldn't think of anything to say, so he sipped his beer and looked at her awkwardly.

"I remember some of the cover stories and theme issues you used to do," she recalled.

Schor nodded, studying her lovely entrancing features.

"Theme for your next issue: Who owns New York?"

The editor chuckled. "That's a good one. We might just do it."

Their eyes met. Schor grew desperate for a way to jump-start the conversation. His frustration was bottomless. He'd just begun to get to know her as a person, and politics, politically correct motives and expectations, had cast a pall over the entire discussion. This woman was inexpressibly beautiful. As he studied her face now in the dim light, with Duke Ellington's fluid melodies filling the space all around, he was aware of a ghostly oval apparition channeling all the feminine beauty he'd ever encountered or imagined in his life.

"You know, you really shouldn't believe in the starving writer trope. Not nowadays. I'll tell you, the woman in my life, whoever that turns out to be, will *never* have to worry about money!"

To his dismay, she excused herself now on the pretext of going to the restroom. He waited patiently, finishing his drink and starting on another, but she did not return. Perhaps she had some intensely private feminine need to attend to, or maybe she'd left the restroom and retreated to a corner of the darkened place without his noticing. Half an hour passed. In an alert state, Schor might have waited longer or probed the mysterious depths of the wine bar for the woman, but he was drunk and his feeling of humiliation was overwhelming.

Heading north on the wet pavement of Eighth Avenue, Schor noticed something curious on the edge of the sidewalk a few blocks below 14th Street. Here on the curb was a distribution box for the *Village Oracle*, but someone had flipped it so that the lid faced the street rather than the storefronts on the other edge of the sidewalk.

Kids, Schor thought, advancing to the end of the block and making a right.

Soon he made it over to the East Village. His breath billowed out before him. He was drunker than he'd been in months and was lurching but it was only a couple of dozen yards to his front stoop. Now it was fifteen yards . . . ten yards . . . five yards . . . A gloved hand closed over Schor's mouth and he felt an awesome force pulling his body toward the curb. He tried to cry out, swung his arms and legs ineffectually. Now he felt his attacker and another party loading his body horizontally into the back of a van. Someone, he thought it was the first attacker, slammed Schor's head with a crowbar again and again until he lost consciousness.

Schor woke up in a filthy windowless room, with his wrists and ankles bound so tightly he wanted to cry. A lone dusty bulb in the ceiling cast a sleazy sheen over empty rusted paint buckets, a rake, a wheelbarrow, a few molding paperbacks, nails, shreds of paper, wrappers, bits of glass, rags, and dust. Schor rubbed his forehead and the back of his head. There were several bloody gashes. He thought: *Tanenbaum! I'LL KILL YOU!* Unable to believe where he was or what had happened, he closed his eyes and managed to fall asleep. When he woke, there were three others in the room. One was a huge man in his late twenties or early thirties, with thin dark hair combed unimaginatively across his scalp, wearing a black leather jacket and a pair of dungarees. The second was a younger and shorter man who wore his ash brown hair mohawk style and wore a black denim jacket with patches on the elbows and a pair of worn blue jeans. The third was a girl, twenty or twenty-one, with straight black hair and prominent lips recalling an early-career Fairuza Balk. She wore a white tank top and both her jacket and pants were of black leather.

The younger of the two men unbound the captive's mouth. The larger man loomed menacingly, as if to warn Schor that any cries or screams would bring a kick.

The youngster with the mohawk said, "I sure wouldn't want to live in a world where Disney tells me where and when I can walk and bathe and eat and shit and jerk off. How about you, fella?"

Schor could only shake his head, with raw naked terror in his eyes.

They told him how it was. The *Village Oracle* was going to publish a 3,000-word essay decrying the corporate takeover of Times Square and the city in general, and calling the conniving backstabbing bloodsuckers who orchestrated the whole thing exactly what they were. If Schor didn't like it, they'd pick up one of the larger pieces of glass and jab it through both eyes repeatedly like someone's cock working in the heat of intercourse. They had the essay saved as a Word document, and all that remained was for Schor to fire it off to a subordinate with orders to run it, in print and online, in the paper's forthcoming edition.

Schor told his captors he wanted to cooperate but he felt so rattled at the moment, he couldn't remember his name, let alone the name and e-mail address of the subordinate who must receive the essay. The young woman said surely the names and e-mail addresses must be on the home page of the *Oracle*. No, Schor said, my managing editor is on vacation and the guy I need to write to is a new hire whose name isn't on the site. The captors sighed, cursed, seemed to weigh jamming a shard of glass into Schor right now, but decided to let him rest and clear his head for a brief while.

"Hey . . . can I have a drink of water?" Schor asked as the punk with the mohawk began to bind his mouth again.

"Fuck you," the punk answered, and the captors left.

Time passed. At a couple of points, the male captors came into the room, viewed the terrified quivering form on the floor with distaste, and administered kicks. They gave Schor bruises and split his forehead. He bled and wept but dared not cry out. Hours or possibly days later, the dark-haired girl came back into the room and unbound Schor's mouth.

"Are you ready?" she asked.

"Uh . . . almost. I need some water."

She left and returned with a chipped mug filled with an opaque liquid. Schor grabbed it and drank hurriedly, then sat there heaving and panting.

"I—I need to know," he said, each word costing a monumental effort. "Excuse me?"

"I'm unlisted. H-how . . . How did you find out where I live?"

"Oh, shut the fuck up," she said before walking out and closing the door.

It was the young woman in the wine bar, he thought. He'd made the elementary mistake of leaving his briefcase while he went to the juke.

No—it was Tanenbaum, the sly bastard! It had to be!

No, he was overlooking the still more obvious likelihood that Herrick had settled a score with his boss. How had Schor made the mistake of hiring that kid without proper screening?

Schor resolved he was going to send the essay to Herrick, then find a way to kill him! Unless, oh, unless in fact it was Tanenbaum after all. He found the thought impossible to dismiss as he sat cross-legged on the floor and wept.

Two hours later, the girl returned.

"Is your memory clear now? It's really not in your interest to wait any more," she said.

"It's getting clearer, bit by bit. Things will fall into place if you tell me how you found out where I live."

"Fuck you."

But looking into the eyes of this poor lass, mentally plumbing the depths of her existence, Schor sensed that she was the least zealous of the three and that she would just like to go back to smoking weed and listening to punk rock in Tomkins Square Park.

"How did you find out?"

Her eyes shifted toward the door, then back toward the captive.

"Come on," he pressed.

She mouthed two words at him before disappearing through the door again. Her lips seemed to describe two words: *Emily Lofton.*

Indeed, he had made a poor choice as to who should guard his briefcase. He never suspected the impression his zeal for taking down tiny newspapers on Martha's Vineyard and the Jersey Shore had made on that young lawyer.

"If you decide you still aren't ready, they're going to come in and beat your brains out with the crowbar," the girl said.

"I'm ready."

She came in with the laptop. Of course she had to unbind his hands now. Schor logged into his personal e-mail account, wrote a brief message addressed to Herrick saying here was a statement he'd decided with much deliberation the paper should run, attached the MS Word file containing his captives' manifesto, and clicked send. His message read, in part, "I feel possessed by the idea of another Manhattan." But Schor thought the shrill, overwritten anti-corporate manifesto said nothing that people hadn't heard before, and its impact would be minimal, particularly when he got out and told the world how these lunatics had coerced him to publish it. These goons would accomplish nothing. He was not going to argue with the captors. To his mind, they weren't bright enough to grasp how a strong and often litigious corporate empire is the ideal vehicle for a progressive agenda.

When the girl bound Schor's hands after he'd sent off the file, she did so sloppily, without the professionalism of the big captor who'd done it earlier. As soon as he was alone, Schor managed to wriggle his right hand out and then free himself completely.

Many hours later, the girl came into the room with the chipped mug. Schor leapt up, pushed the girl into the grimy wall with all his force, and dashed through the door into the main part of the disused warehouse, which he already was mentally placing in the meatpacking district. Within this large space, the older and bigger captor languished on a couch against the wall on Schor's left as he ran across the floor. On the captor's face,

Schor glimpsed the tranquility of a heroin rush. Across the room, on Schor's right, the young guy with the mohawk sat on another couch staring at a TV.

"Hey," was all the dude with the mohawk said as Schor rushed past and out the front door into the cold night.

Reactions to Schor's re-appearance in the world proved mixed. His friends were glad, but the owners of the *Village Oracle* had harsh words for him. It turned out that Herrick, suspicious of the circumstances of Schor's order to publish the manifesto, had run it with a disclaimer saying that Schor had gone missing and some kind of plot might be afoot. Nonetheless, the developers of Times Square properties took quite a bit of placating and a few of them went so far as to pull their ads from the *Oracle*.

Schor couldn't go back to work there even if they wanted him back. His post-traumatic stress was so acute that long-suppressed drug habits returned, and he took to wandering the streets of Manhattan in a dazed state, gibbering, leering, cursing out or threatening strangers. Even before they evicted him from his building, he was quite like the homeless wrecks he'd so often viewed with distaste. He got deeply in debt to his heroin dealer, and few people wanted to talk to or look at him.

Revolted at the contempt with which sedate, moneyed New Yorkers treated him, and burning with fury at the corporation that wouldn't have him back or even give him a letter of reference, Schor decided to put his litany of complaints into writing. He had a good many other things to say about life in New York these days, and four of the homeless guys he stood on line with at the soup kitchen in the basement of a church on Sixth Avenue, just below Eighth Street, were unsung writers themselves.

They began writing on scraps of paper donated by the soup kitchen. A short ways up the avenue, the Jefferson Market Library had Xerox machines where Schor and his new pals could reproduce their handwritten articles and diatribes for nickels. Thus four writers and one committed editor brought an alternative publication to the world.

Regarding Whitlow

Here is what I think happened.

But hold on, there's something I ought to say first. Just so that you are fully prepared, gentlemen (and one lady) of the executive committee, let me tell you that I am going to give my account of the disaster in an unaccustomed style. As General Counsel for what I refer to in internal communications as The Company, I'm quite used to doing things a certain way. I talk to survivors of events that happened under The Company's aegis, and I draft a report that protects our interests while hewing more or less to the truth. The facts are verifiable, and there is nothing that would embarrass anyone under cross-examination. In recent instances, like the case of a mid-level manager who preyed on female interns, or the director who violated a confidentiality agreement over ten whiskies, my job has been easy and the final report has been dry and legalistic. I have set out the facts as a chain of bland generalities and have recommended that we settle and move on. That's how it usually goes. There is no invention, no departure from a legalistic style. But here before us now, gentlemen, is a case where doing things by rote might be catastrophic. In common parlance, *We're in deep shit.*

We have tried to anticipate every possibility and manage our "human resources" smoothly, competently, efficiently, and ethically. My task as I see it now is to show you the hole where the rodent got into our well-managed corporate environment, where an element of *force majeure* no one could have foreseen or prevented made itself felt as abruptly as wildfires ravaging a thousand acres between L.A. and San Diego. As I said, the misfortunes we have encountered up to now have generally lent themselves to the most comforting, the most banal, the most pat classifications. But the case of Stephen Whitlow is different.

Personally, I would never have authorized the decision to send this employee from our New York office on a trip to California in the first place, but my authority extends only so far. Mr. Whitlow, hereinafter called "Steve," had a few spots on his record—tense interactions with managers as well as subordinates—and his psychological profile was complex. He accused people within this firm of being liars. More than that: he accused people of lying for a living. Furthermore, employees of The Company knew through hearsay of Steve's frayed personal situation. He lost his mother, a lifelong smoker, to a heart attack eight years ago, and his father's physical and mental health has been rapidly declining for at least as long. Steve dwelt in a brownstone in one of the outer boroughs with his invalid father, and paid live-in Jamaican helpers $150 a day to take care of the senior Whitlow, spoon-feeding him, changing his adult diapers, calming him when he grabbed the rails of his mechanized bed and began wailing about strangers or rhinos or tigers entering the room or began calling his deceased wife's name. Though Steve's compensation by The Company has been competitive for the type of work he does, it has barely covered all the costs associated with helpers, groceries, utilities, repairs, and monthly mortgage payments. I might mention that Steve's father, when long past the point of *compos mentis*, took out a reverse mortgage to satisfy the demands of a crooked "social worker" in the neighborhood, who made extravagant promises while using the power of attorney the senior Whitlow had given him to loot the Whitlow family's assets, including almost every cent from the reverse mortgage loan. There was nothing Steve could do about the thief's dishonesty. He could only chafe at one more symptom of a brutal lying world. I did not mean to digress, but to illustrate that Steve's situation at home was desperate and getting worse every day. All of this was fairly common knowledge within Steve's department. Yes, he was desperate, but then so are a lot of people nowadays.

So now for the things no one imagined. Steve had been quiet around his colleagues when he was not in conflict with them. For hours he sat at his computer in his cubicle on the 22nd floor, never making eye contact with other denizens of the floor. He was quite fascinated with the funds our company manages, and people who passed him in the hallway and breathed on him in elevators were distractions at best. But Steve had an active, not to say fevered, literary imagination. He had friends, and one of them, a disreputable bohemian by the name of Bryce Allen, had actively encouraged Steve to be a writer. Given how little he spoke to colleagues, no one at the firm could ever have suspected Steve of harboring any unpractical ambitions or conceits. (Let me spell it out for you, members of the executive committee: I think we're pretty well protected there.) Much less could anyone have suspected Steve of developing an obsession with a young screenwriter and performer named Caitlin Murray, who did not even live on the same coast. But the world's so hyper-connected these days, and between his reviews of margins and returns and management fees, Steve may have snuck in peeks at the Facebook page of young Ms. Murray, which she filled with gossip about upcoming comedy shows featuring her or about her ongoing collaborations with A-list actresses. She had plenty to talk about. The 2013 release scripted by Ms. Murray, *The Dry Spell*, more than recouped its $20 million budget, feeding interest in a sequel. Caitlin Murray was young, pretty, funny, saucy, gifted, and full of promise. Don't worry, though. Steve did most of his long-distance gaping and fawning and God knows what else at home. In any event, perhaps you are beginning to discern the hole where the rodent got in.

In retrospect, it is hardly surprising that Steve volunteered, not once, not twice, but on three occasions, to set off on the mission to L.A. The Company needed someone to go out there and meet in person with the principals of another asset management firm with which we've been eager to form a joint venture, with an eye on investing in a chunk of hot Qatar real estate. The mission would also involve meeting partners in the L.A. office of a global corporate law firm whom we wanted to advise us on the joint venture. Steve's contention was that he understood our VI and VII funds, and cross-border transactional law, better than anyone else who'd be available to go to California the third week in April. Steve just may have been right. But there had been fairly serious problems in the past when Steve had received visitors from out of town and used the corporate card. Misplaced receipts, unapproved expenditures, instances where Steve in effect claimed to have been in two places at once. A manager in Steve's division, whose name is a matter of record, reluctantly o.k.'d dispatching Steve to L.A., but cautioned Steve that he'd be flying economy, not first class, and would have a "walking around" budget of only $500 for four days and three nights on the West Coast. Surely Steve got the impression that The Company's faith in him went only so far.

The flight from JFK to LAX lasted six miserable grueling hours. The airline promised passengers comfort, but it was a dirty and dishonest venture like so many things. Steve's first meeting in L.A. took place just forty minutes after he came off the plane, on the twenty-sixth floor of an immense gleaming tower on Flower Street downtown. As Steve milled around in the spacious lobby of Howell Venture Partners, waiting for someone to lead him to a conference room where he'd meet the principals, he got to enjoy a view of the city, the hills of North Hollywood, and the Santa Monica Mountains denied to most mortals. Looking north from the firm's aerie just above Route 110, he stood admiring the nearly infinite variety of neighborhoods stretching away in the clear afternoon to the base of the hills adorned with the famous Hollywood sign and the D.W. Griffith Observatory. In all that expanse of neighborhoods before him there were hardly any tall buildings to rival the one he was in and its neighbors on other downtown blocks. To Steve, the skyscrapers were ultramodern protrusions in a land of mystical hills, sentinels maintaining a vigil over a town untroubled by riots or fires or earthquakes or terrorism, by any excrescence from subterranean currents that had inspired terror in the distant past. It was so balmy outside that even for adults, Steve thought, to feel joy at being alive must not seem trite or cloying at all.

After five minutes, a twenty-one-year-old brunette in a taffeta blouse and a svelte black dress strolled into the lobby and invited Steve to follow her down the hall from which she'd come. He followed her past framed reproductions of Klimt and Rodchenko until they both entered a conference room with a long window looking out on exactly the same scene, or almost exactly. Maybe the view here was clipped just a bit compared to the view from the lobby. The principals of the fund, a man and a woman who were both about thirty-six, appeared within moments. Unlike Steve, the man was fit and trim and still had all his hair. The woman was in good shape too and her body carried faint hints of an extravagant lifestyle—a necklace with a ruby in the corset, a ring on a finger of her left hand bearing a glittering white diamond. For about forty minutes, they discussed the joint venture. By all accounts the meeting went quite well, and the principals took the edge off it with the obligatory cute jokes. At the end, the woman smiled and proposed that she and Steve meet up for coffee the next time he was in town. I think at this moment Steve grimaced inwardly, at the knowledge of how unlikely it was he'd be out this way again anytime soon, but also at an awareness of what the limits of their talk would be if he ever met this professional woman outside of an office. We know from his remarks later that he thought about how riddled with lies were the private placement memoranda that Howell Venture Partners, and the firm he worked for, issued to investors. (That was and remains Steve's position, and to challenge it is not within the scope of this report.) Five minutes and twenty-two seconds after the meeting in the bright pristine conference room, Steve re-emerged onto Flower Street thinking he'd covered up his exhaustion pretty well. Now he had nearly twenty hours to get through before his meeting at the corporate law firm.

From his online research, Steve knew that Caitlin Murray had a show coming up that very evening at a venue on Franklin Avenue, in the border area of Hollywood and Los Feliz. She was part of a troupe of young entertainers who called themselves the Catalysts. They specialized in stand-up comedy, and nearly every week they were in a show at one of the clubs or theaters beloved of undergrads. They weren't the only performers in the show, but they usually got top billing. The Catalysts have a reputation for brilliant improv. They'll turn abruptly to the audience and ask for a topic, any topic. Someone out there might say the word "spoon," and the Catalysts, with zero preparation, will enact a skit where one of them complains about a spoon in a fine restaurant having a spot or a touch of rust on it, another retorts that the complainer was born with a silver spoon up his or her ass, they argue about who's willing to rough it and who's a prude, and the latter question leads to a back-and-forth about blow jobs. The Catalysts absolutely excel at what Saki once called "romance at short notice." Steve was dying to see them perform and watch Caitlin Murray do her thing from only a few feet away. He got his chance, all right.

Almost everyone in the packed little theater was a student. The forty-year-old man with a patch of bare scalp sitting in the dark, a bit hot in slacks and a sports jacket, looked out of place to people in the audience, like a professor at a keg party. Before he got to see the Catalysts, Steve had to sit through an act by three young guys who weren't all that funny. Their dopey skits were mostly about relationships, and there was a routine in which one of the trio accuses another of murder. The only amusing parts were when a member of the audience got up to go outside and the actors on the stage pretended to take offense. As Steve sat in the dark on one of the flanks of the little stage, he clapped politely with the rest of the audience but did not laugh. Though he didn't enjoy the act very much, he thought this was improv as it should be. There were a couple of chairs on the stage, and nothing else. If the actors wanted to use any kind of prop, they had to convey it through gestures, summoning an object out of thin air.

As soon as the Catalysts came onstage amid a mad swell of applause, Steve knew that almost all the pictures of Caitlin Murray he'd stared at were recent. Her pale pink cheeks were as fresh, her shoulder-length whey-colored hair as lovely, as in the pictures he'd obsessed over. In keeping with the general nonchalance of this event, she wore jeans and a green cotton shirt that drooped modestly below her neck. The Catalysts included two other women and three men, but Steve wasn't aware of those five as performers or as people. There was a woman on the stage who'd grown up in Monmouth County and was about the same age as Kirsten Dunst, another famous former resident of that county in New Jersey, a much-reviled state that produces beautiful people. And soon something would happen to remind Steve that Caitlin shared the renowned actress's bluntness, her willingness to say whatever is on her mind.

The Catalysts performed a skit about a lone American tourist in trouble with a *caudillo* dictatorship, another about two parents trying to persuade their teen daughter that her calling in life is to be a porn actress, another about a halfway house where the junkie patients rebel against the staff, then yet another about a rivalry between two campus factions that can't agree on which show should play on TVs in the lounges on Tuesday nights. Steve didn't recognize the names of the shows in the latter bit, but he thought it was extremely funny. They all were. Though the Catalysts seemed to be making everything up as they went along, they timed all their lines perfectly and never once bumped into each other when darting about the little stage. Like the previous act, they pretended to take umbrage on the rare occasions when someone in the audience got up to leave. The audience laughed loudly whenever this happened. The thought that anyone could walk out on the Catalysts, even to use the restroom or smoke a cigarette, was itself hilarious.

The penultimate skit was about a famous actress meeting with her therapist. Little does the patient know, at first, that her greedy shrink has accepted huge bribes to record all that she tells him in supposed confidentiality. The bribers in turn will sell her secrets for far greater than they paid. Caitlin Murray played the actress. How it amused Steve that she was playing the role of an unnamed actress so soon after reminding him of an actual one. He watched with fascination. He wanted to punch himself for failing to anticipate the twist about halfway through. The actress realizes what the shrink is up to, but this doesn't deter her from divulging personal things. On the contrary, it emboldens her. She's unafraid to be who she is, and to hell with her image. What she reveals is frankly astounding. "You want to know what I have brought myself to confront through this therapy? I have faced the fact of my long-running insecurity. That's a fact about me and I'm not afraid to tell the whole world. You want to know what I've faced? Well, I've faced down one old demon. My breasts aren't particularly large. You heard me: Caitlin Murray's breasts aren't particularly large! And you know what? Despite how I may have felt as a vulnerable teen, I don't want them to be bigger. They are average and they are nice breasts and that's fine. I'm fine with who I am and I don't think I've felt genuinely embarrassed about my body since I was eighteen, since an occasion when I was out on the street and I realized I didn't have any tampon money. *I'm tired of lies making the world go 'round and I refuse to be embarrassed and I'm willing to have these words appear on every website on the planet!*"

Everything Caitlin said had a ring of verisimilitude to it, her voice was smooth, her tone was utterly natural, and Steve came to the realization that she was talking openly, ingenuously, to this room full of strangers about herself. She was candid, she was honest, in a very real sense she stood naked in this room full of strangers. There were no hoots, or cheers, or claps, but a profound, respectful quiet.

Minutes after the show ended, Steve lingered outside on the crowded pavement of Franklin Avenue. Already a long line had formed for the next show. It was the same crowd, thrill-hungry college kids. Steve had a vague idea of what might happen when the Catalysts came outside and he approached Caitlin. She might be guarded at first, but would warm to him when she saw just how earnest a fan he was. But to Steve's bewilderment, the Catalysts did not come outside. Steve waited, trying to be inconspicuous. He waited some more. He grew anxious, then faintly angry. They must have gone out the back. Or they were still in there, laughing and talking without a care in the universe. It wasn't right. It seemed cruel in an oblique, mocking way.

Steve walked up the avenue a bit, past the front windows of a fairly crowded bar and restaurant adjoining the theater. At the table adjacent to the wall nearest the theater, the Catalysts were sitting and talking animatedly over drinks. He wondered how they'd gotten out of the theater and in there so fast, but he didn't care. There, at the seat nearest the wall on the side of the table further from the entrance, was Caitlin Murray, the most ingenuous and unpretentious person Steve had ever seen, grinning, exclaiming, laughing in response to her five companions.

Steve walked in, took a seat at one of the narrow flanks of the bar counter spanning nearly the length of the place, ordered a glass of the house chardonnay. He was at the point furthest to the left of anyone who walked through the entrance, and the Catalysts were furthest to the right. They were far too absorbed talk and laughter to notice the lonely man at the bar, yet he feared his staring must provoke them sooner or later. Oh yes, it must.

He studied Caitlin Murray in that bright happy company. He thought of the misery, the hell he'd gone through to be here now. The petty, ugly, bureaucratic wrangling. The six-hour flight. The distance between here and home was a dark, squalid, reeking tunnel through which he'd crawled on his belly for six hours for the tiniest gulp of fresh air, the briefest experience of light. At this moment, the longing he felt for Caitlin was as intense as the impossibility of satisfying it was absolute. For he saw no way he, a weirdo far outside Caitlin's preferred brackets of age and attractiveness, could partake of her sweet, unabashed, charming, disarming, and as yet underappreciated honesty.

But there must be a way.

There must be a way.

Once again Steve thought about walking right up to Caitlin and introducing himself. Though hot, tired, and deeply insecure, he thought he would do it. But before he could get up the courage, thoughts and imaginings intruded as the wine went to work on Steve. He thought of walking, staggering, lurching, arm and arm with Caitlin to the peak of one of the red-ochre mountains in a range in Riverside County, a peak topped with snow even at May's threshold, he thought of them fighting their way to the top just to be able to embrace there in a space others saw only from planes, just to relish the shining indestructible moment. He imagined them walking together, naked, on one of the beaches in Caitlin's native Monmouth County on a tranquil afternoon before the brutal crowded months. At low tide, the little waves tickled the beach right at the point where the tough sand just began to lose its consistency and pairs of footprints grew both larger and less distinct. Next Steve imagined a cool spring in a remote place. In late April of the year he envisioned, rain fell heavily on the green folds of the valley. The few rectangles of wood and brick were stolid, lonely forms with no smoke coming from the chimneys, no other evidence of life within. But in a window of one of these remote structures, there is light. And inside, at a table in a sparsely furnished kitchen, the smile of an otherwise self-effacing blonde has a mesmerizing effect on the man in early middle age, who cannot speak or rise from his chair. In yet another month, in Switzerland, an economic forum is over and sharply dressed people are sitting at dozens of tables among which waiters weave, holding trays topped with glasses of exquisite Montrachet. There is no reason to be jealous of most of the wealthy people here. How little they truly know of love, of longing, of deliverance, of the joy of fulfilled desires after infinite afternoons under the relentless weight of severe depression. In the throng of guests, one man, one member of a couple at a largely overlooked table, understands these things.

Oh, the places he could go with her. . . .

But he'd brooded too long. When Steve next turned his head, the Catalysts had dropped some bills on the table and split. He leapt off his stool and moved out onto Franklin in time to see a few bobbing heads dozens of yards up the avenue, on the far side of the theater.

On the following day, Steve was downtown again. It was time for his meeting with a couple of partners of the corporate law firm we wanted to represent us in the joint venture with Howell Venture Partners. He entered a shiny tall building on Flower Street and rode an elevator to the eighteenth floor. Once again he was in a fancy, tastefully designed office with a magnificent view of the city, the hills, the mountains. Here were Persian rugs and framed Picassos. These were nice digs. Looking around, he already had an idea of how elite and selective the firm must be, how accomplished and professional people must be to work here. It was enough to make you feel tiny. But Steve had a plan. His extensive research in the legal press, print and online, had revealed that one of the partners he was to meet with, Justine Getz, had brought a $100 million malpractice suit on the firm, alleging a conflict of interest. A few months ago, Justine had represented a Chicago-based investment manager in a proposed investment in a fund domiciled in Luxembourg. She'd allegedly advised the investment manager not to proceed with its original plan, but to pursue what she hinted would be a far more lucrative investment in a Cayman-registered fund she had represented in the past. When this little fact became known to the Chicago investors, they were understandably furious. She'd really violated their trust.

When seated in a conference room on the eighteenth floor, Steve saw that Justine Getz was an attractive lady in her late thirties with a warm yet oddly detached manner. Her pale brown hair flowed demurely over the tops of her ears, leaving a clear view of the tasteful, expensive aquamarine gems adorning the lobes. Her smile was acutely professional. There was no warmth in it whatsoever, Steve decided. He thought of how much The Company had already invested in the joint venture with Howell Venture Partners.

Steve looked Justine Getz in the eyes.

"Look, now, Justine, you don't have to come clean about your views on anal sex. But could you at least be honest about your conflicts of interest?"

Within seconds, the law firm's elite security personnel were in the room.

Well—so much for that relationship.

After they ushered him back out onto Flower Street, Steve wandered around downtown, found an internet station, and fired off some really malicious messages to the Howell principals, the contents of which I won't repeat here. Suffice it to say he considered them an unworthy venture partner, he thought there was a basis for all the lawsuits undertaken by former investors. Then he pulled up a list of the names and e-mail addresses of all The Company's current investors, did a mail-merge, and sent them a colorfully worded message about how the parasites who managed this organization had lied blatantly in every single private placement memorandum for the last six years and the investors were too busy sucking their own dicks to realize it. (Yes, his words, in case you're wondering.)

Steve guessed there was something unromantic and maybe a bit pitiful about queuing up again, the night after the performance that had so impressed him, outside the theater on Franklin Avenue. Once again, passersby on the street noticed a man twice the age of many of the undergrads waiting to see the Catalysts, a nervous fellow turning his head in either direction every few seconds, wishing the line would budge. He kept thinking of Caitlin, kept imagining her saying yes to a question whose exact content he couldn't even formulate. He thought if she did say yes to that question, he'd just be all the more frustrated because she was saying it to someone else, a boyfriend or would-be beau.

"Who's your favorite member of the Catalysts?" asked the scruffy twenty-year-old in front of Steve on the line.

Steve wanted to say, *Shut the fuck up and mind your business.*

"Amanda Rhodes," Steve said.

"You mean Amy Rhodes," the youngster replied.

"Uh, yeah. She's my favorite."

"You're so obsessed with her you can't get her name straight," the kid said with a grin.

Steve let this pass. When seated in the dark space inside, Steve wondered how he could possibly sit through the first part of the show. He gnawed the presumption of the theater's managers who'd made the Catalysts part of a package, so that it was hard to see them without suffering through at least part of the amateurish opening performance. Steve had no doubt it was a trick to get people to notice performers whose antics would otherwise appear in YouTube videos hardly anyone ever saw. After the bumbling opening act, Steve watched with relish as the Catalysts came onstage. Caitlin wore a pair of beige trousers one might wear to work, and a white cotton shirt through which Steve could just make out the outlines of her bra when she turned her back to him. Again he found himself wondering what would happen if you responded to her ingenuousness with openness of your own, if you told her what she represented to you and asked whether she could recognize and respect your kindred nature. What would she say? Maybe that was the wrong approach, maybe the first thing was just to ask her for a date. As he sat there, uncomfortable in the stuffy space, he realized how preposterous it was to be having these thoughts now. He took off his jacket.

Caitlin's smile as she sat looking out at the spectators in front of the stage, ignoring its flanks, was as unaffected as ever. The viewers craved the clever interplay of words and movement. Caitlin effortlessly rode the levity of the moment. The improv segment began. One of the Catalysts made an appeal to the audience for a word, any word.

"Lust!" exclaimed someone in the third row.

Caitlin and Amy launched into an argument about who had suffered more in the past month: Amy, who had been through a breakup, or Caitlin, who had stumbled upon three clothed co-workers while she was wandering nude on a clothing-optional beach. Whose rawness was more powerful, more affecting, more savage, more overwhelming? The banter of these two Catalysts was quite hilarious, as Caitlin related how her colleagues, bound by strict decorum and sexual harassment training during the week, had leered, gibbered, whooped, and drooled at the sight of her, and Amy's *Schadenfreude* was quite obvious. Amy did not want Caitlin to eclipse her in the eyes of the earnest undergrads. She ramped up her lines with references to crying in public, lambasting her ex in her sleep and waking her roommates, having to leave work early when the barren day looming before her instilled more terror than any adult had a right to feel. Amy appeared to be winning out, she was investing her appeals to the audience with more urgency than Caitlin achieved. But for one member of the audience, it was Caitlin who justified the Catalysts' existence, Caitlin who was a walking breathing artistic manifesto. Again he imagined her saying yes to an unknown question. Amy went on about the travails of the newly single life, about having to correct people when they appeared on a subliminal level to be saying "you" in the plural form rather than the singular, or at least when they appeared to her to be doing so, and this made the audience bellow and roar.

If incongruity is the essence of humor, and people were here to laugh, then perhaps they shouldn't have gotten upset when the forty-year-old in the slacks and blue work shirt leapt onto the stage and tried to embrace Caitlin.

He exclaimed: "A break-up's nothing. Look at me, Caitlin Murray. Know me. This is raw and this is real. I see you for what you are and I'm exactly the same. Will you accept me? *OH, CAITLIN, CAITLIN, I'VE LUSTED OVER YOU IN PRIVATE DOZENS OF TIMES!*"

Her eyes did not betray fear. She did not retreat. For a moment she stood there, regarding this incoherent stranger at the edge of the stage, gazing in a direction she'd avoided looking in all evening, a placid bemused expression on her face, her eyebrows only slightly raised, a mercurial quality in her lucid eyes the color of a lake in remotest Monmouth County. For just a moment, he was aware of the absence of alarm, of someone viewing him with total comprehension.

Caitlin Murray said, in a clear voice, "Wherever've you been all my life, sweetheart?"

The uproar from the audience was nearly enough to muffle the sounds of two UCLA football players as they leapt from the first row onto the stage, one of them pummeled Steve him the gut, and the other slid behind the forty-year-old freak and got him into a headlock, interrupting the traffic of Steve's windpipe so severely that the pretty face before him melted into blackness.

Gentlemen of the executive committee, if you think I had a hard time in the past convincing prospective venture partners that *force majeure* clauses exist in contracts to protect both parties in a deal, imagine the time I am having now. It is true: You never know when a war, riot, revolution, hurricane, or eruption from subterranean depths will derail a project. We are never safe. Such a calamity is before us now. But in this case the only way to craft a legal defense that will stick is to compose an account owing nothing to legal conventions and forms, or in short: To be a writer. Which brings us to a further irony.

Gentlemen of the executive committee, I have spent many sixty-hour work weeks reviewing our internal policies and protocols. Without question, it will be necessary to administer tests to ensure that all candidates for work at The Company cannot write in a literary form and lack any literary imagination or aspiration to write. Moreover, we must ensure that they do not live or associate with any known writers. That is the only way to insulate our firm and our interests from another catastrophic invasion of *force majeure*.

And there will be another time, as I think Steve knew, for the fulfillment of a wish can also be its denial. For Steve, it was agonizing to imagine her giving an answer he'd always longed to hear—to someone else.

Yes, a painful vision. But what do you think is happening as you read these words?

On a cool fresh evening, a twenty-six-year-old blonde enters the second-floor apartment of a house on a quiet leafy street in Los Feliz. The phone on the wall is ringing. Caitlin lifts the receiver to her ear, listens for a moment with a burgeoning smile.

"Of course," she says.

In the Proudest Country

No one back home could understand the terror Bryan felt in France one summer. Nobody at home would get it if Bryan said Paris was the last place on earth he wanted to be, because you have to fight through the crowds in the sweltering air to feel the revulsion that overcame him one day in July 2007. He was glad to step onto a bus bound for Angers, in the Loire Valley, where he'd rest for a night before going on to a village where his sculptor friend owned a little house. As the dreary tenements of La Midi slid past, and the old couple in the seats ahead chatted about a scandal embroiling the National Front, Bryan reclined in relief and tried to banish the horrendous cliché looming in his mind: that he was escaping to "the real France." The cliché could make you vomit.

Minutes later, the humidity passed its climax and drops began to dot the dusty road and the white and black roofs amid the patches of swaying stalks on either side of the bus. Back in Montparnasse, in the area around the hotel where Bryan had stayed, people must be retreating to the cafés and the apartments, but the crowds would never be gone for long, they would swarm soon enough in their pursuit of wonder. To Bryan, they were so many locusts.

Before nodding off, Bryan thought about his friend Peter, who had grown from a bullying C-student in grammar school into an obsessive artist at the New School and then at SUNY/Stony Brook. Peter's paintings had appeared in exhibitions at Lincoln Center, he'd done a bust of a celebrity, and now he was taking advanced sculpting classes with about thirty Americans and Canadians in this village in the Vendée. Bryan could only admire how serious his friend was and wonder how to find the same drive in his writing. Twenty-five, and he'd barely completed a story, let alone gotten one published. To date, the majority of his works were abortive, misbegotten attempts to fashion a tale out of an odd idea or scene that had occurred to him. Maybe he and Peter were just wired differently. The question of Bryan's accomplishments came up again and again when friends of Peter's got done talking about art and directed their curiosity toward his quiet friend. Maybe in a month in Les Cerqueux, Bryan could reverse the ratio of planned and completed fictions. Honestly, he'd be happy to produce one.

Bryan had another thought: *Lurking in the mind of every American visitor to this land is fear.* And a question: *Outside of easy, social settings, are the French quite as civilized as their reputation suggests?*

When he woke, the bus was hurtling through a zone where sodden green alternated with the tarmac as far as he could make out, a place where all nations, all uniforms and customs and holidays and drinking songs, seemed to Bryan like inventions conceived to stave off insanity. In about a half hour, he'd have to seek out another dive on the streets of Angers. The bleakness outside dimmed as the humming of the engine and the banalities passed back and forth by the elderly couple lulled Bryan until he nodded off once more.

When he arrived the next day in Les Cerqueux, Bryan could recall little of the night in Angers. He felt like lying down and kissing the streets of this anti-Paris where the only other being in sight was a lame dog that ambled up the cobbled street beside the church with its tongue lolling, jubilant to see the visitor. The houses across from the church were squat, a series of two stories and drab façades joined by thin plaster walls. Adequate, no more. Further up the road, Bryan made out bigger houses where the mayor and other local officials might have lived, and the road running perpendicular to where Bryan stood led to a one-story café and a *dépanneur* and then to a grey region of hedgerows and corn.

He thought: *Fear. It encroaches, climbs, darts and weaves. It insinuates itself into thoughts and gestures, it distorts your face when you're not thinking about anything in particular.*

Bryan knocked on the door of one of the drab houses, which opened to reveal a forty-fivish man in glasses, trousers and a blue short-sleeved shirt from which two hairy arms extended. Beside him was a blonde in overalls, maybe thirty-eight, with a grin on her ruddy face. In French, Bryan asked which of these houses was Peter's, and the man told him in English and asked whether Bryan was the writer Peter talked about so much. Bryan happened to have knocked on the door of one of the art teachers.

On Peter's door, Bryan found a note stating that his friend would be back from sculpting class by 6:00, so he sat down in the road—there was no sidewalk—and watched the funny dog, sections of its body bouncing and wobbling as it ambled and turned in the direction of the café, quickly overtaken by a young man on a moped. A Mirage fighter jet roared through the skies, heading east. Bryan considered the church, imagining the still silence inside that had helped fold worshipers' distance from God for so many centuries. Then another guy on a moped shot by. *Damn, those look dangerous*, Bryan thought. *I might rent a bike and that's it. I'd rather be slow than paraplegic.*

When Peter showed up, he embraced the visitor, though Bryan did not like this type of physical contact, and gave him a tour of his modest house, with an easel on the upper floor. The ground floor was quite spartan. There were no books, a fact that reminded Bryan how Peter's artistic skill and Bryan's intellectual curiosity were not even distant relatives. In the hours that followed, Bryan met another art teacher, a rotund woman in her forties with craggy blonde hair, two attractive young students named Cyprian and Lara, and a trio of local officials wandering through the village. From the outset, he liked both Cyprian, a Londoner of Polish descent, and Lara, who'd grown up on Long Island and who sometimes gave hints of a romantic interest in Peter. Bryan's fear became less conscious, less palpable.

The café was where all the Americans and Canadians hung out when not bent obsessively over their art. As soon as he wandered in on his second day in the village, Roy, the first teacher he'd encountered, exclaimed, "Hello, Mr. Hemingway!", bought him a glass of beer, and inquired about his writing, drawing yet another awkward reply.

There was a good deal more to see in Vihiers, the town a couple of miles to the north, so Bryan began walking there and back regularly, sometimes hitching rides. While relishing the scenery, he knew he'd have to get more efficient and rent a bike. Vihiers was not only charming, it had been the scene of dramatic events during the royalist uprising of the 1790s. Bryan hung lazily around, gazed at young women on the street, checked out one of the quiet cafés, bought a few things from the grocer, looked for lizards on the peeling walls between dusty shops, and squinted at the glare of the white pavement at 2:00 p.m. People didn't seek out this town, nor did it try to lure them. It was just exquisite. He didn't mind that a few of the clerks glared at him.

On his way back from Vihiers one day, Bryan hitched a ride with a professional in his early thirties who claimed to know an actor looking for a native English speaker who could sit down with his daughter for a few hours a week and help develop her pronunciation. If Bryan was available, it would pad his wallet. Bryan immediately agreed, and asked who the friend was. It was an actor whose name everyone spoke with reverence, and who owned a castle roughly equidistant from Les Cerqueux and Vihiers. Bryan knew there were castles around here, of course, but he couldn't get over the incongruity of a place where ultrasophisticated fighter jets shot through the air above castles. He thanked the driver, writing out his number and stressing his availability in the weeks to come.

He began tutoring Gerard Depardieu's daughter Camille a week later. She immediately liked the shy American, and told the actor so.

When Bryan woke up on Wednesday of the following week, he urgently had to piss, but the door to the bathroom was shut. Bryan lingered in the dusty spaces on the first floor, clutching his loins and studying the light under the door of the restroom, but Peter was taking his time, so Bryan charged out the back door and up an alley into the yard of a farmer he didn't know, turning away from the expanse of dirt and corn to the west and letting go with immense relief. Then he turned again and gazed right into the shrewd face of the fifty-year-old farmer who'd come out to inspect his crops at the moment that Bryan lost control. The farmer, a friendly man inured to the rhythms of his life, chuckled at the embarrassed American.

"*Ah, c'est sec,*" he told Bryan with a gesture over the fields.

"*Trés sec,*" the farmer added as Bryan zipped his pants and tried to fight off the shame coloring his cheeks and ears.

"*Pas encore,*" said Bryan.

"*Restez-vous une minute,*" said the farmer, "*contemplez-vous mon fils, mon cher Remy. Ici nous aimons les jeunes Americains.*"

Bryan craned his head and caught a glimpse of the farmer's son, who stood at a corner of the field gazing at the American with a mix of wonder and bemusement, with his mighty arms folded into a vise that Bryan imagined could crush his skull like a dome of sand. The father watched Bryan with an indulgent grin. Both he and Remy were curious about Bryan's activities in the village, so he told them about a story he planned, involving resistance fighters and betrayal in the Vendée of the Vichy period, avoiding any mention of the duplicitous French characters. Then they asked about the art classes, which Bryan sat in on from time to time, mainly to see Lara in the nude, and he talked about form and the ways people occupy space and felt the distances between him and the father and son who were perhaps unduly kind to a rude young American. Later, alone, meditating on their expressions and speech, Bryan reflected that the farmer and Remy had listened out of a kind of morbid curiosity. They quite clearly didn't care for young Americans at all, but had to put up with them. Bryan found one thing quite curious. Remy, huge and gangly with a dopey kind of look, didn't resemble his father at all.

A week after his encounter in the field, Bryan accepted an invitation to Gerard's castle for dinner. When he arrived in the dusk outside the looming structure, he set aside the bike he had rented and climbed the slope with trepidation as the fields all around rustled faintly, the same fields from which a kitten had gazed out at him through a gap in the hedgerows beside a road the other day in the glare of three o'clock. He wondered whether the kitten lingered somewhere in the hidden reaches of those fields that bowed and rallied with the winds. Wherever it was, perhaps it shared the tranquility that he felt in his deepest reaches, the sense of a peace and serenity that existed as a thing apart like the sun or moon, nurturing Bryan yet above and indifferent to him. Darkness seeped over the whispering fields as he rang the bell at the front door. A servant let him in, asked him to wait a minute, and vanished. One humble candle burned on a stand beside the door. Bryan knew there were others in the halls and chambers and stairwells all around him, yet for a moment he felt utterly alone. In moments, another servant came and escorted Bryan through a long hall and up a winding stairway to a floor where chairs from the age of Napoleon III lay between frescoes and paintings of angels diving or dancing in luminous landscapes. Within the reaches of this monument of silence, its corridors running through history as through space, Bryan supposed there might be men planning intrigues concerning Gerard's career, his yearning to be the most revered actor on the planet. Bryan realized that he and the servant had yet to exchange a word. Still he followed the tall, square-shouldered man through two more halls until they came to the chamber where Gerard awaited. He did not see the servant depart.

Gerard's aging face betrayed no pleasure at the guest's arrival. It was the face of a man with a quiet faith in the inevitability of certain outcomes, Bryan thought. He sat down and sniffed the red wine in his glass, then looked up at Gerard, who smiled now at the impertinence of a guest whose first thought was wine.

"My daughter speaks highly of you," said Gerard.

"Oh, she's a little tart, and a really bright kid. She's a delight."

"Camille might study in America. If she does, I want her to be as comfortable as possible."

Bryan sipped his wine and felt it soothing him.

"Well, I think I'm a pretty typical American slob."

"Slob?"

"Never mind. She's making excellent progress and this is working out for both of us."

"Teach her all the little feints and parries until she can hold her own in conversation."

Besides a father's protectiveness, Gerard seemed aware of the dislocations, the weirdness that would befall Camille when walking through a grinding steel and concrete city or a college town in the Midwest.

"It saddens me that it's the dreck of our culture that stares out at you from billboards—the worst junk, we call them B-movies at home, ones that I wouldn't spend money on. For you, that's 'American culture,'" Bryan said.

"Not for the educated here."

They talked for a while about Bryan's writing, his desire to infuse it with verisimilitude by living and working among the farmers and the *ouvriers* in a remote part of the province, a place even educated folk mostly ignored. Then Gerard cautioned Bryan not to wander too far from the village by himself at night, with so many marshes in the environs.

"Has no one told you this?"

"No. I'm sure you glad you did."

Then Bryan asked without preamble about getting an additional thirty francs per hour for tutoring Camille, in light of their progress. The answer was yes.

The next day, Bryan sat at a table in the café in Les Cerqueux with a glass of beer when a pretty blonde strolled in and ordered a croissant and tea before turning to the timid American and introducing herself as Kirsten. She was a Canadian, was enrolled in Peter's sculpting class, and seemed quite taken with the lanky writer. They traded small talk and she asked why he hadn't flown directly to Paris, so with a shade of embarrassment, Bryan told how he'd bought an open-ended voucher for any seat that might become available on a transatlantic flight. He recounted for Kirsten the train ride from Stuttgart to Strasbourg and the next leg, from Strasbourg to Paris. He'd sat in his window seat thinking of the tales he would attempt once he sat down in Les Cerqueux and really focused, and of the awesome diligence he'd have to summon—no fucking around this time! At a couple of points on the way, he gazed out the window and spotted graffiti equating Le Pen with Hitler. At a point between Strasbourg and Paris, the train came to a halt abruptly. Bryan heard the hissing breaks and then heard nothing, saw nothing in the whiteness outside, and his reverie commenced.

Consider: if most of a nation subscribes to certain values, principles, there's no need for anyone to scrawl them at lonely train stops in the country. But intelligent people have not always prized the liberal and humanistic over the ruthless. I think about the tradition to which this insufferably proud people belongs, about Plato in his Symposium *reflecting on varieties of love— romantic, homosexual, love for one's kin, for one's country, and observing that rarely do we see devotion to country and performance of one's civic duty boil with the ardor of other relationships. So maybe it's not surprising to see Alcibiades welcomed, honored, at the dinner even though he's an infamous butcher. Here's a guy who did his duty to the* polis *and then some, at a time when the chips were down. So with W.T. Sherman in his march to the sea, so with warriors whom the French won't completely disown, Napoleon, De Gaulle, and now, of course, Le Pen.*

Consider: Unrest comes to the Ivory Coast and French soldiers spill out from their base all over the country, shooting first, never getting around to asking too many questions, until nine of them die in the regime's airstrikes and the French demolish the country's air force, they could crush the rebels or cripple the regime, it's an assertion of an ancient colonial dogma either way. It's in the Africans' interest, they say. This was in 2004, not 1904. I suppose it's no more brutal than setting off nukes in populated parts of the South Pacific.

Now Paris has burned on global TV. They're in a horrendous mess, torn between the outrages of la racaille and the memories of Vichy. The tourists come and go and most of them probably don't even know what it is they're swarming after, just that it's all so fucking important. And now—

The train's gears kicked in again and within an hour Bryan was in Paris.

Bryan found himself yearning to be with Kirsten, who combined an aesthetic sensibility with practical qualities. An exhibit of her sketches was coming up in a week in a barn nearby and she hoped that Bryan would come. He'd been planning to meet with Camille at that time, but he said yes anyway, hoping Gerard wouldn't be mad if he rescheduled.

Bryan hung out daily in the café in the hope of seeing the young woman from British Columbia. It was a meeting place for the hopeful creative artists from America and Canada as well as a generation of French gentlemen who remembered Vichy and earlier years, and whose opinion of the young upstarts was, to Bryan at least, hard to fathom. At times, they came out of the back room where they'd enjoyed their pipes and cards to shake hands with the twenty-something kids, and were nothing if not civilized toward the young women, but their manner seemed layered—a sheen of friendliness covering mild curiosity hiding—what, exactly? They answered his questions politely and then their eyes turned ever so slightly and gave one another a look. Then, on Wednesday night, Bryan's circle and several other Americans went a bit further than before. They didn't even realize the back room was in use as they got ripped on beer and bantered so loudly that the patron came out to remonstrate gently. But the loud talk went on, and on, and on, even as the men filed out of the back and through the front exit in their work shirts and berets without even a glance at the revelers, Bryan and Peter and a few others detecting a fierce disdain in the men's eyes, bordering on something else entirely.

Bryan later told Peter how embarrassed he felt and proposed that they apologize to those café folk. They were pretty nice to the youngsters despite the checkered history of foreigners in this area, Bryan reminded Peter. Bryan had heard a story about coal miners from Spain, Italy and Germany passing a fortnight in the town almost two decades ago, and things got out of hand one night and those miners did something awful, oh yes, from what Bryan understood it was in the nature of a gang-bang involving one of the local girls.

On Friday night, Peter invited Bryan to accompany him, Cyprian, Lara, and Kirsten to a night spot somewhere on the outskirts of Vihiers. Here was yet another chance to zero in on that enthralling sameness-within-the-alien. At the most horrifying end of that scale was Paris in July, and at the other end was a working-class woman on the streets of Vihiers with her cigarettes and her coy questions and body language, or the yuppie driving through the hedgerows in his sleek car, or the fighter jets streaking high above the castles and churches. Bryan happily said yes, and a few hours later he sat wedged on a back seat between Peter and Kirsten, with Cyprian and Lara up front. They drove for about fifteen minutes through the cool night with constellations asserting their beauty, took a shortcut through a field and swung into a crude lot where a dozen or so young people had already parked.

The five young people strode into the improvised club, where lights spun and illuminated a grinning face, a girl bending forward to light a cigarette, a farmer's son striding toward a table with two or three drinks in either hand, his friends waiting to consummate the joy of being young on a cool clear night in the Maine-and-Loire. Cyprian and Peter walked up to the bar as Bryan, Lara and Kirsten wandered to one of the tables, Bryan striving to appear more at ease than he felt around the ravishing Kirsten.

Cyprian and Peter came back with a round of drinks and the talk turned to sculpting class, where Lara made nice money exposing her body to the pupils. Peter thought some of the young sculptors vastly more accomplished than others. Peter did not seem nearly as turned on by Lara as vice versa, which Bryan found sad because of how nice and open Lara seemed. He kept noticing her gazing at Peter while the latter was deep in conversation with Cyprian about this or that. Now more kids arrived and merged into the throbbing scene. At length, Bryan excused himself to use the men's room, paused at the bar on his way back, and that was when he met Claude. The young man had blond hair like gold flattened into a sheet in the manner of pewter, and intelligent blue eyes set in a nicely angled face, almost like a younger version of Gerard, Bryan thought. Claude studied the American for a moment with a look neither warm nor cold. When Bryan had another round of drinks ready on a tray, the young man broke the silence, in the type of voice a shopkeeper uses toward a vagrant loitering outside. He asked whether Bryan was a Canadian. Bryan gave curt answers: American, writer, Les Cerqueux, et cetera.

The calm face studied Bryan for a moment. Then Claude stated his name and said that he lived a mile outside Vihiers, and that it was not common to see Americans, who took little interest in the town even when studying in Les Cerqueux.

"But then," added Claude, "if you don't care about those who go through life as amputees thanks to you, then who cares about a little place like Vihiers?"

Bryan smiled by default at his interlocutor. Now the music shifted to a snappier, more danceable song and the throng in the center of the place swelled. Bryan could not see his friends.

"Relax, I'm just making a joke with you," said Claude. It was one of the solecisms that result from literal translation.

"Glad you told me, because I'm not sure what's funny," said Bryan.

"I'm sorry?"

"Never mind."

"I'm not saying you would blow up houses full of people in Afghanistan," Claude continued. "I don't know, you might be a good guy."

"I'm not too little to come to your country in spite of all that's happened."

"Because we've got the best women, *n'est-ce pas*? Like that one," said Claude with a gesture at a girl three stools down, a brunette whom Bryan thought actually had kind of crude and homely features. He wanted to get back to his friends now.

"She's the best, eh? You'd like to go together with her?"

Go together?

"Oh sure, it would be kind of like eating cardboard," Bryan replied before cutting away from the bar, around the dancing kids and back to the table where his four friends were chatting.

Even as he moved further away from the bar, he felt the fear return.

Lara had maneuvered herself next to Peter, and she was leaning close against him and resting one hand on his leg as she spoke to him. Desultory talk was going on between Cyprian and Kirsten as they sipped their beers and followed the action on the floor. Bryan thought of his stateside friends with vastly better social skills, reflecting that they would have no trouble pulling Kirsten away from her non-conversation with Cyprian. But Bryan's tongue lay ugly and dumb in his mouth, like cordwood. Kirsten returned his glance with a warm smile and he knew he had to come up with something.

"I don't think we made a great impression on those old men in the café," Bryan finally managed to say.

"You know, Peter and I talked about that, and I don't think they took us seriously enough to take offense," she answered.

"I think a certain amount of—I don't know, dislocation—was likely for us, and there's a right and wrong way to deal with it."

"Maybe so. It's easy not to think about all the layers of history and tradition, you just see a white road and a café and then feel the red wine working on you."

Across the table, Lara and Peter appeared to have gotten somewhere in their conversation. Peter was explaining a point to Lara and she was nodding as disappointment creased her lovely features, following Peter's logic perhaps, but not at a loss for another approach to her goal. The throng in the center of the room had thinned a bit, the music segued into a ballad exhorting you to *"changer de vie,"* and for the first time, listening to the ballad, Bryan thought he knew why it had been a British invasion in his parents' day and not a French one. Cyprian got up to fetch another round, Lara and Peter talked further, and soon the intimacy of Les Cerqueux beckoned once more. Claude sat on his stool with his arms folded, gazing coldly at the five as they filed out of the club while Remy, the tall muscular son of a Loire Valley farmer, sat counterpoised to Claude with a faint smile and a look that said *whatever it is, let it go.*

"So, Bryan, you'd rather flirt with French teenagers than talk to us," said Cyprian as the car hurtled through the clear night, and as always, Bryan couldn't tell whether the Londoner meant what he said.

"Leave him alone. Shut up and drive!" Peter said.

Bryan sat wedged between the women on the back seat and gasped as Cyprian swerved to navigate a hedgerow, and then there were two more hedgerows, so the car was not going too fast when a bang made Bryan lose control of his bowels and others in the car screamed and cried. The car spun 180 degrees and flew in a wild dance with the spinning mass it had hit and landed in the viscous earth on the far side of the third hedgerow.

Peter, his forehead bleeding profusely, hissed at the driver.

"Why the hell did you take this shortcut?"

Lara was unconscious.

"Are they out there?" Kirsten murmured.

"Fuck. Fuck!" from Cyprian, still clutching the wheel. Bryan couldn't tell whether he was bleeding or not. He was the only one in the car who felt more or less the same as before.

"Did you just hit a farmer?" Peter asked.

"I think we hit a cow," Cyprian muttered. He climbed out of the car and examined it from all sides, then strode over to the dying beast that would have proved fatal to the humans at a higher speed. Kirsten, Bryan, and then Peter climbed out and stood staring at the mass that lay flopped on its side with its tongue lolling, its impenetrable black eyes gazing up at the bipeds that had destroyed its simple dignity, and no one could guess what depths of loathing and murder lay in the distances of those eyes. The cow breathed heavily and wheezed and they knew it had minutes to live. Cyprian looked at Peter and something passed between them.

Bryan heard the sculptor whisper to Cyprian: *"I'm twenty-six and this could fuck up my entire life."*

At this point, Bryan's concern was for Lara.

"We need to go to the police, and Lara needs an ambulance," said Kirsten.

"You just better shut up," Peter said, glaring at the woman he'd mostly ignored all night.

"Kirsten, hey," said Cyprian. "Lara's a little dazed, that's all. I want to take her back now and let her crash out on my couch. This is nothing, this is not our fault, let's leave now."

"No, we've got to go to the police," Kirsten replied. "And we've got to get Lara to a hospital and call her parents."

"*Shut up, you fucking bitch!*" Peter screamed and started towards her. Cyprian and Bryan both moved into his path and half forced, half remonstrated with the sculptor until he backed off.

"We can't go to the police," Peter repeated several times as they eased him back into the front passenger seat, his skin jumping and shivering as something burned terrifyingly beneath it.

"Bastard. Bastard," Kirsten moaned as the men forced her into the car. Bryan's tongue felt like lumber again as the car pulled away from the dying cow in the cool air and the vast reaches of corn.

The next morning, Bryan woke with a dry sensation at the base of his throat, wondering where Peter was. He looked out the window and saw none of the young people who made this an artsy place where you stood on the threshold of infinite possibility, just the lame dog ambling up the street past the church. Bryan felt acutely lonely in the spartan room with a few wrappers and cans he'd neglected to clean up.

His heart almost stopped when a knock came at the front door.

I'm only twenty-five, a year behind Peter, and this could be it for me.

Now he looked at the back door. Beyond it was a muddy alley, and then endless reaches of corn where he could maybe hide and creep toward a bus stop in another town. The brightness outside beckoned, beckoned.

But he walked to the front door and flung it open, and there was Cyprian.

"Listen, Lara's fine," he assured the American with a queer grin. "She just needed to rest her head a bit, and she's been listening to CDs and joking for the last couple of hours. Peter's calmed down too, he's not mad at Kirsten."

It was more and yet less information than Bryan needed.

"And, oh, you might be interested to know that they've made an arrest. Remy Brulotte is in jail for hitting that cow with his car," Cyprian added.

"Remy?"

"That's right."

"But he didn't—"

"Oh, shut up, sure he did. But listen, you're not to talk about it to anyone," said Cyprian, and it was not a request. "Just forget that it ever happened."

"I can hardly do that. I never thought I could feel so terrified. They *hate* us. They want an excuse to kill us. Cyprian—"

"*Bryan.* In case you haven't figured it out, we're really not worth hating. The proudest people in the world aren't going to lower themselves to despise us."

And so the well-dressed young man from London turned and retreated up the cobblestone street toward the café. Bryan guessed Cyprian had resolved the situation to his own satisfaction, at least.

When Bryan returned to the actor's castle for dinner the following night, he strode into the dining room, sat down, and studied the inscrutable face across from him. Minding his manners this time, he did not eat or drink until the actor began. Gerard talked at length about Camille and the possibility of applying to schools in the United States, soliciting Bryan's views on which to go for and which to avoid. Gerard was more lively and talkative than last time, he slammed down a second glass, a third, a fourth, and soon had to call for a new bottle of wine. If Camille were to study in America, Bryan said, it really would not be an ordeal at all. Don't worry about the "freedom fries" issue, there are thousands of campuses where she'd have fun.

Gerard asked about the art classes, about Bryan's writing, and finally about the repercussions of Remy's arrest.

Bryan fell silent. He sighed, stared at the table, at his empty glass, and then at Gerard's handsome aging face. He summoned all his courage to break the silence.

"Gerard . . . uh, listen . . . Remy Brulotte did not hit that cow."

The actor's look was inscrutable.

"He was definitely traveling from Vihiers to Les Cerqueux that night."

"Yes, I know. *But Remy didn't hit the cow, my friends and I did.*"

With a faint smile, Gerard asked whether Bryan pitied the farmer's son because he was slow-witted.

"No, that's not it. I feel terrible because I don't even think Remy was drunk that night. He was a lot more responsible than we were."

Gerard noted that Remy did not have a clean record, that complaints about his behavior reached all the way back to an episode in 1995 when the cat of a girl who spurned him suddenly disappeared. Bryan insisted that was irrelevant, but there was no persuading Gerard, who pointed out that the local gendarmes had found molecules of paint in the hide of the dead cow matching Remy's car, not that of the five youngsters.

"That's impossible!"

But Gerard insisted it was so. He went on to tell Bryan that French-American relations were precarious enough as they stood, that there was nothing the world needed less than an episode where rustics in the Loire Valley rounded up a group of Americans and Canadians on charges of dubious merit, but the whole issue was moot because of the physical evidence in this case. At one point, Gerard called Remy a bastard. Bryan studied the aging face, the intelligent eyes that had witnessed so many sunrises and sunsets over the valley and become inured to the cycles of the crops' planting, appearance and maturity in the quiet of a timeless cycle amid the hedgerows, and who cared for the land and its people as perhaps for his own soul, and Bryan once again regretted his impertinence, the rudeness of an immature drifter, he wondered how to put things right again. He felt a fawning respect for the actor who effortlessly evoked laughter or pity or fear or empathy in his celebrated roles on the screen and stage. He wanted to plead with Gerard, to make him grasp that not everything was lost on the young interloper who drank his wine and took his money, but he felt numbed inside the distances of the castle and the darkness that all but obscured the aging face beyond the flickering candle in the center of the table.

Bryan was too drunk to ride his bike back to Les Cerqueux, so one of the servants gave him a ride, and soon he was gazing out the window at the rows of corn and nodding off.

Consider: Our soldiers in Afghanistan have shot X number of goatherders, and incinerated houses where insurgents hid among women and kids. Some of them say that if they weren't doing those jobs over there, it would be draftees with no zest for the role. Yet they don't get a lot of support. France is a different story. Here, it seems to me more and more, there is nothing unfashionable or impolite about racial consciousness. De Gaulle understood this when he blatantly championed racial solidarity, purity, when he stood at a podium in Quebec and appealed to the cheering crowds' deepest need for recognition, affirmation, survival as members of the very same race.

Oh, as for these people in my life. I think I get Peter and Lara and Kirsten. But Cyprian = cipher. I don't get him at all. Even if Remy is a bastard, he's not inscrutable.

The chauvinism and fury can as easily turn inward as they can look beyond the country's borders. I was terrified of what these people would do. I've known a low-intensity kind of terror since I set foot here, in the proudest country, but at last, at last, I think I know why I am free and safe and Remy is not. Remy's real father is not the man who saw me taking a piss in his garden. Remy's father is one of the foreigners involved in that gang-bang. They've hated him, the bastard born of invaders, as much as or more than the immature rabble my friends and I represent. We're not worth hating. France's standing in the world is worth considerably more than getting back at us.

Bryan was lolling in the café with his forehead in his left hand and his notebook before him again when a thin black-haired woman in her late twenties strolled inside. She noticed the awkward, lanky guy with sensitive blue eyes and a tired face and asked whether he was a painter or sculptor. Neither, he told her, and gave her the spiel. The woman introduced herself as Nicole, saying she was an experimental artist who had come to Les Cerqueux to study under the teacher Bryan had met on his first day in the village. Trying to look interested, Bryan asked what sort of experimental stuff she did.

"Inverted landscapes, sometimes. But right now I'm interested in trapezoids—how the depth of suffering can emerge within cold clean angles—and I'm branching out to include other forms and patterns. Right now . . . ."

Bryan wasn't sure he followed, but he listened indulgently as mopeds sped by outside and farmers chatted about corn and rain and the months to come.

Fatal Element

Anton put his knees together and spread the map of the province out before him. The bus rattled and bounced pretty severely at times, but he managed to focus his attention on the area around Panciu. He hoped that the transfer point, where you caught another bus going down to Berca, was coming up in a few minutes. In Berca he'd meet up with a friend. He almost didn't mind the fact that the threat in the skies had been no bluff, and snow had been coming down heavily for a few minutes now.

The map's makers had not had Western eyes in mind. A number of the towns had the names of obscure soldiers, organizers, and party officials from various stages of communism's history. The scarlet of the characters on the map mixed pleasingly with the black contours of mountains and the dark gray of municipal borders. But there weren't many mountains or hills in the area the bus moved through now, and towns of any size were vast distances apart. A blank space greeted Anton's eyes as he tried to gauge precisely where he was. Even in their ideological fervor, the map's makers had found nothing to put in an area of about three centimeters between a town named for a labor hero of the 1930s and an airfield heavily bombed by the Allies during the war. The map's propagandistic qualities were obvious, but even now Anton felt some sympathy for the revolution. He had even dreamed about a role in perpetuating it. He fancied himself a smart man with nearly unrivalled gifts for identifying, assessing, sorting, processing.

All around the bus were wide blank spaces that fed a vague anxiety. As he might have expected in so barren an area, the bus had few passengers. In the seats around him were an old woman with the edges of a ragged black shawl visible beneath her gray coat, a teen in a red parka, and a couple in their forties in worn jackets. Everyone had a bored air. The couple looked as if they were at one of those banal in-between moments in a relationship that you never think of until they arrive. Whenever Anton wondered about the *terra incognita* of marriage, he kept coming back to the thought that marriage would probably deny him much time to study in solitude. For Anton, who often felt quite insecure about his looks and social skills, intellectual growth was virtually the only thing with the potential to ennoble him and make him feel the equal of or better than others. Anton found endless fascination in the feuds of historians of unsurpassed intelligence who never made any concessions to each other. It was a panorama of irresistible forces and immovable objects. The discipline could ennoble someone who got really serious about it. So what if you were part of what they call a "dying order," Anton thought. With training, and rhetorical skill, you could puncture holes in just about any argument or position.

The snow came harder now, but it did not quite obstruct Anton's view of the fields on either side of the road. This part of the country reminded him of the American Midwest. The province might be beautiful in other seasons, but in winter the ubiquitous dull brown could not fail to affect your mood. Anton looked at his watch. He shouldn't be waiting too long now. Soon he'd be on another bus, with another handful of strangers, going through the depressing landscape, moving inexorably closer to the town where a friend he'd met in grad school, an intellectual and historian like himself, waited. Soon they'd be drinking wine coolers or one of the local beers and talking about capitalist exploitation and the growth of labor movements in the cities in the 1920s and 1930s. But they wouldn't talk too loudly. It was a time of severe unrest in this part of the world. The dictator Ceaușescu had fallen and the country was more open, but people were far from calm and trusting. Fierce arguments broke out as the regime crumbled and images of the execution of the dictator and his wife played on screens around the world.

The bus came to a halt. Anton stood. While most of the others ignored him, the eyes of the teen in the red parka seemed almost to dare him to step off the bus. Anton ignored the little punk. Things were okay outside, he decided. The middle-aged driver didn't look at Anton as he stepped off onto a patch of dull earth and lifeless grass. Soon the bus was a receding shape far off to the east. The taillights were the last parts to vanish in the intensifying snow. Anton looked around. Here were a bench and a pole with a printed schedule inside a little glass frame with rusted blue metal edges. The stop was a tiny outpost in a nondescript place, a brown barren world where you could wander for days only to find more mocking plainness. Yet Anton felt an old confidence coming back. Yes, the trip had been dull so far, but Anton was so much more serious about completing his doctoral thesis than any number of other candidates. He'd taken the trouble to come all the way to this remote place. After meeting his friend, he'd move on to interviews with scholars who had vast expertise in the fields of labor or intellectual history.

But right now, he was all alone in the gathering snow. As he lingered by the pole and the bench, the snow seemed far more aggressive and determined than he could have predicted from the relative comfort of the bus. What had appeared through the bus's windows as a shifting curtain with many tears in it now had the appearance of innumerable white wraiths hurling themselves diagonally at the barren brown. The wraiths could not hurt him individually, but their gathering fury blotted out the awareness of things in virtually every direction. Again he looked at his watch, and compared the time with the hour printed on the paper in the little case. His connection should have come by now. He stood in the falling show, humming, wondering what his friend in Berca was doing.

An hour passed. Another hour. He grew furious at the ineptitude of the bus driver who should long have come and left. Anton was of Romanian ancestry but had grown up in a city in America where buses were usually on time. He'd never expected this. He waited anxiously, telling himself he must not let his emotional maturity fall away at an annoyance. For surely the bus's headlights would appear at any moment. But another hour crept by. Morning was long over now. Anton wanted to pull the screws out of that case affixed to the pole and rip the lying little schedule into bits. Snow had gathered in the spaces between his neck and the collar of his parka. His feet felt frozen, and it wasn't just due to the sensitivity of those parts of the body. Anton stamped his feet, did a jig in an effort to send blood rushing down there. With a growing sense of futility, he looked up and down the deserted road. He still hoped he'd see the beams of a pair of headlights and would climb a little flight of steps and forget his anger quickly and totally, like a hangover.

He looked around. He thought about what to call snow. It was a form of frozen water vapor, so he wasn't sure whether to refer to it as an element. But if it wasn't an element, then for all his erudition he had no idea what to call it. Snow came and came. The headlights failed to appear, despite the logical necessity of their appearance. Anton stamped his feet, rotated his body 360 degrees, took in the road, the plains, the bench, and the solitary pole with its mendacious little schedule. He thought desperately about what to do. In another age, perhaps, people would have little phones they could whip out in an emergency. Anton had no way to get in touch with anyone. Here was a world whose functioning depended on people being where they'd promised to be without fail. He stamped his feet, compared the time on his watch to the time on the schedule again. Another miserable hour passed.

Anton made a decision. The probability of dying was not much lower if he struck out into the white landscape than if he stayed, but he had to try. Once more he looked around at the gathering snow. He tried to recall the last hour of his ride, to recapture images of buildings the bus had passed, but nothing came to him. Was it better to follow the bus, to keep moving east? That might just take him further out into nothingness. He knew how crazy it would be to leave the road. Surely a vehicle must appear before too long. Of course he didn't know there were no buildings back to the west of where he was. He'd been looking out from only one side of the bus, and only at intervals. Maybe there was a town somewhere back there. He had to find out. He felt he owed his potential as a scholar at least that much.

Anton moved west on the road with desperate eyes. Though the snow showed no sign of relenting, it did not yet impede movement. He recalled occasions in the past where drivers had yelled abuse at him for straying onto a road. If only that could happen now! He'd do anything for someone's attention. He trudged ahead, feeling more flakes perch on the bare flesh between the collar of his coat and the ends of his ash brown hair. Gusts sent snow into his face in rude angry streams. An old dreaded feeling came to him. He was a child, full of protest, needing to vent his anger, but with no one at all to listen.

Neither side of the road had any features. Here was brown earth rapidly disappearing beneath white. He trudged ahead. This was just pitiful. Anton, a man who had practically defined himself through his intelligence, was walking without direction in a place he didn't know, and was at risk of succumbing to one of the most elementary dangers of all, one that should have been easy to avoid.

He wanted to stop and rest, but the snow was coming even harder now. If he paused, he might get stuck between drifts. Anton grew aware of a decisive change in the complexion of things. His feet crunched rather than clumped on the surface below. The sheet of snow was getting rapidly thicker. Looking across the fields, he saw growing mounds and fierce horizontal flurries. The cold was so harsh now that he felt moisture dart from his eyes in zigzagging moves. He forced his legs to plod on, plod on. Still there was not a hint of traffic in any direction.

At last he spotted something. His position on the eastbound bus, where he'd slumped against a right-side window, had denied him the sight of a structure over on the northern side of the road. Way out there, he made out a rectangular building. It had the shape of a hangar, but looked a bit small for one, at least from here. More interesting to Anton were the five cylinders topped with flickering orange out in front of the structure. Yes, there were fires in those barrels. Here was a prospect of warmth and safety. At last, at last! Anton tried to run but his movement was little more than a stagger. Even so, the structure and the cylinders grew steadily in his vision. As he lurched and nearly fell and pushed ahead, his feet crunching on the snow, he came to find something almost primal about the scene. Here was the vessel that had brought to the planet a race that had never really made more than a wary, temporary adjustment to the climes. This impression grew stronger when Anton drew near enough to make out the bundled faces above the flames. He saw three men and two women. The faces visible inside the hoods of the parkas had a pinched and cracked look. He thought of Eskimos and was far too desperate to reflect on the vulgarity of the stereotype.

Anton's desperation was obvious enough. He hurried forward in the expectation that the five strangers would make a quick assessment of him, and indeed they did. The aged weathered man at the barrel furthest to the left had a look of peculiar detestation in his dark brown eyes. Anton did not see the carbine until the opening at the tip was two dozen yards from his face. The noise that came now was loud, but more of a *clump!* than a roar, as if the snow had muffled it. Anton felt a displacement, a whizzing and sucking, in the air just to his left. The bastard had fired at him and probably had not meant to miss. He turned and fled, in the direction of the road, as the enemy fired three more times. As he raced, cursing and crying, away from the five strangers, he realized he couldn't see the road and didn't know quite where he was going. He had come further north than he'd realized in his effort to get to a structure he'd equated with security. Anton thought that at this point it made no difference whether he was on the road, there were no vehicles going either way. Maybe an official *diktat* was in effect, or maybe it was just the locals' sly sense about the weather. He guessed they knew it was impossible to get help in time if they broke down in a blizzard out here.

Though Anton didn't know where he was heading, he thought his course was generally westward, roughly parallel with the road. He thought he'd really failed to imagine the kind of disorder that might flourish in this country so soon after the fall of the dictator. For surely those five strangers hadn't been afraid of a desperate, terrified, five-foot-seven foreigner. Their hostility came from a guess as to who he was and what he stood for in the context of this land's agonized history. But he couldn't believe that structure, which he was still lucid enough to identify as a garage rather than a spaceship, stood out here without any purpose. It must play a role in the perpetuation of some kind of order.

Anton trudged ahead, his feet making increasingly sharp crunches and crackles. He wanted badly to have made the right decision. Of course he didn't know what lay on the far side of the road, but he wanted to vindicate his choice of a direction through the belief that the land to the south was a place that found all life repellent. It would tolerate nothing and nobody, and people avoided it. Such thoughts kept Anton from becoming too aware of the density of snow on the back of his neck. It was so cold he wanted to scream. Anton had respected himself as a bright man with the potential to command and lead his intellectual inferiors. Here he was, ready to dance around naked for the first stranger he encountered, if he could only do it in a warm, safe place.

Anton saw a house up ahead. Maybe he was closer to the road than he'd realized. He saw now that perhaps he did deserve credit for his guess about the garage way back there being part of a kind of network. Though the driveway of the house looming before him was not visible, he couldn't imagine it wending for miles. As for the house, it was a strange building, like two great humping rectangles, one on top of the other. The cement was only a bit darker than the snow whirling and crashing against the walls. The windows were dark but it would hardly have mattered if they weren't, given how far ice had encroached. He could not see the entrance. It almost seemed to want to evade him. Anton moved rapidly in the direction of the road, his eyes fixed on the front end of the building's east side. Finally he made out a narrow black portal in the middle of the big house's façade.

Anton walked up to the door and turned the knob. To his amazement, the door opened. At last he was going to be indoors! His desperation almost superseded his deeply ingrained habit of stamping his feet, but he did so quickly before moving inside and pulling the door shut. Now he saw just what a nasty place he'd discovered. The building was of concrete inside as well as outside. It had been a while since anyone made much of an effort to maintain the place. He was at the front of a dank corridor running to the other side of the building, with three doors on his left at intervals of twenty feet. On the right side of the corridor, a staircase led up into darkness. A dripping came at once to his ears. Drops were coming through the hall's ceiling, suggesting that water ran freely, madly, in an upstairs room. He noticed puddles on the staircase, and grime in every corner. Again he thought that the building he'd happened upon must be one of a number of structures with an underground infrastructure in common. The water came from somewhere but he hadn't seen a reservoir on the roof.

Anton urgently wanted to find someone who would understand and accept his reasons for trespassing. With tentative steps he moved down the hall. The first door on his left would not give. He guessed there were people in there who were busy with their lives and had achieved such total fulfillment that it was beneath them to answer a knock on the door. When he moved down to the next door, he discovered a larger room than either of the adjacent ones. The door was open. Anton walked into the room and stood a matter of yards from a chair with an official personage slumped in it. Here was a thin middle-aged man with trim white hair, wearing a pair of designer pants and a blue dress shirt whose sleeves reached all the way to his inert hairy wrists. All his clothes had big crimson stains on them. The weathered quality of those five strangers at the garage was not entirely absent from this man's face, but it carried a hint of urbanity, of erudition. All that was necessary to complete the official image was a pair of eyes.

But this man had no eyes.

The man had languished there as blood leaked out of the holes. Anton guessed that someone had stabbed him in both eyes and then guided him to the chair, or allowed him to stumble there. But the latter seemed unlikely if the man could not see. Now to Anton's amazement the man spoke.

"Boy. That's not a coat for these parts."

Anton reeled. Even more astonishing than the man's use of English was that he could see. The two facts were clearly related. A glance at Anton, even a glance through the tiny slivers of pupil, iris, and schlera on the fringes of those bloody sockets, was enough to determine that Anton was not a local, he was part of a transnational elite. Anton looked more closely now at the two sockets. Yes, remnants of the man's eyes poked and slithered around the edges like worms. They were so small and ragged but obviously could relay bits of visual data to the stranger's brain. Anton tried to imagine perceiving, feeling, thinking with that instrument.

"I did not plan for a blizzard, or for the absence of vehicles."

The man gave the faintest of laughs.

"You may have wondered why you waited hours with no cars passing. It's the remnants of the *securitate*, you know. They've commandeered all private vehicles."

Anton felt the stirrings of a rage whose expression belonged to a distant time, an unimagined place.

"They didn't care that there might be people out there who need rides?"

"These are my friends you're talking about here."

"Ah, sir. Is there anything I can do for you?"

Again that faint flutter of laughter, the recognition of a preposterous incongruity.

"I suppose my need is a bit more dire than yours."

"Is there anyone I can call, anything at all I can do for you?"

"How does your neck feel?"

Though utterly incredulous at this non sequitur, Anton realized now that the snow had built to the point that his neck felt totally numb and he had no idea how responsive it would be to commands. Without removing his eyes from the mutilated man, Anton swatted the ice from his neck for nearly a minute.

"Thank you, sir. Now is there anything I can do for you?"

"Yes, of course there is. Persuade the zealots running around here that I am not Ceaușescu's brother."

Here was an official, a commissar, whom the anticommunist insurgents had accused of wielding undeserved power, living ostentatiously, and surveying his domain with the utmost pomposity, almost like a grotesque parody of the landowning classes before communism. The parallels were so disturbing that they had necessitated a bit of surgery.

"What I meant to ask was, is there anyone I can call to help you in your immediate situation—"

The man laughed, loudly and sharply this time. Nearly simultaneously, there came a hoarse cry from the far reaches of the dank hall. Anton barely had time to turn before a drooling shirtless figure, with hideously jagged teeth and hair down to the crack of his ass, came rushing into the room, clutching a narrow object in his right hand. Anton recoiled, retreated a few steps, but not nearly fast enough. He was aware of a flashing motion and the parting of skin on his forehead. He screamed. With another swift motion, he had a huge gash on his left cheek. The commissar laughed in a low key, taking this all in with relish. The skinny attacker raised the weapon again. Anton darted through the door, up the hall, and out of the building. No sooner had he gotten out into the frigid air than he began wiping his forehead and cheek in an effort to contain the liquid before it congealed into ice.

He could not fathom the distance between here and the road, and he did not care. He might never reach the road. The only distance that mattered was that between him and the structure of socialist modernist design behind him. Anton knew the mutilated man's concern for him had been wholly ironic. He could have warned Anton had he chose.

Anton ran and ran, his feet crunching on the thick white sheet. The pain was so sharp he could think of little but the need to move. But he wished for a mirror so he could gauge the extent of his wounds. He ran, lurched, stumbled, picked himself up, never daring to look back at the hideous structure on the plain. He just knew that he had to keep running, and if he died from the exertion, it was preferable to other possible exits. The ground before him kept vanishing under his feet. It was freezing. He had to negotiate, to plead for every breath he drew now. His thoughts were a jumble and he could not hold to the same course. He zigzagged repeatedly before veering in a direction that felt westerly. In a general way, he was going back in the direction from which the bus had come, or so he thought. Anton ran in this direction for a while before the ebbing, the lack of vitality in every limb and muscle, sundered his control over his movements.

Anton fell face first into the snow. He felt the will to get up ebbing out of him even as the awareness of death's inevitability grew. At length the need for less labored breathing made him rotate his body, which was vanishing beneath the white, until he was facing a distant point where the road might have been. Then again the road might be far behind him. He had no idea anymore. He rotated his body again, this time to take in the full scope of the planet's invasion by the hurtling flakes. The snow did not take the edge off Anton's wounds. After watching the invasion for a while, he rotated his body once again, until his lacerated face was deep in the snow. The flakes made a thickening quilt on his back. Anton lay freezing for agonizing minutes until he felt his awareness giving in. There came a loss of clarity about where or who he was, then an onrush of darkness. The snow built and built, and all around the world was silent, and still but for the millions of white wraiths.

He felt a gloved hand on his left shoulder. Then a pair of strong arms rotated his body until he looked directly upward. His eyes alighted first on the man's cap. It was of a distinctly military style, deep olive with a band just above the visor and a red hammer and sickle on the front. The face belonged to a young officer, no more than twenty-nine or thirty, with a bold clean-shaven face and a look of pity, if not quite tenderness, in his lucid blue eyes. The officer pulled Anton to his feet, seemingly with minimal effort, and then a couple of other soldiers helped him move the nearly lifeless American in the direction of a dark green, thick-plated military vehicle. The vehicle was idling and emitting a bit of smoke into the air around the road on which Anton had traveled by bus at a distant point in the past.

Anton found himself on a back seat of the vehicle. One of the soldiers got beside Anton with a first-aid kit on his lap. Soon Anton's arm was out of his parka and a needle channeled a translucent liquid into a vein. Then the soldier dipped swabs into a little container, reached up, and wiped Anton's forehead and cheek methodically. This went on for about ten minutes as the vehicle moved through the silent landscape, with slivers of white visible through slits on either side. Anton lolled in the seat, his pain finally fading, as the young soldier applied bandages. The ease and lassitude of the vehicle's movement through the province was infinitely calming.

Up front in the passenger's seat, the officer turned back and said something, but to Anton his voice was like water squirting against glass, weak and indecipherable, and Anton liked it that way. He sat there in a state between joy and oblivion for half an hour. Finally the vehicle came to a halt and Anton was once again an object pushed and pulled by strong young men with a tough professional demeanor. Within seconds they had him out of the vehicle. The cold and the snow didn't feel quite so aggressive here. The land was quiet and peaceful. On either side of the road, Anton saw houses, real houses, not the kind of socialist monstrosity where he'd met the eyeless commissar. Here were brick and wood houses with porches, steeples, and spires, houses Anton would not have found out of place in Binghamton, New York. They had an appealing, reassuring homeliness. Here were the residences of real people to whom virtually anyone could relate. Here was a community. He did not know whether the road on which he now stood was the road on which the bus had come. He dimly remembered the military vehicle changing course.

Anton ceased appraising the houses and gazed down the road, to the west. Or was it to the east? Down there, he saw the rear wall of a squat building made entirely of brick except for the shingled roof buried under three feet of snow. One of the soldiers said Anton must not know where they were taking him. Although he was nearly certain this was a joke, Anton shut his eyes as they pushed him over the snow, into the building, through a short hall, and into a room. Anton opened his eyes. He was in the staff room of a filling station. It was a plain room with dark brown strips of oak for walls and a grimy concrete floor. Anton sat in a plastic chair a few inches from the door. He faced a desk where bundled papers and a filthy ashtray rested. On the wall beside him was a calendar with no images, just boxes and letters. For a few minutes Anton sat there alone. Then the officer brought in a cup with steaming coffee and left it on the desk. Anton drank the coffee with immense gratitude though its taste was rather turgid. As the liquid passed into his stomach, he felt parts of himself at last begin to stir again. He alternated sips of the coffee with aggressive rubbing of his hands and movements of his joints. Soon he had his circulation back and would not need the young men to help him move. It was delightful to feel, physically, almost as he had before his ordeal. But he wasn't well yet.

He wanted to sit here in this humble but comfortable place for hours. He felt virtually invulnerable in the care of the soldiers, who appeared to understand his needs exactly. One of the younger soldiers, and then the officer, came back to give Anton more coffee and check that he was warm and cozy. On his third visit to the staff room, the officer chatted with Anton. He wanted Anton to know how lucky he was to be alive, but it was fairly clear that Anton already knew. Without varying his tone, the officer said it had been necessary for state operatives to commandeer private vehicles. It was up to them to organize an effective response to the blizzard, but that was hardly the only reason. The counterrevolutionaries were making all kinds of mischief. They had enlisted the worst sort of men to help them mete out what they felt to be justice against state officials. Felons from the jails, murders, rapists, pedophiles, and child killers who had been in solitary confinement and had not eaten a proper meal in many months, were at large in the countryside.

The officer left again. When he returned twenty minutes later, he had a roll and a plastic container of citrus juice. Once again Anton thanked him profusely. The officer stayed there, talking calmly, while Anton ate and drank. He had questions about Anton's background, which Anton answered without much thought. The officer said he could tell by looking at Anton that here was a young man of exceptional intelligence, precisely the type of man the *securitate* needed in the present state of disorder. There was such a lack of clarity about who was a legitimate citizen and who was not.

The officer reached out and touched Anton's wrist, and in that moment Anton felt something extraordinary happen. He saw the room, the filling station, the whole white landscape fall completely away. Anton saw himself in an entirely new setting. He held a coveted place in a courtroom. Seated at the back of the room, Anton had a comprehensive view of all the men and women who came through the big double doors at the front to plead their case. What struck him immediately was the utter, abject deference in the features of these people. They were so simple, so unlettered, so naked in their wish to persuade him of their desire and ability to obey, if not grasp, the socioeconomic doctrine Anton espoused. The doctrine that had taken root in the country over the course of a decade, but was even now too sophisticated for some. It might have all manner of complexities, but if you failed to get it or failed in your devotion to it, the commissar seated at the back of the room would make a quick decision about your worthiness to live at this point in history.

Anton's strange vision continued. He looked at a man in a rugged farmer's outfit, overalls and soiled boots, studied the creases and splotches all over his face, made a guess as to how many times the man had bellowed and laughed at the rationale put forth in a smoky tavern for turning over the direction of the state to a rarified, Paris-educated intelligentsia. He issued a decision, and two guards in stiff uniforms seized the farmer by either arm and led him outside. Next there came a woman with stringy blonde hair teased with gray, who had urged her five kids to study abroad not in order to become a doctrinaire Marxist, a commissar like Anton, but in order to imbibe what she called the whole range of ideologies. Anton had no doubt that when she hectored her brood about the vastness and diversity of doctrines, she had a target in mind, she wanted to undermine these bright but impressionable young people's sense of their duty in the revolutionary state. It took seconds to decide her fate. Then there came a bearded man in a tweed jacket and a pair of slacks. The restful quality in his dark brown eyes marked him instantly as a counterrevolutionary. The proceedings were over in seconds. Dozens more people moved into the room and met Anton's judgment.

Next Anton found himself in a much larger room, a stark place where perhaps thousands of cattle had died. Flanked by soldiers with epaulettes on the shoulders of their crisp jackets, Anton oversaw the herding of dozens of known counterrevolutionaries into this ugly lot. Here were men and women, city folk and rubes, young and middle-aged and elderly people, all with one thing in common. They were naked. On Anton's command, they parted their thighs to allow a better view of what lay between, stood there in the chill air, rotated their bodies, grasped their buttocks, and repeated the parting motion. Little did they realize that Anton had determined their status in advance, and only they held illusions about what their obedience might achieve.

Anton was absent from the scene that followed, at least in a physical sense. Here was the bohemian sort of café, almost as common these days in Bucharest as in Brooklyn, where stunted flowers and the commingling of classics and paperback dreck on the walls encouraged patrons to question, and to violate, all the assumptions they'd ever held about anything. Here was a man in a blazer and a pair of silk trousers, raising a glass of Ursus to his lips, pontificating to his wife and daughter about the correspondence in which he has engaged with a mathematician in the United States. To some people, the content of the exchange he is describing might sound dull. The man has sought guidance with respect to the literature on a persistently problematic hypothesis. Although he is not yet ready to write a new paper, the fact of his having engaged in an exchange with a scholar in a society where rules and norms of expression are fundamentally different appears to have a liberating effect. The man is talking volubly if still casually to his wife and daughter.

The stranger who enters the café now has nothing in common with the drooling ravenous shirtless men who have plundered the countryside. On the contrary, he wears an olive shirt with crisp symmetrical pockets and a pair of dark slacks conveying seriousness of purpose. In his right hand, he wields a Tokarev TT33 pistol. He quickly aligns the barrel with the scholar's forehead, and then the rear wall of the bohemian café is a tableau of red spray and tissue like so many meatballs cast out of a fancy dish for their ugliness. This assassination, carried out on Anton's orders, helps affirm an authority, a purview, extending over the lettered as well as the simple classes.

Now Anton is out on a plain. The outer reaches of a plain, the fringes where the concrete of a self-important facility gives way to straggling grass and indifferent dirt. Dusk has arrived. There are hundreds of shadows on the ugly barren ground, belonging to naked people who have previously appeared before Anton and undergone the most detailed scrutiny. There are shadows, too, on either side of the commissar. He stands between and slightly behind two pairs of crews manning long, sleek Cugir machine guns. Anton gives a command. All four of the machine guns unleash their contents on the dozens of rows of naked cattle. Screams fill the dull white air as bodies fall with flesh and muscle torn and displaced in infinite ways. Anton feels a bit of distaste at how rapidly the bursts from the weapons cut off all protest, but his work on this gray dull day is just beginning. Under his authority as commissar, the soldiers have amassed not dozens or scores or hundreds or thousands but tens of thousands more naked men and women who have treated the revolution, and the principles behind it, as a joke. At this point in the vision Anton knew that his nasty intelligence was the most fatal element of all.

Anton came out of his reverie in the staff room of the dingy filling station. No one else was there. He got up, flung open the door, ran down the little hall, opened the back door, and dashed out into the snow. Now it did not crunch under his feet so much as grudgingly give way, as if in acknowledgment that it could not last forever. Though Anton could not think in a linear way, he still had memories of the houses on the other side of the road. He looked over there, to the north, and the second building to the right looked inviting. It may have been the least comfortable place in this country, but the blue-eyed officer and his men had no particular reason to expect to find Anton there.

He dashed across the road, mounted the porch, and rapped hard on the door. A blonde teen opened it. In hurried but articulate Romanian, he explained that he had been the victim of a robbery out on the road, he had reported the matter to the police, and now he urgently needed to get down to Berca. The girl regarded him coolly. She could not mistake the gashes on Anton's face. She turned and called out. Her father, a tall thin man with a horseshoe of gray hair, came down the stairs and beckoned Anton inside.

Anton sat in the living room, sipping coffee, listening to the father talk on the phone in the kitchen. Then the father came in and explained that the official requisition of private vehicles was set to expire in the morning, at which point he would be happy to give poor lost Anton a ride down to Berca. Tonight Anton would sleep in a guest space between the girl's room and her parents' chamber.

The hosts went into the kitchen to prepare dinner. As he sat there on the couch, Anton noticed a magazine on a little table before him. He reached for it, turned it upright, and regarded the front cover. A bronzed, shirtless teen from some pop band looked up at him. Anton took in the image for several minutes. It was totally moronic. It was utterly beautiful.

The Envy of Nations

The sun was high over the cliffs to the east when the riders appeared. They came on so fast and furious that it was all the Confederate soldiers in Mesilla could do to rouse themselves, grab their weapons, and take up positions around the town in time to meet the attack. Private Robert Claudel's mind would return often to those moments after the cry came from the wagon at the outskirts of town. Men darted out of houses, ran over to the mules that grunted and milled anxiously in the streets, opened packs at the animals' sides, took out cylinders and springs and levers, and pieced together tiny howitzers. As the noise of the oncoming cavalry drove the men deeper into a frenzy, Private Claudel looked in vain through the dust and chaos for his regiment's commander.

No one had hazarded a guess as to the number of Federals in New Mexico. They were based in the forts along the Rio Grande and at a few points in the mountains, their presence a welcome thing to people afraid of the Apaches. If Confederate Lieutenant Colonel John R. Baylor's dream of new ports on the West Coast and access to the gold lying in the hills was ever to become reality, it would take a shattering rout of the blue hordes, but now the Confederates were wondering whether they could survive the next hour. Corporal Scott Martin was trying to direct the aim of two men who had mounted howitzers on the rampart made of crates, while Corporal Thomas Fleming shouted and waved at several troops rushing up from the center of town. They took up positions and aimed at the Federals, close enough now to tell their age or whether they had shaved that morning.

Private Claudel ran into the hotel thirty yards north of the main street, leaping up the stairs and into a room on the upper floor. As he leaned out the window, there came the hot queasiness no training could have averted. He had never been to an opera, but from his cousin's account of one, the same grandeur was on display below and around him. Way back behind the cavalry, he could make out the pennants and colors of a group of Federals, that just might have included the hated Lieutenant Colonel Edward R.S. Canby, watching and commenting in their urbane way.

The first horses leapt over the rampart and whirled back to face the defenders, who were stunned at how little their preparations mattered. Private Lionel Foster fired his pistol at one of the mares, which reared back on its hind legs and quickly straightened out, allowing its rider to put a bullet through the defender's skull. Two other Confederates fell screaming to enemy fire as more steeds jumped the parapet, and a Cajun kid, sixteen or seventeen, his face streaked with blood from a gash in his forehead, staggered backward and tripped over Private Foster's corpse. The attackers kept coming.

At the window, Private Claudel aimed his Enfield rifle, paused for a moment, and fired. One of the riders' backs erupted, spraying another horse, and the rider tumbled into the dust as his steed lurched. The Union soldier whose horse and saddle were crimson turned toward the hotel and fired his pistol. The round whined past Private Claudel's ear before he processed the fact that he was no longer invisible, fired his rifle again, and ducked to the windowsill, watching three more horses jump over the rampart as a boom came from the distance. Then it was as if one of the houses north of him met the impact of a god's hammer, glass and wood spinning outward in a lethal shroud. Now another twenty Confederates rushed up from the other end of the town, all training their fire on the Federals. In the same moment, two riders fell from their horses and a third grasped his neck, screaming hoarsely. A Federal with crisp yellow epaulettes on his sleeves emptied his pistol furiously before five bullets tore into him. Private Claudel did not see the rest because, just as he rose, another boom announced a blow to the base of the hotel, and the private gasped as splinters raked his face and the ground came up to meet him.

A face glimpsed in these parts might be that of an Apache or a Mexican, or a priest administering your last rites, but was always, irredeemably, a face. Visages that came and went over the bed of an injured man might not hasten his return and readjustment to that alien and hated thing: the world. Private Claudel had met men from the cities whose inhabitants swarmed like so many insects, had talked with those for whom one project would never be complete; a process of stripping down the world from one level of social organization and density to another until the deserts, cliffs, and hills were just as the earth after the floods of Genesis, with no traffic, no debts, no selfish women to pursue the men like specters. But Robert Claudel was no misanthrope. On the contrary, he lived in the hope that the distaste he felt for successive groups of people he had run into would fall away as a new force overtook him, the inspiration of fighting alongside men who displayed traits that the louts and cheaters in the red light district of New Orleans lacked. Serving with bold, decisive warriors, he would feel enervated at the fury with which they rose to meet the blue hordes, and he would imbibe the wisdom of the thinkers who advanced the cause in geopolitical terms. He was hardly one of those ill or suicidal men walking among the professional soldiers of the South. Lying stoically under a gas lamp, the private watched blurs hover over him and vanish. He had suffered many bruises and a broken wrist but otherwise was not in a bad way.

"Lucky dude," said the doctor coming into relief against a background of pain and mangled limbs into which he had just discharged morphine. "We only got so much morphine, and you gonna have to take your pain like a man."

For four days, more blurs came and went, and then the fire withdrew from his body, until Private Claudel was once again able to report to Corporal Fleming. He learned that his side had intelligence indicating that the Federals, having despaired of taking Mesilla or holding out at Fort Fillmore, had set out across the desert toward Fort Stanton, some 250 miles to the northeast. Here was a chance to pounce and cripple the Federal presence between Texas and California.

So the next morning, a train of men and wagons set out for the northeast, Corporal Martin and Corporal Fleming riding in the wagons near the head of the column and the doctor and priest at the rear. The eight mules wore bags full of meat, ammo, and the parts of howitzers. The men's faces bore the sun like a lash as they moved toward the mountains. On occasion, someone pointed out a buzzard, a coyote, or a patch of cacti twisting into a bizarre shape. No one liked to see a coyote, whose eyes were more intelligent than they had a need or right to be. At least there was pretty terrain as the men trudged on, with the cacti segueing into lilac bushes in many places and the green of the sage and the yellow of the creosote forming a visual call and response throughout the valley.

In the growing shadows, near six o'clock on the second day, the men at the head of the train spotted a few figures kicking up dust two hundred kilometers ahead. Privates Claudel, Perry, Gibson, Wheeler, and Sandefur ran up to the three stragglers, who might just have seen a demon emerge from the hills and bite the head off one of their number, so blanched were their looks. When the Confederates caught up with guns raised, the stragglers at first appeared hardly upset at the prospect of trading their agonies for a new condition. When the one on the left reached for his holster, Private Claudel jumped behind him and pulled his arms into an X across his back while Private Perry took the pistol from the Union man's belt. In a distinct County Limerick accent, the soldier blurted, "If ye's goin' to kill me, let me talk to Dan for a minute about my accounts." The other two Federals gazed ahead stonily.

"Never mind, just give me the pistol so's I can blow me brains out," the man muttered.

"Don't worry, we'll find plenty of uses for your brains," said Private Perry. "You look like a freak in one of Claudel's dad's circus acts."

After they got back to the troupe, Corporal Fleming sat the captives in one of the wagons under the ghoulish sheen of a gas lamp, as men organized shifts to gaze with vigilance at the plateau on whose reaches coyotes howled as if speaking an awful prophecy under the circling buzzards.

"Our souls be damned, there's no way we'll perform in a circus for you," said the man from County Limerick.

"Fellow's delirious," the corporal remarked.

"I ain't no lion tamer nor no clown. I couldn't be sad in a controlled way before all them kids, I'd loose the inner freak and invoke hellfire and damnation, sittin' up with me whiskey and wonderin' if the Injun bitch bled the night before and if her man's gonna come and gut me. I ain't prayed much..."

The second man was no more coherent, but Corporal Fleming gleaned from the third, a stout twenty-five-year-old from the Sixth Colorado Regiment, that the Federals had gotten fifty miles from Fort Fillmore when the officers decided to stop. Then something drove the horses wild with terror, a sound from the hills like the braying of a wounded demon, and then the attackers came, the fearsome Apaches, cutting men down and making others dash off in ten directions, the three stragglers being one such splinter. Little groups of Federals, some including a captain or a lieutenant, were still wandering out there.

The detachment that set out in the morning in pursuit of one of these groups included Corporal Fleming, Privates Claudel, Perry, and several others. A few hours into the venture, Private Claudel was already thirsty, but he had to conserve the water in his flask. As he licked the roof of his mouth and rubbed his wrist again, the private's eyes scanned the jagged contours of the canyon. The sun will back down, he told himself, just like a fighter that's been goin' at it all day. After several more hours of marching, the other men looked as beat as he felt. Squinting hard, Private Claudel processed the fact that they were coming to a village, the tiny houses of brick and adobe shimmering in the haze. Corporal Fleming knocked on the door of the first one which opened after a moment to reveal a haggard middle-aged man in a sombrero. Don Mateo invited the party inside and gave everyone a sip of water from a decanter of faded crystal. The reasons for his mournful look grew clear when he told the tale of a raid by the Apaches that had decimated the town's populace and deprived it of the roosters and mules on which its livelihood, in large part, depended. Since the attack, the survivors had been stealing out to patches of cacti, skewering the prickly pears that grew on them, and peeling the pears to get at what few nutrients lay in their cores. His words seared into Private Claudel's mind: Look out over the length and breadth of the valley, you will see gutted homes where miserable women breast-feed the infants who survived and wonder about the months to come. When you engage the Federals, you destroy the dikes that have channeled the red fury away from the towns in this valley.

"My Lord, what have we done?" Private Claudel murmured to himself. Then the host's daughter, Dona Emilia, came in, a lithe young thing with cloths over her breasts and loins and her flesh the color of diluted honey, her face a study in controlled despair. Though Private Claudel did not know a word of Spanish, he sensed well enough what that face had witnessed.

"I promise we will not let them get away with it," said Corporal Fleming. "You and your daughter will reestablish something like the life you had once we've thrashed those tribes."

They thanked the host and filed out of the scene of sadness and hunger. It was not the only time that day that Private Claudel enjoyed the hospitality, of sorts, of a stranger. For after another five miles, the private saw the white house perched way up on the mesa, and being the first to point it out, received the order to go and check it out. Maybe the owner had seen the Federals. He climbed the slope and walked through the dust to the whitewashed front door, which was not locked. Beyond it, smoke drifted to the top of a nicely, but not extravagantly, furnished room. Seated under a moose's head with a huge pair of antlers, a middle-aged man with thin red hair puffed on a cigar and looked at the private coldly. About twenty pounds overweight, and with an unkempt beard, he had the air of Ulysses Grant about him, though Private Claudel, of course, had no idea of his sympathies. A pistol lay on a stand beside the man's chair. He gestured for the private to sit down across from him.

"You fired so many cannonballs at Fort Sumter," the man broke the silence by saying, "and made the Yanks give in quickly indeed. Flushed with that victory, you're taking a long view of the war, wondering how you can barter with Britain and Switzerland for goods and munitions. Cotton is one thing your planters in the Carolinas have in abundance, and you know the Brits crave it, but you think how much more clout you would have with all the gold of California, the envy of nations, sitting in your treasury. That's the logic behind this escapade, isn't it, my boy?"

Declining to answer at first, Private Claudel glanced at the pistol on the stand, the antlers above the man, the musty bookshelves beside him, and the faded globe resting on the mantel between two windows.

"I don't think—"

"Listen, my boy," the man cut him off. "If you ask Stephen Lambert, no one needs you here. The Union men kept up a sort of equilibrium in these parts, and you've wrecked it. I've listened to the arguments of your man George Fitzhugh, and he obviously takes a theoretical rather than an empirical approach to the question of race. God knows, there are so many good and intelligent blacks and so much white scum. I could show you so many of the deviants, the robbers and opium addicts and killers and whores, until you felt sick and cried out and swore you never wanted to see another white face."

Once again, the private began to raise an objection, and the man cut him off. "That gold is not yours, boy. California is not a playground for your motley array of criminals and gamblers and drunks. You will not harness it for trade. You will lose this war, I promise, both for your strategic ineptitude and the greed and viciousness with which you conduct this affair. Come with me to the window, boy."

The window looked out onto a vista where the parched earth receded from the mesa and then grew into other hills several miles off.

"Look out there, look at those hills, you have no idea what's out there. You don't know how long it took me just to learn about Fort Sumter. Maybe the spirit of the North is aroused, maybe the tides have already turned. Is Richmond in flames right now? Or how about Charleston, Nashville, Atlanta? You don't know that your comrades aren't all lying dead at this very moment. You have placed yourself inside a pincer, between Forts Thorn and Stanton, and I guarantee you'll not emerge in one piece."

Private Claudel thanked the host for his time and set out to rejoin his comrades, ambling back down the side of the mesa and finding them very much alive for the moment.

"He ain't seen the Federals. I reckon we're a hundred miles from Fort Stanton." They walked through the still heat with their rifles and pistols at the ready, the sun falling between the bleached crags rising off to the South and the stunted trees at the other side of the valley. Private Claudel thought that if he spoke, his voice would echo into every crevice in which an Apache crouched with a bow and arrows. If he died out here, his existence would be almost like the tree that no one hears fall in the woods, unappreciated except by the vultures, yet his mind kept returning to the urgency of his cause, for Confederate ports on the West Coast were a few prizes among many. The gold would enable the South to unleash massive fire on the blue hordes.

About twenty minutes later, Corporal Fleming found the bullet case.

"Now what did they fire at?" Private Sandefur asked.

"Apaches ain't far," came a reply.

The case had appeared just off the trail, not far from where a slope bore several pairs of footprints, winding up into a chasm in the canyon wall.

"They traded fire with somebody here and took off that way," said Corporal Fleming with a gesture toward the slope.

"It's time we took the fight to those sons of bitches," said Private Wheeler. Some of them would have liked to rest, but the party needed to go ahead before the light waned too much. As they climbed up the slope, and Private Claudel turned over Stephen Lambert's threats in his mind, the tiny sip he took from his flask did not begin to slake his thirst, but made him realize how little water was left. They passed through a tangle of curving weeds and branches covered with sage and made their way through a pass between the walls of ochre rock that seemed to act as a magnet for the heat. With a glance upward, the private realized how easily the enemy could cause the party to suffocate by knocking stones and sediment loose from the top of the channel. The sun was losing its prominence to the faded blue of six-thirty. Though the slope was less steep now, the private still ambled like a human scarecrow. At length, the corridor widened into a grotto where a thin stream ran from far up the canyon's scarred face. Private Claudel and three others went to the stream, cupped their hands, drank, and filled their flasks as the corporal gazed at the empty spaces way over their heads, as if sure something would materialize.

"All right, this way," he declared with a gesture toward a trail leading off in the direction they had been going. They walked for another twenty minutes until they came to the corpse of a Union soldier, the blue cap still tight over the skull from which the left eyeball dangled, while the right one gazed intently. The rotting flesh reached almost to the rifle clutched in his right hand, a defender of Lincoln and the North until his last wheeze. Private Perry reached down, pried the rifle from the corpse's hand, checked it over, and discarded it before the party continued.

"Looks like a jam made all the difference for that poor fellow."

"They were in such a hurry to get out of here," said Private Gibson, "that they couldn't make a gesture toward Christian ritual."

Soon the party came to a plateau where a few lonely trees bedecked with anemic growths of creosote mingled with the cacti. How the Federals must have reeled when they came to this view of the mountains way off in the northeast mocking the idea of escaping to Fort Stanton so many miles off, in a land where shadows took bizarre shapes in the late afternoon and the cry of an eagle reminded you of everyone you had ever hurt. They walked on the plateau until they came to a pool whose streams led back toward the brook they had encountered before. Now it was hard not to retch at the sight of two more rotting corpses, their limbs jerked into odd positions as if they were the puppets of a child with emotional problems, their bloody faces blending horror and incredulity. Privates Perry and Evans began plucking the ammunition off one of them while Private Claudel strode over to the other. It briefly escaped his notice that a couple of small shafts had pierced the Union boy in the arm and rib cage. Upon pulling out one of these and inspecting the blade, the private thought he detected a type of sap on its tip, an amber thickness he could not name. The look on the dead boy's face spoke of unfathomable agonies. Here was a place where the lazy trickling of the water over pebbles and sand seemed to channel all the hellish moments of the white man's experience, all of his fear and self-doubt, into a hypersensitivity to the mocking trivial moments that said *Here's the substructure of all existence. Why not die now?*

No one wanted to linger, but the corporal's curiosity plied the scene for a minute before they began to trudge on toward the forest at the distant foot of the mountains. With growing unease, Private Claudel felt the damp places on the back of his shirt. What if we run into the bulk of the Federal force out here? They moved on through the scrub and the dirt until they spied what looked like a broken-down wagon ahead and tightened their grips on their weapons.

Then came the whistling noises. The first arrow sailed straight through Private Gibson's neck and made him scream and fire his rifle at the sky before he flopped onto his back, kicking wildly, no one grasping what was happening. Privates Wheeler and Evans spun around as the corporal fired once at the trees and bushes, adjusted his aim, and fired again. More shafts flew, and by the time anyone saw the attackers, they had fatally wounded Privates Gibson, Evans, Wheeler, and Sandefur. The cry of a tortured lion, or so it sounded, pierced the air as the warriors emerged from the trees, Private Claudel and the Corporal fired frantically, their rounds tearing up the torso of one attacker. Private Gibson gagged and tried to pull out the shaft that had bisected his throat. Crouched behind a tree, Private Perry reloaded his pistol; another massive exchange followed, at the end of which Private Claudel and the corporal limped off into the bushes to the north of their ripped-up comrades, an arrow staying just millimeters inside Private Claudel's arm for only a second before he yanked it out and snapped it in two. He ran through a thicket of sage and thorns that rent his face and would have made him scream if he were not desperate to elude the Apaches.

Three hours later, he was lying by the side of a mighty cactus looking at the stars, thinking, *Maybe that shell and the first corpse didn't fall where we found 'em! The Feds ain't dumb, they wouldn't have continued in the same direction if they thought they'd strayed into a red trap.* In the dawn he woke, squinted, wiped a bit of the blood off his face with spit, and tried to stare into the distance as the sun tormented him. He tried to rise and sank with a groan, then he drifted off again with his face down, tasting the dirt. When he woke minutes later, the face of Don Mateo filled the whole sky, laughing at him and the rest of the party. Don Mateo, who hated the whites for reasons unrelated to the imaginary destruction of his village. Don Mateo, who had a vision for the future that the private could not begin to fathom. *Maybe I drank the mescaline at Don Mateo's, or maybe it was in the stream, or maybe the shaft brought it home. Or maybe I'm delirious like that Irishman.* Private Claudel was painfully aware of the evils done to both the Mexicans and the Apaches as he drifted off into his dreams. Then he was on a train with his mother and older brother, George, whose hair was darker, but that was not the chief distinction. They stood in the midst of crates and trunks, a squawking chicken on the right and bags of flour to the left, wishing the line would budge. The attendant at the counter up ahead had his hands full selling pretzels and lemonade. The black nine year-old standing just inches from Charlotte Claudel had noticed George's stump and could not avert his eyes from it.

"What happened to your hand?" he asked. George gazed out the window, pretending not to have heard.

"What happened to your hand?" the boy persisted. George turned halfway to the kid and put the stump forward, and the boy took it in both hands, feeling, rubbing, and inspecting it with fervor, as if this was the most fascinating thing he had ever seen, but soon the boy had other questions too, namely whether the absent father was some kind of mutant.

They had a father once, a little, vain, depressed drunk, whose jokes fell on still air and who could not have failed worse in his career as an entertainer.

"I can't stand to be around you," Robert said after his father came home drunk one night, remembered that it was Robert's birthday, and tried to make his son laugh with jokes that the boy had endured before. Robert's words cut the father short in the middle of a line about the donkey and the forty pounds of butter. His father went into the foyer and opened yet another bottle. Yet again, Paul Claudel would drink until he blacked out. Young Claudel retired to his and George's chamber and stared at the wall.

Months after the funeral in March 1859, Robert had a dream in which Paul Claudel appeared in the likeness of an absurdity from the circus, his torso and limbs enclosed in wooden boxes as if he were a kind of robot. He moved with ungainly steps down the street toward the boy, not taking his eyes off Robert as he made a stop, a movement of one unbending leg, then the other, and another pause to master his new position.

"Er, Rob, I, ah, need some time here. But you might get to hear about the bear and the fox, or the hunter and the great big mountain. Just hold on, I might need a hand, heh heh . . ."

The cloud of what Robert had said to his father hung over the man until the sharp bisector came down and lopped off the box protruding forward from the robot's right shoulder, and it clattered to the ground.

"Oh, heh heh, Rob, I might need help here, you know what the hunter told the mountain goat—"

Retreat, said the boy's eyes, retreat from this place. The partition came down again, taking the left arm, and blood spurted from both sides now.

"Er, Rob this, uh . . . you are glad to see me, aren't you?" The dad creature toppled onto its back and flopped several times in the blood.

"Rob, if you help me, I'll tell you about . . . Rob . . . er . . ."

Torrents of blood came as the torso moved spastically and the creature's syllables reached the air. It was about to die, yet its words touched on points so remote from the fact.

"Rob, do you know what made the monkey dance? Rob...Rob!" Now the voice grew lower as blood came seeping down the street toward the boy.

After they buried Paul Claudel, Robert threw himself into drinking, smoking, chewing tobacco, and hanging around at all hours of the night in the red-light part of New Orleans, prey for the denizens of dubious health who reduced the rewards of the flesh to a transaction. Then came the brawl with a kid who tried to talk to Rob's girlfriend. He might have gone to jail if the state's decision to secede had not shifted everyone's attention so decisively.

Once again, Private Claudel tried to get up and sank into the dirt. Even as he cursed his pitiful state, he saw all the Confederacy rising in the form of an angel, spreading its wings and setting out from its perch into an infinity of azure. All of the new nation's might, all of its potential to stride the stage of the world and shake up and trade and wrestle with other nations was here, contained within the spread of its majestic wings, and now he yearned to be a particle of the nation, to see his failures and agonies and humiliations resolved into the soaring glory of the triumphal country, reaching from the beaches of Tidewater, the Carolinas, and Florida to the shores of California, bedecked with the gems of Mobile and Pensacola and San Antonio and New Orleans. The breadth and diversity of it, and now the gold, would furnish the men and material with which to repel those killers and rapists so ill qualified to lecture anyone about civil rights. Then the southern states would go unmolested, its belles would stand on porches sipping wine in the evening as the scent of wisteria drifted on the faintest of breezes.

The next morning, he rose and stumbled through the haze until he saw the pennants flying way off in the distance. They can't dare join the battle without me, the private thought as he staggered through dirt and sagebrush, dimly aware that his wound had re-opened and more blood had left him. But when he reached the twenty Confederates, among whom Corporal Scott Martin stood prominently, they hailed him and handed him a new, clean rifle, and asked if he would accept the honor of leading the charge against the Federal position. Surveying the other brave men in gray, he knew they would have made able leaders. But it was he who led the charge off into the valley, not caring how many shots the enemy fired at him, the thunder of millions of aroused tempers echoing through the vast reaches of sand and sage.

The Reckoning

Charlotte watched in awe as the revolutionaries herded yet another group of well-dressed men, their hands bound by cuffs behind their backs, into the huge rectangular room with cracking walls. The sight was nothing new, of course. She'd watched the day before, and the day before that one, as Marat and Robespierre oversaw the transfer of financial sector professionals into this room and thence to the adjoining cells, but repetition did not dim the impact. For someone who'd grown up in the days of Wall Street's dominance, it was utterly shocking. The Jacobins were in charge now, they were rounding up thousands of white-collar rogues, and no one in the world could stop them.

Back in the early days of Occupy Wall Street, Charlotte reflected, the public never imagined such scenes as were unfolding now. That was long ago! Oh, yes, it was before President Joseph Biden, despondent over the cooling of elation following his victory in the 2016 race, had caved to his own fury at those who'd failed to support him, and had vowed not to deploy the army to protect anyone. It was before he'd disbanded the National Guard by executive order. It was before the police, still brooding over the anti-cop rhetoric that had led to the murder of officers on Mayor Bill DeBlasio's watch, had called a general strike. And it was before the man whose identity was a secret, but whom everyone called Robespierre, had taken over TV and the internet, had begun broadcasting his messages about how things got to this point, and had dumped thousands of guns on the street.

Now Charlotte watched as Robespierre went back outside, leaving Marat to direct the processing of prisoners, with help from Louvet and Brissot. The latter two relied on a corps of clerks, in loose-hanging dress shirts and pants cut off below the knees, to take down the prisoners' personal data and listen to the whining, the futile protests. The revolutionaries who made the arrests had already stripped the captives of items of value, leaving them only with driver's licenses. Cell phones, ATM cards, and credit cards were out of the question, as were photos of family or pets. These white-collar rogues were here to suffer, to provoke their captors into sneers and laughter as they babbled in the idiom of hedge fund managers and law firm partners. Clearly Marat was enjoying himself already. As soon as Mirabeau came in from the courtyard dividing the big room from an empty school, the two leaders began bantering with a cocky air, making many gestures at the professionals. The captives stood with their heads bowed, sullen and miserable, muttering answers as the clerks scribbled on pads.

Once again, as Charlotte studied the faces of these dejected men, she felt an emotion she'd never dare mention creep back. She pitied the captives. She could relate to them, for she wasn't allowed to have a cell phone either. It had been more than three months since Charlotte had talked to her parents, a bohemian artist and dancer who'd begun dressing Charlotte in a black leather jacket and giving her hits from a joint on the stoop of their East Village apartment when she was just eight. She missed her parents more every day, and the fact that they were a twenty-minute walk from where she was now, or at least she believed them to be, fed her frustration. If she talked to Marat about the matter, he'd mutter about revolutionary courage and sacrifice before turning to something really worth his time. Charlotte didn't dare broach the topic with Robespierre. She was sad a lot of the time, but not suicidal.

The revulsion she felt at what she was witnessing grew more powerful every day, yet something tempered it. The radical educators Charlotte had studied under at City University had done an admirable job of clearing away outmoded ideas and assumptions and getting Charlotte to see the world as they did. The indoctrination had been fierce, and relentless.

Now a little object skittered across the floor, away from the captives, and came to rest near the wall against which Charlotte leaned. Charlotte thought she noticed a scuffle going on in the midst of the crowd. No, it wasn't a fight at all, she saw now. One of the captives, a fat man with thinning red hair, wearing a blue dress shirt and a pair of dark slacks, was frantically trying to push and slide his way out of the crowd so he could retrieve the object. He wheezed, cried out, flailed his limbs madly. His voice was hoarse, like that of a submarine commander in combat for hours. The man had severe asthma, and the object someone had kicked across the room was a plastic inhaler. A couple of guards moved to the crowd's flank, denying the fat fellow exit. Charlotte rushed to the inhaler, picked it up, and turned to the crowd. In her peripheral vision, a figure came up so fast that she had no time to react or avoid the gloved hand that closed over her right wrist.

With a cry, Charlotte dropped the inhaler and turned to look into the eyes of Marat, who had been watching the captives' processing from the back of the room. His eyes were the colors of a tsunami, with irises so focused and angry Charlotte feared her bones might come loose at the joints. Now the crowd was in her peripheral vision, so she hardly saw one of the guards sock the asthmatic fellow in the gut. Marat spoke to her, calmly but menacingly, as the fat captive fell to his knees, wheezing and weeping. Charlotte nodded in desperate assent. Finally he released her wrist, moved on to the front of the room, and went outside to catch up with Robespierre.

A few of the captives gently helped the fat man to his feet, talking consolingly. Now Charlotte noticed she still was not unobserved. A young man in the crowd, a slender thirtyish fellow in gray slacks and a white dress shirt with pink stripes, looked directly at her. After making sure that Louvet, Brissot, and the clerks and guards weren't watching, Charlotte made eye contact with this stranger, who indicated with moves of his eyes that she should pick up the inhaler and bring it to him. She looked around again. Louvet and Brissot were explaining things to a cluster of clerks, while the guards made menacing gestures at a captive, a balding man who might have been president of one of the investment banks under the Old Regime, so haughty was his manner. Darting, whirling, gliding across the floor, Charlotte brought the inhaler to the young man, who slid it into a pocket of his slacks and flashed her a wink. With a mixture of embarrassment and the *frisson* of being in on something, Charlotte resumed her place at the wall, just as Louvet and Brissot got done edifying the clerks.

Within an hour, the clerks had taken down all the data and assigned the white-collar captives to holding cells. The rounding up over the last few weeks had not gone nearly as briskly as Robespierre and Marat had hoped, and a couple of factors were to blame. For one thing, the revolution had communicated its aims too early, putting the guillotine to use in public when the arrests were just underway, giving the white-collar people a chance to flee to points all over the country, though they could not go further, what with the borders firmly shut. Secondly, the parties that went out to round up the aristocrats of high finance had acted, at least in the beginning, on a faulty understanding of who the targets were. Naturally, enemies of the people included the heads of banks, exchanges, asset managers, corporate law firms, and global corporations. But one must also understand them to include accomplices, mid- and low-level hirelings, anyone with an interest in the system of exploitation, anyone who acted like a member or latent member of the one percent. This was a great many people indeed. But there was a music to this way of thinking, the Jacobins insisted. Just imagine how odd it would be if a partner of one of the global law firms stood in a crowd such as had just filled this room, under the supervision of guards or clerks who had been associates at the same firm and had worked with the partner, not three months before, on the takeover of the last independent energy distributor in Guatemala.

On the following morning, Charlotte thought once again about her parents. They'd never been well off, never been cheerleaders for the banks, yet she couldn't help wondering what they made of the revolution. They were nice, decent people. She began to recall scenes from her youth in a cramped but cozy apartment in the East Village, lolling on the couch with her dad as he read the Tolkien books to her, sitting in the kitchen as her mom served hot chocolate and asked what she wanted to be for Halloween. She ended up going as a fairy, and the costume her mom made wasn't terribly good. Her parents couldn't afford a fancy costume, but she didn't hold that against her mom and dad. Charlotte knew that not all kids had parents who took the trouble to read to their kids.

One of the clerks, a boy with knotty blond hair down to his shoulders, jolted Charlotte from her memories. He was furious that Charlotte had been leaning against the wall of the huge room in a dreamy state. She sure hadn't been acting like a revolutionary. The clerk told her he sincerely hoped it wasn't time for a discussion with Marat. Charlotte hurriedly apologized. Admittedly, she had neglected her duties. The idea was to keep the white-collar rogues alive long enough for processing and punishment to take place. It was Charlotte's task to bring bottles of water and bags of crackers from the truck that parked outside twice a day to the doors of the holding cells in this big room and on the far side of the courtyard. The truck had now been idling for three minutes.

Charlotte hurried to the front of the room, grabbed a big wicker basket, and went outside. A minute later she returned and began making the rounds with the bags of crackers and bottles of water. Captives in the cells on the left side of the room moaned and whined about their meager rations. It was two bags and two bottles per cell. Only when she got through lots A through C and began to move up the opposite wall, toward the entrance, did she meet a different reaction. At the door of Lot D, the fat man who'd had the asthma attack appeared before her, a wide grin on his face. He thanked her for retrieving the inhaler, which the thin thirtyish fellow had managed to slip to him just before the guards broke them up. Behind him loomed the important-looking, balding fellow who had angered the guards, an inscrutable look on his prim face. Now Charlotte moved to the door of Lot E. To her astonishment, she was face to face with the guy who'd directed her to grab the inhaler. Behind him in the cell, people lay slumped against the wall, weeping or pressing their hands to their faces.

"Hi. What's your name?" he asked.

"Charlotte."

"Charlotte, I'm Phil. Thanks for your decency."

His voice was easy, mild. He did not wish to pry, but he sensed she had secrets, and he was curious. Yes, his tone invited her to stay and talk. Like a startled cat, she hurried off to the next lot without even recognizing what had frightened her.

But the next day, Phil was waiting in the same position at the cell door, his blue eyes calm and lucid. Charlotte resolved not to get scared again, like a silly pet. There were no guards or clerks in here at the moment anyway.

"It's all right, you can talk to me, Charlotte."

"Why do you want us to converse?"

"Oh, well, that was a really nice thing you did the other day, and don't imagine I'm the only one who noticed. I've got this sense that you're not helping the Jacobins because you want to."

After looking around just in case Marat or Robespierre might have glided in here, Charlotte indulged her curiosity and let Phil indulge his. They chatted about the people they'd been before the Revolution. Charlotte talked with remorse about the parents she'd been unable to communicate with for all this time. For his part, Phil described a girlfriend of three years whose whereabouts he didn't know. He made clear that all the captives in his lot were feeling ache and loss. This aroused Charlotte's suspicion.

"Well, now, Marat told us to expect talk of this nature. You're sounding, what's the word, oh, you're sounding mawkish, Phil. Marat told us we must never forgot you're all a bunch of little Eichmanns!" she said.

"Little Eichmanns?"

Charlotte nodded. That was the phrase Marat had picked up from radical professor Ward Churchill and had made more popular. Marat reminded all the guards, clerks, and aides of the crimes that the little Eichmanns had committed daily against the rest of the world until the Revolution unseated them from their aeries in the gleaming towers.

"That's a horrible phrase to use. Take me, for example. Do you have any idea what I did?" Phil protested.

Charlotte shook her head. She guessed it was something pretty terrible, if he was here in this cell. The Jacobins were smart men. Though Charlotte felt compassion toward the captives, it hardly seemed possible to her that they'd be here for nothing.

"I was a financial news editor down on Wall Street."

"Ah, yes. A parasite," Charlotte replied.

"Why would you say that?"

"You dwelt in an utterly exclusive world, manufacturing news to lull people into false optimism about the economy and a state of ignorance about the systems of exploitation and aggression that underpinned this economy," Charlotte retorted, repeating verbatim lines from a talk that Louvet had given to a roomful of young revolutionaries.

Phil had such a ready reply you might have thought he'd rehearsed it for months.

"Charlotte, I was the editor who commissioned a report warning that we'd forgotten the lessons of '08. It was one of the most-read articles on the web for three months, and it had a direct effect on the volume of CDS and CLO issuances for far longer."

Charlotte had no idea how to respond. She swallowed, shuffled her feet.

Phil continued: "And, as to exclusivity, that may be true to a point, but you don't seem terribly interested in the reasons why it's true. Certainly not because we didn't try to expand the scope of our recruiting."

Her curiosity piqued, she looked at him encouragingly.

"Sure, a lot of the people I worked with were the same, rich suburbs, trust funds, the Ivies, the master's programs. But I hired this black journalist, in fact I chose him over six other candidates, against the reservations of people who said he didn't have enough of a news background. I hired him because I liked him. As soon as he started the job, I was mentoring him, teaching him how to write in a more 'business' kind of style."

"Really? What was his name?" Charlotte inquired.

"His name was Kevin."

Charlotte wondered why Kevin wasn't here. Maybe it was just too much of a stretch to tag *him* as a little Eichmann.

"So how'd it go?" she asked.

"Oh, there were people who wanted to cut Kevin loose. But I made sure he stayed on, and I mentored him pretty intensively until his work got better. I was glad I did, Charlotte. Kevin was a little difficult at first, not really welcoming of any criticism or guidance, but I think he saw his work really was substantially improving and I wasn't there to belittle him."

"Oh, how nice. So tell me, Phil, just how many people were there like Kevin in this company of yours?" Charlotte inquired.

Phil had already answered her question. It was purely rhetorical.

"Never mind. That doesn't detract from anything they taught us about Wall Street," Charlotte said, though she felt she was arguing for its own sake.

"I don't know what they told you, Charlotte, but—"

Phil didn't get to finish his sentence. Charlotte was unaccustomed to a captive contradicting a revolutionary with anything remotely like eloquence, and it discomfited her more than a little.

"Now you're going to tell me about food donations and renewable energy projects, is that it?" she retorted, recalling a lecture where Louvet and Mirabeau had drawn attention to the rhetorical tricks of the bourgeoisie.

But as the week advanced, Charlotte could not deny her longing to engage with Phil again, to see whether he really was evil beyond redemption. She pitied the captives. She didn't know who could help them, but she felt someone must. Even now these feelings were at war with her ingrained dislike and fear of what her instructors at the university had called "the racist-capitalist system," and those associated with it. The professors had made Charlotte write over and over, in papers and exams, that once people had fouled their minds and souls by working at a big bank or fund, there could be no redemption.

On the following day, she had barely reached the door of Phil's lot when the commotion began. A dozen guards came in through the front door and streamed to the mouth of Lot A, across the room from where Charlotte stood. One of them produced a big key and unlocked the door, and then the guards were in the cell. As they pushed their way further in, the furious voices of the fallen CEOs and asset managers rose abruptly, mixed with the ringing of cell phones. With a start, Charlotte realized that a few of the rings were just feet away, inside Lot E. As the guards manhandled people in Lot A, the latter tried to connect with their lawyers here in Phil's cell. She heard a few of Phil's cellmates answering and offering counsel. "Ah, no, they can't do that without due process, of course. Calm down. *Calm down.*"

Within minutes, the guards had organized all the captives of Lot A into a file and were moving them out of the cell, through the big room, and toward the rusting metal door leading to the courtyard. Charlotte positioned herself so she could peer out there. As soon as the door opened, she spotted a few of the Jacobins, waiting under a pale sky. Yes, there was Marat, and there was Louvet, and there was Brissot, and there, at the courtyard's northern edge, where the wall of the next building met the chain link fence topped with barbed wire, stood Danton, his blond locks and angular features recalling, to Charlotte, an Aryan athlete more than an intellectual leader of a glorious revolution. Charlotte nearly jumped when Danton made eye contact with her across the distance. The captives moved into the yard and gathered into a cluster at the center, glaring, miserable. Marat fairly drooled with glee.

Not only did Danton have an Aryan appearance, but Charlotte saw now that the leaders had chosen to marry the imagery of 1789 with that of the Third Reich. Far down near the front of the yard, a few feet from the fence, they had propped up a couple of *Machinengewehr*-42, sturdy and polished, ready for duty. The babble and bleating from the herd of captives rose as they noticed these tools of the revolution, and reached a pitch as a couple of guards took up positions at the weapons. Perhaps the Jacobins thought that here was poetic justice for the Eichmanns. The steel door closed. Charlotte sank to her knees and desperately covered her ears, but failed to shut out either the roar of the machine guns or the screams.

She thought, *It must stop!*

On the following day, she had no chance to engage with Phil at all. No sooner had she reached Lot E than Louvet appeared before her in the cold gray, bearing orders directly from Marat. The latter desired Charlotte's presence in a room across the courtyard. Too timid to speak, she followed Louvet through the yard, where they hadn't yet cleaned up all the blood, and into the building whose unknown reaches had intrigued and terrified her. They moved through a corridor painted a dull institutional beige, turned into a perpendicular hall, advanced thirty feet, and entered a large room Charlotte guessed had once been a classroom. Here Marat and the other leaders had assembled a couple of dozen clerks and aides before the spectacle of twenty choir girls, who'd gotten arrested while trying to flee back to their town in Indiana. The girls stood in two rows, watching the assembled Jacobins and clerks nervously, their blue and white uniforms still just barely creased. Marat's eyes were on Charlotte. He flashed her a giddy conspiratorial look, as if to reinforce her grasp that the revolution was many things but was, above all else, an opportunity to witness things you'd always yearned in private to see. The other leaders had proud faces. Only Danton's look was, to Charlotte, unfathomable. Charlotte guessed that perhaps his mind was in that courtyard even now.

But then, quite abruptly, Danton stepped boldly forward and gave orders to the choir girls. At the front of the room, the guards brandished their batons and carbines menacingly. At once, the nice proper girls began to shed their blue dresses with prim white collars and their tasteful leather sandals and black socks. Before they were all fully nude, some of them broke down in confusion and fear. They kneeled or got on all fours, still with a bra dangling from one strap or a sock on one foot, and began kissing, fondling, probing, masturbating each other, emitting shrieks or sobs or the cries of rabid bitches, to the delight of the Jacobins at the wall. The clerks and aides generally enjoyed it too, but the guards kept up a menacing demeanor.

Marat came forward. He'd already grown impatient, Charlotte saw. The Jacobin approached a pair of guards and demanded their batons. Equipped with these tools, he strode imperiously into the center of the room and commanded a pair of choir girls to begin going to work on their cohorts one at a time. The girls screamed as cold metal entered them from behind.

Charlotte thought, again: *It must stop.*

The next day was the day they cleared out Lot B. Now precedent reduced the shock ever so faintly. In contrast to the other day, Charlotte was able to talk with Phil for a bit. To Phil, the course of lot clearances was obvious. Yet he talked in an even voice about the company where he'd worked as an editor, about family, girlfriends, and weekends on Long Island. Charlotte wanted to scold herself for thinking *How fucking classic. He's got the job on Wall Street and the house in the Hamptons.* That reaction was a reflex, she chided herself, the product of all those hours of indoctrination, those days when she'd absorbed so much political correctness that she'd lost all perspective.

She wanted to know more. Phil talked, haltingly at first, then more fluently, of weekends he'd spent at a house by the beach, in the company of his girlfriend and two other young couples. They'd frolicked in the waves rolling up on the beach from Long Island Sound, had drunk wine in cafés in the picturesque town nearby and on the porch of Phil's house, and had danced late into the night to reggae or zydeco or jazz or even, when the mood took them, J.S. Bach. One of the guests, a guy named Andrew with unruly red hair down to his shoulders, drank way too much, but it quite violated the spirit of these get-togethers for Phil to say so. At times Andrew sat there all alone on the porch with a bottle of merlot or malbec or champagne, drinking and breathing in the scents of the ocean and the wind as the others sat on pillows inside watching the last quarter of a game. The others were indulgent. There was something about the way Andrew reclined there on the deck chair, his head lolling with infinite serenity toward the scuds of cloud scoring the monotony of blue. He'd escaped from life in a way others wished or pretended to but rarely did. When they all went down to the beach to frolic, the women grew increasingly bold, removing their tops more and more readily. They laughed and frolicked and mock-fought in this place of amber sand and blue.

The water was full of mines. Lacking a boat, they couldn't sail anyway, but that was okay for now. They never even felt the temptation, so acute in the past, to drive three miles along the coast until they came within view of the skyline, shimmering, radiant, inviolable. No one wanted ever to return to the city. There came the news on TV and the appearance of a fluttering cloak at the most unlikely places in town. They kept up the leisurely life until one afternoon when Phil picked himself up from a cushion, walked out the back and down the steps to the beach, knowing that Andrew would want to know why no one had brought booze around for hours now. Andrew followed Phil down to the beach, sand getting caught under his toenails. For a few minutes, Andrew spoke clumsily, pleadingly, as Phil looked out at the waves. Andrew grew irritated at his friend's silence, not knowing that Phil had been in town earlier in the day and had seen something quite odd through the window of a little antiques shop, a man in anachronistic dress standing in the middle of the sunny street.

Finally Phil turned around and gazed past his friend toward the edge of the dune, where not a person, house, or vehicle was in sight, just a long ridge of sand with a quality of fading brightness, with blades of grass that swayed and rallied with the light winds.

"I'm sorry, Andrew. We can't see the city from here, but you should have figured it out anyway."

"Huh?"

"I'm sorry, Andrew, but they're here."

Charlotte was still pondering Phil's account the following morning. It could not be long before the Jacobins resolved whatever clerical issues stood in the way of clearing the remaining lots. If Phil was to share anything else with her, it had to be soon.

She thought: *This is not a better world. The killing and the mistreatment must stop.*

The next time Charlotte went to the door of Lot E, she found Phil in the company of a fellow in his early thirties, with trim black hair, wearing a pair of John Lennon spectacles.

"Good morning, Charlotte. Have you met Sol?" Phil ventured.

Here was a journalist, like Phil, but with a more cerebral air. Charlotte doubted that Sol had spent quite as many weekends getting drunk and stoned at the beach. She could more easily envision Sol playing chess in a park with bearded retired professors, or talking existentialism with them. Sol was no fool. He was aware of the effects that exceedingly didactic talk have on the listener. At the same time, he'd spent years studying modern Europe's history at a post-graduate level. In an even voice, Sol talked to Charlotte for a couple of hours about the origins of 1789 and the histories of Mirabeau, Louvet, Brissot, Danton, Marat, Robespierre, and a good many others, and he compared this history to what was going on now, dwelling with urgency on one question: *When would Danton become Danton?*

Charlotte had to reflect on this question before it could even begin to make sense to her. But, in time, it did.

She thought: *I don't want these men to die. The killing and the mistreatment have to stop. There has to be a way. There has to be a way.*

On the next morning, punctual as trash collectors, they cleared out Lot C. Now there were thirty-nine fewer parasites, crooks, little Eichmanns, or whatever term one might prefer. As the morning advanced, Louvet interrupted Charlotte's routine again, relaying an order from Marat. She must appear, now, in the classroom across the yard.

Once again she walked in on a council of supreme Jacobins. In Marat's eyes she saw a flickering, irrepressible light magnified several times since the choir girls had sex here. Danton looked as youthful and ready as ever. Louvet and Brissot were not youthful or attractive. Charlotte moved to a position at the front of the room, amid the clerks and aides, a position affording a clear view of the fifteen Boy Scouts in the room's middle. It was a long way from Salt Lake City, and these troopers, who had come to Manhattan to visit Ground Zero and the 9/11 Museum, would never pray in an LDS church again. They were here and the Jacobins aimed to have a bit of fun.

One of the captives, a pudgy thirteen-year-old, dressed in the familiar tan-colored uniform, stared at Charlotte, fuming at the impudence of *her* staring. His closest pals, a pair of eleven-year-old boys, stood a few feet behind him, glaring over his shoulders at the audience. Yet another of the captives was about twelve, a tall and lanky youngster with trim dark hair, whom Charlotte mentally tagged as Alfalfa, though he lacked the disobedient lick of hair. These youngsters had testosterone roiling in their developing glands, they were not so timid as the last captives herded in here. They were willing to fight, but they knew there could be no resisting the phalanx of revolutionary guards brandishing batons and carbines, watching without remorse.

Marat, the master of ceremonies, stepped forward. In one hand he clutched a saber, and in the other an axe. The pudgy scout, his two pals, and Alfalfa regarded the Jacobin warily as he advanced to a point near the middle of the room, paused, then with a flourish tossed the weapons in the air. Everyone watched them land with a *clang!* No one doubted that the captives understood what was to take place here, but they were unwilling to begin. Marat nodded at one of the guards, who came forward, raised his carbine, and shot one of the pudgy boy's slender cohorts neatly through the forehead. The victim had not hit the floor before the guard turned his carbine on Alfalfa. Screams and cries filled the air as a dash for the weapons began. Alfalfa got his hands around the hatchet and, in moves nearly too fast to see, decapitated the fat boy's remaining pal. But the fat kid had training, too. He seized the scepter and swung furiously at Alfalfa, cleaving paths through the dry air, left to right and right to left, making Alfalfa retreat until he tripped backward over a boy who lay on the ground, weeping, clutching his palms to his ears. Alfalfa got up and tried to move away from the cluster of flailing limbs. Within seconds, clumps of his brain decorated the nether parts of the room.

Fighting to keep control of her bowels, Charlotte dared not move. All around her, spectators whooped and cheered, but she knew how fast their manner could change. She calibrated every twitch of their faces, every rotation of their eyes. No, she must not move. Once again, she thought: *The killing and the mistreatment have to stop.* Marat decided they had a wonderful spectacle going and it was time to exploit the opportunity. With a gesture at Louvet and Brissot, he gave the order for the choir girls to come in here from a nearby room, and join the fray.

On the following morning, Charlotte spotted Danton lingering at the front entrance of the huge room. With a glance at the clock above the door, she made a quick assessment. Boldly, decisively, Charlotte walked up to the strapping blond revolutionary and bid him good morning. He turned to her with an indulgent look. What could this child want?

Charlotte began to talk to him in her loose melodious voice. She reminded him of times when he'd never dreamed of being Danton. She brought him back to the years when he was a semi-employed "artist" living in SoHo, drinking wine in cafés, hanging around with her father on the benches at Sixth Avenue and Houston on the edge of the huge basketball court, drinking beer in brown paper bags. They loitered for hours on those benches, sometimes with their kids present, more often not. On one of the former occasions, Charlotte recalled, the man who would become known as Danton pointed out to her a smartly dressed chap ambling up Sixth Avenue, and said, "See him, Charlotte? That man is a partner at a corporate law firm. What it takes your dad a whole year to earn, that fellow makes in a few days." Charlotte had heard the awe in the pre-Danton's voice, mingled with something like envy.

Most of the time, Charlotte didn't mind not being with her dad and his friend when they sat there on the benches amid litter and grime. One exception was Halloween. How she'd enjoyed watching from atop the benches as the thousands of revelers in their freakish glory advanced up the avenue. Every member of the parade was a catalyst to a bright girl's fancy. Her eyes lingered with a voyeur's relish on every member of the Beatles, the Stones, Led Zeppelin, U2, REM, the Grateful Dead, Aerosmith, Journey, and dozens of other bands, on Leatherface, Michael Myers, Freddy Krueger, Jason Voorhees, Chucky, the Terminator, Lara Croft, every character in the Star Wars universe, and hundreds of less-known characters from assorted franchises, one-offs, and rip-offs. There were radioactive mutants, ghouls, corpses, witches, ghosts, aliens, robots, and androids without number, there was Zeus, the Pope, Doctor Who, Charles Manson, Hitler, and Harry Potter, there was Buddha, there was Beelzebub, there was a man inside a giant penis costume (at least she assumed it was a man), around which women swirled with flailing and fondling gestures. More outlandish than all the above, there was Bernard Madoff, yes, Charlotte was sure she saw him, flanked by a Wookie and a Klingon, ambling up the street with a knowing grin. *You thought I was in jail, huh, folks?*

Curiously, the spectacle had provoked a serious discussion between Charlotte's father and the blond man whom the world would soon know as Danton. Charlotte's father said that Danton hated a lot of people. This parade had a message, he continued. Although some of the costumes had violent themes, that message was really one of tolerance, it had to do with people's right to be whatever they chose, be fucking Bernard Madoff if that's your calling, part of what made this country wonderful was its infinite capacity to accept such diversity, the real kind and not the p.c. kind, to have the Devil and his succubi walk arm in arm with the Pope. Rarely had Charlotte heard her father speak with such eloquence or conviction about any topic. The pre-Danton's counter-arguments were half-hearted, and everyone knew it.

Now, as Charlotte recounted that discussion, it had a visible effect on Danton. The young man's brash manner began to crack. He paused, tried to respond, stuttered, mumbled, shut up again, looked at his feet, gave voice feebly to his annoyance. Why was Charlotte tormenting him now with this recollection? He was Danton, a leader of the most glorious event in modern times. Ignoring his protests, his manifest and rising insecurity, Charlotte tortured him further with accounts of the choir girls and the Boy Scouts. She saw, now, that Danton, beautiful blond Danton, was crying.

"Charlotte, I'm *so* sorry—to you and your dad. Maybe there is still some way I can help people?"

She reminded him of the fate of the lots. Three were empty, three left to go. Danton was someone the other Jacobins would actually listen to.

And so, on that day, Danton became Danton. When the guards moved to the door of lot D, the last one they had to clear before they got to Phil's lot, Danton planted himself before the door, giving them a fierce look. Charlotte observed the scene through a crack in the doorway of the women's restroom, at the back of the vast room. She watched as the guards yielded before this great figure's insuperable authority. A few of them began to apologize for trying to do their job, and one of them wept.

Then, at the edge of Charlotte's vision, the fluttering of a robe disrupted the stillness further down. Marat strode up to the cluster of people outside Lot D, followed by an entourage of clerks and gendarmes. The looks he cast at the Danton, and at the guards who'd yielded before him, could have melted iron. He gave curt, indignant orders to his gendarmes. And so, indeed, Danton became Danton. Guillotines are bulky, inefficient instruments, but they did not hesitate now to put one to use. It stood just blocks from here, in a deserted park. The instrument was so much truer than the *Machinengewehr*-42 to the imagery of 1789.

Danton's head had barely rolled into the basket when the clearance of Lot D proceeded.

When Charlotte next spoke to Phil, he had quite unexpected news.

"They didn't get all of our cell phones, Charlotte. There are places in the body they never bothered to look."

"So what, Phil? I can't imagine whom you'd talk to or what difference it could make," she said.

"Charlotte. Not everybody believes in what the Jacobins are up to. I don't think *you* do. But I mean on the outside. The Vendée uprising has begun," Phil replied.

"What?"

"We have someone out the outside. One of the gendarmes. He's one of the handful of people left in the world who don't believe you should kill those who disagree with you, and he's extremely distraught over all the massacres. This fellow is going to bring a pistol to the street corner outside. This is the only chance to save my life."

With hardly any deliberation, Charlotte agreed. She would do it. She'd assassinate Robespierre and the revolution would fall apart. Though she'd hardly ever seen Robespierre in person, she felt such loathing for him at times that she felt she could kill the Jacobin with her bare hands.

At dusk, Charlotte reminded herself that she could now measure by hours the time before the clearing of Lot E. By now, she reflected, enough people had died to make up dozens of the parades she'd watched as a little girl.

Charlotte crept to the front of the big room, opened the door tentatively, and peered out at a barren dimming street. The air had a dull depressing quality, making her think of the rehearsal for a funeral. She moved outside, looking around nervously. The first time her head turned up the street, westward, toward the Hudson River, her gaze was too fleeting to take in the figure lingering under the street lamp near the corner. Turning again, slowly, cautiously, with gathering dread, she saw him. Here was a young black man in a gendarme's coal-colored pants and deep green tunic. He looked at her intensely, almost accusingly.

She stole up the street toward him. The transfer took place without a word. The gendarme fled toward the river. Charlotte held the object aloft in the waning light. With this fleeting encounter on a dusky street, she was more powerful than at any point in her sad thwarted life. She moved onto the street running north to south, parallel to the river. There was a time when she could easily have recalled the *ancien régime* name for this street, but the Jacobins were renaming everything and preserving dated memories would have been disloyal in the extreme. Charlotte moved into a space below a window of the building where she'd witnessed the fate of the choir girls and Boy Scouts. She wanted to caress the .45, to smell it, to lick it, but in her peripheral vision there came the terrifying flutter of a cloak. She held the gun in both hands behind her back.

Marat appeared before her. He began to speak accusingly, spittle flying from his mouth. She knew how insolent her presence here was. She knew he would never understand, she knew there could be no question of corrupting him and that left her, Charlotte, with one course. The blast reverberated throughout the empty streets as Marat staggered away, fell to his knees, and pitched backward like a mummy in which all the natron had cracked and come apart, his face gone below the nostrils. Charlotte slid the pistol into the right front pouch of her trousers, turned the corner, and walked back to the front entrance of the vast room. With immense relief, she saw on opening the door that the room was as vacant as when she'd left. She stole across the floor, alert for the presence of Robespierre, until she reached the women's restroom at the back. Inside the restroom, she fished out the .45, pushed out the swivel top of the trashcan, and buried the weapon under paper towels and tampon wrappers. Then she went into one of the stalls and passed a good twenty minutes there, thinking about things. Even in her paranoid and terrified state, she doubted anyone could link her to the slaying. Charlotte thought her act would not prevent the clearance of Lot E, but she dared hope it would buy Phil a bit of time. She emerged from the stall and ventured out into the room, to find that Mirabeau, Louvet, and Brissot were assembling guards and clerks and issuing orders with an urgency one might associate with an impending bombing raid.

Charlotte moved to the door of Lot E.

The cell was empty.

She finally knew by what margin she'd underestimated the speed and skill with which the Jacobins could move when they perceived a threat.

On noticing her, Louvet commanded her to move to the center of the room. He spoke in a cool voice.

"Greetings, Charlotte. As you may already have heard, there is rank disloyalty somewhere among us. There may be all manner of rumors and slanders going around, and I truly don't know how susceptible you may be. At this point I would like you to surrender yourself to comrade Brissot."

Brissot, who had not yet become himself in the sense that Danton had become Danton, took her aside. She didn't really feel intimidated by the slightly pudgy middle-aged man, who might have been a meister at poetry slams in the years before the revolution. Charlotte was wondering about Robespierre. She saw now that her audience was not with Brissot alone. Louvet and Mirabeau and one of the others—was it Fabre, or Sieyès perhaps?—restrained both her arms as Brissot, brandishing a syringe with a translucent liquid inside, spoke to her.

"Comrade Charlotte, I don't know the extent of your awareness of this drug. It hardly matters now. I want you to think about the instruction you received at earlier stages of your life. Nothing else matters—forget for a moment that you are in the midst of a revolution."

"W-what is the name of this drug?" Charlotte asked in a weak voice as she felt a prick in her right arm, followed by something cold creeping through the arm.

"This is a new, experimental form of propranolol. It is a memory suppressant. The extent of the suppression is entirely dependent on the dose," Brissot answered.

"Propra-*what*?" Charlotte asked as the alien substance spread further inside her.

"*The same question!* I thought you received information lucidly," Brissot retorted.

Charlotte went out into the yard and sat down. She found she could remember the last few minutes well enough, but if she tried to go back further there was a gap. The gap went only so far. It was the *recent* past she was losing hold of now. Scenes from many months ago were still quite vivid to her, but not the last few weeks. Well, they wanted her to recall her university days. She began to remember the lectures, the rows of yearning minds behind eager eyes in an auditorium where a stern middle-aged woman in spectacles moved back and forth on a stage, delivering her lessons in a searing voice, pausing to allow the graduate teaching assistant a moment to change the slide reproduced on a large screen. At times the images were of corpses in the aftermath of a bombing raid in Quang Tri Province, juxtaposed with images of western-owned tea plantations, and at times the images captured the devastation visited on inner-city Detroit by the abandonment and neglect of the parasitic white-collar elite, as the professor put it. She liked to fill the screen with data conveying the vast, apparently unbridgeable gulfs between the wealth, education, and longevity of demographics X and Y. Virtually anyone you know is a permanent member of X, the professor maintained. How Charlotte had begun to loathe those the professor described as white-collar scum, prim villains who'd flooded the market with toxic securities and denied others economic stability so that they might buy a third house in Montauk. When the students left the auditorium, it was all they could do not to assault anyone on the street who reeked of pampered parasitic status.

Charlotte's conversion to the professor's views had not been instantaneous, of course. On one occasion, Charlotte had dared raise her hand and voice questions. Had the banks *wanted* to loosen their underwriting standards? Was it conceivable that the banks had felt pressure, from the Justice Department and assorted interest groups, to extend credit to those who would otherwise never have qualified? The room was silent as the pair of spectacles on the stage fixed on Charlotte. The question was irrelevant, the professor replied in a particularly nasty voice. The only real question was who benefited and who didn't. Then the professor used a dreaded, lethal word. What was Charlotte, some kind of conservative?

This molding, this fixing of Charlotte's consciousness within narrow parameters was all she could think of now. Thoughts from later periods of her life foundered and died.

Now that Charlotte had received her dose of the radical new form of propranolol, she was ready to be a responsible, dependable revolutionary. It was time to serve Robespierre, they told her. Charlotte fairly jumped.

The blond young clerk who'd blown up at Charlotte when she'd grown dreamy the other day escorted her across the courtyard. The grip of this boy's hand above her left elbow was painful. He said, "I swear we're going to find the dog who killed Marat." He led her into the school building and through a series of halls to a room she'd never seen before, a large and ugly room with rotting yellow walls and a dusty tile floor. Charlotte wondered why they'd sent her to an empty room. Perhaps these were the last moments of her life?

Robespierre appeared in the doorway. She realized just how long it had been since she'd really seen him. He looked bizarrely like a cross between a bum on the street, and one of the retired professors with whom she'd imagined Phil's cellmate playing chess. He wore a pair of baggy black trousers that fell to his ankles, which were inside cracked leather sandals, and a black pullover that could hardly contain his rolling, sagging gut. Robespierre's belly literally dangled a couple of feet from his silver-buckled belt. His arms, bare below the elbows, had so much hair you might have thought him a character in a sci-fi film, mutating slowly into an ape. Even indoors, he wore a pair of dark shades above his droopy cheeks and pouty, inquisitive mouth. Coils of silver hair swung on either side of his large head. As she watched him move into the room, Charlotte was prone to an impression that Robespierre's fingers never moved individually, but in pairs or triplets, like pincers. And his voice! When he greeted her, he managed to sound haughty and coarse at the same time.

Finally, Robespierre explained why she was here. A number of the choir girls who'd entered a melee with the Boy Scouts the other day were, amazingly, still alive. Charlotte was here to give them an example of the revolutionary ideal to which they must aspire. But first, he had to decide which of them were fit to go on living, in this enlightened age. The blond clerk and a pair of guards ushered ten choir girls into the room, then left.

Charlotte thought, *No!* She couldn't recall the content of thoughts she'd had in the past few days, and she knew these girls were representatives of a bad dead order, yet the scene made her uneasy. Though the girls varied widely in height and figure, they all had huge, terrified eyes. Charlotte's unease grew as Robespierre explained that part of the measure of these girls' fitness to live was their ability to fulfill needs of his that had gone unsatisfied for many months. Everyone grasped his meaning practically before the words had fallen into sequence in the air. When Robespierre's shirt and pants were off, Charlotte saw that his gut was even bigger and droopier than she'd realized. Robespierre went to work on one of the girls, a small, timid lass who could not have been more than eleven, stripping her naked, licking and biting her face and ears. If the girl said anything, Robespierre was slurping too loudly for anyone to hear it.

Charlotte's body jerked at a semi-conscious impulse, an instinct of revulsion, but she held her position. Blessedly, the shaggy gray head in the middle of the room did not turn. Charlotte knew that even though her memory of huge blocks of the recent past was noise and fuzz, she couldn't accept what was happening here. The lectures she recalled so vividly had never fully wiped out a need, an urge to help people in states of trauma and terror. She could do it! Charlotte remembered the gun. She could run back to the ladies' room and retrieve the weapon.

No—she'd never make it there and back with the gun.

But she must try. Was there any chance?

Robespierre turned his drooling visage to her.

"What are you standing there for? Help them disrobe!" he bellowed, in a voice so ferocious Charlotte feared for her life.

Charlotte set to work removing the tasteful blue and white dress from a slender twelve-year-old with long amber hair. Robespierre sucked the nipples of his victim for a bit, then pulled his penis over the band of his underpants and began teasing the edges of her vagina with it.

Charlotte thought: *I could still do it. I could get the gun.*

Sensing hesitation, the leader of the glorious revolution and the new enlightened age turned again, and commanded her to get to work on the choir girls still in clothes. His voice, at once hoarse and shrill, nearly made Charlotte's water break.

She knew she had better obey. There was no question of resistance anymore.

To drive the message home, Robespierre turned his head once again and croaked:

"What are you, girl? Are you some kind of *conservative?*"

The Diversion

Max Rose, a frustrated stand-up comic, and Al Duchamp, a failed film director, stood in the drizzle outside a bar near Hollywood and Vine. The tourists had thinned out. The Marilyn Monroe and Rudolph Valentino impersonators had gotten into a bit of a turf war before they and the other nostalgia merchants had packed up and vanished. You would not have expected the purple Cadillac that pulled up to the curb to belong to such a personage as Reid Hamilton, the multimillionaire, but they saw that Reid was in the passenger seat, beside a driver they didn't know. On the back seat was amateur actor and stuntman Steve Rawls. The comic and the director climbed in beside Steve, then the car made its way out of Hollywood, in the direction of the hills between there and Glendale. As the car wended its way through tracts of claylike soil, the drizzle tapered off, and Reid lowered the windows with the push of a button, allowing in a scent from the clusters of manzanita shrubs and the flowers. Soon the air was as crisp and lucid as the evening when Steve first saw Rachel Getz, his beautiful girlfriend. Happily, Rachel did not know what he was up to; as far as Rachel was concerned, Steve was at one of the libraries cramming for the realtors' exam. Reid never introduced the man driving the car, nor did anyone think to ask.

The Cadillac drifted to an exit ramp leading to a curve so tight you'd shoot right off the road if you didn't check your speed. When the road evened out, the men in the car enjoyed a view of Glendale's downtown, such as it is, a barren place where a tiny figure sauntered out of the old Alex Theatre, but otherwise no one was visible, even in the pavilions of the cafés. It still looked every bit the frontier town, with the multicolored columns and domes of the Barnes & Noble and other chain stores in place of barns and saloons. The car veered away on a side road to the north, moved along for a few minutes, then turned east again, the road's altitude creeping up, then leveling off. Here and there were gas stations, crumbling churches, and houses that Steve found a bit creepy, with their rickety porches and air of sad desolation. The car made a right into a cul-de-sac at the end of which loomed a long building occupied by a tavern in the front, and in the remaining parts, by stables where people could sign up during business hours for horseback tours of a few of the vineyards.

"Here it is, the ass end of the sack," Reid said.

The others got out and followed the rich man toward the entrance of the tavern, where a Budweiser sign flickered in one of the windows. In front of the building, rocking on his heels in the breeze, was a man in cowboy boots, dungarees, and a yellow button-down shirt too déclassé for even an L.L. Bean outdoor catalog. He had dirty Hitler-style hair, and had not shaved in a few days. When Reid was within spitting distance, the man said, "Hello my good man, thank you for coming out tonight."

"At ease, Chalmers," the millionaire said.

Everybody strode into the tavern. Al, Max, and Steve couldn't hide their surprise on finding that the bar, tables, chairs, and dart boards took up only the first third of the building. They'd imagined there was probably a big dance floor occupying the middle of it. But Reid led them directly through a door between the end of the bar and the western wall, so that soon they were standing in the stables, their senses assailed by the straw and dust and manure and piss. In a few of the stalls, horses neighed plaintively. The director, the comedian, and the stuntman followed the hedge fund executive all the way to the back of the place, where wooden posts demarcated the bounds of a ring of some kind. A sextet of overweight men in undershirts leaned against the edges of the ring, as gleeful as boys who'd found a copy of *Penthouse* in a basement. Steve and Max surveyed the scene with morbid curiosity; Al stood there and gaped.

"Cock fighting don't cut it no more," Chalmers said.

"No, it doesn't," Reid concurred.

More spectators trickled in from a door in the back, laughing and smoking, men began slapping bills down on the crude railing, and someone brought bottles of beer from the tavern and passed them around. The air grew hazy as the men smoked and drank and spat into the straw. In the stables, the horses weren't making a fuss now. To them, what must happen, must happen. Al, Max, and Steve exuded an air of nervous uncertainty, but for the moment, the novelty of the experience trumped other reactions. With impatience the others whooped, swore, called out to Chalmers, beat a tattoo on the railing.

Now there moved into the ring two men clad only in boxer's shorts. One of them was bald, with a dark mustache and beard, and stood at least 6'1". His opponent, a Russian with tattoos of serpents on each shoulder, made up in muscle mass for any disadvantage in height. The tall man looked calm. The Russian leered and seethed with a feral light in his eyes. For a minute, they stood there eyeing each other at opposite ends of the ring. Then Chalmers raised a starter's pistol, paused portentously, and fired at the ceiling. A few horses neighed and whinnied and kicked the doors of their stables. The two fighters began to circle each other, warily, tediously, as if they must constantly size each other up, lest they miss something about the other's intents and abilities.

"Come on, come on," urged Reid. Al and Max watched intently, as did Steve, but his look contained something inscrutable.

Still the fighters circled each other, until both seemed to decide they could test the patience of those who'd bet money on the match no longer. The tall man swung at the Russian, who raised his right arm just in time to check the blow, then, molding his left hand into the shape of a claw, slammed his opponent in the nose with all his force. He'd acted in the hope that the pain shooting through the tall man's nervous system would provide a window in which to land a second, more painful and disorienting blow with his right arm, but the tall man staggered backward briefly, then lunged at the Russian, pummeling him in the face with both hands. The Russian staggered back a few paces, jabbing his fists upward as if trying to swat flies, until he changed tack and tried to knee the opponent in the groin. The bald man responded with a kick that sent the Russian howling and dancing on his unhurt right limb like Lucifer with a cleft foot, until his adversary punched him in the head so hard the spectators could practically hear his brain cells scream and disperse and try to regroup at a remove from the pulsating agony. The Russian did a spastic jig, spun, fell on his ass, and the bald man joyously took the opportunity to kick him in the face, splitting his lip wide open. *Those tattoos!* Steve thought. *Those damn tattoos. He's so proud of all they signify.* The shorter man spat about a pint of blood, moaned pathetically, and was just beginning to get up when Chalmers moved into the ring and separated the fighters for the next round. Spectators cheered, money landed and moved around on the flat surface of the railing. Reid was getting a delightful *frisson*, while Max and Al kept up poker faces. Steve looked on with an ambiguous expression.

In the next round, the Russian's performance picked up a bit. It was as if his brain had gone into an emergency default mode, and he hammered at his opponent as ruthlessly as he could manipulate his body into doing. The bald man tried to make his retreats look like considered, tactical moves, but he appeared to be recoiling from the fury of the man he'd humiliated. The Russian drove a right hook under the chin of the bald man, followed up with a blow to his abdomen, all the more powerful because unanticipated. Outside the ring, men jeered, blew smoke, slammed bottles down on the railing. Reid cheered, he urged the underdog on, he pretended not to notice when Max and Al exchanged glances. The railing shook as a few of the watchers began pounding on it, jumping up and down in glee. But now the bald man, who had nothing to lose by holding back, landed a hook on the shorter man's jaw which made him stagger backward a few feet. Although not ideally placed on the opponent's nose, the blow made him gasp and spit blood and try in vain to collect himself before the bald man could land another blow. This the larger man did, catching the Russian on the right shoulder, but before he could follow up with punches on the chest and face, the Russian lunged again and did something wholly unexpected. He locked both arms around the bald man's right arm, and bit furiously like a famished animal that knows it will die if its prey jerks away even one more time. The bald man howled, howled again, then he was screaming, as blood mingled with his opponent's saliva mottled his chest and his pants and the straw on which they danced. The watchers hooted and roared. Again Chalmers moved into the ring and separated them, brandishing his starter's pistol as if he would no more hesitate to put down a man than a rabid or crippled beast. Reid looked on exultantly. Max exchanged another look with Al. They saw Steve lean over to Reid, but they couldn't make out any of the exchange between the amateur actor and the executive.

In the third round, the opponents moved slowly, as if pain had reduced their animosity to the studied repartee of a ballet. Surely they could never justify circling, and circling, and circling each other, the onlookers thought. Everyone watched to see whether they had the guts to engage. The bald man's face was streaked with blood, the smaller man's, coated with a cold sweat. They continued to circle, drawing groans, sighs, and finally jeers and curses from the watchers. Finally, engage they did. They understood that they weren't both going to walk out of there.

"Come on, now," Reid prodded, clutching his beer tightly.

"God deliver me," Al said.

Pain appeared to have disoriented the larger man, who lashed out with a punch that might have knocked the other down if he hadn't dodged it. The Russian, not inexpert in fighting, expected that a blow initiated from a greater height or distance would lose force on the way to its target. After whirling out of range, he charged his opponent yet again, hammering him with punches at close range that knocked the wind out of the lumbering giant and made him teeter and lurch and finally drop to his knees. Though cognitively impaired, the Russian recognized the opportunity. Bloody spittle flying from his mouth, he hit the bald man so hard on the bridge of the nose that splinters of bone might have broken away toward the latter's brain. The watchers screamed and laughed and cheered as more blows fell on the bald man's face, and then the Russian kicked his opponent in the abdomen, following up with another kick that got his foot partly tangled in the opponent's shorts, which began to shred away at the foot withdrew. The bald man was silent as if he were praying. Leering, drooling, the Russian moved in. The next blow split the bald man's forehead wide open.

"Hold it," someone said. Everyone ignored him.

"Hold it for fuck's sake!"

Now Reid and a few others turned their heads. It was Steve Rawls. He was smacking the railing with the flat of his hand and beckoning for the attention of Chalmers.

Reid leaned over to Steve and said something Max and Al couldn't hear. Then Chalmers walked over to the blond man, they exchanged heated words, and Steve turned angrily and walked back toward the tavern, Chalmers watching him coldly, pistol in hand.

The bald man lay face down in the straw, but the Russian was just getting started.

When the match ended, Chalmers and a couple of others went into the ring and began to sweep up a bit of the bloody straw. The next pair on the program were a Korean and an Armenian. But before the match began, Reid reached with annoyance into his pocket and pulled out his ringing cell phone. Al and Max saw him nod and mumble into the phone with irritation before he snapped it off and announced he must leave. There was trouble with a business associate, they gathered. They expected to see Steve Rawls out on the lonely roads trying to thumb a ride, but Steve had called his girlfriend to ask her to come pick him up. Rachel, who knew quite well he hadn't been studying for the realtors' exam tonight, had actually thought of Steve as old-fashioned and chivalrous in the best sense of those terms, as a gentleman. Now she knew better.

Scott Jensen's father would have been proud of his promotion by the LAPD to the rank of captain, if the father, who had also been a cop, still lived. The elder Jensen had gone off to Vietnam when Scott was only two. Just a few months into his tour, Ralph Jensen trod on a land mine and the blast sheared away both of his legs up to the knees. Ralph came home a seething wreck wishing everyone around him to feel as miserable as he did. He did not get to see his son grow up, for just over a year after his return, they found him slumped dead in his wheelchair from an overdose of morphine and antidepressants. One of the toughest things for Scott to accept was that it wasn't the Vietcong who had taken away the brave, strong, kind, funny man Ralph Jensen was. Setting the land mine that destroyed Ralph's legs was the work of troops from the Republic of Korea, allies of the United States who had failed to coordinate their operations with American units. Irrational though it was, Scott Jensen at times could not help feeling a twinge of loathing when it came to Koreans in general. One thing that might have endangered his promotion was his way of parsing emergency calls and bulletins to see who or what was in danger. Otherwise, he was an effective cop, with dozens of felony arrests to his credit, who deserved his promotion. Now his purview included Glendale and a swath of the land to the north and west.

He believed he could do a good job of protecting the people in his jurisdiction. It wasn't their fault that cops got so much rotten publicity, what with cell cameras capturing everything. Now there was a furor over the beating of a parolee, Jermaine Wilson, by a couple of UCLA athletes after Wilson tried to steal their car. If a grand jury failed to indict the athletes, there could be riots. The incident had not directly involved the cops, but could potentially strain relations further in a number of neighborhoods.

When the captain first heard, through an informant, about the use of a tavern in the hills above Glendale as a venue for drugs, hookers, gambling, and fighting, his first thought was *Who the fuck cares? If people want to do stupid, self-destructive things, that's their right.* What just killed him, and a lot of other cops he knew, about cases like this one was that you could shut down the illegal operation without too much trouble, but you wouldn't touch those behind it. They lived way out in the Valley, or in affluent Los Feliz, Silver Lake, Hollywood, or West Hollywood, or in the hills above Hollywood. Pornographers, dealers, and other entrepreneurs who wanted to save on their rent were taking over real estate in Koreatown and other choice parts of Mid-Wilshire. Captain Jensen buried his face in his hands, cursing under his breath, with no idea why he was about to risk his life once again. But fuck it, a job's a job. Once the police had gotten a judge to issue a warrant, Captain Jensen organized a posse, diverted three squad cars for its use, and set out with his men into the hills in the modest light of six o'clock.

Many cops say that their experience when responding to a call or acting on a warrant is never what they expected, that they never find people screaming and pointing at the bad guy as he comes running out into the street with a bag of loot in hand. Even so, these officers were in for a shock. The cars rolled into the dusty cul-de-sac, where a pair of men, one of them dressed like a cowboy in the Winslow, Arizona, of 1935, and the other in a green tank top and black shorts, sat playing a card game at a wooden table in front of the tavern. When they saw the cop cars, the man in the tank top gave a friendly wave, not appearing the least bit alarmed. The cowboy said something to his friend, got up, and strolled into the tavern as nonchalantly as if going to get a beer. As the police climbed out of their cars, the man in the tank top rose, babbling, gesticulating, as if he wanted to correct the notions on which both the cops and the cowboy were acting. As he ran toward the squad cars, a succession of flashes at one of the front windows heralded bullets that grazed the man's shoulder and punctured the windshield of one of the cars. The man in the tank top spilled onto his stomach, letting out a cry that people at the outdoor cafés all the way down in Glendale might have heard. Already the officers were returning fire with their service pistols and shotguns. They shot furiously until the flashes at the window ceased. Captain Jensen grabbed a megaphone and bellowed at the man inside the tavern that he must know the futility of any course other than immediate surrender. They waited, and waited. The captain repeated his demand, but Chalmers was not done trying their patience. On the captain's instructions, one of the officers fired a canister of tear gas through the remains of the front window where the cowboy had fired at them. Though the cops well knew that a canister heats up as it releases gas, they never could they have expected what this action triggered. First plumes of smoke came through the window. To their surprise Chalmers began firing again, though surely he could not see his hand in front of his face, let alone see the cops. Then a creeping miasma of orange diluted the purity of the whiteness, then came a moment of utter silence, and then there came screams from inside as the flames swelled aggressively into all corners of the house. *Those screams!* thought Captain Jensen. *There's something about those screams, like agony in the heat of an orgasm.*

The captain heard horses neighing, wailing, screaming, jumping, kicking hard against the walls of the stable. He ordered one of his men to move furtively around to the back of the stables and let them out. Thanks to his quick actions, only one horse died that day. When it was safe, they pulled the blackened, smoking shell of Chalmers out of the tavern. If Captain Jensen felt any remorse, it was only because the incident was like one he'd heard of in Miami where a tear gas canister used during a standoff led to a deadly fire. Years later, the cops involved in that incident were still in a legal mess.

On the following morning, cops forced the self-important executive, Reid Hamilton, through a perp walk in front of dozens of cameras. The reporters got only one comment from him. Reid turned with irritation to a microphone and said, "It's easy for you to stand there and judge me. I'd be a poor host indeed if I never gave my guests what they're after."

Captain Jensen, following close behind, heard the remark.

He thought, *I swear, if there's a riot over this Jermaine Wilson business, every fucking bastard in Hollywood and Los Feliz can burn!*

The Ordeal

"Go ahead, *auteur*, make your move," Max Rose said.

It was Saturday night. Max had proposed we meet up and have a real L.A. adventure. It's a town full of social pretensions and some folks, creative types especially, are comically averse to risk, he'd told me. We were in a club on Pico that gave a bit of a *frisson* because it was on the edge of dicey areas. All around us were kids in ripped jeans and t-shirts with logos of bands I'd never heard of, plus a smattering of middle-aged folk who'd never parted with the scene. Though it wasn't late, a stranger had already approached me and asked whether I knew anyone who had coke. He was a clean-cut guy on whom a denim jacket, dungarees, and two days' stubble looked almost like a Halloween costume. I shook my head and thought *Good luck, officer*. Maybe he'd happen upon a dumb kid yet, make an easy arrest. In the center of the place, the crowd was growing slowly. The place had a retro style so bands on the loudspeakers included The Fixx, The Eurythmics, Duran Duran, Men at Work, and mid-'80s U2. As I looked past flailing limbs and around the room, I tried to make out who the softer targets out there might be.

Max, leaning against the railing of an inside terrace between the entrance and the dance floor, repeated his dare. I strained my eyes. Some of the forms were hard to make out at this remove, but I took in a girl with long blonde hair tied up in a pony tail, wearing a white t-shirt and a pair of mauve trousers, gyrating across from a fellow in a dark suit with a yellow tie who struck me as a doofus, with coarse features and a head of untamed black hair. Heaven must smile on the guy who gets to know that girl during the daytime, I thought. She's pretty and unpretentious yet smart with a cynical edge. A few feet from them, a redhead in a white short-sleeved ruffle blouse and green trousers danced with a young man

216

in a red and black flannel shirt and tan trousers, and next to them was a Latino couple in t-shirts and jeans. I figured most of the unattached women were probably not on the floor but fetching drinks or chatting with their girlfriends on one of the three terraces. Rather than take Max up on his dare, I fought my way over to the bar where a guy in a white Jack Wills blazer and shiny black pants filled glasses with amber liquid. From all around me came sounds that made everyone feel seventeen again, on the edge of a magnificent unknown territory.

For a while I competed with others for his attention until I noticed a woman about my age with frizzy dark hair and features like a softer and more feminine Sigourney Weaver, standing there patiently with bills in her left hand lolling on the counter. I stared at the back of her head as she watched the bartender, craned my neck forward ever so slightly to sniff that frizzy hair, withdrew, tried to think of words to say to her. I came up with something totally banal, leaned toward her again, and spoke but the music was so loud, she gave no sign of having heard me, and I felt ridiculous and didn't try to talk to her again. After getting two drinks I moved off in search of Max near the front of the place but I couldn't find him so I downed both of the beers and then decided I really did have my fear on a leash. I moved out to the floor and danced in an exuberant way while taking care not to be obnoxious to any of the couples I came within reach of. Somewhere within these walls there had to be a girl who liked *auteurs*. I moved around the room. At one point as I made the circuit I felt a couple of fingers pinch my ass, but even as I turned the bodies around me had shifted and there was no question of seeing who'd done it, I just knew that one of the girls here thought I was hot. One of them, somewhere. I danced in a way I'd perfected at parties at USC, rotating my limbs behind and above and around me with alacrity. I slid through the throng, conscious of when the skin of my hand brushed a girl's thigh or ass, scanning the length and breadth of the place for Max. Once again at the side of the floor close to the bar, I whirled to look at the pretty young things so naked in their lust and joy. And once again I began to engage in my moves, my practiced whirls or gesticulations. A few inches from me stood a brunette, wearing a black sweater with the sleeves rolled up to her elbows and jeans that she'd bought maybe three days ago, ever so slightly worn, hugging the contours of her ass. She didn't have a partner. At points nearby on the floor were a

Vietnamese girl in a frilly pink and white smock and a black mini-skirt, and a man in his early forties who resembled nothing so much as a hedge fund manager determined to cut loose. A few Asian and Hispanic kids filled up the remaining space at this end of the floor. From the speakers came U2: "*So we're told this is the golden age / Gold is the reason for the wars we wage. I want to be with you, be with you, night and day.*"

I got myself another beer, returned to the floor, with a confidence I hadn't felt in many months. Navigating a course through the twisting bodies, I thought I saw someone who might have been Max, whirling and swinging his arms well out of the scope of his glasses' tiny but distinctive rectangles. Before I could zero in on his face, the guy turned away, and so I spun once again and maneuvered to the very edge of the floor. There I began to twist and gyrate and set my body on a course of continual revolutions, as fast my feet could go without losing my balance, in a mime of the actions suggested by the blaring backbeats and five-cord progressions. I spun and I spun, clutching my beer in my right hand, and spun some more. The music was ecstatic. At this point my feet felt so light that I could have taught choreography to a roomful of pupils unselfconsciously. When I looked up, a blonde girl in a blue sweater rolled up to her elbows and a pair of dungarees was pressing her face toward my forehead, studying me with interest if not exactly mirth.

"Are you o.k.?" she asked.

I tried to say something but she had already retreated several feet and begun whispering in the ear of a woman in her early thirties who resembled a dressed-down attorney, in a flimsy light brown blazer and a skirt that hugged her knees and buttocks. That woman nodded and looked at me with a strange grin. Then a guy in a white dress shirt with the collar unbuttoned and chinos leered at me with a big smirk and said, or at least I think he said, "You dancing alone? *Coooollll, man!*" He gave me a mock thumbs-up. Suddenly, I couldn't bear to think it but no other possibility asserted itself, I had a suspicion that it was he who'd pinched my ass before. I started to say something and that was when I felt someone kick me hard in the right buttock. When I whirled around I faced a couple of dozen young people, smirking and grinning at each other.

I found Max talking to an earnest-looking girl near the terrace closest to the entrance. When I insisted he drive me out of here immediately, he seemed only faintly annoyed. We walked out and slid into his Mercury Sable. He asked whether I'd enjoyed myself. I said, "Get me the fuck out of here." Max didn't seem at all in a mood to argue as he eased the car out of the lot and east on Pico toward the Harbor Freeway, but he did venture to ask whether anything about the club didn't agree with me. I looked at the man in the driver's seat. He was a stranger with a nasal voice, oily black hair, and a couple of days' stubble. I really wondered who he was. No, it was silly to think that. He was Max Rose, the comedian, the toast of the Strip, and it was in his nature to be playful and ask probing questions. He'd given me a hard time for being just like my millionaire chum Reid Hamilton on a certain level, and really like all people who party in their youth and explore their sensual nature, as the phrase went, before settling down and starting a family in Sherman Oaks or Placentia or wherever. To Max, they were captives of cozy domesticity. Max had ridiculed me for living a life with none of the edginess I wanted my cinematic work to project.

"Just get me the fuck out of here!" I repeated.

He gave a bit of a shrug, gazed out at the streets with shuttered warehouses and shops in an orange half-glow from poles at intervals of forty feet.

"Do you have to work tomorrow?" Max asked.

Now we were moving onto the Harbor Freeway but were turning south instead of north.

"No, of course I don't. Tell me what you have in mind."

"What do you say we get to know each other a bit better."

"Oh, I get it, Max. Everyone knows the stage performer, the comedian who likes to light up the room with his playful irreverence. But behind that façade—"

"No, I mean it, man. Whatever happened to you back there, just put it out of your mind for a minute and listen to me."

"Okay."

"There is a music to the wilderness to the east and south of the places where you willingly set foot."

"You're wasted, Max."

"No, you're drunk, and your tail's between your legs."

He asked whether I thought the highway patrol would be out in force tonight, but he didn't really seem interested in the answer. We were cruising south now on the Harbor Freeway faster than I would have liked but still just within the limit. I resolved to lay back and let Max take us where the action was. We were passing through a student-heavy neighborhood, and thirty or forty yards from us on the freeway were moving heaps in which dark shapes leaning over glowing consoles, on their way home to apartments shared with stoners and deadbeats where, I imagined, the next knock on the door would be as likely to come from the building superintendent and a city marshal as from a dealer. As we moved further south the other cars were fewer and fewer. Then onward we sped through neighborhoods that might officially have been gentrifying, but where the smattering of whites tended to work as perennial extras or waiters looking for film work or as the dreadlocked clerks at cannabis clinics. Both of Max's hands lay slumped on the lower half of the wheel and I began to think his foot had dozed off. As we barreled ahead, I felt that awkwardness that had come over me in the early part of the evening when I thought how little I had to discuss with him and how odd a prospect going out with him was. No, I must not think that way. I made small talk. I veered from asking him for his lawyer jokes to encouraging him to tell me about his family to asking him to slow down a bit, a request I repeated moments later. He said that if the cops had to spit out chunks of donut and work for a change, then so much the better. Time to get this party started.

"Come on, Max, cut the speed a little, will you?" I asked, breathing heavily. Seriously now, I didn't need to get in trouble on his account. Applications at some of studios had a clause asking whether you had a record. If yes, please explain.

"You do plan to use this car again, Max?"

His unresponding eyes fixed on the freeway, dark with splotches of yellow that made other cars look lurid and turned grins into leers. His hairy hands did not twitch.

"Just slow down a bit, o.k.? I'm not going to help you pay for a ticket."

He grinned without mirth.

"You sound a mite nervous there."

"I'm really not."

"Apologies, then, amigo."

"Look, take it down to forty, would you?"

We slowed a bit as we came within sight of an exit ramp, but Max's eyes just narrowed ever so slightly behind their rectangular magnifiers and then the speedometer climbed again as we shot past the ramp. I figured that we had cruised south of Vernon, Slauson, Gage, hell we were probably below Florence Avenue by now. Wherever he had in mind for us to go, it better be good. I pressed him but he mumbled irritably and I felt like a little kid. I didn't know how to talk to him. No, indeed. Right now he looked like nothing so much as a grad student who'd defended his thesis for three hours before a trio of advisors. Soon to my relief he began nudging the car in the direction of a ramp. We didn't pass anyone, and no one crept up behind us. Finally we got to the ramp. For a couple of minutes after we came off the freeway into a plateau of widely spaced single-story homes and little shops joined by ramshackle outdoor loggias, he drove us around the block a couple of times as if trying to orient himself. Then the tires shrieked as he cut around and took us east on a broad avenue, I guessed at first that it was Rosecrans, where the lamps cast cones of orange over identical radiuses of dust and danger over an infinite longitude before us. His foot was crushing the gas pedal now. It might not have been Rosecrans, it might have been Elm or one of the other parallel streets. Or a place far from any of them. How little I knew of my own backyard. He pressed harder now. The Mercury screeched and sped while in my peripheral vision something, a kitten maybe, darted out of the street and into the unfathomable blackness of an alley between two squat shuttered heaps. I leaned back in my seat, feeling kind of queasy like when a kid in the 8th grade with whom you once had a wobbly acquaintance steps out on a windowsill, grabs the criss-crossing bars, and leans into the wind. There was still time to make a loop and circle around to the entrance ramp to the freeway. Now Max pounded on the gas and I stared hard at him. Who was this stranger and in what show or performance had I or anybody ever seen him? I knew then that he'd long ago made an assessment of me. As the Mercury accelerated on the uncomplaining concrete, I thought at first that a kid would run out from between two cars or buildings and get creamed and within seconds we'd have a mob after us. But the streets were a bit like a city in the weeks after mardi gras, their silence saying *So much for all that*. We were doing sixty now. Then sixty-five.

221

"For fuck's sake, you'll get us both arrested, you know that, shithead? Please, Max, turn around and take me home."

I castigated him some more, pleaded, then fairly begged, but he ignored me. As the sheen of the dashboard pulled at my eyes, I felt a runny sensation creep over my forehead. My palms were damp. I looked, really looked, at the man next to me. That grin came again, like when someone puts a disc in a player in a roomful of extended family and the movie turns out to have a blowjob scene in it. The car was going even faster, incinerating the rubber, shredding the CV boots. How obviously he'd written off ever using this car again. My ass shifted painfully in the seat and I was sweating really hard.

"Oh no, I think all the cops that patrol these parts must have got us on their scanner," he muttered with a tinge of loathing in his voice.

"There don't seem to be any cops around here, Max."

"You're damn right there don't."

My ear for sarcasm wasn't what I thought it was.

"Max, would you slow down just a bit?"

"No."

"Just a little? Please?"

"No sir. My Rosemobile."

You can't argue with a five-year-old, I thought. I was going to die. The low dingy buildings skirted by on either side of us. His hairy right hand gripped the wheel with the defiance of a 1980s delinquent who has broken into an arcade after hours. We gathered more speed, and more, and more, and I felt my sphincter tightening. In my bowels was a mass not content to go either up or down, but something must happen to it soon enough. On how many occasions, I wondered now, on how many evenings onstage when his lines had fallen on silent space, would he have killed to be where he was right now, hurtling through streets that minded their business, in near perfect darkness, his sole audience unable to bolt?

"You had a little too much to drink there, fellow. I accept responsibility. Slow down. Come on. Slow down a bit, okay? Please?"

"No!"

My resolve not to beg died spectacularly as we shot past nebulae, galaxies, universes of dingy stucco storefronts, rusting fences, shuttered warehouses, and weed-filled lots. I was sweating like a man burying a corpse near a road at midnight. My hands gripped the seat. I knew if I peered at the speedometer I'd shit myself. I started to glance, jerked my eyes away. I pleaded some more with him but he stared at the hood and the two cones of light before us. Yes, he'd made an assessment of me the moment we met. I was so slow, mentally, that I'd thought he kind of liked me. In my mind, I began compiling an inventory of what I had with me, thinking of what I could use to puncture Max's throat, or his eyes if I could rip those glasses off him. Just maybe, I could. I'd have to be quick though. Get something into one of those sockets and use it as a lever. That was the trick.

"Please! SLOW DOWN!"

"Shut up."

"What's wrong with you? I asked politely."

"Shut up."

"You want me to shit myself, is that it? You want the satisfaction of seeing a grown man do that?"

"Correct, sir."

He grinned again. My fingers pinched the sides of my seat as we shot eastward on the erratically lit street. I was alone in the universe with this stranger. It was so unfair, how well he seemed to know me. Once more in my peripheral vision I caught a flurry of movement, too quick for the mind to pin anything on it, off in the luridly warmed darkness to my right. The black regions between buildings were longer and more frequent now. We were not on Rosecrans after all, no, but on an ever remoter back road somewhere, I decided, and there were only shuttered warehouses in the area. If I pitched my body to the left and got my hand on Max's door, if I did it fast enough, maybe I could ram him out of the vehicle. Maybe. But he'd resist and even a tick or spasm of his right hand would jerk the car out of its trajectory and then we'd clip a fire hydrant and ram into the metal sliding mouth of a garage and flip over a couple of times before exploding. What would my eyes, my senses know at the heart of that nova? I began to imagine headlines. I realized that at such a moment as this, others would have coolly reviewed who was in their will and how much they had saved where. But a shifting in my intestines overwhelmed all such thoughts, and I found myself debating the merits of just letting it out, for the part of me that would have felt embarrassed was at the bottom of a mine somewhere.

I screamed.

"*FOR GOD'S FUCKING SAKE SLOW DOWN! WHATEVER POINT YOU WANTED TO MAKE, YOU'VE MADE IT! I PRETEND TO BE DARING BUT I'M A CAPTIVE IN MY INSULATED PRIVILEGED WORLD! I'M A MISERABLE TWO-FACED DILDO-LIKE SON OF A BITCH! MAX—*"

Max grinned as if he'd sprung the most unexpected punchline in the history of humor. Already I was getting hoarse. I hadn't wanted to acknowledge the damp feeling at the tip of my privates for what it was. It had been such a quick discharge, neither foreseeable nor preventable. Kind of like hair loss, it was inconceivable until it happened, then there it was. I thought if he grinned one more time, then my life just might be worth watching him die. In that matted, shitty black hair I saw every kid who'd ever mocked me from a passing car. Perhaps I could get those glasses off, and the most vulnerable parts of his head would blink nakedly. Maybe, just maybe, I could get something in there and use it as a lever—but now I could feel the car accelerating yet again.

I reached into the left pocket of my tweed jacket, and with a movement so swift I don't think either of us saw it, took out a metal object and pressed the barrel of it against Max's throbbing right temple.

"Stop the car or they'll be vacuuming your brains off the upholstery."

Now I achieved what is beyond most people I know: I made a comedian laugh really hard.

"Hey. Very silly. That isn't necessary. Put it down and then we'll talk about my career a bit, okay?"

"Is that what this is about, you miserable cocksucker?"

"No. But I thought you could be one of those directors who's sort of a paternal figure for the people he employs."

"I could, Max. I could."

As I lowered the silver cigar holder that my millionaire chum, Reid Hamilton, had given me weeks before, I felt the velocity of the car begin to slip infinitesimally, as if gnomes had begun to lean on the pistons and levers under the hood. We finally slowed down. We slowed a little more. Further still. Then, as if to thwart anyone who might be after us, Max made the car dart into a side street, turn east and south again, and proceed south for a couple of minutes. The concrete was barren. All around us in the night the palm trees were still amid the drabness of a place I wanted to call Compton. But surely we were well east of there by now. We'd left Compton in the dust and wound up in a place without a name. I began to say something to the driver in almost a civil voice but checked myself. I was still panting, all right.

Part of me was expecting Max to plow into the first pedestrian we encountered, but at last I saw that there was a plan behind all the movement. Max guided the vehicle around another corner and then pulled into the half-full lot of a squat brick building painted a deep brown and surmounted with wavy arches like a film-set reproduction of an 1875 town hall. He grinned at me as if to say, *Betcha didn't know about this joint.* We climbed out of the car and I followed Max inside, moving kind of robotically. I wanted to cut his throat but he had the keys and I'd never make it home. This place he'd brought me to wasn't at all bigger than it looked from the outside. On the contrary, a claustrophobic feeling came to me. Here were rickety wooden tables and chairs, a bar running along the southern wall parallel to the street, the smoked rim of the counter elegant yet blunt like the barrel of an old Enfield rifle, and a plastic mat and microphone for entertainers opposite the entrance. People at the tables were hunched over, minding their business, and for a moment I thought perhaps it was one of those places that flip their identity every dawn and dusk, perhaps only gamblers were welcome here at night. But when we sat down on stools near the middle of the bar, the forty-four-year-old Hispanic lady behind it smiled and served us, if not promptly, then at least not with outright contempt. I wrung an agreement out of Max that if he was going to drink more, I was the driver for the remainder of the night, even though I was a bit wasted myself. That designated driver stuff seemed like a clever ruse. I was going to impale him. Take one eye, then the other. Max leaned toward me, reached out his right arm, and clapped me on the back like an obnoxious uncle at a reunion who wants you to know he's decent underneath it all. It was so smoky and dusty in here and I briefly had the feeling of languishing in a domain of *bandidos*, in a bistro. No, that was ludicrous, I decided. How far they all were from anything like that, how hopelessly remote. All around us I caught bits of chatter in Spanish or in a gangsta lingo, a phrase here or there but never a sentence. Perhaps for a price someone in here would do what I needed done. Now Max referred to the occasion on which we'd met a few weeks before.

"You didn't have to drive all the way out to Riverside County just to meet Reid Hamilton in person, you know. He's got a place above Hollywood and he's at the studio in West Hollywood two or three times a week," Max remonstrated.

"Yes I know that, Max."

"Good way to ruin things with a guy like that is to act desperate," he said, gulping down beer.

I could have done without this. Over at the end of the place a singer was getting ready. I sensed how rude it would be to banter, but Max kept at it:

"I suppose you're going to tell me you lived in too small a world. Talk about false modesty—"

"Oh, get off it."

He grinned again.

"My man, this town's been under the sway of the CGI franchises way too long. We're gonna bust that monopoly wide open."

"Are we, Max?" I said in a tired voice.

"Shhhhh!" someone hissed from one of the tables.

The singer, a girl of about twenty-three with flesh the color of tupelo honey, in a blue and scarlet shirt with a drooping neckline and worn dungarees, began crooning something by the great Lucha Reyes, I think it was "El herradero." Although Max kept quiet, his lips were twitching with what he'd suppressed and once again his eyes were alive with a knowingness that was not at all pleasant. As was inevitable when I heard a song so beautiful, I began to think of contexts denied to me, but I checked myself. There was a criminal here. Maybe a couple of songs into the act, when the girl had everyone mesmerized, I'd look around and find something I could thrust into Max's throat, I thought. But then I doubted I'd have time to reach into a pocket and grab his keys before they jumped me. There is so much blood inside the body and when spilled it has a way of running where it must not.

The girl's voice was the kind that is so easy to listen to because it practically sucks the listener into other contexts. As she moved into "Traigo un amor" and "Juan Colorado," we had a second and a third round. I went to the men's room and had to apologize twice to people at tables as I stumbled past. I made sure they heard me when I apologized. Back at the bar, I very much doubted Max could get up on his own. When he once again began to talk, I dragged my finger across my lips. His mouth remained shut but that intelligence played about his pupils. I was nearly out of cash at this point so when we slammed our empty glasses down, just as the girl was starting on "La Panchita," Max took out his wallet and fished out bills. As he was paying, I snatched his wallet off the counter and looked at the surly face gazing up from the driver's license: a guy with unruly black hair that he didn't try to comb because that would be like putting all his thoughts in a little box, and glasses that did not make him look charming, as glasses often did for others, but rather too inquisitive. You'd expect to see this guy playing chess in Washington Square Park with retired philosophy profs as the bums and dope pushers looked on. Well there was one opportunity he'd never get. No sir. When I handed his wallet back to him, I saw that he'd gotten us tequilas. It was at about this point that I noticed that seven or eight people had come in and sat down at one of the tables near the entrance. They were from one of the black sections of this neighborhood and moved with the ease of people who came here fairly often. I found something almost fastidious in their look, but I could tell how poor they were. They gazed at me. It was a look you got when you took a wrong turn and detoured through rotting houses and trash heaps. They whispered to one another. I couldn't tell whether the impertinence of our being here was amusing or not. Now as I reached for the tequila on the counter, a Hispanic man bumped into me, hard, on his way between the tables and bar. He didn't apologize. Hammered, I decided, and thought about something else. Although it registered only in my side vision, the eyes of those newcomers fixed on me to the point I wanted to bellow and throw something. But they kept on looking, and looking. In another setting, I would have turned to them and barked, "Something wrong?" Yes, in another setting. Instead, I bent toward the counter, sipped my drink far too often, and pretended not to notice them.

Max and I toasted our collaboration. The director and the comedian. He gulped down the ochre liquid in his cup, flipped it, slammed it dramatically on the counter. Heads turned at this. Smoke drifted toward the ceiling and again I had that sense of being in a bistro in a country that loathed Yankees. We talked a bit longer until Max managed to get up on his own and stumble past the tables and the stage in the direction of the john. When he was gone, I overheard a number of the patrons talking about an incident somewhere out there in the night. Unless I was mistaken, which was possible in my state, the new arrivals who'd been staring at me had left a party where someone got into a shouting match and got shot. Around this place, people were looking with interest at the sole seated white person. The bar was small and compressed by infinite distances all around and damn if I could name a street or neighborhood anywhere around us or say what neighborhood we were in. Now the fellow who'd bumped into me, a middle-aging man in a weathered flannel shirt, jeans, and leather boots, slammed into me again going the other way. This time he turned, making eye contact, but rather than apologize, he said he was collecting tips for the performer.

"Well, now, maybe you are and maybe you aren't."

He studied me, taking in my features for the first time, not with anger, but with a bit of interest—*wellwhat do we have here?*

I shifted a bit on my stool, made eye contact with him, blinked, raised his curiosity another notch.

Everyone in the still and remote place was watching now, everyone. Naturally I couldn't see behind the counter now, but the woman was eying the gringo with loathing.

The stare-down continued. I didn't know what calculations took place behind his eyes. Slowly he began to nod, and then to turn toward the space behind him. The other people here were waiting for his word.

I withdrew the silver cigar holder, dangled it before this menacing stranger's sad eyes, flipped the top, pulled out a bill, and dropped it into his rough palm. He stared at it. He stood there for maybe two minutes, just gazing. I don't think he'd seen a $100 bill in a while. Others were staring. More where that came from? I gave myself about five seconds before they rushed me. I picked myself up, slid between the tables and the bar to the bathroom, and burst in to find Max crouching and puking into the toilet. They wanted to kill us. I wondered whether we'd be able to protect ourselves if they barged through the door. I pulled Max up and tried to position him so he could dash water on his face from the rickety sink above the chipped tile floor, but succeeded only in enabling Max to turn his face to me inside this cramped space, parallel with the sink, his back to the grimy wall. I began to tell him we were both going to die tonight. I don't know whether he heard anything I said before he started mumbling. I guess that's okay because I didn't catch everything he said. The breath that wafted out of him was like the stench of corpses from deep down in a coal mine.

"You been a little hard up for material, Max? Did you just solve that with me in the car? I swear I'll snap your fucking neck. I will. Do you care to contest that, funnyman?"

When Max spoke, he was barely audible, and even less coherent. But I can reconstruct for you the essence of what he said.

Want to make films? Want to make lots of them? How about it, then. I know we're not getting out of here alive, but just listen now. How brave are you? Lots of stuff out there for films. Big chicken men. Two-legged hogs. Suited ghouls and vampires. Poor families that feast on shit. Informants the police hired and then let ago, after they'd compromised themselves. Men who've been tortured for weeks and turned up drooling through teethless mouths on detectives' doormats. Club owners who take candy from stoned babies. But they're not such nice kids, are they? Children raped by the corporations, the state government. Where are all the fathers now? Bring cameras into the ICUs and film old men who fell while their nurse was trying to change their diaper and sliced their forehead open on the TV stand. They've lived off this town all their lives, haven't they now? They have no claims against us. Or better yet, bring a camera into a basement where they've got a Crip who became a Blood, or an informant who one night put his liquor on the wrong charge card and now is parting with his ears. Oops. Something funny—

"Max, you know they won't let either of us walk out of here."

He laughed.

Funny. You need extras, we'll go to Vegas and when they come staggering out of Sands Casino at 1:00 a.m. we'll say, Hey, don't slash your wrists, don't down that potassium cyanide just yet, you can be in our movie.

"Max, they'll come pounding on the door in a second. I want you—"

You want me to start making sense? Well, imagine if we could harness all of this for a higher purpose and make thieves and rogues cower. Imagine. They'll have to found TV stations just to stream our movies 24/7. Imagine the impetus to thought. Imagine when the Prince of Monaco comes and he'll take you to Vegas and he won't be satisfied with what is there so he'll take out his wallet and commission a hotel on the spot, right there, and name it after you.

Of course they can't build in sand. Can't build on sand. Can't build— But you're not an idealist of my stripe so be honest with me. For once.

Have you ever really felt comfortable living in your own country? In a place where lions stare at you from the red hills?

I answered his question with a question.

"Max, buddy, do you have a will made out?"

But he was even less coherent than I was. They were going to come in and kill us and share a damn good laugh. I thought of how gratifying it would be to slam Max's head forward and crack the grimy panel imprinted with floral images directly behind it. I was going to hurt him and it was hard to think of anything else for more than a few seconds. On the far side of the flimsy door was silence. All the eyes out there were on this door.

"Come on, Max."

"Why, another spin in the Rosemobile? Right on, pardner!"

But when I tried to pull him toward me and the door, he slumped as if all his muscles had gone on strike at once.

"Please, you bastard. I'll leave you right here if I have to."

"S'okay, I know you need your warm milk before they tuck you in."

I panted, aware of that awkward lump in my gut again. The eyes out there were on this door. I slung his arm around my shoulder like a wounded comrade in the jungles of Quang Tri. Then with sharp abrupt moves pulled him through the door, and down past the stage. As we shuffled between the tables and the bar, I could not help rotating my head ever so cautiously in the direction of the newcomers' table. Yes, they were all staring. One of them, a twenty-five-year-old with bold handsome cheeks, began to stand up. With my left hand, I began rummaging in the right breast pocket of my blazer. With Max's quivering mass between me and the table, it was just conceivable for about a fifth of a second that I had something in there. Just barely. That was all the time I was going to give them. I shoved Max past the length of the bar, past all the peering eyes, and outside, into the crisp air, toward the Mercury.

After I managed to drag him over the gravel of the lot to the passenger's side, I groped in his pockets. I felt like jumping fifty feet in the air at the ease with which I dug the keys out. I slid him into the dark sleek compartment, onto the very seat where I'd writhed and cried, before moving around to the driver's side. Once in my seat, I glanced at him again and wondered on how many occasions people had decked Max Rose for looking at them the way he regarded me now. The rictus in his lower face stretched back just tautly enough to give him a buck-toothed appearance. In his eyes was the triumph of a high school math whiz who has proven he can get as plastered as anyone. Now this miserable fucker was my captive. He writhed and jerked. His right fingers began to close around my arm. I slammed his hand into the dash hard enough to break a finger or two. I started the Mercury and swung us out of the lot and onto a road that led somewhere, westward I thought. Around us in the dark I could make out but little. Off to our left stood the fence of a lot between disused boxcar-shaped buildings, but I could see nothing on the far side of that lot save dark within dark. To our right there were, I think, a number of single-story houses and a couple of them actually had a Ford or a Lincoln in the driveway, but there were no lights on. I imagined crouching in one of the driveways, in this dark space of absent sound, waiting, begging for a presence to come to the window at the side of the building. Pleading. As we began to roll westward, if in fact that was our direction, I felt the vehicle come up and down a little too far. Yes, we had a flat. It was the front tire on Max's side. I said something to Max. He giggled. You can drive on four flats, he said. He asked whether I cared to contest the point. I made a right up a narrow street and turned left again, and we continued on a wider avenue, maybe it was Rosecrans, then again I would have expected to see a car or two on Rosecrans even at this hour. I took us four blocks, five, six, before I thought no way was this Rosecrans and I made an abrupt left onto a street shielded by palm trees and fences from the sporadic lights on that avenue. We drove for what seemed like eighty yards, turned right, and drove another hundred yards or so before I stopped somewhere between a shuttered bowling alley and the barren lot of a supermarket. Here and there in the spaces around us were houses, with silent dark spaces behind dusty windows, and shuttered bars that might or might not have been open at some point tonight. Nothing stirred in the blackness on either side of the faraway fences that enclosed the space without acting as its parameters, nothing moved under the weight of darkness that terrified and stultified and denied the existence of a respectable lady walking her dog in the palm-fringed fragrance of one of the narrow side streets, of a detective leaning over the dash of a car parked strategically in the most obscure alley, of a mangy kitten wandering over the barren spaces of the lot. I kept the Mercury in drive but leaned hard on the brake.

"What's goin' on . . . ?"

"Get out, Max."

He looked at me with that grin.

"Come on. You're walking home tonight."

"No, amigo. No way. My Rosemobile. Mine."

"You live too far out of my way and you can't drive. There are bus stops around here."

"Fuck you."

"Get out now or I'll cut your fucking throat."

He shook his head.

"So I make assumptions," I said.

He muttered something unintelligible.

"I make assumptions about people, Max."

He shook his head again. I'd misunderstood him earlier, or he just didn't want to engage. Maybe he'd forgotten why we got together in the first place. This was never about *my* false assumptions.

With a darting movement, I slid my right hand behind his neck and slammed his forehead into the dash with all my force. He shrieked. As he jerked back, his glasses began to come loose and he reached for them. I slammed him again, harder because he was in too much pain to resist, and slammed him a third time, hearing a sound like a melon dropped from three stories. I rammed his face into the dash a fourth time. I thought another blow would end him. He moaned and began to sob as a dark syrupy substance on the dash oozed and ran. Now I felt something then I'd felt before and would feel again. I'd never laughed at the right moments and now here I was, moving and reaching restlessly in the dark to hurt a crying man. A few more slams and I knew something would begin to come loose in the most intricate, most delicate regions of his skull. The lights in the distances outside, such as they were, were so garish I felt they were daring me. I couldn't take the car. Or perhaps I could. I could slam his head even harder and loose some tissue from his frontal lobes. That would feel exquisite. Or I get out and walk and walk, until the remoteness of a space under jutting shingles lured me. I'd wake up breathing dust and blinking, gauging the passing shapes around me in the wide day to determine whether the heap in the corner, the blanco, had registered at all.

Or I could just take the car. Take it and then lose it somewhere in the mountains north of Altadena.

Straightening up in his seat, Max began to push his glasses back up his nose. I punched him in the temple four times as hard as I could. He started wailing.

"You're not like me. Get it? You're just not like me at all. You don't make any *assumptions*. You're not like me. So get out. Get out now. Get the fuck out and walk to the metro. All you'll probably see is a cat. Nothing to worry about out there. Nothing. Get out of the fucking car, shitheap."

I didn't have to see that grin because he reached up and wiped the sopping mess of blood and tears his face had become. He cursed me, but in a resigned way, and shook his head sobbing. In the garish light around us I could see the palms in the distance sway a bit as a wind swept down from the valley. As I thought about what to do with him, weighed the different options, I kept expecting something, a rock or a brick or a bullet, to roar through the still air around us and jolt us into flight. That might very well have been Max's best hope, or so I thought, but all around was this dead land defined by what was unseen. Another blow really might kill him, I thought. Suddenly, to my astonishment, for the first time that night, the man I was with addressed me by name. He blew mounds of bloody garb through his nostrils before he spoke.

"Al. Listen to me. I'm not the least bit fucking sorry."

About a week later, I needed time alone. On the coffee table in front of the couch in my bungalow there was a pile of mail including a letter from the alumni office of my high school concerning a reunion coming up in a few weeks. It was full of the cute jokes and gossip you'd expect. I took a look at that letter and thought *No, thank you.* I dumped the mail in a trash bin, shut off my mobile, walked out to my car, and commenced a long drive down to Santa Monica, then southeast on 101 until I reached Harbor Freeway, where I could have turned right on the route taken by Max the other night. Instead I turned in the other direction and pursued the North Pasadena Freeway all the way through Elysian Park and up past

Montecito Heights, Monterey Hills, Highland Park, and South Pasadena. Then I went straight north, right through Pasadena and all the way up into Altadena, a staid community of respectable homes at the base of Eaton Canyon. Lacking an interest in cedar trees or the lights that adorned them every Christmas, I'd rarely made my way up here in all my years of living in L.A. But I drove around, pulling over at strategic points. Out here, if you knew where to look, you could find houses whose components were almost like sections of skyscrapers lying prone amid the sands and cacti and mountains, whose cool pristine interiors gave their owners the time and space to reflect and imagine, isolating bits of memory like bacteria. The cliffs and hills were so vast and barren I had wondered once whether the descendants of Civil War armies that pushed through the desert from New Mexico long ago were still wandering around out there. Anyway, the houses were the attraction here. I sat inside my Saturn with the engine idling, studying sleek panes for a flicker of movement, but my impatience just fed itself, as I thought I deserved to see something after watching for so long and it would be so grossly unfair to me to quit now. No faces ever came. It was dusty and lonely here. At last I turned and drove down to South Pasadena where there were more houses of the same type, divided by strip malls and filling stations and golden arches, with no reason or excuse for turning into the driveway of one of these places if you didn't live there. I changed my direction six or seven times but grew discouraged about finding a vantage point, so I began driving further south, down to Bell, where I knew they'd built a school with kind of a radical design. I had a fancy to sit in my car studying it, letting the cool interiors visible through big windows lull me. It was a really good school. If someone is bright, a setting like this one isolates and magnifies the quality, I thought. Then I began to have kind of a heavy feeling and I couldn't keep up the resolve to drive all the way down there to look at a school, so I turned and began to drive west back toward Hollywood. On either side of my lane, the neon signs for strip clubs were dead, the lots outside the stores desolate, the roads as barren as if air raid sirens had sounded. I'd been down for the past few days, and I felt pretty mad at myself for imagining that if you've been hurt your whole life, hurting back just a little bit can restore equilibrium. So strong was the belief that I'd just barely checked an impulse to kill. It all seemed totally childish to me now. When in a fluid state outside the parameters of anywhere, it hit me how little there was for me in this place or that. Yet I needed to be alone in the universe, I had years to travel through obscure back roads to gain any sense of myself. The roads were still lonely but I was getting closer to Hollywood. I shouldn't have taken this drive, I thought. I really didn't need a house like the Kauffman House, with pools, rooms, terraces, annexes, and wings that you could practically break off and set out on a coffee table. But now I wrestled with the heavy feeling I'd spent my life denying. In solitude, the rightness of my decision the other night at last began to stand out clearly. When I got back to my bungalow, the invitation would still be there in the trash bin, with the other mail. I hadn't done or altered anything at all by throwing it out. I pulled off onto the shoulder and idled there among rocks that had been there for centuries. Then I took out the mobile and flipped through my address book. I needed, if not exactly a friend, then a collaborator and partner. I had one.

Scenes from the Catastrophe

As Steve Rawls, a stuntman, drove east on Hollywood Boulevard with his girlfriend Rachel Getz, a man in a Giorgio Armani suit with slick dark hair like Valentino's, and with a dripping gash on his forehead, dashed up to the hood of Steve's Chevy, rested his palms there for a moment, and stared blankly at the cracked windshield. The man began to say something, but the noise of a huge collision up the street startled him and he ran off. Steve stepped hard on the gas. When the Chevy reached the middle of the next block, another man, naked except for a torn white tank top, ran up to the passenger's side window, puckering his lips against the glass, before Steve hit the pedal again and the car lurched forward, making the stranger topple backward toward the curb. Rachel suggested they help him, but Steve found something more than a little ambivalent in the behavior of these people. Not that they had wanted the riot, but some were more desperate than others to get out of it.

From what Steve and Rachel could gather from reports on the radio, the rioters had mostly broken away from Normandie in favor of points west and northwest. Though no one spelled this out explicitly, Steve figured that the cops who fled the intersection of Pico and Western could not have gone far in that direction if the mobs still clogged Normandie. They drove east for a few more blocks before Steve eased the Chevy to the curb on the right and parked it. He looked at the woman whose smile mesmerized him on an evening long ago with a scent of cranberries drifting on a breeze.

"Please step out, Rachel."

"You're going to leave me here, with all these goofy people."

He chuckled.

"Is that what they call lawbreakers in Brady, Texas? Goofy people?"

"I'm going to say no. Hit me if you like. But you're not leaving me here."

He locked eyes with her.

"You're *not*, Steve."

"I love you. I'll see you in the second act."

"I am *not* getting out, Steve."

So an argument began.

Meanwhile, the terrified people might have been plentiful up here, but were harder to spot at points further south or southeast. They had vanished into hiding places in motels, movie theaters, department stores, and warehouses at the advance of the rioters. In some of the areas from which the rioters had set out, residents had begun a campaign to raise money to cover the fees that a civil suit against racist cops would entail. They went from door to door with paper cups and cutoff cartons asking for a contribution, but their rates of success were wildly erratic. A couple of the collectors got shot for their troubles. 911 calls went out. On these occasions, the police knew full well that if they tried to step in to help the wounded and dying, the fury of the crowds would force them right out again, whereas if they did nothing, there would be accusations and possible legal action from certain quarters. For the time being, they settled for the latter.

Jane Jeffrey, a PR flack who lent her talents to struggling indie productions, had begun to make her way westward on Sunset, on the logic of safety in numbers. By the time she crossed Normandie, she realized how little prospect there was of turning around now. People ran every which way, cursing and screaming and tossing bricks and bottles or their personal effects, for they had no use for wallets or watches in this kingdom of acrid skies. A fat man barreled into Jane as he ran south on Vermont, habit kicked in for just a moment and he began to mumble an apology. Then he tried to leap-frog a distribution box for one of the weeklies only to land on his face on the far side of it. Jane continued westward. People surged up from between the cars lining the north side of the street, pressed against her, and their fury carried her for a couple of blocks before they dispersed every which way, as if they'd forgotten where they were going. A lady in large horn-rimmed glasses and K-mart clothes, possibly a school bus driver, gesticulated to Jane to suggest that they must both get away to the north. Perhaps she thought they'd be safer hugging the letters of the Hollywood sign, Jane thought. Jane began to open her mouth but something which might have been a paperweight or a computer modem sailed through the air and clapped her on the right temple, making her cry out and sink to her knees. The bus driver, if that was what she was, reached down and yanked Jane to her feet, hissing that they'd both get trampled to death if Jane let that happen once more. The force of people heading west carried them, but at times enough space opened up between the bodies before or behind them that they could move in a desperate lurching way.

Bodies came and went in the surging mass, and by the next intersection, Jane had lost sight of the bus driver. Now the momentum of the crowds was shifting. People welled up from the south side of the street, pinning Jane against the booth of a car wash. Jane thought the weight would crush her to death or perhaps damage her reproductive tract. Screaming would no more call attention to her now than setting off a car alarm in a vast lot where all the other alarms were wailing. So instead she made a feeble effort to push outward with both hands, which clutched something soft. It was the white polo shirt of a boy of thirteen, the type of kid whose parents send him to prep schools and squash clubs and who gets busted with drugs and who may or may not change. Jane clutched and pushed. The kid, whose body was nearly horizontal, rotated his head about 60 degrees in Jane's direction and began to form something like a grin. Then the mass inexplicably shifted southward and the kid dropped onto his belly and disappeared. Jane ran and stumbled westward until once again the space around her was too tight to move. She managed to get a hand up to her face to wipe away some of the sweat. She cried. The weight began to carry her again, inexorably, until the next corner, where the crowd began to lose form and direction as people spilled into the spaces north and south of the epicenter of the intersection. About twenty yards up the street, a few people were huddling between cars and when they saw Jane they waved, beckoning her to come quickly.

"Over here."

"Come on over this way, hang out with us."

Here were a mom and dad from Oklahoma City and their adolescent son and daughter. When Jane reached the relative safety of their position, they made room for her and related some of what they'd witnessed over the past hour. A bleeding man chasing a gypsy who wore a dress with an elaborate design but who was naked from the waist up, her breasts flopping as she bounded up the street. A screaming woman with her hair on fire. A trio of punks in tank tops ramming pens into a girl's vagina and anus. As the boy and his sibling shared all of this, their father, a man in a gray sweatshirt and a Kansas City Royals cap, scanned the intersection nervously, his fingers clutching a rear bumper. The mom, a tense lady in a cashmere pullover and jeans, cautioned Jane quite unnecessarily about the likelihood of getting hurt if she tried to move again. So twenty tense minutes later, the four of them were absolutely speechless when Jane rose, dusted herself off with the flats of her hands, and began to move back toward the throngs. She thought she could fight her way westward, then up to the Walk of Fame, and there would really be some things to see. The bodies were flowing again. She got pushed, pulled, jostled, pushed again, kicked in the shins, punched in the gut.

Authorial interpolation. Hello, my name is Al Duchamp.

When the anti-cop rage that had festered for so many months across the nation erupted into riots, I took refuge in a warehouse on Melrose with the crew of a film I'd been directing. It was a relatively safe place and I hoped that my acquaintances at points around the city would join us there as soon as they could. I cared deeply about Steve Rawls, whom I'd given a part in my film in spite of Jane Jeffrey's appraisal of him. There were times I'd felt tempted to kill Jane myself, but of course at such as a critical time we must set aside our petty resentments and think about our responsibilities to others, just as we hope they'll do for us.

There is something deeply reassuring about the first-person singular, you presume. I am alive and I am safely recounting all this to you. Well, let me tell you what else was going on in the city and what happened to my friend Steve and his girl. As the accounts kept coming in over the radio, I asked, where are the National Guardsmen, where are the heroes?

American Airlines Flight #369 began its descent from the clear skies over the valley toward LAX. A passenger who had dozed practically the whole two hours from Denver, a mutual funds salesman named Brad

Cutchins, looked out his window on the left side of the plane. He'd always enjoyed the part of the flight where the desert turns so abruptly into an infinite grid of suburban streets, with a density that defies the eye to linger on any one point, there is so much to take in. As he gazed out the window this morning, the black smoke rose from multiple points on the grid, which looked like a massive computer's hard drive that someone had tossed on a fire. The smoldering points were so numerous it would take hours to sort out where one stopped and another began, and by then, they would have spread and there would be many new fires. Brad, who was of the sub-literate breed of financial services employee, blurted, "My God, it's an inferno."

On the streets, incidents began that would have been like dozens of others, except that reporters in the news helicopters made a point of capturing them and their aftermath. Outside a house near the corner of Aranbe and Bliss in Compton, a teenager named Marcus Knowles grew suspicious that three other teens who claimed to be collecting for the legal fund were pocketing every cent. When they saw him and began to walk toward him over a weed-ridden lot, holding a cutoff milk carton, he simply shrugged, turned, and began to walk south on Aranbe. One of the three promptly raised the barrel of a black .357 Magnum with a strip of masking tape around its checkered brown grip, and shot Marcus in the lower back. Though the aftermath of the incident began to reach TV screens when a helicopter from one of the major stations buzzed overhead, the boy lay there bleeding in the yard of an abandoned house for more than an hour before he died.

As the teen lay bleeding, a different scene was unfolding at East 68th and South San Pedro. The convenience store there was not as defenseless a place as many of the businesses in the surrounding grid of streets had proved to be. The proprietor, Hector Sanchez, had scared four looters out of the store, on different occasions, by brandishing a steel baseball bat. Hector had $60 in the register and another $100 under the counter, and he intended to stay open in order to feed his wife, Inez, his daughter, Maria, and his tiny grandson, Raul, who at this moment lay cradled in Maria's arms in an apartment over a shuttered and boarded bakery on San Pedro. Now, without warning, an object slammed into the grimy window behind the register. While Hector was distracted with the damage to his window, a young man ran into the store and grabbed a loaf of bread. Hector had been a cashier too long for the thief's actions not to register in his peripheral vision. When Hector ran outside, somebody shot him with a Ruger .352 Magnum, spraying the entrance to the store with blood and tissue. He lay there face down in the grime, but the reporter hovering above could just see one of his feet rotating, left to right and back, as a few people on the street pointed, laughed, or walked over to kick or spit at the prone form from which thin red streams eddied toward the curb. *He's alive, folks,* the reporter said into his mike. *If someone can get here in the next ten minutes, he might just have a chance, a slim one, but a chance nonetheless. Perhaps someone watching or listening to this broadcast is in the vicinity of 68th and San Pedro. Someone, anyone?*

Those concerned about ratings need not worry, for the tabloid dramas kept materializing from the colliding circumstances. Los Angeles Fire Department Engine #39 drove east on Beverly, passing Windsor, Irving, Norton, and the outskirts of Burns Park. The driver, forty-two-year-old Pat Gallagher, married and a father of three, had heard a report of a building on fire near the corner of Beverly and St. Andrews Square. On that corner was a pole supporting lines that provided power to a swath of buildings between West 1st Street and Elmwood Avenue, and if they got damaged, it might be quite hard when night fell to respond to emergency calls originating from pitch dark houses. Downed power lines would electrocute some fool along with anyone who tried to move the body. When Pat got near the entrance to St. Andrews Square, a little side street leading off to the south, he spotted the narrow purple house with a fire on the upper of its two floors. He eased the engine to the curb on his right, put it in park, and got out. It was hot and sticky inside his uniform. He could hear the helicopter hovering a few hundred feet up, just to the north. The walkie talkie at Pat's belt crackled and blared messages intermittently to trucks around the city.

The device at his side crackled again, and then a voice informed Pat that a car was moving west on Beverly. Pat disregarded the call and got to work. *When is a car not moving west on Beverly?* he thought. *Sheesh.* He checked over his gloves to make sure there were no rips, unslung one of the hoses, walked toward the burning structure. Here the air could make you think of a cookout where everyone has passed out from the spiked punch, leaving the fire on the grille to grow and the smoke to rise and rise.

Another call came over the walkie talkie. Now the car moving in Pat's direction, a gray Volkswagen, was just over a block away. Pat would see it if he bothered to look. Again he blew off the warning. He studied the house, estimated that rioters had set the fire within the last two hours. Downtown, at a provisional command center for firefighters near 4th and Maple, men were watching a screen in horror, gaping, sweating, cursing, praying out loud.

"Gallagher, the car is approaching fast. I strongly suggest that you not stay out in the open—"

No one knows what the fireman thought, but it might have been something like, *Fuck it, I'm gonna get her done, maybe get my promotion this year. Maybe a trip to Orlando for the first time since '08.*

"Gallagher!"

He went stubbornly about his work. Inevitably, he did raise his gaze slightly as the Volkswagen moved past. He looked up just in time to make eye contact with the thug, a twenty-eight-year-old with dreadlocks and a leering grin spread over his face, and to see the flash from the 9mm Colt pistol, before the bullet sheared away the right third of the fireman's neck. The stunned victim fell onto his back at the edge of the burning home's lawn, blood spurting as if from a busted water main. He gagged, spat blood, kicked his legs ineffectually. Looking toward the sky, he might have thought of the Beach Boys song about palm trees in the sand and girls so tan. He was conscious just long enough to hear the whirring of the news helicopter as it moved south over a studio executive's wet dream.

Steve Rawls wanted so badly to be a hero. Jane had insisted I should have no patience for this also-ran stuntman from Kansas City. She'd have sneered if she knew Steve wanted to help people caught up in the riots, for Steve had no part in an indie film, let alone in a national event, in anything thing with the word "national" attached to it, no matter how gory.

But Steve wanted, expected, to be a hero. I heard the horrific reports coming in over the radio, mesmerizing us as we sat terrified on the dusty floor of the warehouse on Melrose, and I wondered, again, where were Steve and

Rachel during all this? And if Steve couldn't be the hero he'd fantasized so vainly about becoming, who would step into the breach?

Near the intersection of Jefferson and Normandie, a single mother and her two boys climbed out of the basement of their motel and walked outside to their Honda Accord. They too had received intelligence, by word of mouth and from radio reports, that the rioters were busy torching Mid-Wilshire and the approaches to Hollywood, and were no longer much of a presence on Normandie. Jenna Wright, and her sons Ethan, eight, and Preston, eleven, had gone to the fleabag Ambassador Hotel when the trouble started and she knew there was no way she was getting them all the way from Mid-Wilshire, where she'd been shopping, to Culver City, where they lived in the bungalow that had passed into Jenna's name following her husband's suicide two years before. Her credit card was maxed out and the other people in the basement had begun saying things that made Ethan cry, things about eating little boys when the vending machines ran out of Kit-Kats and Baby Ruths. They were all a lot of weirdos and pervs who'd come to the hotel to shoot up and screw. Jenna just wanted to get her boys home.

The progress of the rioters was like the slithering of an asp. Such a creature was more likely to glide forward than backward, but could dart diagonally or horizontally without warning. As soon as the Honda Accord reached the intersection of Jefferson and Normandie and began to turn 90 degrees to the north, the shapes of seven men in their twenties and thirties swarmed out from behind the cars and palm trees. The mass of bodies quickly congealed in the path of the Honda as more rioters ran up behind it. Ethan screamed. Preston looked uncertainly at his mom, who immediately spun the wheel, but the Honda just spun its tires between the thugs in front and those bracing the rear fender. Jenna cried and cursed. To her astonishment, Jenna could hear a helicopter somewhere up above. Mike Donovan and the others in the KHRN helicopter, and conceivably everyone in the world who owned a TV, could see what was happening right now, at this torn-up, barren intersection in Central L.A. The windows were sealed electronically, so Jenna presumed that all she had to do was wait before cops rolled into the intersection like commandos raiding a terrorist's lair, sirens blazing.

"Just wait, boys. Be calm. Wait."

The fists of the rioters could not penetrate the windows, but more effective tools were at hand. The first time the rock hit the rear passenger's side window, Ethan did not register the meaning of it. When it hit a second time, a third, a fourth, and the cracks spread and bits of glass spattered his face and neck, he knew that the people outside were really mad at him and his mom and brother. Had they been rude? Had they forgotten to say *please* or *thank you*? Preston was crying and looking anxiously from one side to the other. Now there came a slamming noise as one of the rioters behind the car began beating a tire iron against the trunk and rear window. Jenna tried to back up again, momentarily disorienting the man with the tire iron, then pressed on the gas. But the bodies in front of the Honda pressed hard the other way, and the rioter behind the car began hitting it with renewed fury. An unmistakable odor filled the car as both kids lost control of their bowels.

"Hold on, boys, they're just trying to scare us," Jenna told them, looking desperately around for anyone, it didn't have to be a cop, just someone whose presence might distract the rioters. Was there a minister around who'd plant himself on the spot, as in '92 saying, *If you want to kill them you'll have to kill me?*

Ethan looked out. One of the rioters in front of the car wore a white t-shirt with the legend "I Fuck on the First Date." Ethan thought it was kind of funny, he'd seen white kids with a shirt like that. Another had a gap in his teeth, giving his grins a psycho look. Yet another had a cleft between two ridges on his forehead, as if he'd neglected to get stitches for a gaping wound years ago. The rioter slamming a rock against his window wore a black bandanna and the kind of nylon shirt that hugs the contours of every muscle in your torso. He also wore shades, so you couldn't tell whether he was looking at the boys as he pounded away. Now there were holes in the window by Ethan's head big enough to insert a finger. The blows at the rear window continued. At the same time, three men on the left side of the car and two on the right reached under the chassis and began rocking it back and forth, back and forth, without quite lifting it off the ground.

"Mom!" Preston wailed. Preston had just shit his pants. Both boys looked to the front seat, but the woman there was weeping softly, her face in her hands. The car rocked so violently that bits of Ethan's blond hair began poking through the holes in the window shattered by the rock, then disappearing as he lurched the other way, colliding with his terrified brother. Jenna gave up trying to steady herself against the keeling of the space inside the vehicle, and wept as she hadn't done since the suicide of Bob Wright, a man whose acute asthma and clinical depression now seemed to have far more legitimate claims on a person's life than they had before.

"Mom! *Mom!!!*" Preston shrieked, as Ethan looked out at the man with the rock, sobbing uncontrollably. Now more rioters were spilling out from the west side of the intersection, and it looked as if the Honda would soon be floating on a sea of limbs.

The blue Chevy shot into the intersection so fast that the rioter with the "I Fuck on the First Date" t-shirt did not have a chance to dodge it. The car clipped him in the gut and sent him sprawling toward the Honda as the driver of the Chevy slammed on the brakes, bringing the vehicle to a halt roughly parallel to the Honda and five feet off toward the northeast corner of the intersection. Jenna removed her hands from her face just in time to see a blond man in a windbreaker and jeans leap out and dash in front of the Chevy with a Colt .45 in his right hand. Jenna did not notice the passenger in the Chevy. The Honda stopped rocking as the rioters on either side of it let go, turning to face the interloper with incredulity. Ethan tried to form words.

When the rioter in the "I Fuck on the First Date" t-shirt began to pick himself groggily up, Steve shot him in the face, blowing off his nose and freeing his left eye from its socket. The roar of the blast sounded like a fighter jet's acceleration. Then when the thug in the tight shirt made a move in Steve's direction, he fired the .45 at point-blank range, again nearly splitting his eardrums, blowing a hole in the thug's chest, and spraying the remains of the passenger's side window with bloody tissue from his chest and kidneys. The others paused. Steve brandished the weapon, his eyes darting from one thug to another, daring them to take a step. When the rioter with the missing front tooth tried to move, Steve shot him in the kneecap. The thug collapsed screaming, rolling his body up into a ball on the hot bloody pavement. At this point, the others were in no need of convincing about what he might do. Waving the gun, Steve indicated that they were to move away from the Honda. The rioters slid a few feet away, and the moment they did so, the driver's side doors opened, allowing three people to get out and rush north up Normandie. Though the feral eyes of the rioters stayed on Steve, they all registered this development in their peripheral vision.

They rushed the blond man. Steve fired the .45 twice more, grazing the head of one rioter and blowing off the pinky and ring finger of another's left hand. Then a pair of powerful hands was around his neck, choking him hard, making him drop the pistol, which went off once more as it hit the pavement under the Chevy's right headlight. Three more rioters who had just arrived at the intersection quickly joined the fray, so that there were seven people choking, punching, and kicking Steve furiously. One of them, a tall man in a gray tank top, pressed both thumbs into the base of Steve's neck, as if searching, probing for something. Then he seemed to find it, for he began pulling hard with both hands, slamming his forehead into Steve's when the stuntman tried to maneuver out of his grip. The hands continued to probe. Steve was still fighting, all right, but was so dazed that his motions were spastic, without an overall design. The hands of the large man pulled hard around something thin and vertical. Within seconds, the assailant looked like a movie extra who'd had a red dye pack burst in his face.

"Steve!" screamed the blonde woman in the passenger's seat of the Chevy. But Steve didn't respond. As soon as they heard her voice, two more thugs raced around to the passenger's side, quickly destroyed what remained of the window, and reached in to grab Rachel by the collar of her denim jacket. At first, she actually tried to ignore them, as if they were squeegee men demanding money. Again she cried out Steve's name.

At this point, the helicopter above transmitted a live feed of the violence at Jefferson and Normandie to a local station, KHRN, whose executives were quite pleased that none other than Professor Martin Russell had agreed to go on the air, to comment on what was happening here in L.A. right now.

"We're honored to have UCLA Professor of Sociology Martin Russell here with us today," said the anchor, Ted Stevens, to his large audience.

"Professor Russell has been studying and publishing articles about urban sociology and economics for longer than some of our viewers have been alive," the anchor added in a weighty voice.

Down at the intersection, one of the thugs was cackling and tugging hard at Rachel's jacket. She clutched the steering wheel as if it were a bit of driftwood on the open sea. Those who tuned into the station got to see a split screen, with Professor Russell on one side and the scene at the intersection directly opposite. He began:

"Thank you, Ted. The economic exploitation, one might even say, the economic enslavement, of residents of South Central and other neighborhoods in L.A. County has been only one component of the chronic animosity expressed toward residents of those parts of the city—"

"—Steve, get in the car, please! Steve, please! There's still time to get out of here if you get in now!" Rachel cried, but all she could see through the windshield was a blond head bobbing back and forth as hands clutched furiously, maniacally, at the bloody neck supporting that head. Rachel had been weeping for nearly two minutes now. Still the thug at the window was trying to yank her out of the car.

"—the longstanding socioeconomic disparities and economic exploitation have had the effect of fostering what I term a cognizance of oppression on the part of the individuals subjected to it—" the professor droned.

"*Steve!* Steve. . . . " Rachel did not want to acknowledge what had just happened to her, but when her sweating body shifted inside the Chevy, there was something thick and sticky down inside her underpants. She cried and screamed.

"—in times when socioeconomic conditions are slightly less strained, this cognizance manifests itself in a range of cultural forms including gangsta rap and peaceful public demonstrations. At times of greater strain, when conservative fiscal policy and the resurgence of regressive social attitudes on the part of the majority contribute to the undermining of opportunities, the cognizance to which I referred can issue in signifying."

They pulled Rachel out of the car, kicked her hard in the stomach, and then, when she sprawled out on the hot pavement, began stepping on her head and looking around for objects with which to pummel her.

"Could you clarify the meaning of 'signifying' for us, Professor Russell?" Ted asked.

"Certainly. Signifying refers to behavior, or a pattern of behavior, that we should not construe as a literal statement of the cognizance of oppression, but rather as the figurative interplay of signs—"

"Steve!" Rachel was able to moan one last time, before she saw that Steve was lying prone in front of the Chevy, his face turned bizarrely up and to the right, as if his neck were made of rubber, while the rioters danced on his body. Blood drenched his torso between the sides of the torn windbreaker. Now someone reached into the Chevy, through the window from which they'd removed Rachel, opened the glove compartment, found a pen, and leaned down over Rachel, stabbing her hard in the stomach, chest, neck, and face. She kept moaning and looking up at the form hovering a couple of hundred feet above, until the pen went through her right eye, at the same time that she felt her jeans being pulled off.

"Thank you, Professor Russell."

"My pleasure, Ted," the professor replied, hoping that his use of the host's first name would please any viewers who might have been disposed to find him a stuffy old academic.

More rioters swarmed into the intersection, while some of those who had originally stopped the Honda went after the three people who'd abandoned it. In all the time that Professor Russell's commentary was on the air, they'd managed to get only three blocks. Jenna couldn't run fast, and the boys didn't want to leave her behind. They tried to pick up the pace. Suddenly a rock from behind felled Ethan. His mother and older brother stopped in their tracks. A bottle landed and burst at Preston's feet, but his mother could think of nothing but getting Ethan to straighten up and move again. The mob behind them was quickly closing the distance. As she knelt over Ethan, who was heaving and writhing on the ground, a rock hit Jenna almost exactly between the eyes. She keeled backward, arms perpendicular to her body, her head hitting the pavement with a smack. Preston looked at the crowd, at his mom and brother on the ground, made a calculation, and fled up Normandie.

Rachel's pants and feces-filled underpants were off, and a thug was sticking the pen in her vagina, rotating it up toward her head, down toward her knees, like a joystick. One of the other rioters newly arrived at the intersection brandished a small saw, and proceeded to saw off Steve's nose, his ears, and then went to work on his right hand, the one that had held the pistol. A boy was aiming that pistol at the cobalt blue afternoon sky, firing triumphantly at nothing. Already the news helicopter had begun to withdraw. When he was done dismembering the body in front of the Chevy, the rioter walked over to Rachel and pressed the edge of the blade against the soft flesh of the woman's neck. Throughout a swath of blocks including Mid-Wilshire and Koreatown, bodies were turning black as flames crept over them, the smoke rising, spreading a scent all around with a greater radius than in a Midwestern leaf-burning ritual. Rioters hauled bodies out to intersections, doused the heaps with gas siphoned from the abandoned cars, or poured gas from portable tanks looted from stations whose owners were either dead or cowering in basements. The mobs paraded through the streets displaying heads, ears, or tongues of people they'd killed, exulting in these status symbols. As blood ran between cars in streams and rivers and tributaries, some of them got quite soaked but welcomed the accompanying sensations.

In the warehouse on Melrose, I held an urgent conference with my friends Mary, Alice, and Reid. We decided we'd better run out onto the street and try to flag down a bus or a National Guard truck before the rioters burned down our refuge. Luckily for us, a bus driver named Anthony Blair, who'd grown horrified at what the rioters had down to his South Central neighborhood, had split away from his route down on Florence and driven the staggering distance from Florence all the way up to Melrose, then cruised around looking for innocent people caught up in the riots. When the bus reached North Cahuenga and Melrose, he saw our little party turn north onto Vine, but couldn't get to us because of the rioters and burning vehicles in the street. So he'd driven up Cahuenga to Willoughby and waited.

As soon as Mary, Alice, Reid, and I were seated safely behind him, Anthony slammed on the gas and spun the steering wheel left, turning the bus north onto Vine, drove straight up to Santa Monica, and then he turned east, not stopping until we were well past the National Guard outpost at Santa Monica and Wilton. The soldiers waved the bus through, and it came to a halt at the corner of Santa Monica and Western. Here were hordes of National Guardsmen, fresh-faced blond and redheaded kids from Bakersfield, desert towns, farms in Riverside and San Bernardino Counties. How fearsome they all looked with their M-16s and hand grenades. The whirring and rumbling of military aircraft joined and quite overwhelmed the noise of news helicopters in the sky. At this intersection, there were lots of reporters, fresh from their undergrad telecommunications or print journalism programs, as well as a few jaded ones in their thirties and forties.

The bus's doors flew open. People filed off, and though their thanks could never be adequate, they offered them profusely to the driver. When Reid held out a wad of bills, Anthony shook his head without making eye contact. Upon getting off, Reid knelt down to kiss the pavement in front of all the reporters and everybody. Alice and Mary embraced in tears. Halfway up to the street to the east, you could make out a bespectacled man with a wizened face, a shock of black hair with streaks of white, and a frame so thin, you might have thought Mick Jagger had become an academic while letting someone else double for him onstage. I was standing just yards away from Professor Martin Russell.

I sighed. I looked around at all the cars that reporters had left on either side of the street, some with the keys inside, so complete was the absence of any fear here. Already I had creative ideas that would not rest. Here was a uniting feature of all the real artists whose work I had encountered over the course of my life, from the shlockmeisters to Dali, Dreyer, and Buñuel.

I found a tar-colored Nissan Primera whose owner, presumably one of the reporters, had left the keys in the ignition and the doors unlocked. The reporter, a thirtyish woman in a light gray trenchcoat, was standing across the street pressing a microphone in the face a National Guardsman who could not have been over nineteen. The soldier blinked, grimacing at the light from the device on the shoulder of a cameraman beside the reporter. Stealthily, I slid into the Nissan, turned the key, and drove east, at five miles an hour, until I reached the corner of Flemish Lane. Here was another security checkpoint. They waved me through, so I drove on past the Met Theater, under the Hollywood Freeway, past Serrano Avenue, until I reached Hobart Boulevard. I made a left and drove up the boulevard, thinking that out there in the hills there were producers with dreams and money. The air coming through the open window of the Nissan was almost too light and too pleasant this evening, as I looked north and west, deep into the land of Wilder and DeMille and Hawks, Coppola and Altman and Scorsese, Howard and Lucas and Spielberg, and other portrayers of heroes. I passed Virginia, Lexington, and made a left onto La Mirada. From here, it was a straight shot deep into the heart of Hollywood. I could not help fancying that some of the producers, screenwriters, actors, and actresses had already begun making their way back to the cafés and wine bars, feeling not wholly secure, but safer, in the knowledge that the rioters had begun to retreat to the darkest alleys, corners, tenements, and bungalows of South Central.

I drove west on La Mirada, not spying a soldier or reporter up here, though there were a number of vehicles parked on the shoulder of the road, beside families talking on cell phones, looking up and down the road nervously. Once again, I passed Western, passed under the Hollywood Freeway, and neared the corner of La Miranda and Wilton. The light was red. I sat there, contemplating, remembering. Behind me on the road was a Ford Explorer with Iowa license plates. The air was so cool and pleasant, I felt I could sit down and have a drink with anyone from anywhere on this evening of my liberation. All kinds of opportunities awaited. I was soon to discover that Jane Jeffrey had made it to safety, and we could sit down soon enough to discuss marketing opportunities again.

The light changed. I drove south on Wilton, passed Lexington and Virginia again, and swung left onto Santa Monica. It should be an occasion for joy; at least from what I could see, the rioters had vanished completely from the streets. I deliberated for a few minutes before driving west on Santa Monica and then up into the hills toward my apartment.

You wouldn't say the present is such a bad place to inhabit. To my relief there have been no break-ins, in fact everything looks pretty much as I left it, though the half-empty tins of egg rolls and noodles on the table where I once entertained the cast of my film have grown fearsomely moldy. There are men with semiautomatic rifles guarding the approaches to the hills and a writer cannot ask for a better setting in which to work. The helicopters with searchlights moving every which way above provide a level of white noise that is almost pleasant. Now there is nothing at all to stop me from spending a couple of days reflecting and committing events to paper.

Nothing to stop me, either, when I drive east again on Santa Monica, until I near the intersection of the famous boulevard and Western Avenue, where four soldiers stand before the piles of sandbags, brandishing their weapons to indicate that they will open fire on anyone who does not slow down immediately. Their M16s look so clean and shiny in the lamplight. There will be nothing at all to stop me when I take a long breath and step on the gas with all my force.

Printed in the United States
By Bookmasters